TO CAM,

FELLOW FALCON-LOVER & FRIEND,

WITH SINCERE BEST WISHES,

The Bronco Contract

Colin Pearce Series V

Chris Broyhill

Published by
Citadel Publishing LLC
Dover, Delaware, USA
2018

ISBN-13: 978-0-9994183-2-1
ISBN-10: 0-9994183-2-7

Hardback

Cover Design and Text Formatting By:
Welhaven and Associates

Acknowledgements

Of all the books in the Colin Pearce series, this one has been the most fun to write – so far. The location, the aircraft, and the plot all came together for me in a remarkable way.

Sedona, Arizona is one of my favorite places on earth and presents an inspiring backdrop for the action.

The OV-10 was my first assignment in the USAF and was a joy to fly for a young lieutenant fresh out of flight school. I had the honor of working alongside many who had flown the OV in Vietnam, some of whom had become so well known that their callsigns were retired when they left the country. Listening to their stories at the bar is one of my favorite memories.

The A-10 was an awesome and fearsome machine. I still smile when I think about flying it. My first A-10 assignment was to the 78th Tactical Fighter Squadron, “The Snakes,” at RAF Bentwaters / Woodbridge in the United Kingdom. I got to fly the A-10 all over the U.K. and West Germany at 250 – 500 feet. As a flight commander there, I was given responsibility for seven jets and 15 pilots for two weeks at a time when we deployed from the main operating base in the UK to the forward operating locations in Germany. What a lesson in leadership at the age of 30! But the best thing about flying the A-10 was firing the gun. Flying “down the chute” on a low-angle strafe pass and feeling that gun rotate as you fired was a rush beyond imagination.

But what was most rewarding about flying both the OV-10 and A-10 was the mission. We supported the real heroes in any conflict, the soldiers on the ground, who engage the enemy eye-to-eye, and knee to chest.

As usual, I have people who have helped me produce this book.

First, my thanks to my wife, Denise Broyhill, who used her literary acumen to help me to hone some of the rougher passages in the book and make them better for the story. Denise is a voracious reader. Her knowledge and insight have made every book I've written better.

My thanks to Matt Bille, my friend of forty years. Matt is a great storyteller and a fantastically gifted writer. His comments and critique are always direct and to the point. His insight is always tremendously helpful.

My thanks to Major Joden "Riddler" Werlin for his technical advice on the A-10 flying scenes in the book. The last time I flew the Hog was in the Spring of 1992 and the jet has come a long way since then. Riddler helped me flesh out the A-10 scenes with more realism and detail.

Once again though, my biggest thanks goes to you, my readers. Your support and encouragement gives me the creative fire to continuing writing and I'd be lost without it. Thank you for keeping Colin "T.C." Pearce in the fight!

Chris Broyhill
Irving, TX
Winter 2018

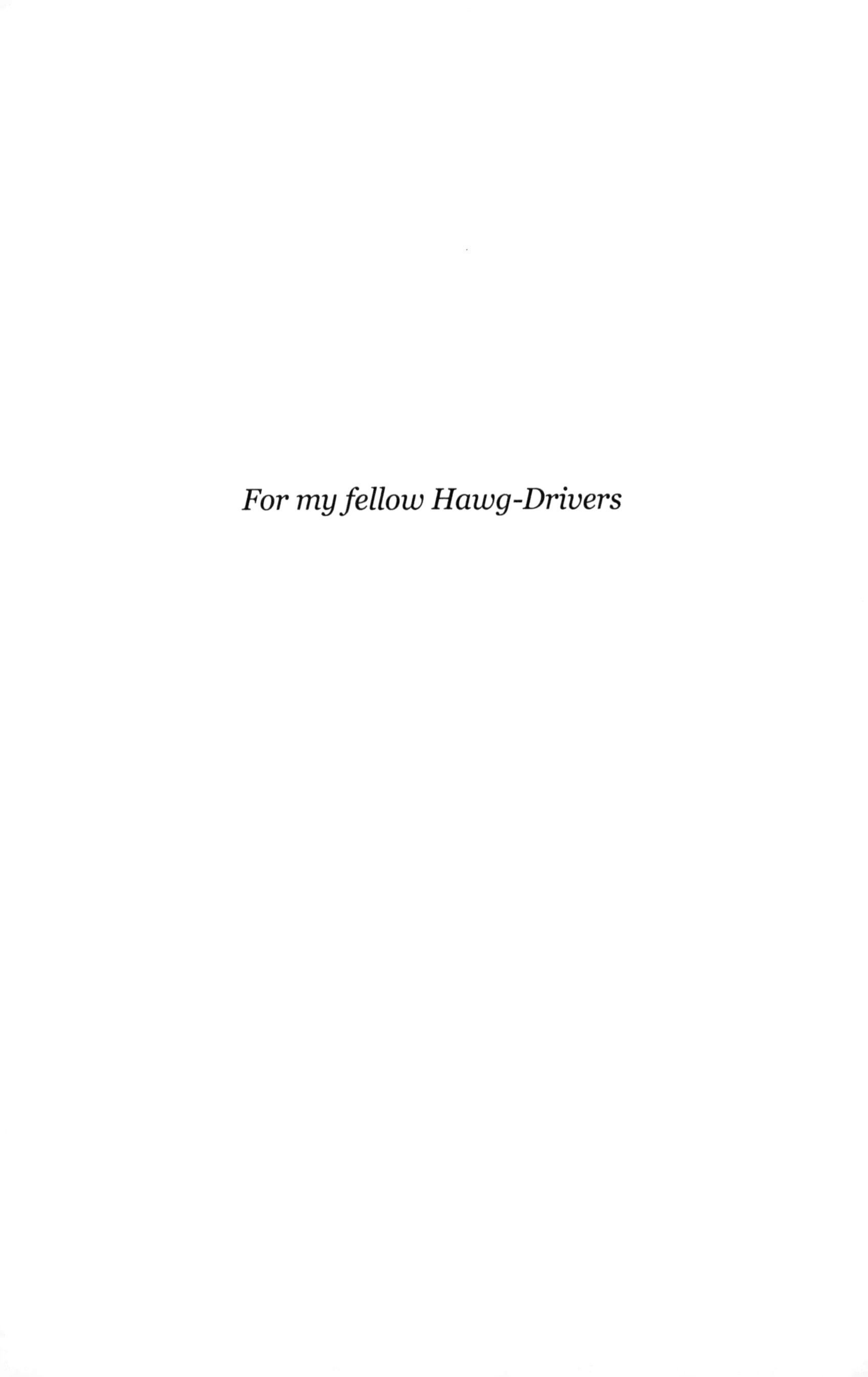

For my fellow Hawg-Drivers

Prologue

It was like my self-imposed exile for the last five years had never occurred. I was back in the cockpit of a fighter again. Flying at low altitude to a target again. Ready to rain death from above again.

The Warthog's cockpit was comfortable and familiar, even though 23 years had elapsed since I had last flown it. The big jet felt good in my hands. I relished its stability and maneuverability as I guided it across the terrain of southern Arizona.

Los Diablos was still alive and well. Miguel Hidalgo's son was in charge. The cartel had taken Ian Brooks, my boss, hostage. But they didn't know what he was or what they had. They didn't know about the device inside him. If they killed him, the consequences would be disastrous, not just for the cartel, but for Mexico and the southwestern US.

We were on the way to extract him. A full CIA ops team flying in two Blackhawk helicopters and me in an A-10. The CIA's job was to get him out. Mine was to clear the way. And between us and Ian lay one of the deadliest anti-aircraft guns ever designed. The Hog I flew was loaded with 1,150 rounds of target practice ammunition and nothing else – no bombs, no missiles, and no countermeasures.

It was going to be me versus a gun that fired 4,000 rounds per minute and a skilled crew. Ian and I had encountered both earlier in the evening when we attacked the cartel's complex in two OV-10 Broncos – and were blown out of the sky.

Now it was up to me, my Hog and the GAU-8 30mm cannon, the most powerful airborne gun system in the world. I smiled under my oxygen mask as I flew to the rendezvous south of the border. I liked my odds.

CHAPTER ONE

Friday, November 13th
0700 Hours Local Time
My Condo
Sedona, Arizona, USA

It was another day in fucking paradise.

I blinked my eyes a few times as I climbed the ladder to full consciousness, looking up at the rich wooden beams of my bedroom ceiling. In my peripheral vision, I could see the bright desert sun cascading through the sheer curtains over the sliding glass door and creating a small sea of golden color on the ceramic tile floor. I turned my head to look out through glass expanse of the door.

The landscape could have come from a Sedona postcard. Cathedral Rock basked in the morning light directly in front of me, its red limestone illuminated spectacularly in the early rays. To the left, the rounded crest of Bell Rock gleamed in the sun, its geology a kaleidoscope of bright, desert-themed color. Beyond both monuments, the red-rocks of the high surrounding terrain provided an intricately colored backdrop and seemed to act as a wall to keep the non-descript world separate and apart from this realm of desolate beauty.

The view was spectacular, as it should have been, given the

$1.1 million I had paid for it. After living in local apartments for most of the last five years, I had finally made a home here, and I had expected to find some serenity and peace with the luxury of my new condominium and grandeur of the view.

I sighed to myself and rolled out of bed. "So much for that," I said to the empty room.

I grabbed my robe off the duvet, shrugged it over my naked body and went into the bathroom to take care of the usual first activity of the morning. I regarded myself in the mirror as I washed my hands afterward. I had turned 55 in July and the years had been somewhat kind to me. I was down to a muscular 210 pounds on my six-foot, two-inch frame and I could just see the outline of the upper two rows of my abs. But the brown hair, mussed by my pillow, sported more spots of gray than it used to, and the hazel eyes appeared tired as they looked back at me in the glass. I shook my head at the reflection, dried my hands and padded into the sumptuous *gathering area* for coffee.

When I had first toured the condo, the real estate agent had called the open combination of kitchen, breakfast nook, dining room and living room by that term and it seemed to fit. It was really all one room, and it sported high ceilings decorated with wooden beams, a rock fireplace that went all the way to the roof and a wall of glass facing the same landscape visible from the master bedroom. I had converted the dining room area into an office and had my bookshelves and desk there, facing the living area where a recliner, sofa and loveseat combination were arranged in front of the fireplace. Between the two, there was a built-in wet bar where my collection of single-malt scotch whiskey was arrayed.

I went into the kitchen area and plugged a K-cup into the coffee maker, retrieved a coffee mug from the dishwasher and activated the machine. As I waited for the coffee to brew, I contemplated the kitchen. It featured the same tiled floor found throughout the condo, 42-inch Maplewood cabinets, tiled countertops and a full complement of gourmet appliances to include a Viking gas range and a Sub-zero refrigerator/freezer. I shook my head as I looked around me. There was no way my meager cooking skills would ever do this kitchen justice.

Coffee in hand, I went to my favorite chair in the place, the recliner in front of the fireplace and sank into its soft leather cushions. I gazed out of the vast sliding-glass doors sightlessly, my eyes seeing the magnificent terrain beyond, but my brain not processing it.

"November thirteenth," I said to myself as I took the first sip of coffee. "Five years. I can't believe it."

Five years ago, today, I had buried someone close to me and begun a period of aimless wandering that had led me here, to Sedona, one of my favorite places on earth. I had discarded the accouterments of my past and taken on a new name, a new identity, and a new life. I had a job I liked, even though I had paid cash for the condo and had enough money in the bank that I never had to work again. I was exercising religiously and was in the best shape in years. My life was simple and uncluttered by drama, violence or relationships. I had accomplished everything I had set out to attain five years ago. I should have been content and at peace.

But instead, I was miserable. And at night, the names still came to me.

Gail Petersen.

Christine Billings.

Susan Turner.

Samantha Everheart.

The four women who had died because of me. Because they were around me.

There was the woman whom I had almost married and the daughter I barely knew. Still out there. Somewhere. Away from me. And away from the danger of me.

The danger of me. That was the other force I couldn't escape. I had once called it 'the Rage' and thought of it almost as an alternate personality or identity. I had done some unspeakable things under its influence. But the last five years had made me realize that what I assumed was a separate part of me, a personality that I became, was something more insidious, and more deeply embedded in me. It was a darkness, a thick, shadowy, darkness that was as much a part of me as my limbs and organs.

During my time in Sedona, I had been able to keep the Darkness repressed, through work and exercise, but it was still there. I could the feel it lurking inside of me, a tangible, powerful force, seeking a means of expression. It reminded me of magma deep in a smoldering volcano, simmering, circling, waiting, for something to trigger it.

As the years had passed, I had re-read the Lord of the Rings trilogy and had been reminded that the Darkness was similar to Tolkien's description of the ring - it wanted to be found. It wanted to be triggered. From time to time, some small stimulus would press the right button in me, and I would have a quick flash of intense anger and feel the release of the adrenaline into my blood and the ensuing heat in my body. My reaction each time was the same. I engaged my internal compartmentalization mechanisms, forced the Darkness back into its place and etched a smile on to my face. The problem was that these incidents were becoming more frequent and the Darkness was getting more challenging to mollify. It wanted to be fed. Soon. And that scared the shit out of me.

Unfortunately, there was no Mount Doom to destroy the Darkness. The only way to kill it was to kill myself. I realized that I missed risking my life. That was one of the things I had enjoyed about working with CIA. Maybe because I didn't care what happened to me. Or maybe because I secretly wanted to die.

I shook my head unconsciously as I allowed my brain to take in the scenic images beyond the glass that my eyes were gathering. I had hoped my self-imposed exile would have dimmed the memories, eased the guilt, and quelled the Darkness.

"But it didn't work," I whispered to the landscape beyond the glass. I took a long, slow sip of coffee and sighed for the second time that morning. "It didn't work at all."

My eyes went to the bar, and I entertained the prospect of a stiff Bloody Mary and crawling inside a bottle for the rest of the day.

"Tempting," I said to myself.

But I had a date with the gym this morning and even though I wasn't scheduled to fly today, there was a chance that Ian Brooks, my boss, would call me for a pop-up flight or if one of the other pilots called in sick.

"Besides," I said to myself, as mental images of my mother's drunken tirades came to mind, "you know where that road goes."

I hung my head and did the same thing I had done every day for the last five years. I said a prayer for the souls of four people who had made my life richer and had paid the ultimate price for it. I said a prayer to a god I wasn't sure existed or even cared. But I didn't do it for me, or even for him. I did it for them. I hoped that in the ultimate math of the afterlife in the universe, the prayers of one wretched soul might make a difference.

CHAPTER TWO

Saturday, November 14th
1930 Hours Local Time
Dahl and Delucca's Restaurant
Sedona, Arizona, USA

Days go by slowly in paradise. And even for a die-hard introvert like me, human companionship can sometimes make that time more enjoyable. So, after a long workout and dinner at home yesterday, I opted for an evening out tonight at one of the best restaurants in the area. Winter was a high season for Sedona and finding a spot at the bar in the small restaurant had taken a degree of patience. Eventually, I found a seat, at the end of the bar, next to a talkative couple. I exchanged pleasantries with them as Luigi, the bartender, walked up.

"So, a-what-a you say, Mr. Connor," he said with the distinct Italian accent that might have been contrived for the surroundings, "de usual? De Plymouth martini, shaken a-hard?"

I nodded at him. Luigi was probably about my age, but carried a substantial gut and a mop of dark hair that was probably a bad toupee. "You have a good memory, Luigi."

"Donna have to have-a good-a memory for you-a," he said. "You come here-a so much-a, you should own-a stock."

I smiled at him. It was true. I loved Italian food, and Dahl and Delucca's was the best place for it in town. I averaged one night a week here.

"I didn't know you had Plymouth gin here!" said the woman next to me. "It wasn't on the list you showed us."

Luigi shrugged and inclined his chin to me. "We a-keep it for a-Mr. Connor there." He's a regular. He kept-a-asking for it."

The woman turned to me. She was a redhead with elegant features and green eyes that were intensely curious. "What's so special about Plymouth?" she asked. "I thought Bombay Sapphire was as good as it got."

"As did I," I said. "Until I had Plymouth in a martini bar in London."

I kept my gaze on Luigi as I spoke. He was making his preparations for my drink. A portion of Plymouth had been carefully poured into a shaker, and the chilled glass rested on the bar in front of him. He sprayed the class exactly five times with a small spray bottle filled with dry vermouth. Then he shook the silver martini shaker with a vengeance for about thirty seconds. Finally, he poured the crystalline mixture of ice and gin into the martini glass and gently eased a slice of lime into it. He nodded to himself and carefully slid the glass across the bar's granite surface to me.

I raised the glass to my lips and took a healthy sip of the drink, allowing the supercooled gin to slide across my tongue and down my throat. I unconsciously closed my eyes in pleasure as the liquid silk caressed the inside of me, and I felt the first tinges of the alcohol glow.

"My goodness!" the redhead said. "That must be scrumptious!"

I opened my eyes, nodded a compliment to Luigi and offered her the glass. "You're welcome to a sip if it won't offend your husband there."

She snorted and elbowed the main next to her. "Maurice, he thinks we're married."

A balding man with a lineless face and an amused smile leaned forward to make eye contact with me. "She wishes," he said. "Problem is that she plays for the wrong team." He winked at me playfully.

I smiled back at him. "Understood!" I offered the woman my right hand. "Connor Price," I said. My pseudonym rolled off my tongue reflexively after five years. I wasn't sure I could have said "Colin Pearce" if had wanted to. "Pleased to meet you."

"Patricia Belmont," the redhead responded, presenting me a well-manicured right hand with long fingers and perfect nails. "Likewise." Her handshake was firm but gentle, and she kept her eyes on mine as our hands touched. She held onto my hand for about a microsecond longer than a normal handshake and then released as she motioned to the man next to her. "This is my very good friend, Maurice Durbin."

Maurice offered me his hand around the back of Patricia's seat, and we shook briefly.

"A pleasure to meet both of you," I said. Then I presented the martini glass to Patricia with both hands. "Please. Try it."

Patricia accepted the glass eagerly and raised it her lips. She took a small sip and seemed to relish it as she swallowed.

"Wow," she said after a moment. "How can it be that much smoother than Bombay?"

I shook my head. "No idea. But it is the gin that the first martini was made with, so there must be something to it."

She smiled at me. "You're quite the knowledgeable one."

"Not really. It says that on the back of the bottle."

Patricia laughed. "So, you can read too," she said, handing me my glass.

"Hard to believe, I know," I said, smiling back at her. I took a sip of the martini and again let the super-cooled spirit soak into me. I looked down at the glass and then back up at her. "Are you folks local?"

"I am," Patricia replied. "But I've only lived here for about five years. I lived down in Avondale before that. Maurice lives in Phoenix and is just visiting. There's a new gallery opening here that he wanted to see." She paused and eyed me for a moment. "You've got to be local as well if you're here so much."

I nodded. "I've been here about five years also, although it took me almost that long to find a place I liked well enough to buy."

'Well damn," Patricia said with an exaggerated sigh. "I'm a realtor. I wish I could have sold it to you. Who was your agent?"

"Maggie Bowman."

Patricia nodded. "With Reeves and Williams, right? I know her pretty well. She's terrific, and she's been in the business for a long time. Longer than me, that's for sure. I've only been a realtor since I moved up here." She eyed me keenly. "Where'd you buy?"

"I bought a condo up at the Summit."

She raised her eyebrows. "Very nice! Eastern view or western view?"

"Eastern. I liked the scenery in the western view a little better, but I didn't like looking down on Route 89A."

"Nice that you had a choice. Those things sell like crazy."

I nodded. "Maggie and I had been working together for a few years, and I couldn't find anything I really liked. As soon as she heard those two units were coming onto the market, she had me in there to see them. We had an offer in before they were even listed on MLS."

Patricia nodded knowingly. "She's been a top producer for years. I'm still learning the ropes."

I allowed my eyes to take her in more thoroughly. After

years of flying wealthy people in business jets, I learned how to recognize the signs of affluence when I saw them. The black cocktail dress she wore was chic and sported a quality of manufacture not found in a department store. I was betting it was Dior. Her matching black shoes featured the red soles of Christian Louboutin. I smiled and nodded to myself slightly. Patricia cocked her head as she saw the look of knowledge in my eyes.

"I obviously don't have to rely on my income as a realtor," she said softly.

I smiled at her nervously. "Sorry," I said. "In a past life, I learned how to recognize clothes that were high end. I didn't mean to stare or offend."

She smiled back at me, but it was a sad smile. "No offense taken. I'm actually impressed that you noticed."

I shrugged sheepishly. "Comes with the turf, unfortunately."

'You're not a cop, are you?" she asked.

It was my turn to laugh. "No. Just someone who observes things." I took a sip of my martini and looked at her over my glass. "I'm sorry to intrude."

Patricia wasn't going to let me off the hook that easily. "So, you're wondering how someone who doesn't rely on their job for income can afford the dress and shoes."

I held up my right hand in a gesture of concession.

"It's absolutely none of my business," I said with an apologetic tone. "Like I said, I didn't mean to intrude."

"You're not intruding," Patricia said. Then she leaned toward me and looked me in the eyes. "There's something about you that is very intriguing, Mr. Price."

It was my turn to laugh. "Respectfully, ma'am, you need to get out more."

She laughed as well but held my eyes. "I meet a lot of people in my job. The few of them who intrigue me are typically married or from out of town or both. You're neither."

I inclined my head toward her in gratitude. “I appreciate that. But how do you know I’m not married?”

She smiled at me and leaned back. “Trust me. I can tell.”

“You don’t seem to be married either,” I said. “I find that quite surprising given your,” I gestured at her with my glass, making a small circle with it to show that I was talking about her appearance, “presentation.”

Patricia laughed and nodded her head in acceptance of the compliment. Then she looked away, and her eyes grew distant. “Thank you,” she said. “My husband passed five years ago. That’s why I moved up here. Since then, relationships haven’t really been on my agenda.”

My mind connected the dots quickly. Patricia’s husband’s death had generated insurance money. Probably quite a bit of it. That’s why she dressed the way she did but didn’t have to be successful at her current job. Money generated by death, even substantial money, was never a consolation for a beloved person lost. When my father had died, early in my USAF career, he had left behind a substantial inheritance for my two brothers and me. But as welcome as the money had been, I would have exchanged it in a moment for more time with my father.

“I’m really sorry,” I said, softly. “I’ve lost people I cared about too, and it totally sucks.”

She nodded, her eyes still fixed on a point across the room. “Yes, it does. Especially when it’s a suicide.”

I was stunned. “Jesus,” I whispered involuntarily. “Then I’m doubly sorry. My mother died by her own hand although she did it over several years instead of all at once.”

“Alcohol?”

I nodded. “Yes, he says as he nurses his martini. She was an alcoholic, and she felt so sorry for herself that she drank herself to death.”

“Wow, that stinks as well. I’m sorry for you.”

"I'm not trying to make this about me," I said. "I just wanted you to know that I might have a small clue about how you feel, although I can't know what it was truly like for you."

"Can I have another sip of that?"

I offered her the glass, and she took a long, slow drink, closing her eyes as she let the liquid slide between her lips.

"Damn, that's good," she said as she lowered the glass.

"Like liquid silk, isn't it?"

She thought for a moment and then nodded in agreement. "That's an excellent description." She looked down at the glass, which now had two distinct lipstick marks on her side of it. "I think I might owe you a new one of these."

"You're welcome to the rest of that one," I said. "I think I owe it to you. I didn't mean to stir up bad memories."

I nodded at Luigi, who was standing a discreet distance away. He returned the nod and got to his work.

"You didn't stir anything up," she said, still looking down at the glass. "It's always been there. You don't ever forget the sight of your husband hanging from a beam in the garage when you return home after a trip to the grocery store."

My ever-active imagination drew a mental picture, and I almost gasped. "Holy shit, Patricia. I don't know what to say."

She took another sip of the martini unconsciously and kept her eyes down. "The irony is that he's the one I was shopping for. He wanted a special meal before..." her voice trailed off. She blinked her eyes a few times and raised them to me. "Let's drink to something happy," she said. She inclined her head to the bar counter to my left.

My freshly-prepared martini had arrived. I reached over and picked the drink up with my right hand. "What do you want to drink to?" I asked.

"How about great people you meet in a bar?" she said.

"I'll drink to that."

We clinked glasses and sipped from them in silence as

we looked at each other. The glow from the Plymouth was taking root inside of me, and I could feel a subtle current of electricity building between us. Patricia continued to gaze thoughtfully at me and then she seemed to make some sort of decision and nodded to herself.

"He was in the military," she said. "And he got involved with something he shouldn't have gotten involved with. He was supposed to turn himself in to the security police at Luke Air Force Base the next day." She looked down again and swallowed hard. "That obviously didn't happen."

A collision of coincidences occurred in my brain as I processed what she said. Luke Air Force Base. A little over five years ago. Right about the time when I was there, taking down Mark Tappan, the wing commander, for selling F-35s to the Chinese.

Damn, I thought.

"I was in the Air Force," I said, without really thinking about it. "I retired a long time ago."

"I thought you might have been," Patricia said. "I bet you flew fighters. You have the look."

I smiled at her sardonically and took a sip of my martini. "My last assignment was at Luke as a matter of fact."

"What was the last job you had?"

"I was the operations officer for the 310th Fighter Squadron," I said. "My commander and I had something of a falling out. I retired shortly after that."

"My husband was the vice wing commander. He worked for an asshole named Mark Tappan who got him into trouble. And my Barney was never very good at standing up to troublemakers."

So, there was more fallout after Tappan went down, I thought. I had known that some of his accomplices had been apprehended, but apparently, the OSI had continued the investigation and found more of them. It was too bad.

I liked this woman. More than I had liked others I had met over the last five years. But nothing could ever exist between us. I had been at least partially responsible for her former husband's death, and the ghosts would never let that go.

"Patricia, dear, we're going to be late for the opening!" Maurice said, in a polite whisper.

"Okay honey," she said, keeping her eyes fixed on me. She seemed to see something in my face that disappointed her a little. I found that I regretted that. "I don't know why I told you that," she said, lifting her glass and finishing what remained of her martini. "I've never told anyone." She put the glass on the bar. "I hope I haven't put you off."

"Not at all," I said, hating myself for lying to her.

"Sure," she said, rising to her feet. She reached into a Prada purse, removed a business card, and placed it on the bar next to me. "In case you feel the urge to buy another house."

She and Maurice left the bar, and I was left to my thoughts and my martini. Again. I turned back to the bar and ordered one of my usual dishes from Luigi without thinking about which one I selected. Then I gazed into the depths of my martini glass and contemplated my life.

"Something has to change soon," I said to myself. "Something has to break."

"Mister Connor?" Luigi asked.

I shook my head at him and continued to stare into my glass. Something did have to change. The ghosts of my past were changing their tactics. They used to just torment me when I was alone. Now they were using surrogates. And the Darkness was increasing its pressure inside me as well. I was going to have to do something. I just had no idea what that would be.

It wouldn't be long before I found out.

CHAPTER THREE

Monday, November 16th
0900 Hours Local Time
10,000 Feet MSL and 250 Knots
Near Sedona, Arizona, USA

It was a crisp autumn day in Northern Arizona, and the OV-10's turboprop engines were chewing their way through the chilly air, generating more thrust than they usually did around here and pushing the stubby aircraft through the air at about 250 knots. For the first time in a long while, I was alone in the sky, without a customer in the backseat. I wanted to take advantage of the solitude and watch the formations of red rocks go by underneath me without having to describe them to someone else.

The maintenance test flight had gone well, and the newly-installed number two engine was performing as required. I had finished the test card a few minutes early and was taking my time getting back to the field, reveling in my airborne isolation among some of the most striking landmarks on the face of the earth. One of the best features of the OV was the canopy, which met the side panels of the aircraft below the level of the pilot's waist and bowed out such that the pilot could look almost straight down without having to bank the aircraft. I took advantage of that visibility as I flew a wide downwind leg to runway 03 at the Sedona Airport, well east of Highway 179, and gazed at Bell Rock in the foreground and Cathedral Rock beyond. The red sandstone formations gleamed in the morning sunlight, and today, looking down upon them, I felt a small release from the guilt and anger inside of me.

"Blazer one, Base," the VHF-FM radio's scratchy audio reached into my ear and pulled me into the moment. Back in the day when the OV-10 was a wartime platform for forward air controllers, the aircraft had five operative radios. This particular plane had three, two VHF-AM radios and a VHF-FM.

I reached down to the right console and turned the MIC TRANSMIT wafer switch to VHF-FM. Then I hit the mic button on the throttle. "Blazer one," I answered.

"Test complete?" It was Ian Brooks' voice, clearly discernible through the scratch of the FM transmission.

"Affirmative," I answered. "No issues. Aircraft is code one."

"Then get it back here," Brooks said. "You're burnin' daylight and we have a paying customer waiting!"

"Roger," I replied. "On the deck in ten."

"Sooner if you can," Brooks said. "Base out."

I sighed and banked the plane up to the right to turn it to the airport more quickly. My time of peaceful contemplation was over. It was time to go back to work and do one of the many missions Brooks Air Service was noted for. While aerial tours and aerobatic flights were our staples, we also performed search and rescue flights for lost and stranded hikers as well as forest fire spotting flights when required. I didn't know what sort of paying customer Brooks had referred to. Most of the time our customers wanted aerial tours in an aircraft that had fantastic visibility and was reasonably fast. But other times, they'd want to get some g on their asses with aerobatics. The 7-g-capable OV-10 could provide them all the g they could handle. I liked the aerobatic flights the most. I loved the feeling of g, even if it meant having to clean some vomit out of the rear cockpit when the flight was over.

"Blazer One, Base." A cold, British, female voice came over the VHF-FM radio this time. Brooks' sister, Anne, performed scheduling and dispatching duties for the small company.

"Blazer One," I replied.

"The Boss wants you to fly an overhead pattern to a low approach and do a closed pull-up to a full-stop." She almost yawned as the finished the sentence. She sounded like she couldn't have been more bored.

For just a moment, I felt the Darkness stir inside of me, like a single guitar string being pulled and released.

Wow, I thought. *Where the hell did that come from?*

I pushed the Darkness down and forced myself back into the moment. Brooks wanted a little show for his customer and was asking me to provide the entertainment. I channeled the adrenaline generated by the Darkness into enthusiasm for the task at hand. "Blazer One, wilco," I said after a moment.

I rolled the OV up onto its right wing and let the nose fall through the horizon as I advanced the propeller condition levers from NORMAL FLIGHT to T.O./LAND. Instantly, the RPM of the two PT-76 engines increased to 100% as each engine's four propeller blades were scheduled into the regime to provide the most instantaneous thrust for the landing pattern. I leveled the aircraft off at 6,000 feet MSL, about 1200 feet above the field elevation for the Sedona Airport. I was now five miles southeast of the airport, on a right base leg to runway 03. I performed a quick descent check, returned the mic wafer switch to VHF-AM 1 and pressed the mic button.

"Sedona traffic, Blazer One, a single OV-10, five miles to the southeast for landing. We'll be flying an overhead traffic pattern for landing with left-hand turns. Sedona."

There was no answer. Sedona was an uncontrolled airport and as such, had no control tower. Instead, pilots reported their positions and intentions on a CTAF, a common traffic advisory frequency.

I applied back pressure to the control stick and pulled the nose around to intercept the extended centerline of Runway 03. Four miles ahead of me, in the distance, the 5,132 feet of runway beckoned to me, stretching the entire length of a small plateau that was 500 feet above the surrounding terrain. As it had so many times in the last few years, the airport reminded me of a geologic aircraft carrier, jutting out of the center of the valley formed by the tall red rocks that surrounded it.

"Sedona Traffic, Blazer One, three-mile initial for Runway 03 at 6,000. Left-hand turns. Sedona."

I pushed the OV's throttles all the way forward to MILITARY, so the aircraft could accelerate to the maximum speed it could attain in level flight. Today, with the cold air and the two PT6s powering it, I thought I might get up to 280 knots.

Back in the day, when I was flying USAF OV-10s at George Air Force Base in the high desert of California, we were lucky to get 200 knots in straight and level flight. Those engines were the Garrett AiResearch T-76s that had come stock on the OV. But Ian had managed to convince the FAA to issue a supplemental type certificate to modify these aircraft with Pratt and Whitney PT6 engines. The Pratt engines were ubiquitous in the aviation community today and much more reliable and easier to maintain than the Vietnam War-Era T-76s. Not to mention the fact that the Pratt engines generated a hell of lot more thrust. I glanced through the head-up display or HUD in the OV's modernized cockpit. The airspeed tape had settled at 282 knots.

"Perfect," I said to myself.

The approach end of the runway went underneath the nose

of the aircraft, and I slowly counted to five. Then, I retarded the throttles to the mid-range, rolled the OV up onto its left wing and applied about five g's worth of back pressure to the control stick to make the 180-degree turn to the downwind leg and bleed off some airspeed. The aircraft's stubby nose tracked smoothly across the horizon at about 15 degrees per second. I looked down through the left side of the canopy. I could see the road that led down from the airport passing below me. Cars were parked along the road, in the small parking lots near the overlooks and hiking trails. Several people in the western overlook were looking up at me as I passed over them. A few were pointing at my aircraft.

I rolled out on downwind, checked the airspeed below 155 knots and dropped the landing gear. When the airspeed decreased through 130, I deployed the flaps to the 40-degree DOWN position. The approach end of the runway went by on the left side, and I continued southwest on a heading of 210. I glanced at the GPS display on the HUD to confirm the winds and saw 040/03 displayed.

"Barely anything," I said to myself. I looked at the flap indicator, the landing gear handle, and the hydraulic gauge and nodded. Then I hit the landing lights switch and moved my hand to the mic button.

"Sedona Traffic, Blazer One, single OV-10, turning a left base to Runway 03, low approach, Sedona."

I glanced over my left shoulder in time to see the approach end of the runway at my left 7:30 position, about 45 degrees behind the wingline. I rolled off "the perch" to begin the 180-degree descending turn to final, with 45 degrees of left bank and 15 degrees of descent. I kept about 1.5g's of back pressure on the stick to help the nose around.

Once the turn was established, I reflexively pushed down on the landing gear handle, glanced at the flap gauge and the hydraulic pressure gauge and the position of the landing lights switch, talking to myself as I performed each task. “Handle’s down, good pressure, flaps are set, lights are on,” I said.

The final turn in an overhead pattern is a precision maneuver. It requires the pilot to make a 180-degree turn and arrive on a one-mile final approach at exactly 300 feet above the runway elevation. Every time I flew one, which was often around here, it reminded me of my years in the USAF and put a smile on my face. Today, I was on my game. I rolled the OV-10 out at 5,100 feet, about 325 feet above the touchdown zone elevation of runway 03.

“Sedona traffic, Blazer One, single OV-10, one-mile final to Runway 03, low approach. Sedona,” I said as I checked my glideslope with the precision approach slope indicator lights or PAPIs on the left side of the runway. Two of the lights were white, and two were red. I was on glidepath.

I drove the OV down to the runway at 110 knots, adjusting the throttles to maintain the airspeed, and intentionally staying a little fast since I had no intention of landing. The black asphalt of the runway surface rose to me, as did the green desert foliage and red-tinged soil around the airport. I leveled the OV off in ground effect, with the main landing gear about three feet above the ground, and held it there for a few moments, to give the observers a good look at the aircraft. Then, I moved the power levers to MILITARY and raised the nose about 2-3 degrees. Once a slight climb was detectable, I raised the gear and retracted the flaps. The stubby prop-jet accelerated rapidly, and I applied slight forward pressure on the control stick to keep the climb rate under control as the aircraft gained speed. When I saw 160 knots in the HUD, I moved the control stick backward, rapidly but smoothly, and the OV shot skyward, the twin turboprop engines clawing at the air and pulling the plane upward. As the nose tracked through 30 degrees of climb, I applied left rudder and rolled the aircraft on its left wing, bringing the nose back down to the horizon and slowing the climb rate. When the nose approached the horizon, I applied a little more back pressure and pulled it into a tight 180-degree turn to another downwind leg. In a few more seconds, I rolled out at 6,000 feet on a 210 heading, perfectly spaced from the runway to make another turn to final.

I rolled out on final about 60 seconds later and kept the power levers at idle to decelerate to the prescribed final approach speed of 85 knots. As the airspeed approached 85, I eased the power levers forward, again marveling at how rapid the power response was with the turboprop engines. In most jets, even the F-16, there was a lag in engine response because the turbine-powered fan blades produced most of the thrust. This led to the pilot having to anticipate most throttle movements and move the throttle before the power change was needed. In the OV, like most turboprops, the response was instantaneous.

I pushed forward slightly to keep the propjet on glidepath and mentally cautioned myself to not pull the power back in the landing flare. Forty percent of the lift on the wings was generated by prop-wash, so a reduction of power in the flare would result in a very firm touchdown indeed. The threshold of the runway went under the nose, and as the runway environment rose around me, I lifted the nose of the aircraft very slightly. I touched down a moment later, checked the airspeed below 70 knots and pulled the power levers back to FULL REVERSE. The propeller blades changed pitch immediately and reversed the direction of the airflow from behind the aircraft to in front of it. I slowed to taxi speed in about seven seconds and cleared the runway.

There was minimal land on top of the plateau where Sedona's airport was situated, and the layout of the plateau dictated the placement of the runway and accompanying infrastructure. The runway occupied the easternmost portion of the plateau, where it was the longest. The parallel taxiway was west of the runway and stretched for nearly the entire length of the runway, except for the last 600 feet of the approach end of 03. The ramp area, with its assorted buildings and hangars, was situated on the northwest portion of the plateau, outside of the parallel taxiway.

Brooks Air Service was at the north end of the ramp. Brooks had somehow managed to buy all the land and hangars on the north end. Then, he razed the existing structures and built a complex for his operation that consisted of hangars, a maintenance shop, offices and a reception lobby for clients. I wasn't sure where he had obtained the money, but he had spared no expense on the construction.

As I taxied onto the ramp, one of the line technicians marshaled me into a 180-degree turn that brought me parallel to the lobby area and facing the runway. I set the parking brake, and the technician motioned for me to shut the aircraft down. I pulled the condition levers to FUEL SHUT-OFF and then pulled the power levels aft to the FULL REVERSE position. The turboprop engines wound down immediately, and the propellers went into the flat pitch locks as their rotation slowed. In mere moments, the ramp was quiet.

I put the safety pin into the ejection seat and unfastened my seat belt, survival kits straps and parachute shoulder harness. Then I removed my helmet and set it on the left console. I opened the canopy door on the right side of the cockpit and climbed down the few steps to the black asphalt of the ramp.

"Code one, Connor?" the technician asked. His name was Fred Collins, and he was the lead powerplant mechanic for Brooks' operation. He was about ten years younger than me and sported red hair and a freckled complexion that made him look like he was in his twenties.

I nodded as I released the leg straps from my parachute

harness and re-buckled them outside my legs. "New engine works like a champ. What generated the engine change anyway?"

"The old number two engine just wasn't generating enough RPM in MIL power," Fred said. "Both Alex and the boss flew it yesterday and said the same thing. And you know how the boss is, everything has to be perfect."

I nodded again. "I do," I said. Brooks was a stickler for impeccable maintenance on his aircraft. It was one of the many things I liked about working here.

"Boss says you need to get inside quickly," Fred said. "If you can sign off the test card, I'll get the rest of the paperwork completed."

I reached inside the right leg pocket of my flight suit and handed him the blue test card. "Already done. Hopefully, I got all the numbers annotated that you needed."

Fred gazed up and down the card for a few seconds, then nodded. "Looks good to me."

"The forms are in the cockpit," I said. "The plane's all yours. I guess you better get her fueled if we're supposed to go right back up."

"Truck's on the way," Fred said as he slipped past me to climb into the cockpit. "I'll have her post-flighted, pre-flighted and ready for you when you get back out here with your passenger."

I nodded and walked around the aircraft slowly, starting at the right landing gear, then around the twin-boom tail and finally to the left landing gear and nose wheel. I paid particular attention to the boom area, just aft of the engine exhaust port and behind the landing gear doors. The post-flight inspection was a crucial final task after every flight. If the aircraft had developed a fluid leak of some sort, or had been damaged in any way, it's the pilot's responsibility to find it, not the ground technician's, or at least that was my philosophy. The OV seemed none the worse for wear. I turned to enter the lobby area, which was easy to detect with its dark glass windows and glass door.

I stepped inside. After the bright sunlight on the ramp, it took my eyes a few moments to adjust to the lobby area. Anne Hanley had aspirations to be an interior decorator, and while her people skills left a lot to be desired, her handiwork in the lobby was impressive. There was a massive stone fireplace against one wall, an oriental rug in front of it and conversation groups of tables and chairs scattered about in perfect Feng Shui arrangements about the room. The ramp and parking lot sides of the lobby were all glass, but the glass was tinted, and the level of light falling into the place was perfect to make it intimate but not dark. To the right side of the room was the reception desk where Anne greeted customers and where Ian Brooks stood, along with a woman whom I presumed was our customer.

"Ah Connor, there you are," Ian Brooks said as his eyes left his customer and turned to me. "Nice little airshow by the way. Do I actually pay you to do that?"

Ian Brooks' appearance was a contrast in physiology. Even after five years of association with him, I found myself fascinated by it. He had black hair and sparkling blue eyes in a face that might have been younger than mine in age, but somehow older in cares and worries. His body was large but not fat, and he carried himself in a precise, even a mechanical way that at first seemed contrived, but the more time I had spent around him, just seemed to be a function of who he was.

"Hi Ian," I said as I approached. "The aircraft is good. Ready for our next customer."

"And here she is," he said, gesturing to the person he was speaking with. "Isabelle, may I present your pilot to you. His name is Conner Price."

The woman, who until now had her back to me, turned to

face me, clad in the standard desert tan Brooks Air Service customer flight suit. She was a woman of color with creamy cappuccino skin and a build and complexion that would have made a runway model jealous. She extended her hand.

"Isabelle," she said. "Isabelle Washington."

The name I knew her by was Sharona Brown. The five years between today and the night I left her bleeding to death in a car just outside of St. Petersburg, Russia went by in a flash. She was still hauntingly beautiful, but the years had aged her beyond the scope of the time that had elapsed. There was a look in her eyes that seemed both timeless and tired.

"Connor Price," I said, doing my best to keep my voice and hand steady. "So, what are you interested in today? A simple scenic tour or perhaps looking at the world while you're upside down?"

She smiled. "Maybe a little of both?"

I nodded at her. "We can make that happen." I shifted my gaze to Brooks. "Have you briefed her?"

He nodded. "And she's been through seat training and life support fitting as well. She was a quick study."

"Standard profile?" I asked.

Brooks nodded again. "Perhaps with an embellishment or two."

"Roger that," I said. I gave her my own briefing about our mission profile, including how the takeoff would feel, what maneuvers we'd perform and our route of flight. I finished the briefing with a review of emergency procedures and asked if she had questions about the material I had covered.

She shook her head.

Brooks listened to the briefing and nodded in approval. When I had finished, he spoke. "Ms. Washington, if you're ready, you can head out to the airplane. Our technician, Fred Collins, will get you strapped in."

She stooped to pick up the helmet bag that was on the

floor next to her and walked toward me. I motioned her to the door and held it open for her. I looked toward Brooks briefly after she walked through, and he smiled at me and mouthed words I had heard him use before.

"Be nice to her," he said. "She paid the full rate. In cash!"

"Of course, she did," I said to myself.

The fuel truck was pulling away as I walked outside, and Fred was helping 'Isabelle' get strapped into the back seat. I did a quick pre-flight inspection and then climbed up the ladder to look into the back seat to double-check that all of Isabelle/Sharona's connections were secure.

I checked that the thruster safety pin on the side of the ejection seat was pulled and nodded to myself when I saw that it was. Fred had apparently taken care of that.

"Pardon me," I said as I reached into her cockpit. "I need to get a bit familiar here to double check that you're all strapped in."

"Fine by me," she said with a smile.

I pulled on her shoulder harness straps and made sure they were in place, and the parachute risers were securely buckled. Then I pulled on her survival kit straps to check that they were fastened as well.

"Excuse me," I said as I reached around to the left side of her waist, found the buckle on that side, wedged between her hip and the console on the left side of the aircraft and gave it a quick tug.

"No problem," she said, the smile still fixed on her features.

Finally, I slid my fingers between her seatbelt and her body and nodded to myself. It was nice and tight. I could feel her ab muscles through the fabric of the flight suit. Her body seemed to be as rock hard as it had ever been.

"I know Ian briefed you but let's go over the seat one more time," I said, extracting my hand and forcing my mind into a more objective place. "I don't know how much experience you have in ejection seat aircraft, but the seat in the plane is a pretty good one, in spite of its age. Once I get the engines started, I'll tell you to pull your pin. Just reach down here, between your legs and pull the pin that's below the D ring."

She nodded at me.

"Do me a favor and let me see you reach down and touch it. Try to find it without looking."

She located it as if she had done it yesterday.

I felt a wry smile etch its way onto my face. *And you just might have*, I thought.

"Once you pull that pin, the seat is hot, and if you pull up on the handle, a few milliseconds later, the seat is out of here. So please try to keep your hands away from the handle unless we really have to get out of the aircraft."

She nodded again.

I gave her another quick version of the egress/ejection briefing, placing emphasis on the word "bailout." She listened and nodded at the appropriate times. As I talked, a radiant smile stayed on her face, and her eyes sparkled. I found myself marveling that she was both alive and here, now. I finished speaking and asked her if she had any questions.

She shook her head. For a moment, I lost myself in her eyes. Her expression was one of pure pleasure and enjoyment. There was no sense of triumph or agenda.

I was leaning on the rail of her open window with my hands hanging on the side of the cockpit toward her. She reached up and took both of my hands in hers. The feeling of her skin touching mine brought a surge of long-repressed emotion immediately to the surface.

"I know what you're thinking," she said. "Don't worry. We'll talk."

""I never thought I'd see you again," I said, fighting to get the words out without my voice cracking.

"That makes two of us," she said. "Now why don't you

get this contraption started and give me the tour I paid for."

"Yes ma'am," I said. "Did Fred tell you how to close and open the canopy, er, window?"

She nodded. "I'm good."

"Cool, see you on the radio in just a few."

I dismounted the steps, fastened my harness straps and climbed back into the OV's front cockpit. In a few moments, I was strapped in. I did a quick flow over the cockpit, checking that the side console, main panel, and HUD controls were where I left them and turned the battery switch on. Immediately, I could hear Isabelle/Sharona breathing into the boom mike attached to her helmet.

"How do you hear me, Ms. Washington," I asked over the intercom.

"Is this line recorded Mr. Price?" she asked.

"Not until when/if we turn on the video, ma'am," I answered.

"Ms. Washington is way too formal. What do you want to call me?"

"Sharona?"

She laughed. "Sure. That works. And it makes me smile. I haven't gone by that name for years."

"I always thought it suited you," I said.

I checked the flight controls, tested the fire detection system, and made sure the power levers were in GROUND START.

"I'm going to start the left engine now," I said. "Once I get it started, it's going to get noisy in here. When the engines are up to speed, I'm going to close my canopy windows. It's cool today so it shouldn't be hot in the cockpit. I'd recommend you do the same."

"Will do," Sharona replied.

I made a twirling motion of my left index finger at Fred, and he nodded. Then I reached down to the upper left console and moved the L START switch to the spring-loaded START position and released it. The left propeller began to turn toward me. I looked down at the digital RPM gauges on the OV's panel. As soon as the RPM rose above 10%, I pushed the condition lever to the NORMAL FLIGHT position. I watched the oil pressure and exhaust gas temperature gauges carefully as the engine wound up to speed and the RPM stabilized at 85% about a minute later. I retarded the left power lever into FULL REVERSE to get the prop off the flat pitch locks and then placed the lever into the GROUND START position.

I repeated the process with the number two engine on the right side of the aircraft and then completed the before taxi checks. Once again, I was grateful that Brooks had paid to have the avionics suite in the OV upgraded from the 1960's technology I had used when I had flown it in the USAF to a modern, all-glass system. There was a pilot's flight display (PFD) that featured a digital attitude indicator and horizontal situation indicator as well as a navigation display and a full complement of digital engine instruments and radios. While the aircraft still had a TACAN, VOR, DME, and ADF from its military days, there were two GPS receivers and even a laser-stabilized inertial navigation system. Brooks had spared no expense. As always, I wondered where the money had come from. The cost to restore, upgrade and equip five OV-10s had to have been well into the millions of dollars.

Like most glass cockpit aircraft, takeoff data was computed by the flight management system. I typed our gross weight and passenger load into the FMS and was rewarded with the correct takeoff speed, runway required and single-engine climb speed. We'd be taking off with no flaps today because it got the aircraft faster more quickly and increased the airspeed margin in the event of an engine failure. I hit the SEND button next to the speeds, and they appeared in my PFD and HUD.

"Are you ready to get some air under our asses, Miss

Sharona?" I asked over the intercom.

"In a big way!" she said.

I checked to make sure the radio transmit wafer switch was in the right position and then keyed the mic button on the right power lever.

"Sedona traffic, Blazer One, single OV-10, taxi from the north ramp for takeoff, Sedona."

"Sedona traffic, Helicopter November-five-six-eight-zulu-sierra five miles south for landing on the south helo pad, Sedona."

"He shouldn't be a factor," I said to myself.

I gave the chocks-out signal to Fred and he went under the nose to pull the wheel chocks out from the nosewheel. In a twin-propeller aircraft, removing the chocks on the main gear, just behind a turning propeller could be hazardous for the person doing the pulling.

I taxied us out to the parallel taxiway and then made the right turn to take us to the approach end of Runway 03. A few moments later, I took us out onto the runway and back-taxied to the end of the runway before turning the OV-10 around to face the northeast.

"So," I asked over the intercom. "Do you want it easy or do you want it hard?"

There was a laugh from the backseat. "What do you think?"

I pushed the condition levers to T.O./LAND and advanced the power levers to MILITARY.

"Hard it is," I said over the intercom. I keyed the mic. "Sedona traffic, Blazer One, single OV-10 departing runway 03, Sedona."

When the propellers reached rated RPM, I took my feet off the brake pedals, and the OV sprinted forward like a hot-rod at a green light. The airspeed increased rapidly in the cold desert air and in mere moments, the indicator in the HUD was approaching our takeoff speed of 118 knots.

"Here we go," I said over the intercom as I pulled back on the control stick. The OV-10 leaped into the air eagerly, and as soon as I saw the altimeter increasing, I reached for the landing gear handle on the left side of the panel. "Positive rate," I said to myself and pushed the gear handle upward as I continued to apply back pressure to the control stick. I peered into the HUD. When the flight path marker reached twenty degrees nose-high, I pushed forward to settle it there, and the red-rock terrain seemed to fall away from as we climbed into the morning sky.

"Wow," Sharona said through the intercom. "I wouldn't have thought a prop airplane could perform like this."

"Well it's not a Viper," I said. "But it's fun to fly, and there's no one trying to kill me while I'm flying it."

She laughed. "By the way, my compliments on the cover name. It's enough like your real name that it keys your ears but different enough to fool search engines."

"It's worked for me for five years," I replied. I banked the OV up on its left wing and let the nose settle to the horizon as we leveled off at 10,000 feet. I keyed the mic. "Sedona traffic, Blazer One, a single OV-10 departing to the northwest, Sedona." I released the mic button and sighed into the intercom.

"What was that for?"

"Don't take this wrong way because it's great to see you again," I said. "But I have to ask the inevitable question. When are the boys going to be here?"

She laughed. "They're not looking for you," she said. "I was the only one looking for you. That's why it took me so long."

"I thought I did a pretty good job hiding," I said. "Apparently not good enough. With no offense intended."

"None taken. Your legend and your supporting material are high quality, but when a new pilot's license appears in the FAA database, that's pretty easy to run down."

"Well shit," I said. "I guess I didn't count on that. The guy who put the legend together for me didn't tell me that was part of the deal."

"Sanford or Connelly?" she asked.

"Sanford," I said. "He was a little cheaper."

I saw her nod in the rearview mirrors mounted on the OV-10's upper canopy rail.

"The work was good. It took me a long time to find you. I've been at it since I recovered from the gunshot wounds five years ago."

I looked out of the left side of the OV-10's canopy as the red rocks of Sedona went by underneath us and swallowed hard. The emotion that had struck me earlier came back in force.

"I felt so badly about leaving you there," I said, forcing my voice under control.

"It was the mission," she said. "I was the one who told you to leave. You did what you had to do, and apparently, you saved the day again. You have absolutely nothing to be sorry for."

"Then you're not here to kill me or anything?" I asked.

She laughed again. It was bright and melodious and a treat for the ears. "I could never hurt you, Colin. You're one of my favorite people. I just wanted to see you again."

It was my turn to laugh. I wasn't sure whether it was relief or joy. Maybe it was both. Isabelle Washington/Sharona Brown was one of the deadliest people I had ever met. If she wanted me dead, I'd be dead before I knew what hit me.

"I'd love to believe that, Sharona," I said. "But you have a reason for everything, and I know that if you were looking for male companionship, there are a lot of guys who are better specimens than I am and would line up to spend time with you."

I saw her head turn in my rearview mirrors. She seemed to be staring at the terrain below us, but I could tell she was thinking about something very intently.

"We have a lot to talk about when you take me to dinner tonight," she said after a long moment.

"Oh, we do, do we?" I asked, laughing.

She turned her head and looked back at me in the rearview mirrors. "Yeah, we do," she said. "And you better take me someplace nice if you want to get lucky."

"Wow," I said. "The evening is getting more promising by the moment. And I think I know just the place."

"I bet you do," she said. "I'm sure you've made quite the run of the ladies in this town."

"You've got more confidence in my abilities with your gender than I deserve. And after watching one woman die in my arms, killing another and almost getting you killed in my last little adventure, I've been staying away from the fairer sex."

I saw her look down in my mirrors. "Actually," she said, "I know that too."

"You have done your research," I said. "So, you've been watching me as well."

She nodded. "Just long enough to be sure you weren't doing more for your boss than working for him."

I felt a lead weight drop in my stomach. "What do you mean?"

"That's one of the reasons I'm here, Colin," she said. "It's your boss, Ian Brooks. When I located you and found out where you worked and who you were working for, I got scared."

My eyes grew wide. "You, scared? I've seen you in action, Sharona. I can't believe you're afraid of anything."

She was shaking her head as I spoke. "I'm afraid of him," she said. "And he has quite the history with the Agency."

I leaned back against the ejection seat's headrest and sighed. "Well that's just great," I said. "I finally find a low-stress flying job, and my boss is an uber-criminal or something." I eyed her in the mirrors. "So, who the fuck is he?"

She was still shaking her head. "He's not a criminal," she said. "He used to be one of ours. And you're asking the wrong question."

"What do you mean?"

"It's not *who* he is that you should care about."

"If not who, then what?" I asked.

She nodded at me. "Exactly. It's *what* he might be that should scare you. It sure scares the shit out of me."

CHAPTER FOUR

Monday, November 16th
2230 Hours Local Time
My Condo
Sedona, Arizona, USA

The meal at the Mariposa Grill had been spectacular, as meals there typically were, and Sharona and I had spent a couple of hours enjoying the food, drinks and the scenic views provided by the restaurant's western exposure. We had made small talk about the food, the weather, and the political climate, and kept the realities of our acquaintance at a distance, along with the associated baggage and memories.

Finally, we adjourned to my condo to enjoy a scotch or two by the fireside in my living room. As I poured the spirit for both of us, Sharona wandered through my three-bedroom home, nodding her head at some of the art on the walls and the décor I had chosen. Finally, she seated herself on the sofa, displaying a fair amount of shapely calf as she crossed her legs in the long, black dress she was wearing.

"And this is?" she asked as I handed her a glen cairn glass with two fingers of whiskey in it.

"This would be the Glenmorangie Quinta Ruban. Glenmorangie with a port cask finish."

I sat down on the sofa with a discrete distance between us and raised my glass to hers. “Here’s to you being here,” I said. “I can’t think of much that has occurred in the last five years that makes me happier.”

Sharona smiled deferentially and raised her glass to mine. “I can think of something that might, but we’ll discuss that later.”

I nosed my whiskey with abandon, smelling the berries up front with a hint of cereal in the background. Then I tasted it and let the sensation of port wine and sugar rush over my tongue. The whiskey was almost chewy in my mouth. It finished with a long and fruity aftertaste that was quite sweet.

Sharona eyed me as I opened my eyes after finishing my first sip and smiled. She had a note of longing in her eyes as she looked at me. “All those years ago, in Cabo, I never forgot the way you sipped your whiskey. Like each sip was your last.”

“What makes single-malt great is the passion that each bottle has inside of it,” I said. “It’s malted, distilled, casked, aged and bottled by people who have been doing it for generations – by people who have devoted their entire lives to creating the art that is whiskey. It seems the least I can do is to honor that passion.”

“You are about passion,” Sharona said, as she sipped her own glass. “I know that much about you.” She held the whiskey in her mouth for a few moments and then swallowed it, relishing it as it made its way down her throat. “Wow, that is really good!”

I nodded at her and leaned back against my sofa, turning my gaze to the fire. “So, what’s this business about Brooks?” I asked.

Sharona scooted herself closer to me and put her head on my shoulder, slipping her left arm between my body and my right arm as she slid into position.

“The fire’s beautiful,” she said. “What is it, electric?”

I nodded, enjoying the feeling of her next to me. I decided to let the subject of my boss pass until she was ready to discuss it. "It's a wood-burning fireplace," I said. "But I didn't want to deal with the whole ashes and clean-up thing, so I bought an electric insert for it. You get almost the same ambiance with a lot more convenience and a lot less mess."

"It's nice," she said, almost like she was talking to herself. "Maybe when I have a place I actually spend time in, I'll buy one."

"Where are you living now?" I asked.

She sighed. "I have an apartment in Reston, Virginia. But I'm never there."

"I take it you're still pushing as hard as you were when we worked together?"

"Harder," she said. "Once I got out of the hospital, I felt like I had been out of the game for too long and I had to make up for the lost time."

I laughed humorlessly to myself and took another sip of scotch. "You remind me of me," I said. "It's one of the reasons I took this job. I have to fly, and on the days I don't, I miss it. I just look at the sky and want to be up there."

"Two lost souls," she said.

"So, it seems."

"Why'd you end up here?"

"I had fond memories of this place. Both from my time at Luke and from the F-35 business here several years ago. It seemed like the right place for me. It's out of the way, not too populated, the climate is mild, and the scenery keeps me grounded. Nothing like millions of years of geology to remind you of your place in the universe."

"Did you buy this place right away?"

I shook my head. "No. I lived in apartments and kept most of my stuff in storage for years. I just couldn't find something I really wanted to buy, and I also wasn't 100 percent sure I wanted to drop roots anywhere. Then, a few months ago, two of the units in this complex came up for sale and the agent I had been using sprung on them. We made an offer that day and closed in two weeks."

"It's a great place," Sharona said. "And you've decorated it well."

"It's comfortable, and it feels like home. Whatever that means."

Sharona kicked her shoes off and pulled her feet up, tucking her knees underneath her body and moving even closer to me. She squeezed my arm slightly. "Colin?" she asked.

I turned my head to gaze down at her. I could see a mixture of longing, affection and desire in her deep brown eyes. The playful competitiveness that used to live there appeared to be gone. At least for now. She trusted me, and she needed me.

And at this moment, I needed her.

I lowered my mouth to hers.

CHAPTER FIVE

Tuesday, November 17th
0722 Hours Local Time
My Condo
Sedona, Arizona, USA

The warmth of the sun on my face awakened me. As I blinked my eyes, I saw Sharona learning against the railing of my balcony, looking out over the houses below and red rocks beyond. She was naked, and her cappuccino skin seemed to sparkle in the morning sunlight. The curve of her highly-toned ass beckoned to me. I arose, found a robe in the nearby bathroom and donned it as I walked out onto the balcony with her.

"Good morning," I said in a soft voice. I slid in behind Sharona, and wrapped the robe around both of us, reveling in the feeling of her skin upon mine as I nudged up against her. As my body touched hers, I could feel a specific part of me becoming engorged as the possibilities of that contact came alive in my brain.

Sharona sighed and reclined against me.

"Did you get any sleep?" I asked her.

"Not much," she said. "But it was worth it."

I nodded against her shoulder. "We understand each

other," I said. "That makes the physical thing work better, I think."

"Yes," she replied. Then she exhaled slowly and deliberately and seemed to retrieve herself from the place where we were and into a more operational one. "I only have bits and pieces about Brooks. His file is classified at a level that is way above mine."

It took me a moment or two to catch up with her but then the import of her words struck me. "A level higher than yours? You do some of the most secret shit imaginable."

She nodded against me. "It surprised me too. I had heard the name around the Agency, but I didn't think the things I heard about him could be true. Almost like there was this mythology associated with him. I didn't press hard to find out more until I heard you were working for him. Then, I pulled out all the stops and asked everyone I knew, and no one would talk."

"Wow."

"I even asked Bart and Bruiser," she said.

I smiled as I recalled Amrine and Smith's handles. Amrine was a blonde and looked a little like Bart Simpson, so the "Bart" handle was obvious. Dave Smith was "Bruiser" because he was deadly with any kind of weapon imaginable.

"What did they say?"

"Only that they had worked with him in the past and didn't think he was cut out for long-term fieldwork."

"That's it?"

She nodded, still resting against me. "But I found one of the officers assigned to his original case. He wasn't willing to talk at first, but a lot of alcohol and poker helped me to open him up."

I tilted my head and pictured Sharona working her magic on an unsuspecting male. Apparently she had a full bag of tools available. Her prey had no chance of resisting her.

"And?" I asked after a moment.

She sighed. "Like you, Brooks is former Air Force. He was a test pilot at Edwards. But he was involved in some sort of accident in the early 2000s, and it took him out of flying for a while. He disappeared for the better part of a year. Then he showed up as part of some new project, and he became an in-house asset for us. We used him until..." Her voice trailed off.

"Asset? You mean assassin. How long was he with the Agency?"

"Until 2010. Brooks had the best closure record in the NCS. One hundred seven confirmed kills. Then, one day, he just left."

"Resigned?"

"No. He left."

"How do you just leave the CIA?"

"Good question. He vanished for about a year and then reappeared in a small town in Colorado. We sent a crew to retrieve him. They were...unsuccessful."

My eyes widened. CIA operations teams, the folks in the black tactical gear, were forces unto themselves. Most, if not all of them were former SEALs, Recon Marines or Army Special Forces. They were highly trained and utterly lethal.

"How does one man overcome a CIA ops team?"

"Not one team, two," Sharona said, quietly. "He wiped the first one out – down to the last man. Then he vanished again and reappeared here. That's when we sent the second team. He didn't kill those folks. He wanted them alive to send a message. But he broke them apart. Some of them will never walk again."

"Jesus," I said. "What the hell is he?"

Sharona shook her head. "That's the part I can't find out. All the records concerning his project have been expunged."

"What was the message?"

"He just wanted to be left alone. That was it. We paid him 'quiet money' even though he didn't ask for it and that's when he started the flight operation he has here."

I nodded. "That explains the money," I said. "Ian obviously didn't know you were from the Agency when you met with him yesterday."

She shrugged against me. "Maybe. Maybe not." She turned in my arms to face me. Then she leaned back to look up at me. "More importantly, does he know that you used to work for us?"

"I never told him anything. That doesn't mean that he doesn't know."

She nodded and lowered her gaze to my chest as she moved in closer to me. I could feel the warmth of her body against me, and the electricity between us began to flow again. She reached down between us, grasped my engorged member and squeezed it.

"Does this thing ever take a break?" she asked.

"It's been on break for five years. Maybe it's making up for lost time."

She smiled and lifted her face to mine. "So am I," she said.

##

Sharona left while I was showering for work. I discovered her note on my dresser when I was searching for socks.

Thank you for a wonderful night and morning. Never been good at personal good-byes. Be careful of Brooks. Have a feeling I'll see you soon.

XOXO Your "S"

PS - You should pay a visit to 1721 Stuarts

Drive, St. Charles, IL sometime. You'll like what you see.

I sat on the edge of my bed and read the note several times. I was no stranger to being left after a night of sex, and I was not surprised that Sharona had exited this way. Had circumstances been reversed, I might have done the same thing. The night we shared had been amazing, but we had both known it was a temporary thing. Oddly enough, that was one of the things that had made it special.

I left for work a few minutes later with a smile on my face.

CHAPTER SIX

Tuesday, November 17th
1200 Hours Local Time
Brooks Air Service Terminal
Sedona Airport (KSEZ)
Sedona, Arizona, USA

"Well you've got a shit-eating grin on your face, Price," Ian Brooks said as I walked into the crew office. "Did you get laid last night or something?"

Brooks' words startled me from my reverie, and I realized I had been smiling as I entered the building. My mind had drifted back to a few hours earlier when Sharona had wrapped her leg around me on the balcony. I marveled again at how two people who had nothing in common other than a few shared life and death experiences could meld so well. The sex had been utterly satisfying. The best I could remember other than Sarah, the woman I had almost married.

"Well?" Brooks demanded.

I snapped my mind back into the moment. The office was empty except for Brooks, Anne and me. Anne was sitting at her reception desk, but there was no one in the lobby, so she had pivoted her chair around and was observing me. She had a look on her dour face of intense suspicion. The brunette hair, which was typically pulled back into a severe ponytail behind her head, hung loose today and I realized that she was wearing a bit more makeup than usual.

Brooks leaned against one of the flight planning tables with his arms crossed and a look of suspicion on his own features. His tan flight suit had hiked up a bit, and I could see that he wore white athletic socks underneath his flight boots. For some reason, I had expected him to be a dark sock kind of guy. The legs that stuck into the socks seemed thick and muscular, but like the rest of his body, there was something disproportionate about them. His normally disheveled black air was neatly combed, and his blue eyes were not sparkling today.

I waited a moment or two and looked back at them. "Wow. I come in to catch up on a little paperwork, and this is my reception. Maybe I should have stayed at home."

"How long have you known the passenger you flew yesterday morning?" Brooks asked.

That's what this is about?

I had to struggle to keep my facial expression in check. Sharona's words from our conversation this morning were swimming in my head. "Why do you ask?" I asked, probably a few seconds too late.

"Because," Brooks said, his eyes squinting at me, "if you didn't know her, then your dinner at the Mariposa Grill would have been a violation of our 'don't socialize with the customers' rule. And if you did know her, you managed a perfect impersonation of someone who didn't when you met her."

I could have smacked myself. One of the things Brooks was very strict about was non-professional interactions between employees and customers. He had been burned a few times in the past when male and/or female crew members had slept with customers and clients and had then attempted to wield some sort of power in the organization as a result. The Mariposa Grill was one of the best restaurants in town. Sharona and I should have gone to someplace far less visible.

"I didn't recognize her at first," I said, which was technically true since she had her back to me when I first saw her. "But while we were flying together, we talked about things we had done, and we realized we shared some history. We went to dinner last night to talk about it." I raised my hands in an expression of apology. "Totally my bad, I forgot about the policy. You don't need to worry about it affecting operations though, it was my understanding that she was leaving this morning."

Brooks and Anne traded looks, and after a moment or two, Brooks began to nod slowly. "Okay, Connor. I'll let it slide, but I need to know something."

I raised my eyebrows at him.

"What sort of *history* did the two of you share?" he asked.

I had to think for a moment or two before I answered. I didn't have a story ready, and I was pretty sure that Brooks would detect a lie.

I crossed my arms and looked between the two of them. "Ian, I enjoy working here. You've got some cool planes, they're well maintained, and the flying is fun. But one of the main reasons I'm here is because you don't typically ask a lot of questions and I can maintain some anonymity. I can tell you that I've never done anything unlawful, but beyond that, I'd prefer to keep the rest of my history to myself."

Brooks exchanged glances with Anne again. I watched him closely and waited for his verdict. His face remained impassive, but I could tell he was struggling not to ask more questions. I leaned against the wall behind me and set my jaw into a determined expression. Brooks looked at me, and I watched the internal debate going on behind his eyes. Thanks to Sharona's revelations from earlier, I knew he had secrets of his own, and I was counting on that to curb his curiosity. Finally, after another few moments, he nodded slowly and rose from the table.

"That will have to be good enough," he said. "At least for now."

I nodded back at him. "I appreciate that. And no more dates with customers. I promise."

The phone on Anne's reception desk chose that exact moment to ring, and the tension in the small office was broken. Anne answered it and listened for a few seconds. "Let me get Ian for you," she said. "He'll pick up in a moment." She motioned to Brooks to pick up the call on a phone mounted next to the navigation table.

Brooks retrieved the handset and punched one of the line buttons. "Ian Brooks," he said. He listened for a few moments. "You bet. We can have an aircraft onscene in 30 minutes. Maybe less." He turned to the table and wrote something on the table's clear plastic surface with a grease pencil. "Got it. We'll have someone airborne ASAP. Our pleasure to help." He turned around to face me as he finished the call. "Our man will contact your unit on scene as soon as he gets there."

Brooks terminated the call and turned back to the table, which featured a 1:250,000 scale map beneath its plastic surface. "Get your ass over here, Price. I've got a mission for you. The highway patrol just called us, and we're the quickest responding asset available. You up for a little search and rescue today?"

I smiled as I walked over. "Now you're talkin'."

"The folks at the Goodwin Gliderport lost a glider. He pointed down to the map on the west side of the mountains between the towns of Cottonwood and Prescott. "The pilot made a call on 121.5 that she was losing altitude and going down just north of the town of Cherry."

I retrieved my publications bag from my locker on the

wall of the room, next to the planning table. While I had an iPad with charts and maps loaded on it, some things were better the old-fashioned way. I pulled out my own area map, a duplicate of the one Brooks had on the table, found the area he was talking about, and drew a circle around it with a black grease pencil.

"That's all we've got?" I asked.

He nodded.

"No chance she could still be airborne?"

Brooks shook his head. "Apparently not. She was a student pilot on her third solo."

"Might have gotten caught in some downdraft from the mountain wave we get this time of year," I said.

Brooks nodded. "Possibly. Now get into the hangar and help Fred get 876 out onto the ramp. You need to get airborne ASAP, find that girl and guide the medevac helos to her if required. Her mother was the Highway Patrol officer who called it in. She was on duty in the local area when the glider went down. She's pretty upset."

I looked over at him. For a moment, I thought I could see a little moisture in his left eye, but I thought I had to be mistaken. Brooks didn't do emotions. He didn't smile, didn't laugh, didn't show anything. But as he turned his back and left the room, I realized one thing. Usually, there was a remark about the money a particular sortie would make. Today, there wasn't.

Holy shit, I said to myself as I folded my map and put it back in my bag. *Ian has a tender spot for little-lost girls.*

I retrieved my helmet from the locker, stuffed it into my helmet bag, grabbed my pubs bag and made for the door of the crew room. As I walked to the door, Anne rose from her chair and blocked my way. She stood there with her arms crossed and a peculiar expression on her face.

"Who was this woman from last night?" she demanded.

Again, for just a moment, I felt the Darkness flash inside of me. For the second time in two days. I swallowed hard and pushed it down. "Just a friend from long ago," I said, forcing my voice into a normal tone.

"You sure seemed to be cozy with her."

I exhaled and shook my head as I looked down at her. "You were there," I said.

She nodded. "I work the bar when they need extra help. I made your martinis. You gave the server some pretty specific instructions."

I had to make a conscious effort to keep from raising my eyebrows. Anne? Working at a bar? Hard to believe. "And you followed those instructions well," I said after a moment. "The martini was excellent."

"I could make you another one sometime," she said, "In a more relaxed...locale." She allowed a smile to etch its way onto her normally sour features. It didn't look natural there.

At first, I thought I had misheard her. Anne and I had worked together for the last five years, and she had barely acknowledged my existence, let alone exhibited any interest in me.

"Excuse me?"

Go there! The Darkness flashed again, and it was all I could do to force it down.

Anne tried to keep the smile on her face, but an expression of impatience seeped into her features behind it. "Geez, you fighter guys can be dense. I was asking you if you wanted to come over one night and have a martini."

I breathed in and out very slowly as I waited for the adrenaline to dissipate. To say I was taken aback would have been an understatement. I couldn't decide whether I was a repulsed or curious. Maybe I was both. Anne was a transplanted Brit, with a pale complexion and a skinny build. She had pert breasts that were probably fake, and a nicely curved ass that seemed natural. She wasn't unattractive, but the pinched look on her face and the fact that she carried herself like she was slightly better than the rest of us made her undesirable. There could be only one possible motivation for her newfound interest. She wanted information. I wondered whether Brooks had put her up to it or whether she was working on her own.

Go there, said the Darkness. This time more insistently. *Go there.*

"So, what do you say, Connor? Does your social agenda have an opening? It would be nice to get to know each other a little after working together for so long."

The adrenaline was coursing through my veins, and the energy of it forced me into speech before I was ready. "Sure," I said. "But what would your brother say?" I asked. "He might object to two of the workers socializing."

A conspiratorial expression worked its way onto her face. "He'd probably never know. He does *things* at night. Or he sleeps. I hardly ever see him."

Interesting. "When is your schedule open?"

She nodded at me, and the smile returned to her face. "I'll pencil you in for Friday night," she said.

"Sounds good," I said. "Now I've got to get moving, or your brother is going to fire me."

She moved to allow me to pass and I did so quickly, feeling my skin crawl underneath my flightsuit. But inside of me, the Darkness was content. And eager for Friday night. I found that I was a little breathless.

"What the fuck, Pearce?" I mumbled to myself.

Fortunately, entering the hangar enabled me to shut that door in my mind and open another one. As I walked in, I was impressed by it, as always. It was 100 feet deep, 500 feet long and had 30-foot ceilings. The five OV-10's lined up in the middle of the vast floor seemed dwarfed by the place. Fred

Collins was attaching a remote-controlled tug to the nose wheel of the second aircraft in, N876PJ.

"You want to throw your gear into the cockpit, Connor?" he asked as I approached. "I'm going to need you to walk one of the wings as I pull this thing out."

"No problem, Fred."

Brooks and his Director of Maintenance, TJ Costello, were very strict about the procedure for towing operations. Moving an aircraft required three people, one person controlling the tug, one monitoring the left wing and another monitoring the right wing.

"Sure, Fred," I answered. "Who's going to walk the other wing?"

"TJ's around here somewhere. He'll be out here in a minute or two."

I nodded and walked up to 896, opened the canopy, and put my gear on the front seat. Then I shut the canopy and stepped back. I glanced over in the corner of the hangar, where there seemed to be two more OV-10-sized masses under a large tarpaulin.

"What's over there?" I asked. "I don't remember anything back in that corner."

Fred smirked at me. "You need to get into the hangar more," he said. "That's the boss's latest project. They showed up last month. Two more OV's but I think they might be D models. The boss works on them at night when no one is around. He says it helps him to relax. Maybe he has some new business idea for them."

"Huh," I said, looking at the tarpaulin-covered shapes." I didn't know Brooks had an A and P certificate."

Fred shrugged. "None of us did until these showed up."

"The D models were flown by the Marines," I said. "They were modified with forward-looking infrared radar, radar warning gear, countermeasures and some even had

20-millimeter gun turrets. I wonder what the hell he has in mind."

"Who knows," Fred said. "As long as I don't have to work on them, I don't really care. Keeping these five aircraft flying is a full-time job as it is."

"Sorry I took so long," a gruff voice said from behind us. "Fucking Pratt and Whitney. Getting stuff from them is like pulling teeth sometimes."

We turned to find TJ Costello walking across the hangar floor towards us. TJ was about 5 feet ten and stocky with closely-cropped black hair and a mustache of epic proportions. He smiled easily but he was meticulous about the maintenance of 'his' aircraft, and he didn't tolerate negligence or stupidity when it came those who operated them. I did my best to stay on his good side, but it was a daily challenge.

"Can you get the main door on your way over, TJ?" Fred asked.

Costello nodded and walked over to the door control panel next to the door to the lobby. He pressed and held the two bottoms marked OPEN and immediately, two massive electrical motors kicked on and the five-section hangar doors began to open slowly, each section rolling along in its individual track in the floor. In about thirty seconds, there was an opening between the two doors wide enough for an OV to pass through and Costello released the buttons and walked over to us. As soon as he was in place on the other wing, Fred actuated the remote-control unit hanging from straps around his neck, and the tug began to slowly move backward, towards the ramp, pulling the OV out of the hangar into the desert sun. I walked just outside of the right wing with my right arm held high and a 'thumbs up' displayed.

"Any idea how much gas is loaded on this thing," I asked as we walked.

"It's full," Fred said, looking over his shoulder to steer

as the tug left the hangar and ventured out onto the asphalt ramp. "I checked it when I preflighted it. The Boss texted me about the mission, so I made sure you have a pair of gyro-stabilized binoculars in the cockpit."

"Well done," I said. "Don't bother chocking this thing when we stop. I'll just get in the cockpit and set the parking brake."

Fred nodded as he brought the tug to a stop. I walked to the cockpit, stepped up and opened the canopy. Then I pulled parking brake handle on the bottom of the center console.

"Set!" I said.

Fred had already disconnected the tug from the OV's nose gear.

"Let me get this thing back into the hangar, and I'll come right back out and get you started."

I nodded at him and began a quick exterior pre-flight inspection. It didn't take long. The OV was a reasonably simple airplane, and TJ and his folks maintained them immaculately. As I came back around to the right side, Fred met me with the maintenance forms.

"No open write-ups," he said. "We replaced the right main tire yesterday. The plane is about 50 hours away from the next inspection."

I nodded as I paged through the 3-ring binder. The maintenance forms were duplicates of the ones I had used in the Air Force long ago.

"Looks good," I said, handing the book back to him. "Did you get a chance to secure the rear cockpit."

"I did, but you should check it."

"Roger that."

I stepped up on the boarding step and looked into the rear cockpit. When a pilot was flying solo, the seatbelts in the rear cockpit were buckled and cinched down to keep the seat cushion firmly in place. I checked the seat belt and ensured the radio and avionics settings were appropriate for solo flight. I scanned the cockpit for loose items and then shut the canopy, taking care to get the locking pins fully engaged.

I stepped back down to the ramp and buckled the leg straps on my parachute harness. Then I climbed into the front cockpit and strapped in.

CHAPTER SEVEN

Tuesday, November 17th
1223 Hours Local Time
Sedona Airport (KSEZ)
Sedona, Arizona, USA

A few minutes later the OV-10 leaped off runway 21, eagerly climbing into the crisp December air. As soon as I was safely airborne, I raised the landing gear and eased the control stick to the right to stay to the west of Cathedral Rock and follow highway 89A for my journey to the search site. In mere moments, I had leveled off at about 1,000 feet AGL – above ground level. I left the power levers all the way forward. Speed was my friend today. I needed to get to location Brooks had given me a soon as possible. The FAA had informed the Highway Patrol that an ELT, or emergency locator transmitter, was being received on the emergency frequency, 121.5. That meant one of two things, the pilot of the glider had actuated the transmitter, or more likely, the glider had crashed, which set off the ELT automatically.

As I made my turn to the west, the red rocks below and to my right went by in a kaleidoscope of color. I smiled as I gazed down at the landscape and took a brief moment to reflect on my good fortune. I had just experienced one of the best nights of my life with a beautiful woman, and now I was airborne to perform a mission that actually had some meaning. For the moment, life was good.

I lifted my eyes to the 8,000-foot ridge in front of me, about 12 miles away. The last known location of the glider in question was on the west side of that ridge. I glanced down at my altimeter. I was at about 6,000 feet MSL right now. I was sure the OV had the energy to climb over the ridge as I got closer. For the moment, I trimmed forward on the control stick and kept the propjet at 6,000 feet as it continued to accelerate through 280 knots. I smiled to myself. Between the extra thrust from the PT6 engines and the cool air, the OV was going to be a speed monster today.

I crossed Highway 89A and continued west. The highway led southwest down from Sedona to the town of Cottonwood, then north to Clarksdale and then east, through the picturesque village of Jerome, which was located about halfway up the eastern side of the ridge. From there, the highway went over the ridge via a series of S-turns and then descended into the valley where the town of Prescott lay.

Prescott, like Sedona, was a destination city in Northern Arizona and featured an 'Old-West' atmosphere for the tourists who came to visit. It was also home to the western campus of Embry-Riddle Aeronautical University, one of the premier aviation schools in the world. Embry-Riddle had a large flight school at the Ernest A. Love airport, just north of the town. I had often encountered aircraft from the flight school as I had flown in the western valley, distinctive with their blue and gold paint schemes. They were flown very professionally, and when the students or instructors spoke on the radio, they did so with precision and purpose, not like typical civilian pilots who tended to babble.

Ernest Love field was also home to an extensive glider operation, and the west side of the ridge between Sedona and

Prescott featured strong updraft air currents that could lift the sailplanes well into the atmosphere. While the updrafts were typically stronger in the summertime, sometimes the mountain wave airflow that occurred during the autumn/winter could provide spectacular lift, and it would draw glider pilots from the airfield to see how high they could climb and how long they could stay airborne. I had flown about 10 hours in a glider at the USAF Academy, many years ago, and I still remembered the quiet peace of flying the unpowered machine. It was almost as if I had been at one with the air.

I sighed at the memory as the town of Jerome appeared in front of me, about halfway up the eastern side of the ridge and about five miles away. A former copper-mining town, Jerome had since become a tourist stop with art galleries, curio shops, and a few distinctive restaurants. I had spent more than one afternoon on the porch bar of the Haunted Hamburger restaurant, nursing a few drinks and gazing to the east at the spectacular landscape that lay below.

I eased the control stick to the right and guided the OV between the towns of Clarksdale and Jerome, doing my best to maintain good public relations for my boss. Everyone in the local area knew the company that flew the distinctive-looking propjets and Brooks didn't like apologizing for the antics of his pilots. I kept the aircraft level and maintained about 290 knots, the maximum speed I could coax out of it. I approached the ridge at a 45-degree angle, aiming at a section of gray stone that protruded from the eastern side of the mass of trees and rocks, just north of Jerome. Tactical ridge crossings weren't something I got to do much these days, and I was going to take advantage of the opportunity. I kept the aircraft level until I was about 3000 feet from the rocks, then I pulled back on the control stick and rotated the OV's stubby nose to 30 degrees above the horizon, pushing forward slightly to hold the aircraft at that attitude. The aircraft shot skyward, trading airspeed for altitude. I watched the trees and rocks go by on the left side of the plane, and I slowly rolled the OV onto its back as I reached the top of the ridgeline. Then, I smoothly applied back pressure on the stick to pull the nose back down to earth and bring the aircraft in an arc across the top of the ridge and headed southwest across the back side of it.

As I rolled out, descending toward the crash site, I allowed myself a wry smile. Times may have changed, and I might have become older, but I could still get an airplane to do precisely what I wanted it to. I checked that the number three radio was on the proper FM frequency for the AHP unit monitoring the event and keyed the mic.

"Alpha-Hotel-Papa-Four-Zero-Seven, Blazer One, approaching your coordinates."

There was a burst of static in my headset, then a woman's voice came over the airwaves.

"Blazer One, AHP Four-Oh-Seven, we can hear you. You're only a few miles north of us."

I briefly wondered if the speaker was the pilot's mother before I responded. "Roger, Four-Zero-Seven. Have you received any better position information, or do you need me to do a DF on the ELT?"

"The satellites have narrowed it down a bit, Blazer. We have better coordinates. Tell me when you're ready to copy."

I nodded to myself as I released the control stick momentarily and retrieved a grease pencil from the kneeboard strapped to my right thigh. Then I keyed the mic in answer.

"Blazer One, ready to copy."

"Blazer One, lat long, 34 degrees, 42 minutes north, 112 degrees, 8 minutes west."

I took the control stick with my left hand and wrote the coordinates on the right canopy while she spoke, smiling to myself as I flashed back to the forward air control missions I had flown so long ago. I replaced the grease pencil and read the coordinates back to her while I programmed them into the OV's navigation computer.

"Coordinates are good, Blazer," the AHP officer replied, "site looks to be near the top of the ridge."

I leveled the OV off at about 7000 feet and began a slow right turn away from the ridge while I plotted the coordinates on my map and checked them in the digital display on the avionics.

"I agree Four-Zero-Seven. As I complete the turn, I'll step up there and take a look. Has the NTSB been called?"

"Affirmative, Blazer."

"Helos on standby?"

"Affirmative. They're at Love Field, waiting for your call."

"Copy that."

"Blazer, Four-Oh-Seven. Do you have time for a quick question?" The tone of the AHP officer's voice was different this time. It was tentative but curious in an urgent sort of way.

"Yes ma'am," I answered.

"Do you have a lot of experience at this sort of thing?"

I nodded to myself. It *was* her girl up there. "I used to be a Sandy, a search and rescue flight leader when I was in the Air Force," I said. "I've had the best training available. If she's up there, I'll find her."

"Thanks, Blazer," the accompanying sigh of relief was almost audible through the airwaves. "Please find her quickly."

"Count on it," I said.

I continued the right turn back toward the ridge as I called up a steering cue to the latest coordinates from the AHP. I rolled the OV out of the turn a few moments later, centering the steering cue and pulling the nose up to get back to the top of the ridge. I kept the power back as I climbed, letting the airspeed wind down so that I could conduct the search at a slower speed and give myself more time to inspect the terrain I was flying over. I was hopeful that the glider would be easy to find but depending on where it had gone down and how fast it had been traveling at impact, there might not be much left of it. I swallowed hard at that thought. It wasn't a message I wanted to convey.

I pushed the stick over at about 8,000 feet on the altimeter, about 200 feet above the top of the ridge, and adjusted the power to maintain 150 knots. I left the condition levers at T.O./LAND to keep the propellers at 100% RPM. I didn't think I'd need to maintain a lot of time on station and flying just above the top of a rocky ridge, I'd need the extra response from the engines if I got into trouble.

The trees on top of the ridge flashed underneath me as I headed toward the crash site. This area of the ridgeline had groups of trees interspersed with areas of rock outcroppings or boulders and the occasional vertical indentations, almost like small canyons. I hoped the glider didn't come to rest at the bottom of one of those.

One half mile to the crash site. I offset to the right slightly and slowed the OV another 20 knots, pulling the gyro-stabilized binoculars from their case and resting them on the right console as I flew. At an altitude of 200 feet, I wasn't sure I'd need them but wanted to keep them handy in the event I did.

Pine trees seemed to comprise the bulk of the vegetation, so there was a lot of green on the ridge below me, interspersed with areas of grey-brown where the hardwood trees had gone dormant for the winter. While the evergreen trees contrasted starkly with the rocks below them, the color of the hardwoods almost blended with that of the stones and I found myself blinking to ensure I didn't lose detail between the two as I looked downward.

Three tenths of a mile. I raised my visor to provide the maximum visual acuity as I scanned the terrain below. I also glanced ahead of the aircraft to make sure I wasn't going to run into the ridge or anything sticking up out of it. I didn't want to add to the number of rescue missions scrambled today.

One tenth of a mile to go. While I had faith in the coordinates provided by the satellites, which could triangulate on an ELT signal with high accuracy, the coordinates were only as accurate as my eyeballs or the computer could refine them. The distance between degrees and minutes of longitude varied the higher or lower latitude became, but latitude was constant with 60 nautical miles between degrees, so each minute of latitude was equal to one nautical mile or about 6,060 feet. Even if I flew precisely to the coordinates given to me by the AHP, I'd still have approximately a 12,000-foot diameter circle to search after I got there.

I reached the coordinates. Nothing there. I nodded to myself in acceptance and began a slow turn to the left as I started a methodical search pattern for the area.

"AHP Four-Zero-Seven, Blazer One has reached the coordinates. I'm beginning a search pattern over the area."

"Four-Oh-Seven copies, Blazer," the officer responded. "Hope you find her soon."

I nodded to myself. "Me too," I said into the intercom.

I alternated my gaze between the terrain to the inside of my turn and the front of the airplane, adjusting the power as required to maintain 130-150 knots and the optimum altitude over the ground. As my circle widened, the pattern of evergreen trees, hardwood trees, stone, and the occasional cleft in the rocks seemed to repeat itself. But there was no sign of the orange-colored glider, which should have stood out clearly against the terrain features below.

I shook my head as I continued to circle. "Damn," I said to myself. "Where the hell are you?"

I flew over a clearing and saw several gray shapes that

seemed to be moving. It took me a moment to understand what they were.

"Wolves?" I asked myself. "Really? Like we didn't have enough to deal with."

"AHP Four-Zero-Seven, Blazer One, I haven't found the glider yet, but I have found a pack of wolves, about eight to ten of them. That might make things more complicated if we bring the helos in."

"Thanks, Blazer," the AHP woman replied, with a note of apprehension in her voice. "Will advise rescue."

"What are they going to do? Bring a rifleman?" I asked myself as I continued to circle. Then I thought for a moment. I tightened up my turn to maintain sight of the pack. "What do you smell?" I said as I watched them. "Where are you going?"

I had owned dogs in my younger days and had always enjoyed the company of canine companions. As I had reached adulthood, my constant travel had made owning a dog implausible, but I still had a soft spot in my heart for them. I remembered how infinitely better a dog or wolf's sense smell was than a man's and how precisely they could detect possible food using only their noses.

"Damn," I said to myself, "you can smell her, can't you?"

The wolves were making their way across the terrain under me and slowly heading southwest across the top of the ridge. Their movement was intermittent but methodical. As I watched, I could see a few of the wolves in the front of the pack raising their noses to the air, like they were sniffing it.

"Holy shit," I said to myself. "You do smell her. Jesus."

I did some mental math. Love Field was about 20 nautical miles from here. At 120 knots, a helo would take about 10 minutes to get here, not counting the time it would take them to climb to this altitude. I continued my turn to the left and again checked to make sure I would clear the terrain as I orbited. Then I gazed down at the wolves as they continued to move to the southwest. As I banked up to fly around the pack and keep behind them, my eyes were drawn to a splash of color that was barely visible in a small group of evergreen trees. The shape was rectangular – like a wing.

"No way," I said into the intercom.

And then as I looked, a female in a blood-stained flight suit crawled out from behind the shape. I couldn't get to the mic button fast enough.

"This is Blazer One," I said. "I've got eyes on one survivor. She's alive and moving. Launch the rescue helo ASAP."

"Oh my God!" The officer said, her voice just barely cracking with emotion. But she quickly recovered herself. "Blazer One, AHP Four-Oh-Seven copies. Chopper will be scrambled."

"Four- Zero-Seven, Blazer One, can you get a rifleman aboard that chopper?"

There was a pause as the AHP officer considered my question.

"The pack of wolves is headed for the survivor," I said. "If we don't get some ordnance on them, they might attack her before you guys can rescue her!"

"Understood, Blazer," the officer said, her voice shaking just a bit. "Standby and I'll coordinate."

I looked down to see the wolves closing the gap to the wreckage. They seemed to be about three hundred meters away.

"Like hell," I said into the intercom. "She'll be dog food before you guys get your shit together."

Without thinking about it, I threw the OV's power levers forward and banked the aircraft on its left wing. I pulled the nose around to the pack as it moved toward the wreckage and the survivor and fell through the horizon. Then I rolled out and aimed the OV right at them. The aircraft accelerated as it descended, and I pushed the control stick forward to bring it to treetop level. While not as intimidating as the noise from a jet engine in full afterburner, the OV could make a little noise in its own right with both engines at military power and both props at 100% RPM. I just hoped it would be enough.

I flew over the pack seconds later and pulled the nose up like I was recovering from a bombing pass. As the nose broke the horizon, I stood the OV up on its left wing and looked to the inside of my turn to evaluate the results of my pass. Some of the wolves had scattered but a few of them, the ones that had been at the front of the pack, were continuing forward.

"Shit," I said to myself.

I checked my airspeed in the HUD. 120 knots. Not a lot of smash for a heavy OV flying in the mountains. But it would have to be enough. I eased the nose back around toward the pack, trying to maintain my airspeed as I kept a slight back pressure on the stick. The last pass had been downhill. This one would be uphill. I hoped I'd have the energy to recover the plane and not bust my ass on the rocks.

I gently applied some left rudder to help the nose around and pushed the stick down to make another pass. The OV floated downward and accelerated a bit. I aimed the nose at the pack leader and eased it down as low as I could stand it. The tops of the trees seemed to reach up for me as I descended, the branches appearing as willowy arms grasping for my aircraft and determined to pull me into the mountainside. I found an open area between the rows of trees as I rolled out, and I allowed the OV to get even lower. The tops of the trees were abeam me now, and the rocks of the forest below were large enough in relief to get my attention. The lead wolves were clearly visible in the windscreen ahead of me, and the one at the very front of the pack turned to stare at me. For a moment, I thought I could see into a pair of cold, grey-blue eyes above an impressive array of teeth.

Then, I looked upward and saw that as I had become

mesmerized by the wolves, the clearing around me was ending, abruptly, in front of me. I pulled the stick into my lap and felt the aircraft shudder with an accelerated stall.

"Fuck," I said. "Too hard!"

I eased off the back pressure, and the OV climbed upward, even as I heard and felt something scrape the left wing.

"Damn it, Pearce," I said to myself, in relief. I had only been milliseconds away from becoming a permanent part of the ridge. "Watch it! For God's sake!"

I stepped on the right rudder and brought the nose back to the horizon. I looked back to the inside of the turn and saw that nearly all the wolves were nowhere to be seen. All of them but one. The single, alpha wolf, the one I had matched eyes with, was still moving toward the survivor, only about 100 yards from her now. I could see the unkempt blonde hair of the survivor shaking as she saw the wolf walking toward her. She had survived an airplane crash, and now she had a wolf stalking her. It was a bad day all the way around.

"Blazer One, AHP Rescue," a voice announced on the VHF-AM frequency I was monitoring, "Two minutes out. We have you in sight."

"Two minutes," I said to myself, "I hope she's not dead by then." I keyed the mic. "Rescue, Blazer copies. We have a pack of wolves advancing on the survivor. I've been trying to scare them away, but one of them hasn't taken the hint. I'm going to make one more pass, and you guys will be cleared in. Just keep your eyes on me, and you'll see the clearing that I'll fly over. The survivor is just under the trees on the south side of the clearing."

"We see the clearing, Blazer," the helo pilot responded. "Is she near the wreckage on the south side?"

"Affirmative, Rescue. She was just trying to crawl out from behind it when the wolves showed up."

The lead wolf was only about fifty yards from the survivor.

He stood by himself in the middle of the clearing, his head held high and his eyes focused on his prey. His grey coat gleamed in the sunlight and even from my distance, I could see the muscles ripple under his fur. Any other time, I would have been lost in admiration and wonder over such a magnificent specimen. But not today. Today he was a hostile and that made him a target.

"I'd kill for a gun on this thing," I said, banking the aircraft to the right and easing the nose around with a little g on the control stick. I had more airspeed this time, about 170 knots, and the nose tracked smoothly. I picked my avenue between the rows of trees and rolled out, pointing the OV directly at the wolf and shoving the power forward as I pushed on the stick. I was going to need every ounce of energy possible to recover from this pass.

The wolf turned to look directly at me again as I descended towards him. The grey-blue eyes looked stubborn and defiant, but he stopped in his tracks and regarded my approach. I could see the corners of his mouth move upward in a snarl as I drew nearer. I felt my own muscles bunch in anticipation, and for a fraction of a moment, I felt my mind wander into a place where it contemplated the timeless contest between man and beast that had existed over the millennia of human existence. But the moment passed, and the shape of the wolf grew larger on my windscreen as I accelerated towards it at 200 knots.

210.

220.

I leveled off below just below the treetops, mere feet above the rocks and vegetation below, so low that the prop wash generated by the aircraft was stirring up debris around me as I flew.

The wolf stared at me defiantly with a primordial look in its eyes. "She's mine," it seemed to be saying as I flew towards it. "She's mine, and you aren't taking her."

I looked back at the creature through the OV's HUD and narrowed my eyes. "Not today, pal," I said. "Not today."

The trees in the clearing were closing in, but I had the geometry clear in my mind this time. At the last possible second, I pulled the stick into my lap, and the OV rotated upward, out of the green and into the blue. I cleared the wolf by mere feet, and the prop wash and downdraft from the wings blew down on him. I rolled the aircraft left and pulled the nose around to assess my pass. The wolf was nowhere to be seen, and the path to the survivor appeared to be clear.

I breathed a sigh of relief as I reversed my turn and climbed into the desert sky.

"Rescue, Blazer One," I said. "You're cleared in. Blazer will orbit until you've recovered the survivor."

"Blazer, Rescue copies."

The rescue crew was professional and quick. In mere moments, the S-76 was established in a hover over the clearing and officers were rappelling down to the glider pilot on the ground beneath them. They had no sooner touched down than a stretcher was lowered to them. A few minutes after that, the stretcher was on its way back up to the helo, with the glider pilot strapped into it. Then the two officers on the ground were retrieved, and the helo transitioned out of the hover and headed back toward Prescott.

"We've got her from here, Blazer," the helo pilot said. His voice had just a touch of Chuck-Yeager-West-Virginia in it. "She's actually in pretty good shape, just a little banged up."

"Good to hear, Rescue," I replied. "Great work. Next time I make my way to Prescott, I'll buy you guys a beer."

"It's us that will be doing the buying, Blazer. If you hadn't found her and chased those wolves away, who knows what would have happened."

"Happy to serve," I said.

##

I landed back at Sedona about thirty minutes later, once again taking my time to enjoy the scenery as I flew. Two solo flights in two days was an unheard-of luxury, and since this flight would be paid for by the AHP, I didn't think Brooks would begrudge me a few extra minutes flying above God's country.

I shut down the OV in front of the Brooks Air Service Terminal and handed the aircraft back to Fred and TJ, after annotating the maintenance forms with the flight time and the number of landings. The airplane had performed superbly, and there were no maintenance discrepancies to report. I thought I was finished until Costello confronted me after doing a quick inspection of the aircraft.

"Hey cowboy," he said, standing in front of me with his hands on his hips. "What the fuck do you think you're doing with my airplane?"

I was at a loss for a moment until I remembered the scraping sound I had heard on one of my passes to scare the wolves away.

"Uh, I might have gotten a bit low out there," I said.

"Ya think?" Costello's expression was one I had seen several times, a mixture of anger and disbelief. Anger that one of his 'babies' had been damaged and disbelief that a pilot could be so stupid as to do it. "You totally scraped the paint off the end of the left wingtip, and the navigation light is trashed."

"There were...tactical circumstances," I said. "I had to improvise."

"Hmmm," Costello said, his eyes narrowing. "No air show bullshit?"

I shook my head. "Never. I know better. I found the

survivor of a crash, and there was a pack of wolves trying to move in on her. I scared them away the best way I could."

"Which included dinging up one of my birds."

"A few of the wolves were somewhat persistent."

"I see. I'll have to let the boss know of course."

"Of course," I said. "I was going to debrief him anyway."

Costello and I walked into the terminal to find Brooks at his desk in his office and on the phone. He motioned for us to come in as he continued to talk.

"Thank you, Captain," he said. "It's our pleasure to help the Arizona Highway Patrol. I'll have my business person contact your accounting department to handle the billing."

Brooks hung up and looked at me. "Aren't you quite the hero."

I raised my eyebrows at him. "What do you mean?"

"Saving the helpless survivor from a pack of wolves? Doing low passes in one of my aircraft to scare away the wildlife?"

I nodded, looking back at him. "Seemed to be the thing to do at the time. But it worked out ok. The survivor made it out."

Brooks nodded back. "Indeed, she did. With rave reviews about her rescuers and a wild story about being saved by some brave pilot."

I heard Costello exhale next to me. "Great," he said. "Just great."

"Relax, TJ," Brooks said. "We won't be making a practice of this sort of thing. But it will be great publicity for us." Brooks paused for a moment and looked between the two of us. "Any damage to the aircraft?"

"I seemed to have scraped the left wingtip up and broken the position light there," I said. "I think I got a little lower on one pass than I intended."

"How long to repair, TJ?" Brooks asked.

"It will be ready to fly tomorrow," Costello answered. "Assuming we don't find any structural issues when we finish stripping the paint on the wingtip."

Brooks nodded. "Seems like a fair trade. This time. Just don't forget that I want the hangar to myself from 2200 to 0400."

Costello laughed. "No worries there, boss. None of my guys want to work that late anyway."

"Let me know if you need anything, TJ," Brooks said, indicating to Costello that his presence was no longer required.

"Will do," Costello said. He turned to go but gave me an angry look on his way out.

"So, Connor," Brooks said, leaning back in his desk chair and putting his hands behind his head. "Some poor survivor is out there on her own, about to be attacked by wolves and you risk your life to save her?"

"She was somebody's daughter," I answered, without hesitating. "It's what they taught us at Sandy School. It's all about the survivor."

"The mission comes first," Brooks said. I wasn't sure he was talking to me or talking to himself.

I nodded. "Always." Then I laughed to myself as a thought occurred to me.

"What?" Brooks said. "What's funny?"

I shrugged. "Nothing, really," I said. "This business today just reminded me of doing Sandy missions in the A-10. Made me miss not having a gun on the aircraft. That's the first time it's occurred to me since I joined you."

Brooks looked at me, his gaze even. "A gun, huh?"

I nodded again. "Yeah, I know. Silly, right?"

"Maybe," he said, a wry smile etching its way onto his rugged features. "Maybe not." He motioned me out of his office and returned to his paperwork.

CHAPTER EIGHT

Tuesday, November 17th
2347 Hours Local Time
My Condo
Sedona, Arizona, USA

It was almost midnight when I heard the rhythmic hum of turboprop engines outside of my windows. I was sitting in front of my fireplace and contemplating the electric flames with a glass of single-malt when the noise reached my ears. The sound startled me for a moment. I had never heard airplane noise this late in the evening, but my condo was closer to the airport than the apartment I had rented for most of my time in Sedona. For a moment, I was tempted to pass the sound off as a consequence of the location of my new residence.

But then my brain processed the sound further, and I realized that I recognized it.

"No way," I said to myself as I rose from the sofa and walked to the sliding glass door. "That sounds like an OV."

I opened the door and walked to the railing of the balcony outside my living room. My condo was located a few miles southwest of the airport, just to the west of the extended centerline of Runway 21, so I searched the night sky directly in front of me and to my right. But even as I looked, the sound was receding. I looked further to the southwest, trying to detect the red rotating beacon or strobe lights of the aircraft.

The sky appeared to be empty, but the sound was still there, slowly fading in the distance. As I squinted my eyes and gazed further to the southwest, a combination of moonlight and clouds briefly created an illuminated backdrop, and I saw the distinctive black silhouette of an OV-10 appear, just for a moment.

"Son of a bitch," I said to the night air. "He's flying blacked out. I wonder why."

##

After tossing and turning in my bed for a few hours and straining to hear the sound of turboprop engines, I rolled out of my bed, threw some clothes on and drove to the airport.

"Goddamn it, Pearce," I said as I guided the Dodge Challenger down a nearly deserted route 89A, "why the fuck are you doing this?"

My adventures with the CIA five years ago had been fueled by the inquisitive side of my brain. Four times in a row, I had almost gotten myself killed by answering a phone call and allowing curiosity and certain feelings inside of me to become invoked by what I heard, feelings that were grounded in personal relationships. In every instance, once the buttons were pushed, my innate stubbornness transformed me into an unstoppable force, pushing inexorably toward a resolution of the situation, usually through violent means.

The old buttons were being pushed again, and now, like five years ago, I was powerless to keep myself in check. Maybe it was the guilt that had haunted me over the last five years. Maybe it was seeing Sharona, alive after all this time and maybe it was the interval we had shared together. Maybe it was what she said about Brooks. Or maybe it was the way Brooks and Anne had behaved after her visit – like there might be something to hide.

There was more. Brooks was a bit gruff and unusual, but he seemed a decent guy, and he had treated me well. I didn't want to believe he was involved in anything the CIA would find untoward, especially with the history between him and the organization.

"Damn, Ian," I said as I made the right turn off 89A on to the airport road. "I hope you're not into some shit."

I kept mild pressure on the Challenger's gas pedal as I spurred it upward on the airport road, climbing to the mesa where the airport was situated. While I didn't spend the 70K to buy the 700 horsepower Hellcat engine, I did have 500 horses under the hood, and the slightest extra pressure on the gas pedal would create a loud muscle car roar if I wasn't careful. I wanted to be as stealthy as possible for my errand tonight.

I reached the mesa and idled up the roadway and made a left turn to follow the road down to our hangar complex. I pulled into our parking lot a few moments later and doused the headlights as I entered. I parked next to the main doors, retrieved a flashlight from my center console and exited the vehicle, taking care to shut the driver's door as quietly as I could.

As I approached the doors and found the key I needed to open them, the hum of turboprop engines became barely audible in the distance. I froze in my tracks.

He's coming back, I thought to myself. *He'll be here in minutes.*

While the return of the OV answered one of my questions for the evening, I was still curious about a few others. I unlocked the door and slid into the lobby, quickly moving to the alarm panel to disarm the system. But someone had beaten me to it. The alarm was already in the standby mode.

Was someone here?

I stepped into the pilot office, grateful that I had remembered to wear rubber-soled shoes to avoid clicking on the tile floor. The office was dark, and the door to Brooks' office was closed. There was no light coming out from under the doorway.

I nodded to myself. Another question answered. "He's the one flying," I whispered to myself.

I stepped out of the pilot office and across the lobby floor to the hangar door. As gently as I could, I rotated the knob and eased the door open, trying to stay as silent as possible.

The dark, quiet hangar mocked me as I looked in, devoid of activity or personnel. For a moment, I was tempted to turn on the overhead lights, but I thought better of it as I heard the sound of turboprop engines growing louder. He was on final approach. I only had a few minutes.

I turned on the flashlight and shone it about the hangar. The ground support equipment all seemed to be in its normal place. The tug and portable fire extinguishers were properly stowed. As I swept the flashlight about the open space, the beam illuminated the OV-10s squatting there in the darkness. I stepped across the floor, eager to see which one was gone for the evening, but as I approached, the beam illuminated the aircraft, and I realized that all five of them were still there, neatly aligned with military precision.

"Well shit," I said to myself. "What the hell is he flying?"

I heard the sound of turboprop engines going into reverse thrust, and a cold chill ran up my spine. I spun on the floor and shined the light on the corner of the hangar where the OV-10Ds were kept, squinting in the darkness to discern the shapes under the tarp that covered them.

My jaw dropped when I saw what was revealed, and I half-walked, half trotted over to the corner. Outside, the OV-10's engines outside came out of reverse thrust, indicating it was turning off the runway. I blinked as I shined my light into the corner, searching all portions of it to make sure I was seeing what I thought I was seeing.

One of the OV-10Ds was gone.

"Holy shit," I said to myself. "He's not fixing them. He's flying them."

I extinguished the light and hurried out of the hangar as quickly as I could, sneaking out of the lobby and back into my car. I started the car and idled out of the lot and down the parallel road, hoping that the Challenger's distinctive engine sound would be covered by the noise of the OV-10's engines. I had just turned off the parallel road and onto the access road when the night went silent, the OV-10's engines winding down and the props engaging the flat pitch locks.

I shook my head as I looked down at the clock on the Challenger's center console. It read 4:33 AM.

"Jesus, Brooks," I said as I guided the car down the access road. "What the fuck are you up to?"

CHAPTER NINE

Thursday, November 19th
1745 Hours Local Time
My Condo
Sedona, Arizona, USA

The discrete brown package was waiting on my doorstep when I arrived home from work. I nodded to myself as I retrieved it and stepped through the front door. I walked into the kitchen, threw my keys on the granite countertop and pulled a paring knife out of the wooden block next to the stove. Then I slit the package's seals and dug into the small box. Inside, wrapped in Styrofoam and plastic were two black, rectangular objects about the half the size and thickness of my iPhone. GPS trackers provided by the CIA, or at least from Sharona.

"Wow," I said to the empty room. "That's amazing."

I dug my phone out of my pocket and sent a text message to the private number Sharona had given me. PACKAGE RECEIVED, I wrote.

My phone rang immediately from the same number.

"Yes, ma'am?"

There was a low chuckle over the airwaves. "Don't you dare call me ma'am after the night we spent together," Sharona said. "It's not like I tied you up or anything."

"Might be an idea for next time," I said. "I'd like to ask where the hell you are and what the hell you're doing, but I'm sure it's way classified."

"Not today," she said. "I'm sitting in my apartment, staring at my new electric fireplace, and thinking of the last time I did this."

I smiled as I turned the rectangular object over in my hands. "Thanks for the toys."

She chuckled again. "Well, you asked so nicely. Besides, it seems like the least I could do. You gave me the only non-self-induced orgasms I've had in a long time."

I laughed. "Glad to be of service. So, what's the range on these things?"

"Theoretically, unlimited. They feed to a satellite and only answer when they're interrogated."

"Who will be monitoring the feed?"

"Just you and me. We're the only ones who have the tracker numbers, and you need the numbers to plug into the website to see them."

I nodded. "Perfect."

There was a pause. "What do you think he's up to, Colin?"

I shook my head even though I knew she couldn't see me. "Absolutely no fucking idea. But I'm going to find out. He flew again last night and was gone for about five hours."

"That's a long time."

"Yes, it is and who knows how long he's been doing this. Assuming he's using the D models it's only been about a month, but if he was using some of the A models, it could have been going on a lot longer."

"You mentioned that you heard him that one night. Wouldn't you have heard him before.?"

"Maybe. Maybe not. I only moved into this place a few months ago and if I was asleep or...otherwise distracted...I might not have heard it."

"We *were* making a little noise of our own, weren't we?"

"Yes, we were. I'm not sure I would have heard a hand grenade go off in the next room."

Sharona laughed. "Maybe we can do that again some time."

"Maybe we can."

She sighed. "What's your plan?"

I exhaled. "You know me. I really don't have one. I'm going to sneak into the hangar, find an unobtrusive place to put these on the two D-models and wait to see what happens."

"Be careful, Colin," Sharona said. "If he thinks you're up to something..." her voice trailed off.

"Don't worry. I'll be careful. I have to at least stay alive so that someone I know doesn't have to self-induce self-satisfaction."

"Good point," she said, chuckling. "You do need to keep at least one part of you safe."

"I'll do my best."

CHAPTER TEN

Friday, November 20th
1633 Hours Local Time
Brooks Air Service Terminal,
Sedona Airport (KSEZ)
Sedona, Arizona, USA

The sound of Anne's car starting in the parking lot was my cue. I stayed at my desk in the pilot area for five more minutes, trying to look busy in the event she came back into the building.

"Don't forget about martinis this evening," she had said as she walked out of the office a few moments ago.

The Darkness bubbled inside of me, and I could feel the accompanying adrenaline surge. "Wouldn't miss it," I responded, trying to keep my voice under control. "What time would you like me to be there?"

"About an hour from now, maybe? I have to pick up a few things and then get myself put together."

I had felt the maniacal grin stretching my features. "Sounds good."

Now I was alone in the building, and the Darkness was in its place. At least for the moment. I retrieved the two GPS trackers from my backpack and made my way through the lobby and into the hangar. The overhead lights were off in the hangar, but the sunlight streaming through the glass panes in the sidewalls created patterns of light and shadow on the highly-polished concrete floor.

I clicked my flashlight on and made my way around the five OV-10As parked in the center of the hangar to the tarpaulin in the back corner. The darkness and shadows in the corner made discerning the exact size and shape of the canvas difficult, but the general bulk of it seemed to confirm what I suspected – both OV-10D models were under it. I made my way to the edge of the tarpaulin, where it met the wall of the hangar, and slipped under it.

Both OV-10Ds stood side-by-side under the dark cloth. As I shined my light on them, I didn't notice any panels opened or any pools of hydraulic fluid, oil, or fuel on the floor. Both aircraft seemed to be in perfectly flyable condition. I let the beam of my light roam over the metal surfaces of the two OVs, looking for differences between these aircraft and the ones out on the floor.

"Sponsons," I said to myself. "These have sponsons. I wonder why."

Sponsons were stubby, wing-like structures that protruded 2-3 feet from the bottom of the fuselage, under the high-mounted wings. Back when I had flown the OV in the USAF, 7.62 machine guns could be put inside of them, and rocket pods and bombs could be hung from them.

"Weapons?" I asked myself. "Seriously?"

Other than the sponsons, the two D-models looked identical to their cousins on the other side of the tarpaulin. I approached the OV nearest me and opened the cargo door on the back of the fuselage. Looking around briefly in the compartment, I placed one of the GPS trackers on the underside of one of the stringer beams on the side of the compartment. Unlike a civilian aircraft, the interior supporting structure of the fuselage was often exposed in military planes. I nodded to myself as I looked at my handiwork. The tracker was impossible to see unless the observer knew exactly where to look.

I shut the compartment door, walked over to the other D-model and repeated the process. As I closed the latch on the door, the beam of my flashlight caught something shiny hanging from the sponson on the right side of the aircraft. As I trained my light on the sponson, I could see a metal wire hanging down from it to the floor.

"No fucking way," I said to myself.

I walked up to the sponson and crouched down to look underneath. The wire was hanging from one of the bomb racks mounted into the hard points on the sponson. As I regarded the other racks, I couldn't see any other wires, but I could see the copper-colored swivel links still sticking out of the solenoid slots at the front and rear ends of each rack. The links were two metallic rings joined by a swiveling connection. One end of the circle was inserted into the solenoid, and the other protruded below.

"14-inch lugs, dual-fused," I said as I looked at them. "Jesus Christ. What the fuck are you dropping, Brooks?"

I pinched the wire with my right thumb and index finger and rotated it between them.

"Damn," I said. "Must have broken off when the bomb was released."

The racks were designed to suspend and release 500-pound class weapons, typically 500-pound bombs. The bombs had lugs screwed into them that engaged the actual mechanism of the bomb racks. Wires to arm the nose and tail fuses were tied off on the lugs, routed through the swivel links inserted in the nose and tail solenoids and then inserted into the nose and tail fuses themselves. Fusing was selectable from the cockpit. When either nose or tail fusing was selected, the nose or tail solenoid would stay engaged at release, and the appropriate arming wire would be pulled to arm the associated fuse. The opposite solenoid would release the swivel link, the arming wire wouldn't be pulled, and that fuse would not arm. If both nose and tail fusing were selected, both solenoids would stay engaged, and both fuses would be armed. Occasionally, one of the wires would break off at release and get tangled in the rack. But, judging by the presence of all the links, Brooks had dropped all the weapons with both fuses armed so it wouldn't have mattered. All the bombs would have detonated.

"Makes sense," I said. "That's the way I would do it."

I stood up and shook my head at what I had found. Brooks wasn't just flying, he was bombing things or people or both. I felt a chill go up my spine as I remembered my first adventure with the CIA, many years ago, where an entire mercenary squadron was doing the same thing on a larger scale.

"It's déjà vu all over again," I said. "That's just fucking great.

CHAPTER ELEVEN

Friday, November 20th
1745 Hours Local Time
Brooks' House
Sedona, Arizona, USA

I pulled into the long driveway that ascended the hillside below Brooks' house about fifteen minutes later, having driven down from the airport and circumnavigated the airport mesa around its north end on highways 89A and 179. Brooks' house was located on the east side of the airport mesa, on a small plateau about 300 feet above the valley floor. With its southern exposure and massive windows, the house held spectacular views of Cathedral Rock, Courthouse Rock and Bell Rock to the south and the Chapel of the Holy Cross on the other side of the valley.

This wasn't my first visit to the property. Brooks hosted a yearly employee Christmas party at the house, and I had enjoyed more than a few cocktails as I had roamed the 270-degree deck on the upper level of the structure. As I entered the circular driveway and regarded the house, I found myself marveling at it again. It was two stories with a five-car garage on the bottom level and boasted at least 5,000 square feet of living space as well as a nicely sheltered private pool behind the house. Brooks had opted for a Mediterranean style of architecture instead of the southwestern adobe style so favored in the area. I commended him for his choice. The white stucco walls and red-tile roof seemed much more hospitable and welcoming than the mud-like adobe.

The sun was already behind the hills to the west, and the entry area was cast in shadow. Small pathway lights had illuminated, and they bathed the stone entry walk in a vibrant yellow glow. The windows of the house's main level were aglow as well. The place looked very inviting and enticing. It was a shame that the errand to be conducted there was so distasteful.

I stopped the Challenger in front of the covered entryway and shut the car down. Then, I retrieved the small bouquet of store-bought flowers, ran a quick hand through my hair and stepped out of the vehicle. I put the flowers on the roof of the car and reached into the back seat for my sportscoat. I slid into the jacket, grabbed the flowers and shut the car door behind me.

As I walked around the back of the Challenger and up the walk, I contemplated my reasons for the visit, while trying to slow my pace to the door. There were competing feelings of reluctance and eagerness at odds inside me. The hesitation came from the rational side of me, the part of me that saw tonight's visit as an information gathering mission and dreaded having to deal with Anne for the evening as that chore was conducted. The eagerness was generated solely by the Darkness, and I had no idea what its agenda was. And that scared the shit out of me.

"Here goes nothing," I said to myself as I reached the ornate wooden double door and pressed the doorbell button.

Inside, I heard the familiar Westminster chimes and smiled. They sounded very similar to the ones in my Grandfather clock back in my condo.

Anne swung the door open mere moments later like she had been waiting just behind it. She wore a black sheath dress that clung to her body in a way that was meant to be enticing but didn't quite succeed. Her brunette hair fell to her shoulders and shone in the light of the entryway fixtures. At work, any make-up she wore was perfunctory at best. Tonight, she had given herself the full treatment with eyeliner, eyeshadow, rouge, and bright red lipstick.

It was everything I could do to keep my mouth from dropping open in surprise, shock or horror. I couldn't decide which. For a moment, I felt a touch of empathy for this woman who was trying so desperately to be attractive and had the looks and body to pull it off but also had a personality that subtracted from it all so profoundly that it left her presentation with a negative balance.

But the Darkness liked what it saw and deep inside of me, I felt something begin to stir that I couldn't quite identify.

"Excuse me, ma'am," I said in an attempt to move beyond the moment. "Do I know you? I'm looking for someone named Anne. I think she lives here."

She shook her head and gave me a crooked smile. "Smart ass." She put her hands on her hips and stuck a model-like pose. "So, I clean up okay, do I?"

I nodded. "I'll say. I've seen you out of your work clothes at the Christmas parties, but never like this."

"A girl needs to indulge herself from time to time. Tonight seemed like the perfect occasion."

I bowed my head in deference. "Well thank you for doing so for me." I presented the flowers, suddenly feeling more dishonest than I had felt in a long time. "My mother said I should never show up at a beautiful woman's house empty-handed."

"Sounds like you were well trained," she said, accepting the flowers with a pleased smile on her face. "And they're lovely."

She opened the door wider to allow me into the foyer and shut it behind me after I entered.

"You might want to keep your jacket on," she said. "I thought we'd have drinks outside on the deck. I've got a fire burning in one of the chimeneas out there."

"Sounds great," I said. "Ladies first."

She nodded and walked up the wide, curved, stone staircase to the upper level. I followed her and deliberately avoided looking at her ass as she climbed in front of me.

The lighting on the upper level of the house was dim and romantic. The staircase terminated in between the formal dining room and kitchen area. Beyond the kitchen area lay the family room and a gas fire gleamed in the massive stone fireplace at the far end of the room.

After retrieving a vase, filling it with water, and placing the flowers in it, Anne led me outside to the deck. Just as she had said, a roaring fire glowed in a large chimenea between the outdoor bar and the southern railing of the deck.

"Have a seat," she said, motioning to one of the two armchairs facing each other on either side of the chimenea. "There are some appetizers on the table, and I already know what you want to drink."

I walked over to the railing and gazed out over the southern valley, watching the sun's last rays illuminate the uppermost regions of the red rock monuments and the eastern wall of the valley.

"You know I've obviously been here for the parties over the years, but I never forgot this view," I said. "It's quite spectacular."

"This year's party is next month," Anne said from behind me. "I take it you'll be here for it."

I nodded. "Of course."

"By yourself?"

I shrugged. "Probably. It's not like I have an aggressive social agenda to meet anyone."

"And why is that?"

I turned to face her, still leaning up against the railing. She stood behind the granite-covered bar with two frosty martini glasses in front of her. Each one held a slice of lime inside it.

"Vermouth in, swished around in the glass and then dumped out, slice of lime and then the gin, right?" She asked.

I nodded. "You have a good memory."

"For some things."

I looked around on the surface of the bar. "All that remains is the vigorous shake."

Anne reached into a compartment below the bar and retrieved a bottle of Plymouth gin, obviously fresh from the freezer. "Why shake it when it's already chilled?"

I nodded and inclined my head toward her. "Said like a true professional or gin lover or both. That's the way they make them at one of my favorite bars in the world."

"Where would that be?" She asked as she poured the syrupy nearly-frozen gin into the glasses.

"The Bar at the Dukes Hotel in London," I said. "It's probably where Ian Fleming invented the James Bond martini."

"Ironic that they don't shake there," Anne said as she retrieved the two martini glasses and brought them over to me.

"You know, I never thought about that. But it is ironic indeed."

She offered me one of the glasses, and I took it.

"Cheers," I said, raising my glass to her.

"To the evening," she responded. "Thank you for coming."

"Thank you for the invitation."

I took the first sip of my martini and tasted the smooth, silky goodness of the gin slide across my tongue and down my throat.

"Damn," I said involuntarily. "That's good." I took another sip and relished the taste again. "You make a mean martini, Anne."

"I've had a little practice." She took a sip of her own drink. "Wow, they are quite good, aren't they?"

I nodded at her and searched for a safe topic to continue the conversation. "Plymouth is the gin used to invent the martini," I said after an awkward pause.

She smirked at me. She tried to make it playful, but it came off as slightly contemptuous. The Darkness flashed inside of me again. If I hadn't had a glass of such outstanding gin in my hand, I would have been tempted to throw it in her face. "And what *research* did you have to do to come up with that little factoid?" she asked.

"None," I said, looking right into her eyes. "It's written on the back of the bottle, and I pay attention to things."

"All those years pouring gin and I never thought to read the bottles."

"Bars tend to be busy places. I'm sure you had other things on your mind. Which reminds me, with all of this," I made a gesture toward the deck and lavish house attached to it, "why do you moonlight at the Mariposa Grill?"

She sighed, either from exasperation with her circumstances or impatience. It was difficult to determine which. "Mostly to get out of the house. I tended bar in London before I came here," she said. "And it's like I told you. Ian is gone or sleeping a lot in the evenings. I don't enjoy being alone that much."

That's funny, I thought. *You sure do a good impersonation of someone who doesn't want company.*

"Now back to my previous question," she said.

I raised my eyebrows at her.

"Why don't you have a social agenda to find someone?"

I looked across the top of my glass at her. "Does there have to be a 'why?"

She eyed me suspiciously. "Maybe not for some people. But you're different."

"What makes you say that? Maybe I'm just lazy."

She smiled crookedly as she took a sip of her martini and then shook her head. "Not you. Don't forget, I schedule the flights and keep the books. You fly more than anybody else, and when you fly, you're the first pilot in and the last one out."

A compliment? Holy shit. I resisted the urge to put my hand to my chest in a gesture of mock cardiac arrest. "I might just be slow," I said after a moment.

Anne gave me what was intended to be a playful smack in the arm. It came off awkwardly, and I barely felt it. There was a look of surprise in her eyes as she lowered her arm. She didn't know about the hours I spent in the gym. "You're not slow either." Then she cocked her head and looked into my eyes. Even in the shadows of the deck, I could see curiosity in the dark eyes. "You're avoiding this question. Why?"

I turned away from her and leaned against the railing of the deck, looking out over the headlights on the roads and the house lights below.

I thought for a moment about how to continue the conversation and settled on the obvious. "How much do you know about me, Anne?"

She seemed to be taken aback by the question, and it took her a moment or two to respond. "Well, your background check and PRIA forms came back clean. You're a retired Air Force pilot and former contract business jet pilot. You have no FAA violations, you've never been married, and you have outstanding credit."

I nodded, still looking out over the darkening desert. "You've done your homework."

"Our search firm is pretty thorough."

"But?"

"But what?"

"You have some unanswered questions," I said. "And that's the whole reason for all of this." I waved my glass at the two chairs on the deck and at her without looking in her direction. "It's the reason I'm here. Now."

Anne walked to the railing next to me and leaned on it, taking a slow sip of her martini as she watched the darkening valley alongside me. "Maybe I'm interested in you and wanted to find out more about you," she said after a long moment.

I shrugged. "That's certainly possible," I said. "I'm a pretty damn interesting guy, of course." I turned toward her and flashed her a self-deprecating smile. "But as much as my ego might want to believe that, if you were interested in me, you would have shown it before a recent evening at the Mariposa Grill with a certain woman."

She stiffened a bit. "It wasn't because I wasn't interested," she said, choosing her words carefully. "I was just...busy."

"Doing what?" I asked. "Besides the obvious. Running the operation. Minding the schedule. Keeping the books."

She turned to me abruptly. "Who are you Connor Price?" she asked sharply. "Other than certain records, which are easy to fake, you didn't exist before you joined us five years ago. Now you're here. And after not showing any interest in women at all, this client comes along, and you're all over her, claiming that you have a common past. Well, it turns out that she works for the CIA. Does that mean you do too?"

And there it was. I had assumed we'd be verbally sparring for hours before we got to this stage. I paused for a moment to consider my options. I could either play it straight, and probably get nowhere, or give a little and see what it got me. I also knew, from my interrogation training years ago, that the best lies have elements of the truth in them.

I walked away from her and went over to the chimenea.

I sat down in one of the chairs near the fire and stared into its depths. After a few moments, Anne seated herself in the chair opposite me.

"I'm not here to cause you and your brother any trouble, Anne," I said after a long moment. "All I want is to be left alone." I lifted my eyes to her and then looked back into the fire. "That's why I've kept to myself, social agenda-wise. I don't want any intruders in my life."

I could see her nod in my peripheral vision. "Are you running from something?" she asked after a brief pause.

I shrugged. "Maybe."

"What?"

I stared into the depths of the fire like I was lost in thought and took a long sip of my martini, relishing the warmth of the alcohol as it coursed through me. "Life doesn't always go the way you expect it to, Anne. Sometimes you try to do what you think is the right thing, for yourself, for others, maybe even for your country, and people you care about...get caught in the frag pattern."

"You sound like Ian," she said. She meant the words to sound empathetic, but there was a hollowness in them.

I nodded. "Happens to the best of us." I drained the last sip from the martini glass. "Anyway, that's essentially why I'm here, and why I'm not pursuing a 'social agenda.' I made my mind up that I wouldn't endanger anyone ever again."

People have a nasty habit of getting dead around you. The thought came out of nowhere, and I nodded unconsciously in response to it.

"I see," Anne said.

She reached over to take my glass and rose to go to the bar. "May I offer you another?" she asked.

After a moment, I got to my feet and followed her. "What brought you and Ian here?" I asked as she set about the martini chores. I noticed that her glass was empty as well. It seemed we both had needed some alcohol-based reinforcement this evening. I knew why I needed it. I wondered why she did.

Anne shrugged as she cut two slices of lime for the next round of martinis. "Ian called, and I came," she said, with resignation in her voice. "We're all each other has."

I nodded, thinking of a similar call. I smiled as I recalled Sarah Morton and our daughter, Colleen. "I know the feeling."

Anne's eyes narrowed as she swirled dry vermouth in one of the glasses. "Who called you?"

"A former contract pilot client. She was in trouble, and I helped her out of it."

"Are you still in touch?"

I shook my head. "Not so much."

She swirled the vermouth in the other glass and then dumped the contents in the sink. "By your choice or hers?"

I looked at her carefully, wondering if she had any information about me that I hadn't revealed. She retrieved the gin from the freezer and poured the syrupy stuff into the glasses with a flourish. Then she dropped the two slices of lime into them.

"Well done," I said. "The last time I saw something like that was in London about five years ago."

She handed me my glass, and we clinked them softly.

"You're doing that avoiding the question thing again," she said.

"I'm not really," I said. "The answer is more complicated than a simple 'her or me,' and it's a sensitive subject for me. That's all."

Anne nodded and gave me a knowing look. "I understand sensitive subjects," she said. "Between Ian and me, we could write a book on them."

"So, let's change the subject. Why Sedona? Why here? I mean, I'm not complaining, I love it here, and I'm glad you guys are here too, but it's kind of out of the way."

"Ian wanted to come here. He needed help runnng the business. I was living in London and had no reason to stay there."

"Nothing to keep you there?"

She shook her head. "Not really." She took a sip of her martini and looked away for a moment. I watched her in profile, and she seemed to be doing some kind of mental calculation as if wondering what she should share with me. She looked down for a moment or two and then seemed to make up her mind.

"I fell for a younger guy," she said. "A pilot," she glanced over at me for a second and then looked back to the scenery in front of her, "for British Airways. It turned out that he was married. What a tosser. And eventually, I told him to bugger off, but not before I was up the duff."

She glanced over at me. I must have had a curious look on my face.

"Pregnant," she added.

Well, I thought to myself. *That explains a hell of a lot.*

"And that was the last thing I fucking wanted," she continued, with a disgusted tone in her voice. "My mum was declining and living with me. Every moment I wasn't working I had to take care of her: feeding her, changing her clothes, bathing her and wiping her ass. I didn't need another fucking human parasite to deal with. Right about then, Ian called. I took my mom to the first nursing home I could find that had an opening and left her there. Then I came to America and had an abortion. And here I am."

The callousness in her words and her tone called the Darkness forth like it was invoking an incantation. I saw an image of Colleen, my daughter, in my mind's eye and adrenaline was forcefully injected into my bloodstream. The sudden power of it made me catch my breath involuntarily. My muscles began to coil in anticipation, and I wanted to go berserk and lose myself in the madness.

But, instead, I took a long sip of my martini and pushed the Darkness back into its place, behind the doors of my mind. I had the mental image of forcing the door shut on an immense, rabid dog, with fangs bared and a homicidal intensity in its eyes. I found myself grateful that I had one drink already in me and the better part of a second on the way down.

I came back to myself a few moments later. I realized that Anne had been watching me closely as I had fought the internal battle. I turned to look at her. Her eyes were narrow slits, and her lips were half open. I could see her breathing had grown more rapid and it looked like her cheeks were slightly flushed. Like triggering me had aroused her somehow.

Damn, I thought. *She knows exactly what she's doing.*

And inside of me, I felt the Darkness smile to itself. *I want her,* it said.

"So how is your story about the woman who called you more complicated than mine?" Anne asked. Her voice had turned softer now. It was almost seductive.

I turned and placed my forearms on the deck railing as I inhaled deeply. Then I drank the remaining liquid in my martini while I looked out into the night sky. I tried to focus on something good. On Sarah and Colleen. Probably the only good things in my miserable life. When I could trust my voice, I spoke. "All I can really say is that I don't know where she... where they...are. And it's safer for them that way."

I didn't know whether that was true or not. It had been five years since I had any news or contact about Sarah and our daughter. In theory, now that I wasn't working for the CIA any longer and Miguel Hidalgo, the drug lord who had threatened her, was long dead, there shouldn't have been any barriers to me rejoining them. But something had kept me from reaching out. Part of it was that I would have had to refresh my contact with my former CIA handlers to find out where Sarah and Colleen were. But the other part it, the real rationale for it, was that I just thought they were better off without me.

I watched Anne in my peripheral vision and willed her not to pull at any more of the threads of my life. The Darkness was barely under control, and I wasn't sure I could keep it that way if she said something else that triggered it. I saw her nod slightly as if she was accepting where the conversation had led. After a moment, she joined me at the railing.

"Ian always liked it here," she said in a surprisingly wistful tone. "He loved the rocks, and he loved the peace and quiet. He always told me that the day he could afford to live here, he'd come here and never look back." She looked down at her glass. "And the change of scenery has been good for me. I've enjoyed helping him build the business and run it."

She paused for a moment, and I could feel the "but" hanging in the air.

"But it has been a bit...lonely," she said, turning toward me. She touched my arm with her free hand, and I forced myself to turn to her as I pushed the Darkness even further down inside of me. I looked down into her eyes and saw the oddest expression of both lust and anger in them. I had never seen that combination before and it both intrigued and inflamed the Darkness inside of me.

"You're hard," she said, stroking the muscles in my upper arm. "You must work out like a fiend."

"I spend a lot of time in the gym these days," I said automatically.

She put her glass on the railing and stepped into me. For some reason, I was powerless to resist her. I tried to justify what was happening for the sake of gathering information. But I knew there was more to it. I wanted it. The Darkness wanted it. And I hated myself for it.

I could feel her body against mine and her nipples, erect

under the fabric of her dress, pushing into my chest. And to my dismay, I could feel my penis stirring against her.

Goddamn it.

"But I don't really like you," I said without willing it.

She laughed. Her first genuine laugh of the evening. "That's perfect," she said in a husky voice. "I don't like you either. But that will make it angry. That will make it better." She lifted her mouth to mine, forced my lips open with her tongue and buried herself inside of my mouth. The kiss was both passionate and loathsome, and the Darkness loved it. I lost myself in it.

"Where's Ian?" I asked when our lips parted several moments later.

"He's here, but he's sleeping," she replied breathlessly as she pushed the sports jacket off my shoulders. "Recharging is what he calls it. He'll be down for at least twelve hours. He won't hear us. Now shut up and fuck me."

CHAPTER TWELVE

Saturday, November 21st
0715 Hours Local Time
Brooks' House
Sedona, Arizona, USA

I wasn't sure what roused me first, the sun's rays through the bedroom window or the raging headache behind my eyes. I forced my eyes open and came back to myself.

'Cause the sex is so much better when you're mad at me.

I pushed my head back into my pillow and sighed involuntarily. The words were from a song by a group called Hinder, from several years ago, and they rang true. Sadly.

The previous evening had been one of raw lust and unbridled, animal-like sex. There was no foreplay, no caresses, or tenderness. There was no looking into each other's eyes and enjoying the union of two human souls. There was no bonding in the act. There was only pure, angry, porno-like fucking. Anne wanted it hard and she wanted it fast and in as many positions as were humanly possible at our age. Eventually, we wound up in the bedroom, with her braced against the headboard of the king-sized bed and me behind her, slamming into her again and again until we spent ourselves.

I'd never experienced sex with someone I didn't like

before, but the Darkness loved it and couldn't get enough. The contrast between last night and my time with Sharona was profound and disturbing. I had felt good after Sharona. I felt like a low-life this morning.

I turned to look at Anne. She was still sleeping, curled up in the fetal position, about three feet away on the king-sized bed. She had the sheets bunched around her midsection, leaving her limbs exposed in the morning light. After a night of hard sex and with worn-off makeup, she wasn't at all appealing. Her brunette hair was disheveled and hung in untidy ringlets around her face. As I looked at her face and her pale body, the phrase 'ridden hard and put away wet' came to mind.

What the fuck was I thinking? I thought as I looked at her. But that was the problem; I hadn't been thinking.

I was reminded of all the one-night stands in my life, and all the women I had left in the morning hours. I had enjoyed every one of those interludes and regretted very few the next morning. The trysts had been about mutual satisfaction between two enthusiastic and consenting adults, nothing else. But last night was different. I had not wanted to have sex with Anne. The Darkness had wanted it and had driven me to it. In my wildest dreams, I would have never anticipated that. I had competing sensations of intense self-loathing and utter bewilderment.

I quietly rose from the bed and headed to the hall bathroom, clothes in hand. I needed to pee, get dressed, and get the hell out of there as quickly as I could, hopefully avoiding Ian in the process. I bit my lip as I tiptoed down the carpet toward the bathroom door. The boss finding me skulking about his house would create questions anyway, but seeing me naked, fresh from his sister's room, wouldn't do wonders for our employer-employee relationship.

I exited the bathroom a few moments later and began to make the left turn for the front door when a blinking light caught my peripheral vision. I looked to the right and could see a door ajar at the end of the hallway and a blinking red light plainly visible through the narrow opening. I fought an untimely battle with my curiosity, lost it, and headed down the hallway towards the light.

As I approached the door, I could hear heavy breathing beyond it, and I nodded to myself, realizing that it was Brooks and he still sounded like he was dead asleep. I peered through the opening and was barely able to make out a stack of black, rectangular metal boxes, stacked one on top the other, against the far wall of the room. The red light I had seen was some kind of power indicator for the middle box in the stack. Wires came out of the box at the bottom of the stack and disappeared beyond my field of view behind the door.

I fought another mental battle with myself, and, after listening to make sure Brooks' breathing remained deep and even, I gently nudged the door open a bit, just enough to peer around it. The room was still shadowy, thanks to the heavy blinds across the windows, but I could make out the dark shape of a large person under the blankets on the king-sized bed. The wires I had noticed earlier seemed to run from the bottom box to somewhere under the covers.

Contextualization is a difficult thing sometimes. As I looked at the configuration of boxes, wires, and human being, I didn't have a frame of reference to compare it against. I also didn't have enough information to make any kind of assessment or judgment. But I knew enough about normal situations, like life support, heat pads or even kidney dialysis to understand what I was seeing was not something 'normal.' Sharona's words about 'what' Brooks was came to my mind, and I felt a hook sink into the back of my brain.

Something is not right here, I thought.

I left the house a few moments later, with my brain struggling to comprehend what my eyes had seen.

CHAPTER THIRTEEN

Monday, November 23rd
2315 Hours Local Time
My Condo
Sedona, Arizona, USA

Once again, the sound of OV-10 engines, droning in the quiet late-evening sky, stirred me from a single-malt-induced reverie on my sofa. I put the glen cairn glass aside and leaned forward to the laptop computer on the coffee table. It took me a few minutes to rouse the computer from its sleep state and call up the web address Sharona had given me. I entered the two tracker numbers into the dialogue box that appeared and hit the return key. The map slowly resolved a few moments later. A topographic image was generated in a 100-mile radius of my location and two white airplane shapes appeared on it. One shape was located at the northeast end of the Sedona Airport, where the hangars were, and the other was about 20 miles southwest of the airport and slowly moving in that direction.

"Gotcha!" I said to the empty room. "Okay, Ian let's find out where the hell you're going."

I slewed the cursor to the moving aircraft and right clicked on it. A dialogue box opened.

TRACK?

I left clicked on it and selected the options for storing the route in memory. Then, as an afterthought, I chose the option for an alert when the aircraft stopped moving.

"Nothing to do but wait now," I said to myself.

I picked up the remote control for the electric fireplace and increased the temperature a bit. Then, I retrieved my glass of the Glen Morangie 10-year-old from the side table and leaned back into the cushions.

I had almost dozed off when my computer binged with an alarm tone. "He shouldn't be back already," I said to myself as I leaned forward to look at the screen. I felt a small knot in the pit of my stomach as I typed in my password to kill the screen saver.

The aircraft symbol I had been tracking wasn't moving. It was frozen in an area of barren terrain about 120 miles southwest of Sedona, about 15 miles north of the town of Quartzite. At first, I thought the GPS tracker had malfunctioned, or the feed had frozen or hadn't refreshed. But when I placed the cursor over the aircraft shape, SPEED=0 KNOTS, ALTITUDE=800 FEET, was displayed, in addition to the longitude and latitude. I slewed the cursor off the aircraft and over some nearby terrain. The altitude of the terrain was the same as that of the aircraft.

"What the fuck, Brooks?" I said to the empty room. "Have you landed? Why the hell did you fly there in the middle of the night?"

I picked up my phone and texted Sharona. ARE YOU GETTING THIS? I asked.

YEP, she answered immediately. WHAT'S HE DOING?

NO IDEA, I replied. BUT IT LOOKS LIKE HE LANDED.

WHAT FOR? she asked after a moment.

"And that would be the 64-thousand-dollar question," I said to myself. I thought for a moment. KNOW ANYONE

AT THE NRO? I asked her. The NRO was the National Reconnaissance Office, a national clearing center for all visual imagery gathered by aircraft or satellites. While re-tasking a satellite was out of the question and going through CIA channels would be too visible, if she knew someone at the NRO there might be a chance that a passing satellite would have some coincidental imagery and we could look at it.

OF COURSE, she answered a moment later. BUT I'M GOING TO NEED TO FIND THAT DAMN COSTUME AND THE BOOTS.

I cocked my head at the screen and typed a question mark as a reply.

WONDER WOMAN appeared on the screen.

"What the hell?" I asked myself. I was about to type a reply when another text appeared.

ROLE PLAYING? COMPUTER GEEKS?

I smiled and pictured Sharona in the full Wonder Woman regalia complete with boots and the Lasso of truth. The poor guy didn't stand a chance.

WILL TALK TO HIM TOMORROW. HE OWES ME ANYWAY.

"I bet he does," I said. I looked up at the computer screen and saw the aircraft symbol moving. I nodded to myself, backspaced over what I had typed and wrote HE'S MOVING AGAIN.

SEE THAT, she replied.

I rolled the cursor over the aircraft shape and saw it was about 500 feet over the surrounding terrain, moving south and accelerating through 250 knots.

"Going somewhere in a hurry are we, Ian?" I said to myself. "Where to?"

Then, as I stared down at the aircraft shape, watching it move further to the south and gain more speed, the shape blinked twice. Then it disappeared.

I leaned forward involuntarily. "Jesus!"

My phone buzzed.

WTF? Sharona had texted.

I nodded at the phone. "EXACTLY!" I replied.

JAMMER? she asked.

I shrugged in response, but then another thought occurred to me, inspired by the arming wire I had seen hanging from the OV-10's sponsons in the hangar. OR ECM, I replied. Electronic countermeasures. WE'LL KNOW LATER TONIGHT.

? was her response.

"Because," I said to the empty room, "If it's an ECM pod, he'll have to land again, and have it removed." Then, the full import of the thought struck me, like I was walking from a dim room into blazing sunlight. "Holy shit," I said to myself. "He's got an arming crew on the ground there."

My phone buzzed with another text message. WHAT NOW? Sharona asked.

I shrugged and typed a response. WAIT. IT'S ALL WE CAN DO.

I took the computer into my bedroom, undressed and crawled into bed. I glanced at my watch before I turned out the light. "About four hours or so," I said to myself. "It's a four-hour airplane."

##

The alert from the computer roused me from a dream about robot knights fighting cyborg dragons. The last thing I remembered was me pulling a knight off one of the horses before the horse was immolated by a stream of flame from a dragon with red scales and dark, piercing eyes. The robot had looked at me with a grateful expression, and I realized at that moment that the face was familiar.

Then nothing.

"Damn!" I said to the empty room as I reached for the lamp switch.

I roused the computer, and as the map resolved, I was unsurprised to see the OV-10 on the ground in the same place it had been previously. The GPS tracker now clearly working again.

"This won't take as long," I said to myself. "It never does."

My phone buzzed. HE'S ON THE GROUND AGAIN. SAME PLACE. WHAT'S HE DOING?

DE-ARMING, I replied. HE'LL BE AIRBORNE IN A FEW MINUTES.

The OV-10 began moving very shortly after that, and I found myself shaking my head in grudging admiration.

"You must have a hell of a crew, Ian," I said.

My phone rang a moment later.

"What's this all about?" Sharona asked. "You seem like you have some suspicions."

"He's flying that plane somewhere, near or south of the border, and bombing something with it," I answered without hesitation. "Probably with 500-pound, general purpose, high-explosive bombs."

"That's pretty specific."

I related the story of the arming wire I had found on the aircraft in the hangar.

"Why not load the airplane in the hangar?" Sharona asked when I had finished.

"For two reasons as far as I can tell. First, someone on the maintenance crew would find the munitions, the hangar doesn't have a lot of out-of-the-way storage, and the munitions are fairly large. But, also, knowing Ian, he wouldn't want to have some sort of emergency with live ordnance hanging from his aircraft in a populated area like Sedona. It's the right thing to do, and that's the way he thinks."

"Then why is he bombing people?" Sharona asked after

a long moment.

I thought about the question for a few seconds. “I’m not sure he’s bombing people as much as he’s bombing things,” I said at last. “And whatever he’s doing, he thinks it’s perfectly morally right.”

“Which makes it even scarier.”

I sighed. “Yes. I guess it does.”

“What now?”

I shook my head and exhaled loudly. “Looks like I’ve got a camping trip in the desert in my future. Any chance I can get a night observation scope and some NVGs from you?”

CHAPTER FOURTEEN

Tuesday, November 24th
0705 Hours Local Time
Highway 89A
Sedona, Arizona, USA

I dragged myself out of bed about two hours later and stared at my bloodshot eyes in the mirror as I brushed my teeth and shaved.

"Dude," I said to myself in the mirror. "You look like shit."

After a hot shower and a cup of coffee, I threw a flightsuit on and staggered out of the door of my condo at 0730, heading for the hangar and a morning flight. I briefly considered calling in and pleading fatigue to be taken off the schedule, but the one sortie was all I had today, and I decided to power through it and then come back to the condo and catch a few hours of rest before heading southward for my evening observation session.

"No different than flying a fighter with a hangover," I said to mirror in the Challenger as I entered it. I smiled as I remembered my days in the A-10 and the gunnery deployments to Zaragoza Air Base in Spain. I had been stationed in England at the time, but the weather was so consistently bad that we were unable to execute the bombing events that required higher altitudes, so we deployed regularly to Zaragoza to perform them. "You always used to drop your best bombs when you had a hangover anyway."

Maybe. My conscience replied as I eyed the lined face in the car's mirror. *But you're a lot fucking older now than you were then.*

"Fuck you," I said. "Besides, I didn't drink that much last night. I just didn't get enough sleep."

Same thing.

"What-the-fuck-ever."

I made the drive down Route 89A and to the turn-off for the airport on autopilot, practically allowing the car to guide itself as recalled the details of today's flight from my tired brain. The customer was a local thrill seeker who wanted to do some aerobatics then try to get some 'motion shots' of the red rocks. The motion shots would require me to fly as close to the rocks as regulations would allow and as fast as the aircraft could go. I felt a smile etch itself on to my lips.

"Sounds like fun," I said to myself.

I guided the Challenger up the airport access road and to the top of the airport plateau as I considered different routes for today's sortie in my mind. I was so absorbed in my thoughts that I nearly rear-ended a car that had stopped at the intersection of the access road and the road that ran up and down the west side of the airport.

The car was a black Chrysler sedan, and it was dusty like it had driven a long way. The driver seemed torn about which way to turn and had stopped as he considered the decision.

As I sat there, a battle between courtesy and impatience arose inside of me. As usual, impatience won, and I hit my horn, briefly.

The car started forward about a foot or so and then made a painstakingly slow turn to the north, the same direction I was going.

"Great," I said to no one in particular.

I turned in behind the car and bided my time as we both drove up the road and into the parking lot for the Brooks Air Service hangar/terminal. I parked the Challenger, grabbed my backpack and exited the car. As I locked it and turned to go into the hangar lobby, I looked up to see the black sedan slowly circling the parking lot, not in the aimless manner of someone who was lost and looking for a place to turn around, but purposefully, like the occupants wanted to look around.

The sedan drove to the fence between the parking lot and the aircraft movement area and then began to turn down the aisle of cars in front of the main entrance, where I was standing. It came to a stop next to me. A moment later, the heavily tinted rear window on the passenger side slid down slowly.

"Excusa?" said a heavily Spanish-accented voice?

I felt my blood go cold. Over five years ago, Miguel Hidalgo, the most powerful drug lord in Mexico, had put a ten-million-dollar price tag on my head. Even though he and his brother Ramon were both dead, it was possible other payment arrangements had been made. I silently cursed my complacency and carelessness. The .45 Colt Commander in my backpack might as well have been on the other side of the planet. There was no way I'd reach it in time.

"Excusa, señor?" the voice asked again.

I squatted down to look into the back seat, certain I'd be staring down the barrel of a pistol of some sort. I planned to drop to the pavement, roll behind the car and retrieve my gun. I prayed I'd have the speed I needed to stay alive.

But as my eyes became level with the car's interior, I saw no weapons. Instead, a man was sitting on the passenger side of the backseat with a folder in his lap and a bottle of water in left hand. He had dark, Hispanic features, an angular nose with a bushy mustache below it, and the white flash of a scar on his left cheek. He wore black slacks and a white dress shirt, open at the collar. The shirt seemed to barely fit over the heavily muscled chest and arms. As I regarded the dark eyes, I saw professional curiosity combined with a look I knew well – that of a seasoned killer.

My instincts had been right, but I wasn't congratulating myself on them. I swallowed hard and prepared to jump out of the line of fire as soon as the inevitable weapon was produced. For the first time in five years, my right hand felt empty without a pistol in it.

"Excusa?" the voice asked again. "Thees ees Brooks Air serveece?"

I nodded. There was no use denying it. The sign on the door behind me said as much.

"You half seen thees man?"

The passenger pulled a black and white photograph from the file and passed it to me. I kept my eyes on both of his hands as I took it. Once I had the photograph in my hands, and I verified that his hands were still empty, I glanced down at it. There were three people seated at a table in a chain fast food restaurant. A little girl with blonde hair and big blue eyes seemed to be speaking animatedly to her mother, seated next to her. Her mother was probably late thirties, also blond. While her face was becoming, in the photograph it looked weary and forlorn. The man, on the far right side of the picture, had his arm around the woman's shoulders and a look of loving concern on his face. While his facial features weren't familiar, the slightly odd shape of his body drew my eyes to inspect him more thoroughly. It only took a second or two for my mind to assemble the clues.

The man was Ian Brooks. Several years ago. *You've had plastic surgery, Ian.*

I fought to keep my facial expression neutral as I continued to inspect the photograph. Finally, I handed it back to the car's passenger with a blank look on my face.

"No, sir. I haven't seen this man."

The dark eyes inspected mine for a moment or two. Then the passenger shrugged. "Gracias, Señor," he said.

"De nada," I replied.

The passenger addressed the driver without taking his eyes off me. "Paco, vámonos de aquí."

Even as he said the words, I saw his eyes narrow slightly, and there was a glimpse of recognition in them. He seemed to nod to himself.

Oh shit, I thought.

I stepped back and watched the vehicle pull away, the rear window closing while the car continued forward. As I watched the car retreat through the gate that led out to the access road, I tried to shake off the ominous feeling that was seeping into my mind. The situation was becoming more complicated, and once again, after swearing that I'd never let it happen again, I was getting involved in shit that I didn't understand.

"Damn it, Pearce," I said to myself. "You're such a fucking idiot."

CHAPTER FIFTEEN

Tuesday, November 24th
1730 Hours Local Time
In the Rocks West of Arizona Highway 95
North of Quartzite, Arizona, USA

The light was fading when I made it to the area north of Quartzite. I had traded my Challenger for a rental Jeep SUV, and after spending some time looking for a vantage point, I found a lightly used trail and followed it to a spot to park the vehicle behind a small ridge on the west side of the valley. As I exited the Jeep, I looked back up the trail to ensure the vehicle wasn't visible from the road. Nodding to myself, I opened the rear doors and donned a set of night vision goggles, grabbed my gear bag and threw an AR-15 rifle with a Starlight Scope over my shoulder. Then, I slowly made my way up the small ridge to the west of the SUV, taking great care as to where I put my feet to avoid contact with slithering reptiles that might be out for an evening crawl. It took me about ten minutes to make my way to the top and find a suitable observation position.

After setting up the low-light / infrared observation telescope and camera, I took a swig of coffee from the thermos I brought with me and surveyed the area in front of me. The valley was bisected by Arizona Highway 95 as it ran, straight as an arrow, from its intersection with Arizona Highway 72 at the north end, due south to the town of Quartzite. Apart from a cleared area across the valley and down a few miles or so, there was no sign of life or civilization. There weren't even any power lines running down the highway.

"Couldn't have picked a better place for a landing spot, Ian," I said as I gazed up and down the road through the telescope. "Nice, straight, seldom-traveled road with no obstacles, and a built-in area to pull off and arm up."

I centered the telescope on the cleared-out area. It seemed to have been a landfill many years ago, but now there were only mounds of earth and no fences, vehicles or indications of activity. The OV-10, with its rugged landing gear, built to operate from unimproved airstrips, could easily negotiate the dirt access road to the cleared area and be armed or de-armed there. Then it could taxi out to the highway and takeoff in whichever direction was favored by the wind. Of course, the occasional car would have to be avoided, but a road like this one didn't see much traffic, especially in the middle of the night.

"Damn Ian," I said to myself as I eyed the area. "How long did you plan this?"

I lifted my eyes from the scope and lowered the night vision goggles. The valley went from black to green, and the desert terrain took on a surreal texture as the googles interfaced infrared energy from the rocks and enhanced the light provided by the waning moon. I looked slowly up and down the road to test the limits of my vision. A car appeared on the northern portion of Highway 95, and I watched it make the turn at the intersection and head south on the asphalt road. It remained visible for a very long time before it disappeared from view.

Satisfied that a vehicle couldn't surprise me as it

approached, I retrieved a sandwich from my gear bag and leaned against a nearby rock as I ate it. I glanced down at my watch. It was 1800 hours. I had about 5 hours to kill.

As it turned out, I didn't have to wait that long. At about 2030 hours, two trucks appeared on Highway 72 and made the turn south. Unlike the other few vehicles I had seen up to that time, these two seemed to be traveling together and maintained close spacing between them. I watched them move down the road in front of me and then slow to make the turn into the cleared area. Raising the NVG's, I put my eyes to the telescope and increased the magnification as I peered down the valley.

The lead vehicle was a tractor trailer, and it moved slowly as it negotiated the dirt road toward the earthen mounds in front of it. I panned the lens to look at the second truck. While almost as long as the first truck, it was differently shaped, almost cylindrical. It took my brain a few seconds to recognize and contextualize the shape. It was a fuel truck.

"Of course," I said to myself in the darkness. "Of course, he has to get more gas. What was I thinking? It's not a four-hour airplane when you're in MIL power all the time."

The drivers of the two vehicles arranged them very precisely near one of the mounds and then exited the cabs of their trucks along with their passengers, one from each truck. In moments, the doors of the trailer were open, and ramps were being extended from the truck bed to the ground. I nodded as I watched.

"And I know exactly what kind of vehicle you have in there," I said to the night air.

The sound of turboprop engines reached my ears a few moments later, and I looked at my watch.

"It's only ten of nine, Ian," I said to myself. "I guess you're starting early tonight."

I lowered the NVGs and turned my eyes to the night sky,

searching for the bright yellow glow of an aircraft in the infrared and light enhancing display. The turboprop sound seemed to be coming from the north, so I turned my head to the left and searched the horizon above the highway intersection. At first, the sky seemed to be alive with the light of the stars and even aircraft flying above on their way into and out of the Phoenix valley. But then my eyes fastened on a glowing object that was moving very quickly and very low above the rocks to the north. The aircraft was flying with no internal or external lights activated, so the only way it appeared in the NVGs was as a lighted mass of infrared energy. I watched it complete a turn to line up with the north-south road and then begin to slow as the landing gear and flaps were lowered. About two minutes later, the OV-10 touched down on the asphalt surface, about a quarter of a mile north of the turnoff to the landfill. I heard the engines go into reverse thrust and the OV quickly slowed to taxi speed. In a few moments, it turned off the pavement and headed up the access road. A few moments after that, the aircraft completed a 180-degree turn between the two trucks and the engines wound down onto the flat-pitch locks.

I raised the NVGs and peered through the telescope now, increasing the magnification level further. My observation position was about four miles from the landfill area, but the scope I was using had been designed for long-range surveillance, and the view I had of the trucks and the aircraft was like I was just across the ramp from them.

The OV's canopy was open, and Brooks was crawling down the ladder. I snapped a few photos as soon as his face was visible and then waited for the scene to unfold.

Immediately, two of the men from the trucks began squatting next to the OV-10's sponsons and working on the bomb racks mounted thereon. I had seen the same process on many aircraft. The first item of business would be a stray voltage check, to make sure the OV's armament circuits weren't powered. Then, the racks would be opened, and the compartments for the impulse cartridges would be accessible. The cylindrical chambers for the carts would be unscrewed and then swivel links would be inserted into the racks' front and rear solenoids to accept the arming wires from the ordnance.

As the men worked, an awkward looking vehicle came down the ramp from the tractor-trailer. It looked low and squat, like an aircraft tug and had a driver guiding it from a small cockpit area. But it featured an arm that protruded from the front of it and in the carriage at the end of the arm was a distinctly shaped object that I knew well.

"Jesus," I said to myself. "So, it is Mark 82s. Five-hundred-pounders. Ian, what the hell are you doing?"

It was one thing to suspect Brooks was loading his aircraft up to conduct bombing missions. It was another thing to see it. I found I had been holding my breath without realizing it.

The vehicle was a USAF munitions loader, and it made its way to the front of the OV with the 500-pound bomb on the loading arm. The fourth man guided the driver forward as he assumed a position next to the loading arm, where the controls for the arm were located. He lowered the arm and pivoted it so that it aligned with one of the OV-10's center bomb racks. In moments, the bomb was mounted on the rack, and the weapons loader retreated to the trailer while the two men ran the arming wires to the nose and tail fuses and inserted the impulse cartridges in the bomb rack. The entire process had taken a whopping five minutes.

"Holy shit," I said to myself. "You guys are fast."

The process was completed four more times, and soon the OV was squatting in the darkness with five MK-82's sitting underneath it – 2500 pounds of high explosive destruction. I zoomed the telescope in even further to determine the fin configuration on the bombs.

"Selectable," I said, snapping a few more photos. "So, he can release them high drag or low drag. Who would ever believe an OV-10 could escape the frag on a high-drag release?"

High-drag bombs were released at very low altitude. The high-drag assembly was composed of a nylon ballute, essentially a large cone-shaped pillow that acted like a drag chute when the weapon was expended. The intention was to allow the delivering aircraft to get well away from the bomb before it detonated. A normal OV-10 would not have the speed to get away from the frag pattern of a high-drag bomb. These OVs, with the powerful PT-6s, could generate nearly 300 knots of airspeed and get away easily.

"You thought of everything, Ian," I said to the darkness.

The next item to be loaded was an electronic countermeasures or ECM pod, just as I had suspected. The pod was about six feet long and was cylindrical. The ground crew mounted it on a pylon on the left wing, located about halfway between the engine nacelle and the wingtip. I hadn't even noticed the pylons when I had planted the tracking devices. I didn't know what sort of ECM the pod was capable of, but I was sure it was more advanced than the gear I had flown with back in the day. At the very least, it was capable of jamming a GPS tracker.

I zoomed in on the pod and clicked a few more pictures, still talking to myself as I hit the button.

"So why ECM, Ian? I can see why you need the bombs, but why take the risk of getting an ECM pod?" But the answer occurred to me as soon as I uttered the words and I nodded to myself. The U.S. Border Patrol maintained a network of tethered blimps with radar that looked into Mexico to detect drug-carrying aircraft trying to enter the US at low altitude. "This isn't about hiding from the bad guys. You want to hide from the good guys."

But the loading crew wasn't finished yet. As I continued to watch, they removed a section of the OV-10's nose and replaced it with a turret that held a 20mm Vulcan cannon. That was something I hadn't seen before. I knew early versions of the OV-10D had been fitted with gun turrets, but those had given way to infrared observation devices and the like. I didn't know how many rounds of ammunition the aircraft could carry, probably not more than a few hundred, but with a weapon like that, those rounds could do an incredible amount of damage.

I felt a strange sense of admiration as I watched the crew finish up. These guys were professionals, and they were dedicated. I just wished I knew what the fuck they were up to.

Brooks climbed back into the OV and started the engines. As soon as he completed the after-start checks, he gave a hand signal to the ground crew, and a pair of them pulled the safety pins for the bombs and the gun, taking great care to stay clear of the spinning propellers. Moments later, Brooks was taxing back out to Highway 95. Even from my position, across the valley and four miles away, I could hear when he put the condition levers into the T.O./LAND position, and the powerful engines spun up to 100% RPM. I zoomed in on the cockpit and watched Brooks turn the OV to the left as he reached the highway. I could see him clearly through the plexiglass canopy as he moved the power levers up to MAX and scanned his engine instruments carefully. Then he released brakes and OV began to roll down the highway to the south. The heavily-loaded aircraft accelerated rapidly and then gracefully lifted off into the night sky.

As I turned my attention back to the arming crew, something was pulling at my brain. I knew that while I was watching Brooks, I had just seen something that was incongruous but important.

"Damn," I said to myself. "Damn. Damn. Damn."

CHAPTER SIXTEEN

Wednesday, November 25th
0922 Hours Local Time
My Condo
Sedona, Arizona USA

The buzzing of my phone on the nightstand woke me from a deep and dreamless sleep. I fumbled for the device in the darkened room, already promising myself that I was going to thoroughly chastise the caller for awakening me far too early after an entire night out in the desert. My hand finally found the iPhone and clumsily brought it to my ear.

"Pearce," I answered, trying to clear the cobwebs from my brain.

"Hey there Cowboy," Sharona's low voice crooned into my ear. "I bet if I were there waking you up in person, you'd be a lot more alert right now."

I smiled in spite of my weariness. "That's for sure." I looked over at the bedside clock and winced. I had only been asleep for a little over three hours. "What's up?"

"A little incidental imagery," Sharona said. "Our boy was busy last night."

I rubbed my eyes and willed my head to clear as I processed her words. "I imagine he was. You got the texts I sent you. He flew two sorties down there with a stop to rearm in between. That's why I got back here so late last night."

"Do you have access to the classified drop box?"

"I guess. I haven't gone to it since you gave me the address and login stuff."

"Drag your ass out of bed and take a look at the photos I just uploaded, then call me back." She clicked off.

"So much for sleeping in today," I muttered as I hung up the phone.

After making the usual morning stop in the bathroom and grabbing a robe, I padded into the dining room/office and fired up my laptop computer. While the device came to life, I located the URL address and login credentials from my text message history. Once a browser window was available, I typed the URL in and was rewarded with a dull screen that said "Photo Drop Box" on it in a very plain and uninspiring font. I pulled down the login box and entered the information Sharona had given me. After several redirects, the page stabilized with a single, unlabeled folder displayed. I clicked on it and immediately, the screen filled with the outlines of photographs. As I waited for the photographs to fill in, I scrolled down through the folder. There must have been over a hundred of them. I scrolled back to the top as the first few photos began to populate.

It was obvious that the photos were shot with an infrared camera because of the white, gray and black color scheme. The lighter an object was in color, the more infrared energy it emitted, i.e., the hotter it was. In contrast, the darker an object was, the less infrared energy it emitted or colder it was.

The first several photos showed an empty road in the middle of an unpopulated area. The road was a thin thread of light gray, its surface emitting heat from the sunlight it had absorbed during the day as well the energy transmitted to it by vehicles that had traveled over its surface. The terrain on both sides of the road was a darker gray because the earth had not retained as much heat as the road had. There were large and small spots of very dark gray and black scattered throughout the terrain, obviously rocks and boulders that hadn't retained much heat at all.

"So, it's a road in the middle of fucking nowhere," I muttered to myself.

The rest of the photos were taking longer to populate, so I made myself a cup of coffee while I was waiting. When I returned, the page of photos had filled in. As I began to scroll down, I saw the story they were telling, and I felt a knot in my gut.

"Jesus," I said. "Sweet Jesus."

I dialed Sharona immediately.

"Well?" she answered.

"He's pretty methodical, that's for sure. And disciplined."

"Describe what you mean."

"Well he waits for the convoy to come up the road, drops a bomb on the first vehicle to stop the convoy, immediately drops a second bomb on the last vehicle to keep them from running to the south and then he slowly, methodically, kills everyone that's left with his remaining bombs and the cannon."

"And that was only the first mission he flew last night," Sharona interjected. "We didn't have a satellite in place to see the second."

"Any idea who or what the target was?"

"No. And that's what's worrying me. All we know is that it was in Mexico like you thought."

"Well, who wasn't it?"

"What do you mean?"

"You've got connections, have you heard anything from the DEA or the Federales?"

There was a long pause. "No, we haven't," she answered

at last.

"Then Brooks wasn't after anyone official, and he obviously wasn't after civilians because that's not who he is." I let the words sink in for a moment. "You know who he's after. Convoys traveling northbound in the middle of the night? Doesn't take an international studies major to figure that out."

"He's bombing drug convoys…" Sharona said, her voice trailing off.

I nodded. "And he's got pretty damn good intel. Not only did he know there'd be two convoys last night, he knew exactly where they'd be and exactly when.

"But why?" Sharona asked. "And why now?"

"No idea," I answered. "But I'm obviously going to need to find out."

"Yes, you do. It's only a question of time before this becomes an international incident, especially with all the other shit between us and Mexico and this presidential candidate who is calling for a wall between the two countries." Sharona paused for a moment. "Hell, maybe that's a good idea. Maybe a wall would stop shit like this."

"Not in this case," I said. "This is personal for Brooks. And I may know why."

CHAPTER SEVENTEEN

Thursday, November 26th
0835 Hours Local Time
Highway 89A
Sedona, Arizona USA

I pulled out onto Highway 89A on yet another brilliant Sedona morning, headed for the airport and a 1000 flight. It may have been Thanksgiving Day, but Brooks Air Service flew when its clients wanted to, regardless of the day. The sortie today was one of my favorite profiles. We called it the "northern Arizona tour," and the route featured such landmarks as the Meteor Crater, Monument Valley and the Grand Canyon and we did it as low and as fast as regulations would allow, with plenty of circling where needed so the client in the back seat could get as many photos as he or she wanted.

The red rocks ahead of me and around me were bathed in the morning sunlight, and I took time to appreciate the beautiful scenery again as I drove, trying to put the growing apprehension I had about Brooks on hold. I also tried to ignore the reemergence of the Darkness inside of me and the ease with which Anne could trigger it. I had spent the last five years of my life trying to breathe in the peace of this place and leave the guilt and the Darkness behind. I had accepted that the guilt would never be gone, but I had hoped I could at least make the Darkness go away.

Apparently, it had been there all the time. Just waiting for the right trigger. I shuddered to myself as I remembered the night with Anne and vowed to myself that it would never happen again.

I was so lost in my reverie that I nearly missed the black sedan that had followed me down 89A and now turned with me onto the airport access road.

"Can't be," I said as I looked into the rear-view mirror. Instantly, my mind was drawn to the conversation in the parking lot at the hangar two days ago. The sedan looked identical to the one I had seen, and although I couldn't see into the back seat from my perspective, I was betting the same Hispanic man was seated there. "What the fuck, guys?" I said as I looked back at them.

I drove up the access road, past the overlooks and the seedy motel at the top of the hill and then made the left onto the airfield loop road. The sedan followed me the entire way and made the left turn as well, remaining a discrete distance behind. I had a quick internal debate with myself and surreptitiously reached inside the center console of the car and removed the .45 ACP pistol from the holster inside. I cocked the weapon, checked it to make sure a round was chambered and ejected the magazine to verify it was fully loaded before reinserting it. I placed the pistol on the center console.

I entered the parking lot for the Brooks Air Service terminal a few moments later with the sedan still in trail.

"No way this is a coincidence," I said to myself. "There's nothing else at this end of the airfield."

I found a spot in the front row directly in front main doors and even as I switched the Challenger off, I saw Ian exit the doors and head to his vehicle, a Chevrolet Tahoe, parked a few slots away toward the flight line. He waved at me as he entered the car and squeezed his substantial frame into the vehicle's front seat. The vehicle settled on its wheels as he closed the door. Then he backed out of his spot and drove behind me toward the entrance to the parking lot. And the black sedan, which had entered the parking lot behind me and made a wide circle round the back row of slots, picked up speed and followed him.

I shook my head as I watched the procession and found myself scratching my chin. "Huh," I said to the empty car.

I went into the terminal a few moments later, after de-cocking the .45 and transferring it to my backpack. Anne looked up at me as I entered the pilot room and gave me a crooked smile. She was wearing a tight wool blouse that emphasized the attributes of her upper body and a matching skirt which clung to her hips like it had been painted on.

"Hey, you," she said with a hungry gleam in her eyes.

"Hey yourself," I answered. "Where was Ian off to in such a rush?"

"There's a meeting of the airfield tenants down at the FBO on the south end of the field," she said, rising from her chair. She took me by the hand and pulled me into Ian's office, kicking the door closed behind her. Even as the lock of the door engaged, she was unzipping my flight suit and pushing it off my shoulders.

"I want you," she said as she pushed the Nomex suit down to my ankles and yanked my boxer shorts down.

I was taken by surprise, and the situation was so surreal that I couldn't respond. An internal civil war ignited inside of me. I was both repulsed and energized by her touch. The sensible part of me wanted to run out of the room, but the Darkness had been triggered again, and it wanted her badly.

I felt her mouth on my shaft and lost myself in the lust, ignoring the feelings of self-contempt that were also rising within me.

"The client is running late, and Ian will be at that meeting for at least an hour," she said as she rose from her knees and lifted her skirt to her waist. She bent over Ian's desk, grabbed my erect member and pulled me toward her. "Now get over here and fuck me."

Once again, the sex was hard and fast, and the Darkness pulled me into her, over and over again as in reveled it the act. I felt like I was outside of my body and unable to control myself. My hips moved against her frantically and hungrily. When the orgasm came, I felt as if she had ripped it out of me and I felt her shuddering against me even as I spent myself inside of her.

A few moments later, I removed myself from her and took a few steps back to recover from the moment and reorder my clothes. Anne grabbed a few tissues from the dispenser on the desk to clean herself up and tossed me a few so that I could do the same. We both performed the task, she methodically and unselfconsciously, and me in a bit of a daze. A few minutes later, the tissues were in the trash, and the clothes were back in place. Without another word, she opened the office door and exited, leaving me standing there.

I remained in the office for a few moments, trying to gather myself and comprehend what had happened. I was still trembling with the adrenaline rush brought on by the Darkness, and I tried to even my breathing as I felt the vestiges of the lust seeping out of my body. Before Anne, when the Darkness had been triggered, the result had been violence and death, and in those instances, I had been unable to control myself until there was no one else to kill. But she had found a way to trigger the same loss of control but channel it in a way that didn't result in violence but left me equally helpless to resist. I didn't understand how it was possible.

"Jesus," I said to myself. "She's like green fucking

kryptonite."

I checked myself in the mirror in Brooks' office and walked out. The pilot room and the lobby beyond were still empty although the ramp, visible through the glass windows in both areas, was showing signs of activity. One of OVs had been towed out of the hangar and Costello was performing a pre-flight inspection on it. Anne was nowhere to be seen. I walked to the window and surveyed the ramp and the airfield beyond. The bright Sedona sun was shining down on the airfield and bathing its structures and asphalt in warm, yellow light. I gazed upward at the orb, surrounded by the sparkling azure blue of the cloudless sky and for the second time that day, tried to force the apprehension and the angst down inside of me.

Anne entered the room a few minutes later, makeup repaired and looking none the worse for wear.

"You're invited to come over tomorrow night," she said without preamble. "Ian wants to talk to you about something over dinner."

I raised my eyebrows involuntarily. "Any idea what?"

She shook her head. "Not really."

I shrugged. "Okay. Guess I'll wait to hear it from him."

She nodded. "But," she said with a knowing look in her eyes, "he might go to bed early."

Great, I thought. I inclined my head toward the OV on the ramp outside the window. "Who's the client?"

Anne smirked. "Your favorite."

I shook my head in resignation. "Myra Golf Sierra Barnes." Myra was a well-known and gifted Sedona photographer. I had several of her prints framed and on display in my condo. But she was an infamous client of Brooks Air Service.

"Golf sierra for golden shower, right?" Anne asked. "That's what I heard from the maintenance guys."

I nodded in response. "She uses the relief tube in the rear

cockpit to pee about four times every flight. The maintenance guys have to rinse it out and clean the bottom of the fuselage where it vents. Why the hell does she always ask for me?"

"I asked her that. She said something like 'he's the only one who has seen me pee, and I want to keep it that way.'"

"Nice," I muttered.

"So, spying on the female clientele, Price?"

I shook my head and looked away. "No. Besides, even if I wanted to, you can't see anything with the rear-view mirrors in the front cockpit."

Anne ignored my answer and looked at me intently. "How in the hell does she pee into that little funnel anyway?"

I shrugged. "I tried to talk her out of it the first time. I told her it was built for guys, not gals. But she wasn't having any. She said she used to win bets in the military by being able to pee into beer bottles without spilling a drop."

Anne shook her head. "So that's how you folks in the military spend our taxpayer dollars?"

"She was a Marine," I answered. "And they're all a little nuts. Must be the brain damage in boot camp."

There was the sound of a car engine in the parking lot, and Anne turned to look through the lobby windows and beyond. "Speak of the devil," she said.

CHAPTER EIGHTEEN

Thursday, November 26th
1030 Hours Local Time
Sedona Airport (KSEZ)
Sedona, Arizona, USA

About 45 minutes later, I rotated the nose of the OV, and it shot skyward off of runway 03 and climbed into the blue heavens above the airport.

"Whoo hoo!" said the infamous Myra GS Barnes from the back seat.

I looked at her in the rear-view mirrors. Myra was a 40-something beauty with long flowing brunette hair with red highlights and striking green eyes. She wore a flightsuit of her own and filled it out very well with a body that could have been painted by Rubens. Of course, none of that was visible in the mirrors. All I could see was her helmeted head, mirrored sunglasses, and a wide, toothy smile.

"This rocks, Price! It's like sex but longer lasting."

I smiled to myself and kept the climb going for another few seconds. Then, I leveled off at about 1,000 feet above ground level (AGL) and pulled the OV into a turn to the east.

"Meteor crater in about ten minutes," I said.

"I'll be ready," Myra said. "I want to get a panorama of the crater from about 500 feet. Can we do that?"

"Yep. We can get low over the crater and over Monument Valley. The Grand Canyon is different. We have to stay higher and on a special air corridor."

"That's not a problem. I've gotten lots of pictures of the canyon. I want to spend most of our time shooting the crater and Monument Valley."

"Roger that," I answered. "You're the boss."

"You're right," she said. "I am. Now hold this thing straight and level for a few minutes. I have a sudden urge to pee."

"Of course you do," I said as I made a mental note to keep my eyes locked forward.

Interstate 17 went underneath the nose and I found myself marveling at the diversity of desert flora and terrain yet again. Here, on both sides of the north-south artery between Phoenix and Flagstaff, the vegetation was mostly green and presented a striking contrast to the red earth and rocks amongst which it grew and was interspersed. To the east, where the crater was, the terrain changed color to light brown and tan, and flora became sparse. Those who thought of the desert as a monochromatic landscape had never experienced the actual variety of its beauty.

The crater appeared in the OV's windscreen a few minutes later, and I reduced the power a bit and began a gradual descent.

"Would you prefer a clockwise or counter-clockwise orbit, Miss Myra?"

"Let's go counter," she answered after a second or two. I think what will work better with the lenses I've got and the sun angles we're going to have to deal with."

"Roger that," I said. "Counter-clockwise it is."

The meteor crater had always intrigued me. It was perhaps the best-preserved meteor impact site in the world. When I had flown F-16s at Luke, the air refueling track we had used was situated directly over the crater, and I often found myself looking down on it from the high teens or low twenties, depending on whether we were assigned the low or high-altitude track. It seemed out of place, a large indentation in an otherwise flat backdrop. I knew that it was a mile in diameter, 2.4 miles in circumference and over 550 feet deep. It was formed over 50,000 years ago when a meteorite a mere 50 meters in diameter impacted the surface of the earth at a velocity of over 8 miles per second or 28,800 miles per hour. The resulting force from the collision was equal to the detonation of a ten-megaton bomb. At the time of the impact, the area was grassland and home to wooly mammoths and giant ground sloths. The explosion would have wiped out life for several miles in all directions.

I shook my head in amazement as I looked down on the giant depression in the earth. The gentle slopes and the green tinge of vegetation that lined the sides and floor of the crater belied the violence of its creation. I could see people making their way down the road to the crater's floor and along the path to the observation platform next to the visitor's center. Some of them looked up at us as we flew by, 500 feet above ground level in a gentle left bank, staying just outside the rim of the crater. I glanced in the rear-view mirrors and saw Myra with her camera up to her face, busily focusing and snapping away.

"I think that will do it," Myra said after a few more orbits of the crater. "I think I have everything I need."

"Copy that," I said. "Ready to head north?"

"You bet. But keep it level, please."

"Let me guess. It's that time again."

She giggled. "Yep. Too much coffee, too much water, and a peanut bladder."

I rolled the OV into a gentle turn to the north and leveled off at 1,000 feet AGL.

"There you go," I said as I pulled the condition levers back into NORMAL FLIGHT and stood the throttles up. "Cleared to pee."

She giggled a second time, and I glued my eyes forward once again, checking the fuel level and calling up the next waypoint in the navigation system. Monument Valley was about 150 miles north of the crater and the flight there would allow Myra a little over thirty minutes to complete her task and get ready for the next photo shoot. I adjusted our course slightly to the right to center the steering cue in the HUD, and at that moment, a large bird of prey passed down the right side of the aircraft. I instinctively followed it with my eyes even as I banked to the left to increase the clearance between the OV and the bird.

"Damn, Connor!" Myra exclaimed over the intercom. "I thought you were going to keep this thing level!"

"Doing my best," I replied.

There was silence for a few moments. I presumed she was finishing her task and restoring her clothing. "So how come I never see you about town with a woman?" she said at last. You're in great shape, you're hot, and you have this whole pilot/bad boy thing working for you. I'd think you have them lining up outside your door."

I paused for a moment while I scanned the instrument panel and verified we were still on course. "I lost someone I cared about several years ago," I said, giving her an edited version of my history, "I just haven't felt like pursuing another relationship since then."

I saw her head nod in the rear-view mirrors and I could see that she was working with one of her cameras as we talked. "I get the relationship thing, but don't you just need to get laid sometimes? I know plenty of single women your age who'd be content to just get off from time to time."

I laughed. "My age? Just how old do you think I am, Myra?"

She laughed in return. “No offense meant. I just know you’re probably older than me, that’s all.”

“Maybe a little,” I said.

I could see her smile in the mirrors. “The only point I was making is that women have needs too. And I know at least a few that wouldn’t mind having their needs met by someone like you.”

I nodded and didn’t respond for a long moment. My mind did a quick rewind to the last five years and my lack of female companionship, physical or otherwise over that time until Sharona showed up the previous week. I remembered how good and how right that encounter had felt, especially since neither of us had long-term plans with the other. Then my mind went to the thing between Anne and me, and once again, I found that I didn’t understand it. When I was not around her, the prospect of being with her repelled me. Yet, in her presence, it only took a few words from her to pull me into a place of darkness and action and for me to feel an inexorable need to lose myself inside of her, both mentally and physically.

“I guess the right person hasn’t come along,” I said, after a long moment.

“You sound like a chick,” Myra said. “I think you might be too focused on the right person for a relationship. What you might need to focus on is the right person to just have some fun with. Women want that too. Sure, there are some who want to get attached. But there are some who just want to go out, have fun, get laid and that’s it.”

I thought back to my time with Gail Petersen, the USAF general who had been a partner of sorts for me in the last ‘relationship’ I had. She liked the dinners and the companionship and the sex, but she had been too consumed with her career to expend the emotional effort needed to sustain a real relationship. In spite of all the previous shallow relationships I had before her, I had wanted something more from her, and she had been either unable or unwilling to give it. But in the end, that had been a good thing. When an assassin put a .50 caliber bullet into her and killed her, I was saddened but not devastated. I had never forgotten her last words:

"You were the best thing that ever happened to me," she had said. "Only one who ever got me...so sorry...didn't see it...too much bullshit."

I nodded to myself as the scene of her dying in my arms replayed itself in my head for the thousandth time, and I felt the usual sting in my eyes as I remembered.

"I don't quite know what I'm looking for, Myra," I said as the towers of Monument valley loomed in front of us. "I guess I'm waiting for something. Hopefully, I'll know it when I see it."

She was silent for a few moments. I could see her looking down at her camera gear and getting everything ready for shots she was about to take. For a few moments, I wondered if she had not heard me or had nothing to add. But then, as US Highway 160, on the south border of Monument Valley went under us, she spoke. And it wasn't what I expected.

"We're having a Thanksgiving dinner party tonight," Myra said. "It will be just Spencer and me and some family and friends. We can easily make room for you. If you could join us, we'd love to have you."

Normally, the thought of another dinner alone, would not have bothered me. But for some reason, that prospect seemed bleak tonight.

"Thanks, Myra," I said. "I'll be there."

CHAPTER NINETEEN

Thursday, November 26th
1700 Hours Local Time
Myra Barnes' House
Sedona, Arizona, USA

As it turned out, Myra's photography had enabled her to earn a more than respectable living, and the house she shared with her husband and their two children was spectacular. I had noticed it in the past as I had driven around town but didn't know it was hers until she gave me directions for dinner. It was built into the side of one of the valley walls on the northeast end of Sedona, looking down upon the roundabout where Arizona Highway 179 made the left turn to the northwest to intersect with Highway 89A. I could see it from a distance as I approached from below. It was an adobe structure with gentle lines and color that mimicked the red color of the rocks surrounding it. The back of the house seemed to be all windows that would command spectacular views to the west and the south. I could see a large deck at the rear of the house and people mingling on it as they took in the scenic landscape around them.

I drove up the narrow street and then parked the Challenger at the end of the long, winding driveway. I retrieved the bottle of wine I had brought from the car, and made my way up to the house, winding through several cars that bespoke of a degree of wealth. A saw an Aston Martin, a Ferrari, a Mercedes ML-350 AMG and a Range Rover. I was sure my car was the cheapest one on the driveway, and probably by an order of magnitude.

The sun was setting as I walked to the door, and I had a chance to see the exterior of the house in the waning light. I wasn't a fan of the adobe style that Myra and Spencer had chosen for their home, but I had to admit that it seemed warmer and more inviting than other houses I had seen built in the same motif. Large windows looked out to the circular driveway made of red-colored pavers. The front door was light-colored hardwood and complimented the red-rock theme of the structure. As I approached, I could hear laughter and the clinking of glasses in the air and I knew that the guests were out the deck I had seen earlier. I knocked loudly on the door and waited.

"Who can that be?" a female voice asked. "Isn't everyone here, Myra?"

I cocked my head as I listened. The voice sounded vaguely familiar to me.

"It's our surprise guest!" Myra said excitedly. "He's a last-minute addition." She lowered her voice so I could barely hear her, but I could still make out what she said. "Plus, he's single and he's pretty hot. I didn't think you'd mind."

"You thought right!" the voice said. "I'll let him in."

I heard heels clatter on what I presumed was a ceramic tile floor and then the door opened to reveal an attractive redhead about my age – the same woman I had met at Dahl and Deluca's restaurant almost two weeks previously. She wore a red cocktail dress with a scoop neck that revealed an intriguing amount of décolletage and was hemmed just above her knees. I smiled reflexively and offered her my hand. "Ms.

Belmont, if I recall correctly."

She smiled at my recollection of her name, and her eyes sparkled with pleasure. "Mr. Price," she said in response. "So good to see you again." She took my hand to shake, but instead of letting it go afterward, she pulled me through the door and shut the door behind us. Then she led me down a short hallway adorned with some of Myra's photos and into the kitchen area.

"Is he the surprise?" she asked as we made our entrance.

Myra stood at a large island in the center of the vast, open kitchen and looked back at us. She was wearing a black jumpsuit made of thin material and gathered at the waist with a belt made of gold, metallic links. The outfit complimented her figure perfectly. Her long hair was gathered into an ornate ponytail and hung down to the middle of her back. She turned and smiled broadly at the two of us.

"Yes, he is! And the two of you make a great couple!"

Myra set down the knife she had been using and wiped her hands-on a nearby dish towel. Then she walked over to us on a pair of high-heeled shoes that must have made her nearly as tall as I was. She threw her arms around me and gave me a friendly kiss on the lips. "So glad you came, Conner!" she said. Then she turned to Patricia and gestured to me. "This is my friend and regular pilot, Connor Price."

Patricia had a smirk on her face as Myra released me. "You never told me you were *still* a pilot," she said.

"I don't think the conversation got that far," I responded. "As I recall you and your buddy Maurice were in a hurry to get to your gallery opening." I put the bottle of wine on the countertop.

Myra nodded in thanks. "You two know each other?" She asked.

Patricia nodded. "We had a brief conversation at the bar at Dahl and Deluca's Saturday before last."

"That is so cool!" Myra said. "See Connor, now you have another friend here! Patricia, why don't you show him around while I get the rest of our dinner together?"

"My pleasure, Myra." Patricia guided me away from the kitchen island as Myra turned back to her work. "This, as you can see, is the gathering room. Kitchen, dining room and family room all in one area."

I nodded. My condo had a similar arrangement, but the square footage here was easily three times the size of mine, if not greater. Myra's kitchen was done in white cabinetry and featured red-tiled countertops that matched the floor and the backsplash. The kitchen was shaped like a large "V" with a rectangular island built around a six-burner range. To our left a large, mission style table was set for 12 and occupied a two-sided alcove with a matching sideboard behind it. In front of us, there were huge windows that displayed the red rocks west of us, silhouetted in the setting sun. To the right was a massive stone fireplace that went from the floor to the ceiling and dominated the entire end of the room. Hardwood beams above and the hardwood floor below finished the room and made the massive space warm and casually cozy.

"Wow," was all I could say. "This is a magnificent room."

"It just gets better," Patricia said, and she took me by the hand again to lead me through the tour.

"Let me guess. You sold this to her," I said as we moved into the wing of the house to the right of the gathering room.

She nodded. "It was one of my first sales here. I attended one of Myra's exhibitions, and she and I just hit it off. When she wanted to sell her old place on the other side of town and buy this place, she gave all that business to me."

"That's awesome," I said. "Great way to jump into a new line of work. The commission on a place like this didn't suck, I'm sure."

She smiled at me as we walked to the end of a long, tiled

hallway with a floor to ceiling window at the far wall. "I got both of them," she said. "The sale of the old place and the purchase on this one. Probably the biggest check I've had in my life, other than when..." her voice trailed off.

I squeezed her hand in reply and left her to her thoughts. She showed me the master suite, study and exercise room. The rooms were impeccably finished and furnished.

"I can't decide if I'm more jealous of the study or the exercise room," I said.

"The place you have isn't too shabby," Patricia said. "I went online and looked at the photos in MLS after you and I spoke."

"It's still out there?"

"Nothing ever gets out of MLS once it's entered," she said. "If you're not a realtor you can't see properties that aren't currently active, but everything is visible if you have the right access."

I nodded.

"So, did you do anything to it? Re-paint or do anything with the floors or cabinets?"

I shook my head. "It was turnkey. In great condition with all neutral colors. That was one of the things I liked about it. I didn't need to change a thing." Then a thought occurred to me as we walked down the hallway behind the kitchen to the other wing of the house. "Why did you look up my condo?"

Patricia blushed slightly. "Well the easy answer would be because I'm a realtor and that's what we do," she said with a nervous laugh. "But the truth is that after our conversation, I was interested in you."

"Well, I'm flattered," I said after a moment. "Although I'm not sure what I said or did to earn that interest."

"You were sympathetic about the business with my husband," she said, not looking at me. "I could tell there was something about it that made you uncomfortable, but you didn't judge."

My mind raced back to that conversation and then the one with Anne, at the house just across the valley from here. Last Friday.

I sighed. "Someone who has fucked his life up as much as I have has no right to judge anyone." The words came out of me unconsciously. For a moment, I wasn't sure whether I said them or thought them. When I realized I had uttered them, I turned to Patricia. "Oh my gosh," I said. "Please forgive my language. That just popped out of me."

Patricia squeezed my hand and laughed. "Don't watch your language on my account. I spent most of my adult life around fighter pilots. I'm used to it."

"I'm sure you are," I said, laughing in return. "But I usually have some control of my vocabulary. I'll try to do better."

We were in the south wing of the house now, and Patricia pointed out the rooms where Myra had her home office, workshop, and a small gallery.

"This is the major reason she wanted this house," Patricia explained. "She wanted to consolidate her workspace and her home, so she could spend more time with her kids. She still has gallery space downtown for exhibitions, but she does all of her work here now."

The rooms were expansive and featured Myra's photos on every wall in various sizes. There were the desert landscapes of course, but there were pictures of verdant valleys and streams as well as close-ups of individual flowers. There were also several portraits of people that ranged from her own children to native Americans and Hispanic immigrants. The extent of her work was impressive.

"I have a few of her photos in my condo," I said, "but they're all landscapes. When I've flown her, that was what she was working on. I never knew she did so many other types of photos."

Patricia nodded in answer.

As we wandered the workshop area, I saw a panoramic poster-sized picture of meteor crater, half of it in shadow and half of it in sunlight.

"Damn," I said, "she didn't waste any time on that one. She had to have shot that while we were flying today."

"How long have you been flying her?" Patricia asked.

I shrugged. "Not sure," I said. "Maybe four years or so? She switched to my boss's company because of the type of aircraft we fly. She's such a frequent flyer she bought herself a flight suit, and we got her a name tag to put on it."

"What's special about the planes?" Patricia asked, leading me from the work area, through the dining room and towards the deck at the back of the house.

"They're OV-10 Broncos, built during the Vietnam, War and designed for counter-insurgency and observation. The canopies go down below your waist when you're sitting in the seat, and it's all unconstructed glass. The visibility is outstanding from both cockpits. Much better for taking photos than a regular aircraft. Plus," I looked over at her and smiled. "They're really fast for a prop aircraft, they're fully aerobatic and 7-g capable. You should come out to the airport and get a ride sometime."

She smiled back at me, but her eyes grew distant, and I could tell she was thinking of her dead husband's life as a USAF fighter pilot. She released my hand and opened the sliding glass door to the large deck, motioning for me to step through.

"Go out and introduce yourself. I'll make you a drink and bring it out to you."

I tilted my head at her. "How do you know what I want?"

She laughed. "I'll never forget watching Luigi make those martinis," she said.

I walked out onto the deck and Spencer, Myra's husband, motioned for me to join him at the railing. Spencer was tall, six feet, five inches, and slim, like a bike racer or swimmer. I knew he competed in triathlons when he wasn't flying helicopters for the local tour operator at the field. He had jet black hair, brown eyes, and a swarthy complexion. He could have been a model for one of those Italian designers.

I shook his hand as I approached him.

"Spence," I said. "Good to see you again. Thanks for the invitation."

"It was Myra's idea," he said, with an embarrassed look on his face, "but I'm glad you're here. It will be nice to have another pilot to talk to. Between Myra's family," he gestured toward a group of men and women standing at the rail to the right of us, "and her friends, I usually have to make a quick exit after dinner to keep my sanity."

"Don't you have any family or friends nearby?"

He shook his head. "Not really. My family lives in Colorado, and most of my friends have other commitments on Thanksgiving. We turned our Thanksgivings into an event for Myra's friends and family a few years ago. I just go along to get along."

I nodded. "Until you can make an exit to your study."

He smiled and gave me a knowing glance.

"Patricia gave me the tour, and I saw the room with all the Army gear and photos. It's a great room."

"Thanks," he said. "It was the only thing in the house that I insisted upon. After all," he gestured at the house behind us, "Myra's work is what pays for all of this. I just fly to keep myself entertained while she does the photography thing."

"But that's how she met you, right?"

He nodded. "I flew her on one of her first aerial photography flights after she moved here." He looked away and seemed to perform some mental math. "Wow," he said. "That was like fifteen years ago. Right after I retired from the Army."

"Early 2000s?"

"2001 actually," he said. "I retired in March of that year, and they almost called me back after 911 but ended up not needing me."

"What'd you fly?"

He smiled, and his eyes became wistful, like the eyes of all pilots who remember an aircraft they loved to fly. "Apaches," he said. "It was cool getting paid to fly around and blow shit up."

I laughed. "2,000 hours in the A-10 and 2,000 in the F-16," I said. "And I agree. If I had a glass in my hand, we'd drink to that."

"Drink to what?" Patricia asked as she arrived by my side with a pair of martinis. She handed me one of them and the three of us clinked glasses.

"To flying around and blowing shit up," I said. I took a sip of the drink and the ice-cold Plymouth, with a slight tinge of dry vermouth, eased across my tongue and down my throat. I savored the taste as I always did.

"This is very good," I said, nodding respectfully at Patricia. "You followed the instructions perfectly."

She smiled in response to the compliment. "I have a good memory for things," she said, looking at me over the top of her glass.

I looked back at her and saw something that looked like a glint of knowledge behind her eyes. *You've been doing research on more than my condo,* I thought. For a moment, I found myself wondering if somehow, she might recognize my face from the business at Luke AFB, five years previously.

Then, a distinctive sound penetrated the peaceful night air and pulled me from my momentary contemplation. Across the two miles of open space separating Myra's house from the airport, I could hear a turboprop engine spinning up during the start cycle. It could have been a Beechcraft King-Air parked at the local FBO, but my gut was telling me it was something else. I heard the momentary increase in RPM to take the propeller off of the flat pitch locks and nodded to myself. There was no doubt. It was an OV-10. I had seen today's flying schedule, and Myra's flight had been the only one on it. The conclusion was inescapable.

Jesus, I thought. *He's at it again.*

The second engine spun up and soon, I could hear the sound of the prop blades going out of flat pitch. Then the aircraft taxied for takeoff.

"Is that one of your company's aircraft, Connor?" Spencer asked. "Sure sounds like it."

I shook my shoulders noncommittally. "Could be," I said, trying to keep my voice casual. "Guess we had a pop-up trip for someone."

"Do you think he'll take off this way?" Patricia asked. "It'd be cool to see it."

"Maybe," I said. "The winds were favoring runway 03 earlier today."

As if on cue, the RPM of the aircraft engines increased. I pictured Ian's hands on the condition levers in the cockpit, moving them from NORMAL FLIGHT to T.O./LAND.

"I guess we'll find out in a few moments," I said. "He's about to take off."

We turned to look towards the airport. The valley was now buried in shadow with the setting sun. In the west, beyond the hills and mountains, only a faint ring of light was visible. As we watched, the sounds of the engines and propellers began to shift and grow louder. I nodded to myself. "Yep," I said, stating the obvious, "he's coming this way."

The OV-10 became visible a few moments later, it's square silhouette barely discernible in the scant light of the dusk sky. It climbed sluggishly and made a slow right turn to the south, passing directly over us.

"He's kind of low, isn't he Connor?" Spencer asked. "You

guys typically climb up pretty rapidly."

I nodded again, watching the aircraft closely. There was no reason for Brooks to intentionally keep the aircraft low. Low aircraft are loud aircraft for people on the ground, and they generate noise complaints. I knew Brooks was all about being a good neighbor to those in the valley around the airport.

"What's that thing hanging beneath it?" Patricia asked.

The bank angle of the prop-jet was such that it was in side-profile to us as it flew over and sure enough, below the aircraft hung a long, cylindrical object.

"It's an external fuel tank," I said, as much to myself as to Patricia and Spencer. "A 230-gallon long range tank."

"I've never seen you guys fly with those before," Spencer said.

And that would be because we never do, I thought. I shrugged and gave Spencer an empty look. "Must be a long mission," I said.

"Dinner is served!" Myra called from the door behind us.

##

Dinner was a delicious repast of the traditional turkey, stuffing and all the trimmings, done in a Cajun style. I ate greedily, having not had a proper Thanksgiving dinner for many years. The wine, a crisp Pouilly-Fuissé, complimented the food perfectly. The conversation was lively and light, and Spencer and I did the usual sparring over helicopter pilots versus fixed-wing pilots and Army versus Air Force. The back and forth between us was fun and invigorating. I realized I had missed out on a possible friendship over the last few years. I made a silent promise to myself to have lunch with him sometime soon and get to know him better.

Myra was an impeccable hostess and ensured we lacked for nothing at the table. She was assisted by the two kids,

Darby and David, ten and twelve years old respectively. I was impressed at the kids' respectfulness toward their parents and their willingness to help their mom with everything she needed.

But even as the evening went on, my mind was repeatedly distracted by what I had seen earlier. *Why the 230-gallon tank?* I kept asking myself. *It doesn't make sense. He can get all the gas he needs at his arming stop just north of Quartzite, and he can't hang a full load of ordnance on the aircraft with the huge fuel tank on the centerline station.*

"And I couldn't stop looking at the way he made the martini!" I heard Patricia's voice exclaim, and I was startled out of my reverie.

"So, Connor," Myra asked. Her voice sounded like it came from the end of a long hallway. "You have a bartender in town who keeps a special bottle of gin on hand for you and who makes martinis using your special recipe without you even asking for them?"

Looking. My mind keyed on the word, and it brought my contemplation into focus. *He was looking. He wasn't bombing. It's a reconnaissance flight. He's scoping out a new target. What the fuck are you up to now, Ian?*

I suddenly became aware that the table was silent, and everyone was looking at me. I forced my mind back into the moment and tried to recapture the last bit of conversation I had heard. "Yes, I do," I said, hoping the conversation had stopped where I thought it had. "And I tip him damn well to do it. But there's a small problem."

"And that would be?" Patricia asked after a short pause.

"I think the bastard is drinking my gin!" I said.

There was polite laughter from the table, and the conversation shifted to a different topic. Eventually, we rose from the table and helped Myra clear the dishes. Myra's family and a few of her friends repaired to the family room with after-dinner drinks in hand, and energetic conversation followed. David and Darby went upstairs to play a video game, and Spencer, Patricia and I helped Myra with the cleanup. There was plenty of playful conversation, but my mind wasn't entirely present. All I could think of was getting back to my condo and looking at the GPS tracker to see where Brooks had flown. Assuming he didn't stop and upload a GPS jammer.

As we finished putting away the last few plates, Spencer invited me to sneak off to the study with him to drink whiskey and solve the problems of the world. I thanked him and asked for a rain check. I thanked Myra profusely for the invitation to dinner and made my way to leave after giving both her and Patricia a warm hug.

Patricia followed me to the door of the house, and I turned to face her as I opened it.

"What were you thinking about tonight?" she asked. "It seemed like you were a million miles away for a while there."

I smiled tiredly at her. "I have some things on my mind these days."

Patricia nodded, but her eyes were fixed on mine. For the second time that evening, there was a look of knowledge in them. "That isn't all of it," she said. "There's something else."

I raised my eyebrows at her and remained silent.

"After what happened to my husband, I know when I'm not getting the whole story from a man. What's really going on, Connor?"

I looked at her for a long moment. Part of me wanted to tell her something, anything, to confirm her perceptions. But then, in a flash of sorrowful remembrance, the memories of the four dead women from five years ago ran through my mind. Patricia was nice, and I liked her. But her curiosity could have lethal consequences, and she'd never see it coming. There was no way I was going to be responsible for that.

"Probably nothing," I said.

CHAPTER TWENTY

Friday, November 27th
1830 Hours Local Time
Ian Brooks' House
Sedona, Arizona, USA

I pulled into the driveway at Brooks' house, wondering for the second time in a week, what I was doing there. The driveway was empty, but that didn't surprise me. The five-car garage could have easily housed Brooks' car and Anne's. I selected the garage second from the right and parked in front of it. I didn't have flowers tonight. Instead, I brought two bottles of wine, a nice Chateauneuf du Pape, and a white burgundy. I retrieved them both from the front passenger seat of the Challenger, locked the car behind me and proceeded to the front door. The walkway lights were on tonight, as they had been a week ago, but for some reason, the ambiance they provided was different than it had been last Friday, and the lighting felt gloomier somehow. Last week I had felt apprehensive. This week I was more curious than apprehensive, but my curiosity was mixed with a sense of dark anticipation. I knew what Brooks wanted to discuss. I just didn't know how I'd react when we talked. My stomach was tight with uneasiness. Inside of me, I could feel the Darkness circling, waiting, as if it knew something was coming.

Anne answered the door several minutes after I rang the bell, and she was attired in her standard work garb. She stepped back to let me enter.

"'Ian's not back yet," she said. "He'll be here in a few minutes."

I nodded. "Any chance of a martini in the meantime?"

"Probably," she said, with an unenthusiastic look on her face. "The gin is in the freezer under the bar on the deck. The vermouth and limes are still in the fridge. Everything should still be good. Help yourself."

As I climbed the stairs to the main level, I couldn't help contrasting her mood tonight with that of last week, or even yesterday. She had mentioned that tonight's dinner had been Ian's idea when we spoke yesterday, but she had also hinted that other *activities* might be possible. Tonight, however, there was no hint anything else could be in store. She seemed resigned, somehow, like the events of the evening were beyond her control. I felt a button being repeatedly pushed inside my brain. It was a maddening sensation. I felt like there was something I should be noticing. Something I should be seeing. Something that was right in front of my face. But I was missing it.

I didn't wait for Anne's invitation to go out onto the deck and to the bar. Instead, I walked through the door, turned right, and headed to the outdoor bar. I could sense her behind me, but I didn't look at her. I moved behind the bar, opened the freezer and removed two frosted martini glasses as well as a bottle of Plymouth. The bottle was unopened, and I wondered who had replenished it, Anne or Ian. The limes and vermouth were in the fridge as Anne had predicted and there were a small cutting board and paring knife in the plastic drawer next to the small refrigerator.

"May I?" I asked as I reached for the drawer handle.

"I told you to help yourself," Anne said with an impatient tone.

"I assume you'd like one," I said. "I guess we'll wait for Ian to arrive before we make him one."

"I'll take one," Anne said, looking like she'd prefer to be anywhere else but here. "But Ian won't have one. He can't drink."

I felt another bell go off in the back of my brain. The use of the word *can't* versus the word *won't* dug into my mind. "Well, he'll be missing out, them," I said.

"I guess," Anne said with a dismissive tone. Then she glanced at the small watch on her left wrist. The movement was quick and subtle, but it caught my attention.

What is supposed to happen tonight? I wondered.

I made the two martinis slowly and methodically while Anne took a seat on the barstool opposite me and looked everywhere but in my direction. I finished the process and pushed the drink across the granite surface to her. She took the glass and raised it to her lips immediately, almost frantically, like she needed the tranquilizing effect of the alcohol.

Well cheers to you too, I thought as I raised my own glass. Even as I felt the icy, silky, goodness of the Plymouth ease into my mouth and over my tongue, I watched Anne closely. She had withdrawn into herself and seemed to be in some sort of trance or daze.

From below, the sound of a vehicle could be heard, pulling up the driveway and stopping. A few moments later, a car door slammed, and Anne was visibly startled from her reverie.

But you were the one that said he wasn't home yet, I thought as I continued to watch her. *What the hell is going on?*

About five minutes later, the heavy clomping of big feet on stairs became audible, and Brooks emerged onto the deck, smiling as he saw me.

"Glad you could make it, Connor!" he said, offering me his hand.

I shook it and smiled back at him. "Wouldn't miss it."

Brooks nodded at me with a satisfied look on his face. He turned to his sister. "Annie? What's up with dinner?"

She didn't look at him. "It's in the oven," she said distantly. "They delivered it about twenty minutes ago."

"Hope you don't mind the informality, Connor," Brooks said. "We eat delivery or carry-out a lot. I don't like cooking, and Annie sucks at it. We got Dahl and Deluca's to deliver us a meal."

I nodded at him and smiled. "Sounds good to me. There isn't much food I'd rather eat than theirs."

A few minutes later, we were seated around the island bar in the kitchen with several containers from Dahl and Deluca's on the counter around us. I was eating pieces of Veal Marsala and Chicken Saltimbocca, along with some angel hair pasta in olive oil and garlic. Ian had a huge helping of Lasagna in front of him, while Anne picked at a salad. I nursed a glass of the Chateauneuf, Brooks drank water and Anne had a glass of the white burgundy in front of her that seemed to be untouched. Brooks attacked his lasagna with gusto, smiling as he ate. He asked me about my career in the USAF, and I provided him a slightly edited version of my real history, dwelling more on the jets and the locations than the people involved. He responded in kind, telling me that he started his career in the F-4G Wild Weasel. I learned we had both been at George Air Force in California at approximately the same time. Then he talked about flying the F-16 for two tours before being selected to attend the prestigious USAF Test Pilot School. He spent the rest of his career in flight test at Edwards Air Force Base. I did my best to look unsurprised as he told me of his USAF background.

While the conversation itself was unremarkable, the

timing of it was curious indeed. I had worked for Brooks for nearly five years. He knew I was a USAF pilot from the resume concocted to support my Connor Price legend, but he had never asked me anything about my career other than that required to verify my provided credentials. And we had certainly never swapped anecdotes about our careers.

"Ever see any combat, Connor?" he asked, as he finished the last bite of his lasagna.

I nodded. "I flew the A-10 during the first Gulf War," I said.

"Were you tasked to cover the Highway of Death," he asked, eying me closely.

I nodded again, chewing on a mouthful of pasta.

"How did you feel about it? A lot of the media and liberal historians have said that was a massacre of sorts. All those Iraqi vehicles trapped on the road as they retreated and the merciless allies shooting them up and killing all those soldiers."

I shrugged. "I'm not sure I've thought much about it. I was a soldier, and the people in those vehicles were enemy combatants. It's not like they were waving white flags or anything." I looked across the counter at him. "Were you there as well?"

He nodded. "I led a flight of Vipers in right behind the A-6's who blocked the northern end of the road with Rockeye. We put eight CBU-87s on the same piece of the road right after they came off target."

The Mk-20 Rockeye was an anti-armor cluster munition. The CBU-87 was Rockeye's replacement in the US arsenal. Both weapons featured shaped charges in small bomblets and were lethal against tanks and other vehicles.

"So, you were part of the roadblock?"

He nodded again. "We flew two more sorties the next day against the column with more CBU-87s. By the time we came back for the second sortie, there wasn't much left that wasn't blown up or burning."

"We had the same experience," I said. "In the sector we were assigned there wasn't much left to shoot at on our last sortie of the second day. I almost felt like we were wasting ammo."

"Could you tell if anyone was still alive in the vehicles you were attacking?"

I shook my head. "Not really. We just shot at vehicles that were still somewhat intact. We fired all of our 30mm, but I kept my flight from shooting the Mavericks. They were too expensive for target practice." The AGM-65D Maverick missile was a guided air-to-surface missile with a 165-pound shaped charge in the nose. It was the weapon of choice against tanks or hard targets, and the imagining infrared seeker head could lock on to nearly any target that either generated or absorbed infrared energy.

He nodded, apparently agreeing with my rationale. "So, after you flew the A-10, you got into the Viper. Which did you like better?"

"I've been asked that question many times," I said. "And it's difficult to answer because it's not really an 'apples to apples' comparison. The A-10 was the most fun flying I've ever done. Most of it was low-level VFR during the Cold War, in the United Kingdom and Germany at 250 to 500 feet AGL. Most days the highest we got was 1,500 feet to enter the traffic pattern. The F-16, however, was the most demanding flying I've ever done. There was a hell of a lot going on in that jet, and the power was incredible. I enjoyed air-to-air combat, and I was pretty good at it, but the Viper was nowhere near as good an air-to-ground machine as the Hawg was."

"So, what did you enjoy more, air-to-air or air-to-ground?"

I grinned at him. "Mud-moving was always my favorite. I liked putting iron on target. Nowadays, everything is done with precision-guided munitions, and the pilot just needs to drive to a point in space and release the weapon, and the weapon finds its own way to the target. I liked going down the chute in both jets, watching the pipper track up to the target, and hitting the pickle button. Even with the CCIP in the Viper, you had to be on dive angle, on airspeed and on altitude at release. Dropping iron bombs was an exercise in precision, and I always enjoyed that."

Brooks wiped his mouth, took a drink of his water and sat back in his chair, nodding at me with a degree of satisfaction in his eyes. "So," he said, watching me closely, "how would you like to do it again?"

And there it was.

I didn't need to feign a look of surprise on my face. It appeared there all by itself. "Excuse me?" I said.

A crooked smile worked its way on to Brooks' face. "There's this project I'm working on," he said. "And I'd like to get your help with it." He saw the question mark on my face and he leaned forward with a gleam of secret knowledge in his eyes. "If you had the means and the ability to destroy something that was pure evil, something that took someone away from you that you loved, would you do it?"

I looked back at him and took a long sip of my wine as I considered my answer.

Brooks gazed back at me, but his expression wasn't one of curiosity, it was one of certainty.

I felt a knot form in the pit of my stomach. *Jesus,* I thought. *He knows about me. How is that possible?* I looked him across the top of my wine glass and gave him the best answer I could summon, given the circumstances. "I think you already know the answer to that question," I said.

He nodded at me slowly. "I do indeed," he said. He picked up his water and took a thoughtful drink. "Pleased to make your acquaintance, Mr. Pearce."

I raised my wine glass in acknowledgment and waited

for the other shoe to drop. Brooks didn't make me wait long.

"It seems," he said, "that we are both retirees or maybe fugitives from the same three-letter government agency."

I raised my eyebrows in feigned surprise, and Brooks gave me a look of mock disappointment.

"Oh, come on," he said, smiling at me and shaking his head. "I know she told you about me. Think about it. She could have just met you somewhere. But she had to come here first. She had to see if it was really me before she talked to you about me."

Brooks' words rang true in my ears and verified everything I remembered about the 'need to know' dogma that pervaded the CIA. Even if she had been here for personal reasons, she would have had to confirm the intel before she told me about it. She would have had to confirm the threat before I would have had a 'need to know.' Suddenly, the timing of her visit, her readiness to have sex and her willingness to provide assistance to my mission to find out what Brooks was doing took on a new context.

I looked at Brooks across the counter and shook my head in realization. "I've been played, haven't I?"

Brooks nodded in sympathy. "You have been. But don't take it too hard. It's what they do." He leaned back and crossed his arms in satisfaction. "What did they tell you about me?"

I shrugged. "Honestly, not much." I paused for a moment to recall my conversation with Sharona on the balcony of my condo and locked down all the memories of our physical interaction in the process. "She claimed that she didn't know that much about you. That your file was classified on a level higher than she had access to."

He tilted his head back and forth as he considered my answer. "That might be true," he said. "My story is pretty unique. I'm pretty sure I'm the only one of my kind."

I looked at him questioningly.

He smiled back at me warmly. “I think you and I need to exchange war stories,” he said. Then he leaned forward, and his eyes blazed with intensity. “And I mean *real* war stories.” His eyes swept to Anne’s now empty seat at the counter and then back to me. “In a more private setting.”

At that moment, I knew we were comrades, not enemies. We weren’t employer and employee either. We were brothers in arms.

“I’d like that,” I said. “But if we’re going to do that. I’m going to need scotch.”

CHAPTER TWENTY-ONE

Friday, November 27th
2000 Hours Local Time
Ian Brooks' House
Sedona, Arizona, USA

Brooks didn't have any decent single-malt on hand. The only thing he had was Dewar's, and I can't stand the stuff.

"Stories like this require single-malt," I said after our liquor search had turned up fruitless.

Brooks reached inside the breast pocket of his flight suit and produced his keys. "Go get us some," he said. "I'll even join you, if you can find some Glenmorangie."

I nodded. "The standard ten or something older?"

"The ten will do just fine."

I looked at his keys in my hand.

"I think I'm blocking you," he said. "Sorry about that. I was in a hurry to get up here."

I nodded. "No problem. I'll be back in a bit."

"Take your time," he said. "I've got to clean up things here and deal with a few emails. We've got all evening and a lot to discuss."

I smiled at him. "Looking forward to it."

He smiled back. "Me too."

I took the keys and descended the stairs, confirming that Anne had disappeared while Brooks and I were talking. I wondered if she had gotten bored with the conversation, but somehow that conclusion didn't sit well with me.

I went through the front door, made my way past my Challenger and climbed into Brooks' Tahoe. I started the vehicle, took a moment or two to adjust the seat and mirrors, and backed the car around in the expansive driveway. Then I headed downhill, ensuring I drove the s-curves in the winding street slowly and carefully in the large vehicle. As I contemplated which liquor store I would drive to, I discovered that I was in a better mood than I had been in a while. After five years of self-imposed exile, I had found a possible friend who could relate to my life and my experiences. The ability to talk about what I had seen, what I had done, and what I had felt, filled me with a sense of hope.

I made another 180-degree turn and accelerated slightly on the straightaway in front of me. I was well familiar with this section of the drive to and from Brooks' house. It was about a half-mile section of straight road, and it would tempt a driver to increase his speed significantly, but there was another 180-degree hairpin turn at the end of this section and a hill below the curve that went down about 100 feet to the intersection where the road met route 179 below. I kept the speed under control and watched the street in front of me carefully, ready to slow and begin my turn when required.

I never saw the black sedan.

My first warning was a series of 'thunk' sounds behind me and the sound of glass breaking. I glanced in my left side view mirror and saw the black, Chrysler sedan, the one I had seen before, in the left lane, next to me, gaining speed. A submachine gun with a cylindrical suppressor was extended from the front passenger side window, and I could see the face of the man I had seen before, behind the passenger windshield. Shell casings were spewing from the ejection port of the weapon, even as the sedan accelerated to come alongside me. My brain, rusty after years of disuse contemplating situations like this, reacted instinctively, and I yanked the Tahoe's steering wheel to the left, hard to the left, into the sedan, as I slammed my foot down on the brake pedal. The Tahoe, for all its merits as a sport-utility vehicle, is not a sports car, and it reacted the way most high-rise vehicles would in a situation where the physics demanded of it were impossible.

It rolled.

In less than a second, the Tahoe went into a rapid roll to the right. I was along for the ride and helpless. I watched out of the front windscreen as the world revolved around in front of me, grateful that I had remembered to fasten my seat belt but concerned whether the roof of the vehicle would be able to continually support its weight as it continued to rotate. I couldn't help but compare the vehicle's rotation with what I had seen through the windscreen of aircraft, but with the terrain in much closer proximity. I was surprisingly comfortable in the Tahoe's plush, leather captain's chairs, and I pushed myself into the cushions with a two-handed death grip on the steering wheel.

The sound of the SUV rotating upon asphalt was a deafening series of unpredictable crunches, clinks, and thuds, combined with the sound of moaning metal as it was hit with impossible force and made to realize impossible angles. While my brain processed the sounds and categorized them, a new series of sounds became detectable, and my brain noticed they were not unpredictable, but regular, and fast-paced.

The man in the black sedan was still firing at me.

A series of small thuds made regular contact with the front end of the car, and three bullet-sized holes materialized in the windscreen in front of me even as the plastic dashboard and instrumentation in front of me shattered with the projectile impacts. As the car continued to rotate, I could feel my shoulder strap release from its inertial reel, and I slumped sideways. The bullet impacts then began to move towards the rear of the vehicle, and soon I could smell the acrid odor of gasoline.

Finally, after two more rotations, the Tahoe came to rest on its roof, and my shoulder harness went slack. I fell out of my seat, on to the interior roof of the vehicle, my head slamming into the hard glass of the moonroof. I saw stars in my vision. They looked like small flecks of snow, in a mini-blizzard that only I could see.

As I struggled to regain my vision, I could hear the sound of an engine, revving up to move forward rapidly, and the sound of steps running towards a vehicle. The smell of gasoline was intense and pungent now, and as my vision slowly began to clear, I could see rivulets of it passing by me on the outside of the car, headed to a lower point on the road.

Then I saw the assassin. The same man I had seen before, in the rear seat of the car days ago, looking directly at me and leaning down to put a cigarette lighter next to a stream of gasoline coming from my vehicle.

I laughed at his foolishness. You could actually put a match out in gasoline, but the laugh made me cough, and when I did, blood spattered all over the shattered window in front of me. “Damn,” I said to no one in particular. “Where the hell did that come from?”

It turned out that the man wasn’t foolish after all. The gasoline had ignited, and a river of flame was making its way towards me, reaching out to me like a fiery finger. I tried to summon the energy to crawl across the roof to the other side of the vehicle, but my legs were entangled in the seat belt and shoulder harness, and I couldn’t reach the release button. I looked toward the fire and saw it growing closer. I could feel the first wave of heat as it approached. And beyond the flames,

I could see the Hispanic man watching. He was looking at me and smiling.

"You fuckers," I said. "You knew it was me. All along."

I closed my eyes and tried not to think about how it would feel to be burned alive. I filled my mind with thoughts of Sarah and Colleen, letting my few memories of them replay over and over again in my mind. There was a loud "whump" sound, and I felt the vibration as the Tahoe's fuel tank exploded. Then there was a flash of intense, searing heat and I felt the air ripped from my lungs. I smiled to myself as my lungs deflated. At least I was going to die of suffocation instead of immolation.

"Better lucky than I good," I said to myself inside the car.

And then everything went black.

CHAPTER TWENTY-TWO

Saturday, November 28th
0700 Hours
Verde Valley Medical Center
Sedona, Arizona, USA

It was an odd dream. A surreal dream. I was watching myself die.

The Tahoe was burning, and I was looking at myself, trapped inside, struggling ineffectually and then collapsing as the wave of heat and flame engulfed the vehicle. I could feel the peace inside of me. I was dying, and I was okay with that. I wouldn't get anyone else hurt. I wouldn't get anyone else killed.

And then something happened that changed everything. Ian Brooks appeared next to the truck. It happened in an instant. One moment he wasn't there, and the next moment he was. In a fluid motion, he yanked the driver's side door off the Tahoe and seemed to expend no effort in performing the task. Then he removed me from the SUV as easily as a father lifting a toddler. He carried me from the burning vehicle and set me down a safe distance away from it. He moved so quickly that it was hard for my mind to process.

Then there was a screech of tires, and the roar of an engine and my field of view shifted toward the rear of the vehicle. The black sedan appeared, rushing toward the place where Brooks and I were.

I wanted to scream a warning to him. *Watch out! There's a guy with a machine gun!*

Brooks turned toward the source of the sound, unconcerned. He looked down around his feet and seemed to survey the stones on the red soil. Then, he bent down, picked a stone the size of a softball in one of his huge hands, hefted it and nodded to himself in satisfaction. He got back to his feet as the black sedan closed on us. It was fifty or so feet away, so close that the faces of the driver and passenger were visible, both contorted in scowls of hate. In a motion that was impossibly fast, Brooks cocked his right arm and threw the rock towards the car. There was a muffled 'boom' sound, and the rock went through the windscreen. The driver's head exploded into a fountain of blood and gore.

The sedan veered to the left and departed the pavement. It careened into some smaller pieces of foliage, which slowed its forward progress slightly, but then it impacted a group of trees and came to a sudden halt. The driver's headless corpse smacked the windshield, the bloody neck barely visible in the collage of carnage already inside of the glass.

Brooks turned to my body as it lay on the ground and looked down.

"I'll be right back," he said. "This will only take a second."

He walked over to the sedan, reached inside the open passenger window, and pulled the dazed passenger from the front seat effortlessly. The large Hispanic man had appeared intimidating in the back seat of the car when I had seen him before. He had seemed deadly when he was wielding his gun moments ago. He looked like a sleepy child now. Brooks slapped him across the face a few times, not hard enough to hurt him but painfully enough that it brought the man back to lucidity. The expression on the man's face was one of instant recognition and raw, unbridled fear. Brooks nodded as the man acknowledged him and then he lifted the man with both hands and propelled him, head first, into the wall of boulders just beyond the curve of the road – a distance of over thirty feet. The man impacted the rock, and his skull made a crunching sound as it was crushed on the rock. The lifeless body then slid to the ground, leaving a streak of dark blood and gore on the red stone.

Then, the scene became nearly silent, with just the barely audible crackle of the flames, slowly consuming the SUV and generating a plume of dull black smoke into the sky. In the distance, I could hear sirens. Brooks turned to my body on the ground and began to gently shake me.

"Come on, Pearce, wake up," he said. "We don't have time for this shit. We have work to do."

##

When I came back to myself, I could feel the desert sun on my face and see the light through my eyelids. I should have wanted to open my eyes, but I had this lasting impression of a dream that I couldn't remember. I thought that maybe, if I kept my eyes closed, I could slip back into sleep and recapture it.

"He's coming around." It was a male voice that I didn't recognize.

"Wonderful," said the voice of Anne Hanley, in a tone that clearly communicated she couldn't have cared less. "I'll ping my brother."

"Does he have any next of kin in the area?" the male voice asked.

"No, doctor," Anne replied. "We're all there is."

"I see. So, when the time comes, will we be giving you his

discharge paperwork?"

"You can give it to my brother," she said with a note of impatient distaste in her voice. "He's the responsible one in the family."

I smiled to myself as I lay there and dozed off again. *At least she's consistent*, I thought.

##

Sometime later, my eyes popped open, and I found myself alone in a hospital room. I was hooked up to a monitor of some sort. There was an intravenous fluid bag feeding a liquid into a connection on my left hand. My head was throbbing slightly, and I could feel a dull ache on my right side. I wondered how long I had been here. My last memory was being trapped in Brooks' Tahoe, certain that I was about to die and finding an element of peace in that realization. A part of me was disappointed that I was still alive.

Then the memory of the odd dream came back to me, and I retreated back into myself for a few moments. I could only retrieve bits and pieces of the dream. I remembered being outside of myself and looking down at Brooks as he stood over my body, but I couldn't remember how I got out of the truck. Then I recalled the image of the black sedan moving towards us and seeing Brooks throw a rock at it, then watching as the sedan went off the road.

That doesn't make any fucking sense, I thought.

But there was one more sequence that came back to me that was even more bizarre. It was clear and uninterrupted in my brain, like it had been embedded there. Brooks pulled the Hispanic hitman from the passenger side of the car like he was a stuffed animal. He slapped the man, and the man recognized him.

"He knew you, Brooks," I mumbled to myself. "He knew

you, and you scared him shitless."

Then Brooks threw the man into the rocks that were at least ten yards away. I could still recall the crunching sound as his head hit the stone.

I leaned back on my pillow, closed my eyes and wondered what effect painkilling drugs might have on my imagination.

##

I must have dozed off again for a few moments because the next thing I knew, I could hear voices in the room and I opened my eyes to see Brooks standing at the foot of my bed, engaged in a tense conversation with a young doctor. Brooks was clad in a green *Brooks Air Service* polo shirt and jeans. His arms were visible, and I noticed, maybe for the first time, that while his arms were big, they didn't seem particularly muscular. The doctor was short, young and had chestnut hair that he wore combed back on his head. He reminded me of Michael J. Fox in *Doc Hollywood.*

"He needs to stay here for observation for at least two more days," the young doctor was saying. "He's got two cracked ribs and a concussion. Plus, he's got so many pins and bolts inside him that I can't tell what else might be broken. We're going to need to do more x-rays and maybe a CAT scan. We can't do an MRI with all of that metal inside him." The doctor paused for a moment and looked at Brooks intently. "I don't suppose you have any idea what happened to him in the past, do you?"

"High-speed ejection from a jet," I said, weakly.

Brooks and the doctor turned to me.

"How fast?" Brooks asked.

"The last time I looked at the airspeed indicator it was going through 600 knots."

Brooks nodded and whistled quietly.

The doctor looked between Brooks and me. "I presume

that's fast?" he asked.

Brooks looked at him. "It's rare for people to survive above 450," he said. Then he turned his attention to me and I saw new respect in his eyes. "You're like a fucking miracle."

"I'm not sure about that. It broke just about every bone in my body. They kept me in a drug-induced coma for two months because the pain level would have been too great while I healed from the breaks and surgeries."

Brooks nodded, and his eyes grew distant, like he was recalling a memory.

"I was just lucky to have great medical care. The lead orthopedic surgeon at UCLA medical center worked on me. I was told she was going to write a medical journal article about my case, but I don't know if she ever did."

The doctor tilted his head as if he was trying to remember something and then he looked at me. "When was this?" he asked.

"The ejection was about six years ago," I said.

The doctor thought for a few moments more and began to nod his head vigorously. "I read the article during my internship," he said. "I remember now. Something about the repair of the skeleton after extreme stress injuries."

"That sounds about right," I said. "And doctor, I'd like to get out of here as soon as possible. With no offense intended, I've spent a fair amount of time in hospitals over the last several years, and I don't like them much."

The doctor thought for a moment and shrugged in resignation. "I'll compromise. It's already late in the afternoon. You can spend one more night here under observation, and if we don't see any complications from the concussion, you can be released in the morning." He looked back and forth between Ian and Me. "Fair enough?"

I thought for a moment and nodded.

Ian was nodding as well. "That should work," he said.

"Good," the doctor said. Then he looked beyond Ian and through the doorway to the room. "Looks like the police are back," he said. "Mr. Price, do you feel like answering some questions?"

I looked at Brooks, and he gave me a quick nod.

"Sure," I said. "Looks like I'm not going anywhere for a while."

The doctor beckoned towards the doorway, and two police officers entered. They were dressed in different uniforms. One of them was a large man of color who looked like he could have been a linebacker on a professional football team. He wore the khaki uniform of the Arizona Highway Patrol and carried the standard "Smokey the Bear" hat by his side. The other police officer was a female, and she wore a navy-blue uniform. I assumed she was from the Sedona police department. She was tall, probably five-feet-ten inches and had an athletic figure. She had dark black hair that was pulled into a business-like ponytail behind her head and piercing brown eyes. It was she who spoke first.

"Mr. Price? I'm Sergeant Philby from the Sedona Police Department and," she motioned toward the state trooper by her side, "and this is Corporal Waters from the State Police. We'd like to ask you a few questions about your accident."

Typically, I'm very wary of talking to law enforcement personnel. After my experience with the Air Force Office of Special Investigations, years ago when I was in the USAF, where my own words were twisted and used against me, I made a vow that I'd never speak to anyone in a law enforcement agency again without an attorney present. But in this case, I was a 'victim' of sorts and not a 'subject.' I decided to cooperate with them. At least for now.

"Certainly," I said. "Please forgive me if I don't shake hands. I'm afraid to move with all this stuff attached to me."

Philby nodded and smiled politely. I expected her to ask

Brooks and the doctor to leave, but she seemed not to care if they remained or not. That relaxed me a bit.

Philby moved closer to my bedside and produced an official-looking notebook. "We obviously have the physical details of the accident," she said. "And we've interviewed Mr. Brooks, who pulled you from the car. We'd just like to know what happened from your perspective."

I nodded. "Okay."

"So, please try to describe what happened to the best of your recollection."

"I'm not sure there is much to tell," I said. "I left Ian's house last night on an errand..."

"What kind of errand?" Philby asked.

I smiled at her tiredly. "I was going to buy a bottle of good single-malt whiskey. Ian's selection was a bit limited. We were going to tell war stories, and you can't do that without good scotch."

Philby wrote in her notebook dutifully. I looked beyond her to the state trooper, and I could see the traces of a smile forming on his face. "What store were you going to?"

"I hadn't made up my mind yet. Probably Sedona Liquors. But Spirit and Spice is near there as well. I couldn't remember which one I'd get to first, so I was going to stop at the first one and see if they had the Glenmorangie 10. If they didn't, I was going to the second one. I was optimistic. The 10 is pretty easy to find."

Philby continued to write. "So, you were in Mr. Brooks' car and not your own, right?"

I nodded. "He was parked behind me. Seemed like the logical thing to do and he offered his keys." I laughed.

Philby raised her eyes to mine with a questioning look on her face, like 'what's so funny?'.

"Probably the last time he'll do that," I said, smiling at her.

She kept her face impassive and returned to her notes.

"Please describe everything you heard and saw from the time you left the house."

I recalled the incident as best I could, from the first turn out of the driveway until I passed out. From time to time, Philby would interrupt me with questions. She asked when I knew the vehicle was under attack, and I told her about hearing the sounds of bullets hitting the car.

"How did you recognize those sounds?" she had asked.

"I've been in combat, Sergeant," I said, providing a generic answer to her question. "Once you hear bullets fired at you, you never forget the sound."

"But you were in the Air Force, not the Army or the Marines," she said. "You were a pilot. How would you know that sound?"

I should have known this wouldn't be an easy line of questioning, regardless of my 'victim' status. It wasn't every day that a vehicle is shot up and blown up in a metropolitan city, let alone the small town of Sedona.

"I was shot down during the first Gulf War," I said. "And I was a prisoner of war for a brief time. I was shot at by Iraqi forces and by coalition forces while I was being transported. Like I said, once you hear the sound of bullets being fired at you, you don't forget it."

She nodded thoughtfully and wrote a few more lines in her notebook.

I left one thing out of my description of the incident. I didn't tell her about the look of recognition in the eyes of the gunman before he dropped the match into gasoline.

Philby finished writing, closed her notebook and looked me right in the eyes. "The most important question we have for you, Mr. Price, is why would someone want to kill you?"

I shrugged and made sure I kept eye contact with her. "I don't know," I said, trying to sound as convincing as I could.

Philby sighed audibly and looked back and forth between

Brooks and me. “Gentlemen, we have a problem here.” She looked at me. “So, you’re driving,” she turned to look at Brooks, “your car, and the car is targeted by men who are obviously career criminals. They shoot the car up and then ignite it, clearly intending to kill the driver and you’re both saying you don’t know why this happened?”

“Have you identified those guys yet?” Brooks asked.

Philby shot him an ‘I’m the one asking the questions here’ look, but the State Trooper answered.

“Not yet,” he said in a deep voice. “We couldn’t do facial recognition because of the state of the bodies, so we have to run the fingerprints. If they’re Mexican nationals, they probably won’t show up in IAFIS, so we’ll have to run them through one of the Fed databases like DEA or ICE.”

“The bodies?” I asked, feeling my guts twist inside of me. “What bodies.”

Philby turned to me. “Oh,” she said, showing a touch of humanity for the first time in the interview. “I guess you wouldn’t know. Your attackers were killed when their car crashed.”

“Wow,” I said. Then I asked the question that I already knew the answer to. “When did that happen?”

“At the scene,” Philby said. “There was some sort of freak accident.”

I must have had a questioning look on my face. Or maybe it was apprehension that what I had dreamed had actually been real.

“Damnedest thing I’ve ever seen,” Waters said. “And I’ve investigated over a hundred road accidents. A rock came through the car’s windscreen and hit the driver in the head. I’d like to say it decapitated him, but there was no head left to find. The car went off the road, and the passenger, whom we presume was the gunman, was thrown clear of the vehicle, and he hit the rocks at the end of the road head first. There wasn't much head left to identify."

Jesus, I thought to myself. *It was all true.* Brooks' words about being "the only one of my kind" came back to my ears, as did my conversation with Sharona about "what" Brooks was. I looked across the room at him and found him looking at me intently, with his arms crossed in front of his chest. He had a slight smile on his face, and he was nodding at me gently. Then he raised his right index finger to his mouth and pressed it to his lips in a 'hush' gesture.

I nodded and once again wondered what the hell I had gotten myself into.

CHAPTER TWENTY-THREE

Sunday, November 29th
1600 hours
Brooks' House
Sedona, Arizona, USA

I was sitting at the counter in Brooks' kitchen, regarding the Sedona landscape through the picture windows on the far wall. I had a bottle of water in my hand, but I wasn't drinking it. Instead, I sat there in a daze as Brooks tidied a few things up in the kitchen and rummaged through his refrigerator to find us something to eat.

There seemed to be no lasting effects from my concussion, fortunately. The damage to my ribs had turned out to be minor, and while I kept a decent level of ibuprofen in my blood, the pain was negligible. I was grateful to be out of the hospital and not in an interview room at the Sedona Police Department. Sergeant Philby had not been happy with us.

##

"We're not finished here, gentlemen," she had said earlier today before I was discharged, and she had come back to my room to ask more questions. Corporal Waters had not accompanied her this time. “This sort of thing doesn’t happen in my town. I think you both know who the attackers were and you’re playing dumb. Which means you’re involved in something that brought this violence to my town. We’re going to be watching both of you very closely and if you do anything, anything at all, that looks suspicious, I’m going to have both of you in my jail. Are we clear?”

Brooks had shrugged, and I had nodded.

“And if you get anyone in my town killed in another one of these shootouts, I’ll charge you with manslaughter. Are we clear on that?”

This time both of us nodded, but we remained silent.

“Damn it guys!” she had said, raising her voice in frustration. “I can’t help you, and I can’t protect you if you don’t give me something here.”

“Sergeant Philby,” Brooks said. “With all due respect to you and the local police force. You can’t protect us against these guys.”

Philby had looked at him and narrowed her eyes. “So, you do know who they are!”

Brooks had shrugged. “Probably. What I can’t understand is how they found us. But I can promise you one thing. Nothing like this is going to happen in your town again.” Then he inclined his head over to me. “Now if you don’t mind, I’d like to get Mr. Price out of here.”

Philby tried to press Brooks for more information but he stood his ground, and she left shortly afterward, her face tight with frustration.

##

“Goddamn it,” I heard Brooks mumble. “It was her turn to go to the grocery store this week.”

“Where is Anne, anyway?” I asked.

"At the office," Brooks answered, without looking at me. Which is handy, given what you and I need to talk about."

I nodded. There was a lot we needed to talk about. I just wasn't sure I wanted to hear it.

He retrieved a bag of tortilla chips from his pantry as well as an unopened jar of salsa. Then he found a bowl in one of the kitchen cabinets and poured the salsa into it. The chips went into another, larger bowl, and he brought both and joined me at the counter.

For a few moments, we crunched on our chips, drank our water and didn't speak. Then Brooks cleared his throat and spoke. "You're not the only one who has endured a high-speed ejection," he said. "But yours, as bad as it was, didn't kill you." He took a long sip of water from his own bottle. "Mine did."

I started to open my mouth and he raised a hand in a gesture to quiet me.

"This will go more quickly if you just let me spit it out," he said. "I was at Edwards, flight-testing one the early prototypes of the F-22. There was a problem with the flight control computers, and the jet departed controlled flight. I tried to recover it but couldn't. Then I bailed out, but between the high sink rate of the aircraft and my proximity to the ground, it was way too late. I impacted the ground before my chute was fully deployed."

"Jesus," I said, involuntarily. "But you're..."

"Alive now?"

I nodded.

"I lived for about ten minutes after I hit the ground. The crash recovery folks and medics arrived on the scene very quickly and got me away from the fireball. They did the best they could to keep me alive, but I was too badly injured. I was literally a bag of bones. When I shut my eyes, I thought I was a goner."

He took another drink of water and looked off into the

distance. Then, he took a deep breath before he continued. "And then I woke up in the lab. It was one year later, and I was the six-million-dollar man."

I nodded in acknowledgment of his reference to a 1970s TV show in which an astronaut and test pilot had endured a plane crash and been 'rebuilt' into a cyborg with a 'bionic' arm, eye and legs. But I didn't smile. The reality of what I had seen Brooks do was too terrible.

"Only I think what they did to me cost more like twenty million."

"What did they do?" I asked quietly.

He sighed. "Full titanium endoskeleton, prosthetic arms, legs, eyes, and ears. I have armor plating over all my vital internal organs, most of which have prosthetic components. I'm like the fuckin' terminator." He looked over at me and raised and lowered his eyebrows like he didn't really believe what he had just said. "But I also have to take anti-rejection drugs by the boatload and have to plug myself into a recharging station about once a week to power everything up." He took a drink of water and looked away. "It used to be once every six weeks or so," he said. "Now it's down to once a week. The batteries are dying, and when they go, so do I."

We were quiet for a few moments. I just stared straight ahead, processing what Brooks had just told me.

"Can't they just swap your battery pack?" I asked at last.

"Like a toy? Sadly, no. Keep in mind that they put me together in the early 2000s and technology has come a long way since then. There wasn't a lot of extra room inside my body for batteries, so they used conformal and flexible battery tech installed inside some of the 'bones' in my skeleton. I don't think they can swap the batteries without literally taking me apart. Today they might be able to build me with swappable components. But back then, not so much."

"Jesus," I said involuntarily. "That sucks." I sipped my

water for a few moments and eyed the array of prescription medicines aligned in front of me on the counter. Suddenly it seemed that any physical pain or discomfort I might have experienced paled in comparison to what Brooks had endured. And nothing that had happened to me resulted in a long-term death sentence. Not yet, anyway.

I looked across the counter at Brooks and changed the subject. "When Sharona, the CIA chick, told me about you, she said they used you as an asset."

Brooks nodded. "For several years. I could get to places that 'normal' people couldn't, although I couldn't fly on commercial airlines because of my metal content and my weight."

"Weight?" I asked. "What do you mean?"

"How much do you think I weigh?"

I looked him up and down. "I don't know. Maybe 220? 230?"

He shook his head. "More than twice that. It's the batteries. There are a lot of them." Then he laughed. "The few times they sent me in via parachute, they had to use a cargo chute for me. I was too heavy for a personnel chute, even for a square canopy."

"So what kind of work would they have you do?"

He looked at me with a disappointed expression on his face. "Wet-work," he said. "Assassinations. Didn't you do some of that?"

I shrugged. "I wasn't specifically tasked for it, but that doesn't mean it didn't happen."

"They sent you in to do other things?"

I nodded. "It usually had to do with airplanes. Fighters or business jets. Sometimes both."

"You lucky dog," Brooks said, smiling in appreciation. "You got a better deal than I did. At least you got to fly."

"Maybe," I said. "But they didn't spend $20 million on

me."

He rubbed his brow and sighed. "Well, they got their money's worth."

I nodded at him. "Sharona said you had like 107 confirmed kills."

Brooks snorted. "Well, I guess she didn't really see the file, then. The real number is well above three hundred. There were 107 *assignments*, but many involved multiple targets."

My eyes widened. Brooks didn't notice my reaction. Instead, I got the sense that he retreated into himself for a few moments. I let him have his space. I was well acquainted with the emptiness that killing people can create inside a person who still has a conscience and I knew Brooks did. After a long moment, I spoke. "She also said that you...left the Agency."

Brooks nodded, his eyes still looking off into the distance. I thought he wasn't going to say anything in response, but eventually, after several seconds, he did. "I just got tired of the killing," he said, so softly I could barely hear him.

"I understand that," I said. "It's one of the reasons I walked away myself. That and the fact that people I cared about had a tendency to get dead around me."

"I had that problem as well," Brooks said. "When I tried to leave, the Agency came after me. You probably know that."

I nodded.

"What you may not know is that there were others that came after me as well. On one of my last assignments, I had to perform a direct action against a large Mexican drug cartel. I eliminated a good portion of their senior staff, but a few got away. When I tried to leave the Agency, someone leaked my location to the cartel, and they came after me. They killed two people who were very close to me. Two people who managed to help me forget all the shit I did for my country. At least for a while."

I remembered the photo the Mexican gunman had shown

me and nodded. The chronology of Brooks' actions was now becoming clearer.

"And that's when the Agency sent the ops teams after you."

Brooks looked over at me, held my eyes for a second and then nodded.

"And you kicked their asses."

"I'm not proud of that," he said, looking away. "I was in a very dark place. And the fact that they brought the doctor who put me together didn't help. He gave me the creeps."

"What happened to him?" I asked, thinking I already knew the answer. Thoughts of the tension between Dr. Frankenstein and his creation ran through my mind.

"I killed him," Brooks said matter-of-factly. "And he was probably the only one of the group who deserved to die."

I watched Brooks retreat into himself again. I knew what was happening inside his brain because the same thing had happened to me. He was reliving the deaths of the people he had killed when the ops teams had come for him. Odds were high that he knew at least some of the team members. He had probably worked with them before. But they had crossed a line, and betrayed him and for that, they paid with their lives.

"Sharona told me that you and the Agency had reached a truce, of sorts."

Brooks nodded. "They paid me a lot of money to keep me quiet, and I accepted it and told them that as long as they left me alone, there wouldn't be any trouble from me."

"So, what changed, Ian? Why are we having this conversation?"

He paused several moments before answering. Like he was composing his thoughts. "Remember the question I asked you the other night?" he asked at last. "Something about how if you had the means and ability to destroy something that was pure evil, would you do it?"

I nodded.

"About two months ago, I got hooked up with an intel source who is deep inside a major cartel in Mexico. The same cartel who killed the people who were close to me. He said they had expanded into human trafficking and were kidnapping young girls from affluent suburbs in Arizona and taking them deep into Mexico for the slave trade. I felt I couldn't stand by any longer. That's when I decided to take direct action against them."

"How much longer after that did the OV-10D's arrive?"

He shot me a 'how-did-you-know' glance. Then his face softened. "I had already located them and made a bid to add them to our fleet earlier this year. When the deal closed in August, I had the engines replaced and the cockpit modifications installed. I thought we might be able to do some fire suppression work with them. The fact that I might use them for other purposes didn't dawn on me until I got the call from my contact. The D-models arrived a month later."

"Other purposes like bombing people with them?"

"How did you figure that out?"

"It wasn't difficult. No one can work on the D-models but you? Then there were the late-night flights with the exterior lights off. Of course, as we discussed the other night, the timing of Sharona's arrival wasn't coincidental by any means. They sent me GPS trackers, and I put them on the D's. I even spent the night on a rock north of Quartzite. You've got quite the crew."

He nodded like the news wasn't a surprise to him. "They're fellow believers, like me. People who have lost someone they cared about to opioids or to the cartels. They weren't hard to find. Of course, I still have to pay them."

"From Luke?" I asked, meaning Luke Air Force Base.

He nodded again. "I'm not sure how they get the munitions off the base, and I don't ask questions. I just give them a suitcase of money every time we fly a mission and leave it at that."

"Maybe one of them is the leak that led the bad guys up here."

Brooks thought for a moment and shook his head. "The cause is too pure, and the money's too good. It wouldn't be in their interest to see it end." He paused for a moment and drained his bottle of water. "Although it will end soon anyway."

"Why?" I asked.

"Because," he said. "I've found the mother of all targets. The cartel's headquarters. All the leadership will be there. It's the whole reason I was trying to recruit you. We'll probably only get one shot at it, and we'll need to hit it with two aircraft at once to get the maximum firepower on target as quickly as possible. I want to end this. I want to end them."

I was nodding as I recalled his promise to the Sedona Police Department's finest.

"We're going to cut the head off the snake, Pearce," he said. "We're going to cut the head off the fucking snake and avenge all the innocent people they've killed. Maybe then my life will have meant something. Maybe then I can die in peace."

CHAPTER TWENTY-FOUR

Sunday, November 29th
2330 hours
My Condo
Sedona, Arizona, USA

I was back in my own space and sitting in my recliner in front of the electric fireplace, nursing my first single-malt in a few days. I stared into the depths of the amber spirit, illuminated by the electronic flames, and pondered the events of the last few days as well as the plans for the not too distant future. I also considered what I would or would not tell Sharona, knowing full well that she was passing on whatever I told her to whomever she reported to inside the Agency.

My phone lay beside me on the table, and the screen showed that there were at least five missed calls, all from Sharona's number, or at least, the number she had been using. There were also several text messages from the same number. I hadn't read them yet and wasn't sure that I would. I was getting a little tired of being so easily manipulated and behaving so predictably.

I was glad that my initial instincts about Brooks had held true. He saw his cause as just, and I couldn't disagree with his motives.

Earlier, after Anne had brought home yet another round of takeout food, Chinese this time, I had tried to pull more information out of Brooks about the people he had lost. It wasn't easy to get him to talk about it. I had a feeling the pain still ran too deep. From his limited discussion, I had managed to learn that he succeeded in eluding the CIA for over a year by assuming an identity as a flight instructor at a small town in Colorado. A single mother, named Carina Bertella, was trying to put herself through flight school by working as a scheduler in the school during the day and by waiting tables at night. Brooks was her regular instructor, and throughout many briefings, flights and debriefings, Brooks and the woman had fallen for each other. The woman had an eight-year-old daughter, named Bella, who saw Brooks as the father she had never known and bonded with him. Then something had happened that ruined Brooks' anonymity and set them all on the run, an excursion that eventually resulted in the woman and the girl being killed. It was clear that Brooks blamed himself for the entire business, but he held the Mexican drug cartel responsible as well and apparently needed to exorcize his own demons through the destruction of the cartel.

I understood his pain and his fire. I understood his obsession. I just wasn't 100% sure I wanted to risk my ass to support it. I had left his house without giving him an answer. I told him I needed time to think.

I took a long sip of my scotch and stared into the electric flames, trying to clear my mind and delve into myself, in a quest to find out what I really felt and what I really wanted to do. I thought about how I had lived the last five years, in a perpetual state of denial, avoidance, and mourning. I thought about the numerous times I had spent time alone, with scotch at hand and lost inside myself. I thought about the utter purposelessness of my life during my time in Sedona, and suddenly, I had my answer.

My exploits with the CIA might have been about my curiosity and my need for adrenaline. They might have even served as venting opportunities for the Darkness inside of me. But I realized now that those exploits were far more than that. They were about meaning. They were about me making a difference. Doing something that mattered. And whatever Brooks' motives for the strike he was planning, the action itself mattered. It was a force for good. It would make the world a better place, or at least a less bad one.

Just then the iPhone buzzed on the table surface next to me. I glanced at the screen and saw Sharona's number. I ignored it again. I didn't need to check in with her, or them. I knew they were close by. I knew they were watching me. And I knew they were wondering just exactly what was going to happen next.

My mind went back to the words my former handler, Dave Smith, had spoken to me five years ago when I had told him I was going to quit working with the CIA.

"You'll be back because it's who you are," he had said. "You can't run away from that. Not now. Not ever."

It turned out that he was right. I thought Smith was talking about my addiction to the violence, but that wasn't what he was referring to at all. He knew I needed the purpose. He knew I needed the meaning.

"Damn it, Dave," I said to the empty room, "turns out you had it right after all."

I picked up my now silent phone and hit the speed dial for Brooks' mobile number.

He picked up after the first ring.

"I'm in," I said. "Let's kick their ass."

"Shit hot, Pearce. Shit. Fucking. Hot. Let's meet at the office at 1900 tomorrow, and we'll fly a practice mission, just so you can get back into the swing of things and we can get used to each other as flightmates."

"I'll be there," I said.

I clicked off the call and looked down at my phone and the list of missed calls from Sharona. I considered calling or texting her and filling her in on what I had learned and what we were doing. But I quickly dismissed that idea. I had been used enough. It was time for them to earn their pay.

"Fuck you guys," I said to the empty room. "You're on your own. And so am I."

CHAPTER TWENTY-FIVE

Monday, November 30th
1900 hours
Brooks Air Service Terminal
Sedona Airport (KSEZ)
Sedona, Arizona, USA

I arrived in the office to find Brooks hunched over the map table in the center of the room with two large 1:250,000 scale maps in front of him. Anne was still at her desk, probably going through the day's flights and expenses. She looked up and eyed me curiously as I entered.

"Hi Colin," Brooks said over his shoulder. "Come on over here and I'll show you what I've got in mind."

I shot a polite smile at Anne. She nodded in acknowledgment but didn't return the smile. Instead, her face took on a neutral, even inscrutable expression.

I joined Brooks at the table.

"This map is northern Mexico. Our target will be in a valley southeast of the town of Pitiquito." He pointed to the town and then moved his finger down and to the right to the position in the valley that was marked. "That's where the cartel's HQ is, as well as their stock of drugs awaiting import into the United States. I'm going to hit the HQ, and you're going to hit the warehouses."

"How do we know there aren't any innocents around?"

"My contact told me that all the farms in the area have been cleared out and the last shipment of girls left last night. Nobody there but bad guys for the next three nights."

"You've got pretty good intel," I said.

Brooks shrugged. "My guy on the inside hates what his bosses are doing. He wants to see them go down."

I nodded. "So what kind of structures are we talking about?"

Brooks opened a file and produced some 8x10 black and white photos. "I did a recon run on Thanksgiving night and shot these."

There were 10 photos, apparently taken with a light-enhancing lens. The structures were all shown in shades of green.

"The big manor house is the HQ. It's a hacienda they took over and adapted for that purpose. I'm thinking adobe walls and a tile roof."

I nodded. "Sounds about right."

South of the manor house there were five, long, rectangular buildings. Brooks shifted through the pile of photos to find the best picture of them. He found one that showed them in clear focus. Guard patrols were detectable around each of the structures, and an additional patrol was stationed at what seemed to be the entrance to each building.

"The barns are wood. New wood and even good wood, but still wood."

"Okay. What do you think about ordnance?"

"I want to hit the house with five Mark 82s, tail fusing only."

I nodded. "You want them to penetrate the roof and explode inside the house."

Brooks nodded in response. "Yep. Drop the first four in

pairs and the last as a single. Maximum internal blast effect."

"And for the barns?" I asked.

Brooks gave me a wry smile. "Napalm," he said. "I located some live canisters of that. Perfect for starting a fire that can't be stopped."

"Where the hell did you find napalm?" Napalm was jellied gasoline carried in a canister. After departing the aircraft, the canister opened and dispensed its lethal payload. The gasoline was ignited milliseconds after it was distributed, and it created a raging inferno on the ground. Napalm had been banned late in the Vietnam War. I was shocked that it was still available.

"I have friends in the ordnance business," Brooks said. "I did them a favor when I was...operational. They owed me."

I shook my head. "Wow. Some friends." I looked down at the photos and then at the map again. "Plan of attack?"

Brooks moved his finger across the map to the location of the hacienda and then to the west. "We'll ingress from the west and action about seven miles from the target. I'll action about 30 left, hold down for a minute, pop up and roll in, right down the valley at them. I'll pop up, rip my 5 bombs and egress to the west, across the ridge." He moved his finger across the ridge to the west of the house. Then he traced another line from the south to the north. "In the meantime, you will have actioned right and driven the extra distance to give you the separation you need. You'll come in from the south end of the valley with 30-second spacing for the frag and lay the napalm down on the barns. Then we'll egress north together."

I nodded in approval. "That should work." I looked at him. "What does your intel say about air defenses?"

Brooks shook his head and smiled. "Small arms and automatic weapons, if even that. If we time this right, they won't know what's happened until the bombs land, and by then it will be too late. You'll hit them with the napalm before they can even react, and we'll be out of there."

"Sounds good. Now, where do you want to go to practice this?"

Brooks pulled the second 1:250,000 scale map out and put it on top of the first one. He pointed to a shallow valley west of us, between Prescott and the Colorado River, just northeast of Lake Havasu. "Here," he said. "The configuration of the terrain is approximately the same. We can do multiple run-ins until we get the timing perfect."

I retrieved my map bag from my locker and unfolded my own local area map. Then I plotted the notional target on it with my grease pencil. "Target here?" I asked Brooks.

He nodded. "That will work." He laid his map next to mine and plotted the same point I did. Then he looked west of the target until he found a rock formation that was easily identifiable. "This will be the IP." You can get a protractor out and get the bearing and distance, but it doesn't really matter, we'll just type the coordinates into the nav systems on the planes and let the computers do the math. Tomorrow night, when we go live, the route, IP and target will all be programmed into the nav systems in advance."

"I don't suppose you have a computer around here that has the software for us to crank the parameters for these deliveries, do you?"

He smiled and nodded. "In my office. But you won't have to get too anal about the deliveries. Both of the D models have radar altimeters in them and software that builds the bombing triangle from the radar altitude. Poor-man's CCIP."

I shook my head. "Not so poor. The LASTE system I used to fly with in the A-10 used exactly that technology. You could use the gun to drive nails. The only limitation on the CCIP for either the gun or bombs was that you had to be over terrain that was the same elevation as the target so that the weapon's range was computed accurately."

"We have that same limitation, but the good news is that as slow as we fly, the difference in elevation won't be that critical."

"Where'd you get the software and the ballistics profiles for the weapons?"

"Kyle," he said.

I stared at him for a moment then I recognized the name. "Kyle from the FBO? The kid who drives the fuel truck?"

"You'll notice you only see him around the holidays. His dad owns the FBO and Kyle attends classes at the University of Advancing Technology down in Tempe. He's double majoring in game theory and network security. I provided him the specs for what I needed and the weapon and the ballistics data from the OV-10 dash 34. He did the rest."

I was dumbfounded for a moment. Kids building software for a bombing computer. It was both fantastic and terrifying. Then something occurred to me.

"Were there any OV-10 dash 34 parameters for napalm?"

Brooks gave me a crooked smile. "Let's just say your data will be a bit more theoretical than mine."

"Great," I said.

##

Fifteen minutes later, we had both D models out from under the tarpaulin, and we were tugging them out onto the ramp. After both planes were in place and the parking brakes were set, Brooks closed the main hangar door and then disappeared inside. He came through the lobby door a few moments later with a set of night vision goggles and handed them to me.

"You'll need these," he said. "The headpiece should fit under your helmet."

I nodded and took the NVGs from him. “What about you?” I asked.

“I don’t need them,” he said.

I started to open my mouth but then thought better of it. The technology I had seen Brooks display with his arms and legs was incredible. I was sure his eyes were on an equal if not greater level.

“Let’s get to it,” Brooks said.

CHAPTER TWENTY-SIX

Monday, November 30th
2145 Hours
Brooks Air Service Terminal
Sedona Airport (KSEZ)
Sedona, Arizona, USA

We landed back at Sedona about two hours after takeoff. The practice runs had gone well. It had taken Brooks and me just three attempts to get the timing and geometry to work out satisfactorily. We did seven more runs to hone the precision we wanted to achieve and to ensure we could perform the entire attack sequence without a radio call.

It had felt damn good to do something tactical with an airplane again. The D-model OVs had even more energy than their A-model counterparts, thanks to the monster PT6 engines Brooks had installed. In the clean configuration, as they had been for our practice tonight, the aircraft could maintain 5 gs in a level turn. I knew it wouldn't sustain that much when we had ordnance loaded, but there would be plenty of smash available for off-target maneuvering once we were clean. The CCIP, continuously computed impact point, gunsight seemed to work effectively and featured approximately the same symbology as I had seen before, including a bomb-fall line and a pipper or "death dot" that neatly tracked up the line. The NVGs Brooks had provided me functioned well and integrated smoothly into the lighting scheme of the cockpit. While not as advanced as last apparatus I had used for the same purpose, the NVGs were user-friendly, and I became accustomed to them quickly.

The most curious thing about the evening was the peace I had felt while engaged in the maneuvering. With each application of back pressure on the stick and the ensuing g on my body, I feel myself relax, and I felt the moroseness and guilt ease out of me. The Darkness, which had simmered inside of me for so long, seemed to be sated as well and I found myself involuntarily grinning from ear to ear with each practiced attack. Even now, as we flew up initial as a two-ship formation and pitched out to land, I was relieved and excited all at once. It seemed that I had returned to my calling.

We taxied in, and when my taxi light illuminated the ramp, I surprised to see TJ Costello waiting for us. He marshaled us into our appropriate parking spots and then motioned for us to shut down. We did as directed and the ramp was quiet in moments.

"Fancy meeting you here," I said as my feet hit the asphalt.

"I could say the same thing to you," Costello said with a smirk. "I take it you've been recruited?"

I nodded. "I needed some more excitement in my life."

"I wouldn't know about that," Costello replied. "I just wanted the money." He looked at Brooks. "Sorry I wasn't here for the launch, Boss. Family plans and all that. Planes ok?"

"Code one here," Brooks said.

"Likewise," I added.

"Good," Costello said, looking between the two of us. Then he turned to Brooks. "Boss, when's the next event?"

"Tomorrow night," Brooks replied. "Get 'em ready TJ. Program the radar warning software as well. Just to be on the safe side."

Costello nodded. "Will do."

We took turns wing-walking the aircraft into the hangar and ensured they were stowed against the back wall. Costello performed post-flight inspections on both aircraft after we chocked them and then we covered both jets with the heavy tarpaulins. Brooks and I left Costello and walked across the shiny hangar floor to the office.

"How long has he been part of the war effort?" I asked, motioning behind us to where Costello was still working on the D-models.

"From the beginning," Brooks said. "He and I go way back. He was helicopter crew chief in the Army and an A-10 crew chief in the Air Force reserve. He knows how to take care of airplanes. That's why I hired him to begin with and why I signed him on for this project. Although, I do have to pay him extra for the late-night work." Brooks looked at me. "Which reminds me. We didn't talk about extra money for you to do this. How much do you want? I still have a lot of CIA hush money to spend."

My eyebrows raised. "Wow!" I said. "They must have paid you a butt-load to keep you quiet!"

He shrugged. "Something into 8 figures. It pays the mortgage and keeps the business running."

"I bet."

"So how much do you want?" he asked. "Didn't you get a contract rate when the Agency paid you?"

"Two-thousand a day plus expenses," I said. "But that was five years ago."

"We'll make if five-thousand a day, starting last Friday," Brooks said. "You were injured on my time."

"That's generous, Ian. But the truth is, I'd do it for free. Flying around and blowing shit up is what I was born to do."

He nodded at me and smiled. "You're a man after my

own heart," he said. "I'd do it for free too. But then all that government money would go to waste. I'm not going to be around to spend it. And I'm sure as shit not leaving it for my bitch sister."

I nodded and kept my mouth shut. I understood his logic perfectly.

He clapped me on the shoulder. "Now go home and get some rest. Try to sleep in as late as you can. The mission tomorrow is going to be a ball-buster. We'll meet here at 2000 and try to be airborne by 2200. We'll stop and get armed and then we'll head southbound."

"Roger that."

I stowed my helmet and map bag in my locker and then headed out to my car. I had the Challenger on the road in moments and encountered very little traffic as I drove down the hill and made the left turn on to Route 89A. I gazed through the windshield as I guided the car along the few miles to my condo. The night sky was a brilliant black tonight, and the stars gleamed brightly against the silhouettes of the red-rock monuments around me. I was looking forward to some relaxation in front of my electric fireplace tonight with a dram or two of single-malt to keep me company.

I parked the Challenger in my designated garage, shut the garage door and made my way down the walk and up the concrete stairs to my condo. The night air had a nice briskness to it, and I enjoyed the dry cold on my skin as I strode to my front door. I took my time on the short distance and listened to the silence of the night, broken only by the sound of my feet on the pavement.

The main entrance to my condo was in an alcove shared by only one other residence. One of the things I had paid extra for was a semi-private entrance. The light meant to illuminate the space seemed to be intermittent this evening, and both doorways were cast in shadow. I made a note to contact the management office in the morning as I reached inside the left breast pocket of my flight suit for the keys.

"Well hi there," a female voice said from behind me.

I spun around, reaching for the .45 in my backpack but realizing that I was going to be far too late if the person speaking to me had a weapon.

The body belonging to the voice stepped out from the shadows, and I saw Anne standing there in a light overcoat.

"Might I ask what you're doing here?" I asked.

She smiled at me and opened her overcoat briefly, revealing black and lacy lingerie underneath.

"Isn't it obvious?" she asked.

I waited for the internal rush of the Darkness to respond to her like it had in our previous interactions, and I braced myself for the unconscious lust to unfurl and drive me into her arms and into her body.

But nothing happened.

We looked at each other for a few moments, but the Darkness stayed checked inside of me. I had no idea why it had remained dormant, but I found myself grateful. I exhaled, not realizing I had been holding my breath.

"Let's have a drink first," I said, to break the now awkward silence.

Anne's eyes narrowed, and she nodded impatiently. I unlocked and opened the door for her, and she went into the foyer in front of me.

"Have a seat on the sofa," I said from behind her. "I'll get you a scotch."

As she walked to the sofa, something about her gait got my attention. Usually, there was an arrogant strut in the manner in which she ambled. But tonight, her walk was stiff and unsure. Like she was nervous.

Something doesn't feel right about this. The thought popped into my mind, and I unconsciously nodded in agreement with it.

I put my backpack on one of the stools at the kitchen counter, surreptitiously removed the .45 combat commander from a compartment, and placed it in one of the large leg pockets of my flight suit. Then, I walked over to my bar, doing my best to avoid highlighting the weight of the gun in my pocket as I moved.

"Do you have a preference?" I asked over my shoulder.

"No, not really," Anne replied, seating herself on the left side of the sofa. Her overcoat was tightly closed, and she held her purse in front of her. Her posture was tense, and she sat on the edge of the sofa, leaning forward.

I heard a warning chime in the recesses of my mind. I poured a couple of healthy drams of the Balvenie Doublewood 12 and brought them over to the sofa, placing them both on the coffee table. I seated myself on the right side of the sofa, as far away from Anne as I could be and remain on the couch with her.

I picked up my glass and nodded to her to do the same. Then we clinked glasses and drank. The spirit's bouquet of chocolate and raspberries warmed my nostrils, but it was the rich fruit on the tongue with a slight note of pepper that I really loved. It was an inspiring contrast. The finish was both fruity and spicy.

"So good flying tonight?" Anne asked.

I nodded slowly. "It was fun," I said. "I haven't done anything tactical in an airplane for a very long time." I took another sip of my whiskey and spoke after a long moment. "So how long have you known about Ian's evening excursions?"

She shrugged. "He hasn't been doing them long. He couldn't very well keep it a secret since we live and work together."

"Do you know what he's doing?" I asked.

She gulped the Balvenie and swallowed it instantly like she

was chugging it. I winced involuntarily. "I know he's flying into Mexico and bombing things. I see the maps and charts in his office, and I'm the one who has to get the cash for the bombs that he buys. He told me it was about paying the drug cartel people back for what they did to this woman he used to know and her daughter."

I nodded. "That's what he told me too."

Anne shook her head. "Seems like a waste to me," she said with an acid tone in her voice. "That woman died years ago. It's ridiculous. He's throwing a ton of money away on this vendetta of his."

I shrugged. "It's his to throw away. And besides, you heard him tonight; this will be the last one of these he flies."

Anne nodded, more to herself than in reaction to my words. "That's true," she said.

There was something about the way she uttered the two words – with a tone of certainty in her voice. It was both curious and ominous. I unconsciously moved my right hand closer to the pocket with the gun in it.

Anne chugged another drink of whiskey, abruptly rose, and walked across the gathering area, towards my bedroom, glass in hand. I sat there, dumbfounded for a moment or two, then I got to my feet and followed her.

I found her strolling about the room like she was giving herself a tour. She turned from the sliding glass window when I entered and approached my bed from that side.

"You didn't offer to show me around," she said, with the usual priggish expression on her face. "So, I thought I'd do it myself." She put her glass down on the far nightstand and pushed down on the bed with her left hand.

"Nice mattress!" she said. "What do you say we give it a test drive?"

I felt my mouth open in disbelief. She couldn't possibly be that clueless.

Before I could speak, Anne came around the bed, unbuttoning her overcoat as she walked. The lace lingerie set became visible again, but my eyes didn't focus on that. I noticed that she didn't have her purse in her hand and I knew that meant something. She reached inside the right pocket of her overcoat as she stopped in front of me.

"Anne," I began, "I don't know what you think you're doing, but..."

She threw her arms around my neck and pressed her body to mine.

"Come on, Colin," she said. "You know you want more of this."

How in the hell does she know my real name? Brooks had used it when he and I were talking at his house, but she hadn't been present. I reached up to remove her arms and felt a sting on the back of my neck. I knew what it was immediately, the prick of a needle.

I pushed her from me and backed away. I reached down to my right flightsuit pocket for the gun, but the room suddenly began to spin around me. I found I was having trouble finding my leg, let alone the pocket. My limbs felt like lead.

Anne approached me again, circling me slowly, like a predator. "What you're feeling is Midazolam," she said. "It's a very fast acting sedative."

She pushed me towards my bed, and I was powerless to stop her. It was all I could do to stay conscious. I blinked my eyes and looked at her, suddenly aware of how heavy my eyelids had become.

"I was hoping to fuck you into submission," she said as I struggled to focus on her face. "And drug you in the morning. But you had to make this more complicated."

Anne didn't waste any time. In mere moments, she had my flightsuit and underwear down around my ankles, and she had pushed me onto my back on the bed.

"They didn't want me to kill you," she said as she unceremoniously discarded her clothes. "They wanted me to keep you alive so that they could finish the job themselves. In person."

Anne leaned down to hold my face in hers. "They're going to fuck you up in a bad way, Mr. Colin Pearce. And they're going to do it very slowly. But in the meantime, I get to use you until they get here. They gave me the sedative, but I might have put a little something in there for me." She winked at me with the usual arrogant expression on her face. "Hopefully, that will get you up for the task."

I forced my dazed mind into the moment. "What's going to happen to Ian?"

Anne laughed as she sank to her knees in front of me. "My dear brother has a special surprise waiting for him," she said. "They've got some kind of gun down there. A ZS? Or was it ZSU? There are numbers in the name as well. I just can't remember."

She lowered her mouth to me.

I tried to detach myself from the physical sensations she was generating. *ZS?* I thought. *ZSU?* But the answer occurred to me even as the letters ran through my mind. *Shit! A ZSU 23-4. It had to be.*

I felt my eyelids beginning to close even as I felt my loins begin to stir.

Jesus, I thought as the blackness took me. *How is that even possible?*

CHAPTER TWENTY-SEVEN

Tuesday, December 1st
?????
My Condo
Sedona, Arizona, USA

When I finally came back to myself, it was dark outside, and I had no idea what time it was. I took a few moments to assess my surroundings with my eyes still closed. I could tell I was still partially naked because I could feel the cloth of my flightsuit around my ankles and the boots on my feet. I could also feel the air on my loins. I almost grimaced in distaste as I recalled the moments from the previous evening, but I wasn't sure whether anyone was in the room with me and didn't want to communicate that I was regaining consciousness. The thing I remembered was Anne's mouth on me, and it was everything I could do not to shudder involuntarily.

But then I remembered what she said before I passed out - about the people coming for me. That could only mean one thing. The contract Miguel Hidalgo had placed on me, years ago, for ten million dollars, was still active and funded.

But by whom?

My concerns about the safety of Sarah and Colleen had been justified. I had kept them out of the fray by staying away from them. At least I had done something right. At least they would be safe.

I could hear the conversation outside the closed door of my bedroom, in the gathering area beyond. It was time to do some reconnoitering. I tried to open my eyes, but my eyelids wouldn't budge. They felt like a massive lead weight had been attached to them. I concentrated and slowly forced them upward. As the first strains of dim light hit my eyes, the familiar features of my bedroom greeted me. There was the ornate ceiling above me and the headboard of the bed to my right, the cherrywood gleaming in spite of the scant illumination. I could also make out the bookcase on the far wall and the door to the master bathroom next to it.

As my eyes continued to focus and fight off the drugs, I discovered something most opportune. No one was visible in front of me. That didn't necessarily mean I was alone in the room, but it would allow me the luxury of moving my right foot. When Anne had pushed me onto the bed the previous evening, she had been impatient and had not removed all of my clothes. I took a small breath and carefully commanded my right foot to move. The flightsuit felt light around my right ankle. Anne had taken the gun.

Well, shit.

At that moment, I heard laughter in the room outside the door. It took me a moment to process it, and I realized it was both male and female laughter. Anne and the boys from south of the border. I was sure the conversation had something to do with the ten-million-dollar prize in the next room.

And that was when the Darkness came to life inside of me, in all of its raw, homicidal fury. I could feel the blood coursing through my veins and the heightened sense of awareness that always came to me when it took control. The Darkness performed a quick inventory of my body, and I discovered, to my surprise, that my hands were not tied or secured.

Apparently, my captors had been counting on the drugs to keep me subdued, but their dosage hadn't been correct. They had wanted to rouse me from my slumber just as they began their tasks and set to work on me.

Now they won't get that chance, the Darkness said inside of me. *They are already dead. They just don't know it yet.*

I heard the 'click' sound of heels on the ceramic tile floor. The sound was getting louder like it was coming toward me.

The Darkness smiled inside of me. It was ready.

Without consciously willing it, I felt my body rolling to my right and sideways off the edge of the bed. That was when I heard feet moving behind me and realized I wasn't alone in the room.

It doesn't matter, the Darkness said. *They're still too late.*

I landed on my right side a few seconds later, even as the bedroom door flew open and the shuffling footsteps reached the foot of the bed. I rolled onto my back as the footsteps from both the door and the room came around the side of the bed, and two guys from "Mexican gangster casting" appeared in front of me, dressed in khakis with the usual casual shirt worn over a t-shirt and outside the slacks to conceal a weapon. The two men were swarthy and darker-skinned. They had small green tattoos by their eyes, inked in prison no-doubt, and indicating how many men they had killed on the inside. They were looking down and grinning at me, neither one of them with a weapon in hand and both obviously thinking I was no threat. They were looking down upon an old gringo with his pants around his knees, a t-shirt on and his dick hanging in the breeze. I wasn't sure what kept them from laughing out loud.

The Darkness laughed back at them because it knew something they didn't.

My concerns about the contract on my life for the last five years had led me to take some special precautions. I had many guns strategically hidden throughout the condo because I knew that if the bad guys came for me, I wouldn't be able to predict the room in which I'd have to engage them. In this room alone, there were three. I had an AR-15 with a full 30-round magazine and a suppressor hidden in my closet. There was also a full-size Colt .45 government model concealed in a locking drawer in the nightstand next to my bed. But the most devastating weapon was hidden under my bed. My left hand found it as I rolled onto my back and reached under the bed frame. The gun was a shortened version of the venerable Remington 870 shotgun, chambered in 12 gauge. It was about 26 inches in length with a pistol grip, a 13.5-inch barrel and had five rounds of double-ought buckshot loaded into it. My mouth contorted into a maniacal smile as the Darkness took full possession of me.

The two gangsters were confident in their persona and appearance. Their grins widened in response, and they began to move toward me.

I heard a laugh come out of me that I didn't recognize, and I pulled the shotgun from its mount under the bed, extended it at arm's length toward the gangster on the left and pulled the trigger, at point blank range. The shotgun produced a deafening roar in the confined space. Even with the short barrel and open choke on the gun, the shot pattern didn't expand much as the nine .30 caliber pellets made the short trip between muzzle to flesh. The gangster's chest opened up in a massive hole of carnage that was nearly eight inches in diameter. He was dead before the impact propelled him back towards the door. As he fell, the Darkness turned the shotgun's muzzle toward the ceiling and released the pistol grip, allowing the weapon to slide through my left hand toward the floor. As the gun's fore-end reached my left hand, I grasped the weapon and worked the pump action, ejecting the spent shell from the chamber and loading a fresh one.

Gangster on the right was reaching underneath his shirt for his gun, his dark eyes wide in disbelief. My second round chambered about the same time as his pistol cleared his shirt. By this time my right hand had found the shotgun's pistol grip, and I released the weapon with my left hand and pointed the Remington at the center of his chest. We were looking each other directly in the eyes by then. His eyes, previously confident and even contemptuous, saw something in mine that filled him with fear and gave him pause. The dark eyes grew wide, and his gun hand stopped its upward movement.

Maybe he thought he could surrender. Maybe he thought there might be mercy. But the Darkness was in charge, and it gave no quarter. The shotgun detonated, and the other gangster's chest opened up like a watermelon struck by a hammer. Some of the blood spatter came back upon me, droplets of it hitting my face and neck. The Darkness reveled in it.

I used the adrenaline inside of me to force my body to its knees and then to its feet. I didn't sway or pause. The Darkness had me on high alert, and I was ready to engage. I swept the room with my eyes to see if any other combatants remained. I detected movement just outside the bedroom door, and I quickly shuffled to the right side of the door, charging the shotgun with another round as I moved.

I saw the woman's arm protruding into the room, with my .45 held at arm's length. The Darkness laughed at her.

Stupid bitch didn't even cock it.

Before I could completely understand what was happening, the Darkness smashed the shotgun down on the arm. The woman yelped in pain and dropped the gun. I saw my left hand grab the woman's arm and yank her into the room toward the bed, spinning her around to face me as my right hand brought the shotgun's muzzle up and pushed it into the skin under her chin.

The back of Anne's legs hit the low footboard of the bed, and the force of the collision propelled her backward and onto the mattress. Her eyes were wide with fear. I could see tears forming at the corners of them as she landed on the bed, her legs akimbo. Her coat flew open, and she lay there, naked and afraid.

"Please," she said, "please, don't kill me."

I froze as an internal battle suddenly raged. I could feel my penis hard with desire. The Darkness wanted to use her. It wanted satisfaction from her. It wanted revenge.

But at that moment, I had a vision of a thick, red line, running across my mind and across my life. The Darkness had never led me to do something wrong. To do something immoral. But now it was. It was driving me to do something I'd regret for the rest of my life. No woman, not even Anne, deserved to be raped. If I crossed that line, there would be no coming back. There would be no redemption.

"No." The word came out of me before I was even aware I had uttered it. I replaced my flightsuit, transferring the shotgun from hand to hand as I dressed. Anne watched me and made no move to cover herself or look away. Her eyes had transitioned from fear to shock. I could tell she wanted to say something but was having difficulty forming the words.

"Who the...what the fuck are you?" she asked after a long moment.

I smiled down at her. I knew it wasn't a reassuring smile. It was the slightly maniacal smile of a man who was coming down off an adrenaline high, a man who had just taken lives and had reveled in the act. A man that knew there were more lives to be taken and was looking forward to the killing. It was the crooked smile of a man who had accepted his fate, after denying it for the better part of five years.

"I'm your worst, fucking, nightmare, bitch," I said, in a voice I didn't recognize. "I'm someone who doesn't give a shit about me and doesn't give a shit about you. And that makes both of us fucking expendable if these assholes try again."

Then, I heard a sound a wasn't expecting – the sound of turboprop engines droning in the distance. I glanced at the bedside clock and saw the time was 2145, 9:45 pm. It took my mind a moment to process the time. I realized it was the next evening. I had been out of action for nearly an entire day.

Ian was on his way to Mexico without me. And he was walking into a trap that the bitch on the bed had led him into.

I quickly walked around the bed and made my way to the nightstand, where a series of syringes were laid out on a cloth mat. It seemed that several doses of sedative had been administered to me during the night and ensuring day.

"What, what now?" Anne said as she turned her head to follow my progress, her eyes still wide in shock and anticipation.

I retrieved one of the full syringes from the nightstand and turned to her.

"You don't understand what's going on here, do you?" I asked. "You fucked with the big leagues here, Anne. I don't know what your connection is with these guys, but I can tell you they don't like loose ends. The people in charge will find out that their men are dead, I'm alive, and so are you. That will make you a liability, and they'll come after you. If I don't kill them all first."

I plunged the syringe into her neck. She startled as the needle penetrated her skin and tried to push against me. But the dosage of the drug was too strong for her. For me, the drug had made me tired and malleable. For Anne, who was probably half my body weight, it put her right into unconsciousness. In mere seconds, her body went limp, and she began to snore.

I tossed the syringe on the bed and took stock of the scene around me. The two Mexican henchmen lay in crumpled heaps a few feet from each other, their chests awash in blood and gore. I watched both of them for a few moments to ensure they were, in fact, dead. I didn't see any chest movement or twitching and the fact that I could smell shit indicated that one of them had defecated as he had died – a common occurrence. I retrieved a washcloth from my bathroom and used it to relieve the two gunmen of their weapons so that my fingerprints wouldn't be on them. I placed the guns, a pair of Sig Sauer 9mm pistols, into the locking drawer of my nightstand, closed the drawer and secured that latch.

Then, I explored the rest of my condo with the reloaded Remington in the ready position, at a 45-degree angle to my chest. I went room to room, and carefully cleared the doorways and the hidden corners.

Five minutes later, I concluded that no one else was in the condo. I did find a suitcase full of cutting implements and a video camera in the living room area. It seemed the two gunmen had plans to slowly cut me to pieces before an audience of sorts. I wasn't shocked by the find. In fact, I wasn't even surprised. I knew that when the bad guys finally got me, my end would come slowly and painfully, with me begging for death. I just hadn't expected my betrayal to come from someone I barely knew.

I retrieved a zip tie from a kitchen drawer and walked back into the bedroom. I placed the gun on the bed and then, with the images of the cutting implements in the case in my mind, I roughly turned Anne's semi-nude body over, pulled her hands behind her back and used the zip tie to secure them at the wrist, pulling it as tight as the plastic would allow.

"Bitch," I said as I released her hands and let her continue her slumber on the bed. I looked at the clock again. It was nearly 2200, 10 pm. Ian would be nearing the arming area north of Quartzite soon if he wasn't there already. I didn't have much time.

I looked around me and surveyed the carnage in the room.

There wasn't time to clean it up, and I wouldn't be back for hours. Calling the police wasn't an option. There was only one option available, and it pissed me off.

"Goddamn it," I said as I reached into the pocket of my flightsuit and retrieved my phone. I looked under recent calls and punched Sharona's name. The phone only rang once before she answered it. I didn't let her speak. "I know you're in town with the boys. I need a sanitation crew at my condo. I just put down two Mexican contractors. You need to take Anne, Ian's sister, into custody. She's been feeding the Mexicans information, and God knows what she's given them. You need to get it out of her."

The line was silent for a few moments, and then Sharona spoke in a businesslike voice. Any hint of the former playfulness was gone. It was yet another reminder of how thoroughly I had been manipulated. "What are you going to do?" she asked.

"Get my ass to the airport and jump in the other OV-10D," I said as if explaining the situation to a child. "Ian needs a wingman."

CHAPTER TWENTY-EIGHT

Tuesday, December 1st
2230 Hours
Brooks Air Service Terminal
Sedona Airport (KSEZ)
Sedona, Arizona, USA

I didn't bother taking a shower and washing Anne and the associated sweat off me. I drove to the hangar as fast as I could, smelling like a refugee from a porn movie set. I pulled the Challenger into the parking slot closest to the terminal entance, slammed the car door shut and raced inside.

I ran into the pilot room and yanked open my locker, pulled my helmet out and shoved it into the bag. Then I grabbed my map bag and parachute harness and went over to the map table, hoping that I'd find something that would give me more precise information about what Ian had shared with me the previous evening. There was nothing on the table. No maps, no lineup cards, no target info of any kind.

"Fuck!" I screamed into the empty space.

Then I heard a tapping of knuckles on glass. I looked to my right, out the glass wall to the ramp area and saw TJ Costello looking at me, shaking his head with that damn sardonic grin on his face. He crooked his right index finger to me in a beckoning motion. I jogged into the main lobby and out the door to the ramp. When I pushed the door open, my jaw dropped open with what I saw.

There, on the ramp, sat the other OV-10D, with an external power cart connected to it. All of the external pins and flags had been pulled, and the airplane looked ready for flight. The avionics in the aircraft were powered up, and I could see the cockpit bathed in the glowing light of the LCD screens.

I looked at Costello dumbstruck.

"The boss said you'd show," he said. "He said he just had a feeling." He paused and shook his head. "Me, I wasn't so sure."

I opened my mouth to speak, but Costello cut me off.

"Not now," he said. "You need to get moving. The aircraft is preflighted and fully programmed. Once you get both engines started, I'll pull the power cart, and you can get rolling. The arming crew is waiting on you at the location loaded in waypoint two. The Boss said you were familiar. Land north to south. The Boss will wait thirty minutes, then he'll be off, and you'll have to try to catch him."

I nodded at him slowly, my mind still not entirely in the moment.

"Get your ass in the cockpit Price!"

I nodded dumbly and made my way around to the right side of the OV, donning my parachute harness as I walked. I stopped next to the cockpit and snapped my chest and leg straps into place, then I scampered up the steps to the cockpit and slid into the seat. Costello followed me and buckled the near survival kit strap and brought the parachute riser straps over my shoulder.

"On the left console are your NVGs and your target materials," he said. "Don't worry about them now. You can get the gogs on while you're enroute to Quartzite and review the target materials while they're arming you and fueling you."

I nodded as I pulled the helmet from its bag. I slid the

skull cap on and pulled the helmet onto my head.

Costello surveyed all my connections and then nodded to himself. He took a step down the ladder but then stopped and came back up. He grabbed my upper arm and leaned in close so that I could hear him clearly.

"You need to help him finish this shit, Price," he said. "He needs to get it done. It's fucking killing him. I can't watch that again."

I turned to Costello and looked at him with raised eyebrows.

"I was the crew chief on the F-22 at Edwards," he said, shaking his head. "The one he went down with. A long time ago."

I nodded slowly to him, and he nodded back. Then he went down the stairs. I ran the pre-start checks and motioned to Costello to begin the engine start sequence. He gave me a thumbs up from his observation position to the left front of the aircraft's nose. Even as the propeller on the left engine began to turn, I looked back at him with one thought running through my mind.

"He's already dying, TJ," I said into the intercom, knowing he wasn't connected and couldn't hear me. "And this won't save him."

I started the right engine and quickly ran the after-start checks, removing my ejection seat pin as part of that process. Costello motioned for me to keep my hands clear of the controls. Then he put the fingers of his right hand inside his left fist and pulled the right hand out, indicating that he was going to unplug the power cart. I nodded in response. He went around to the right side of the aircraft and disconnected the power cart cord from its receptacle just forward of the cargo door. He returned to the front of the aircraft and gave me a thumbs up. Then he raised his right hand and twirled his right index finger in a tight circle about his head in the classic "run it up" signal. I nodded and applied power to begin the journey to Runway 21.

The Arizona night was dark with no moon, but the stars twinkled brightly in the heavens above me as the OV and I hurried down the parallel taxiway to approach end of Runway 21. The night was still, and I thought about what it might be like in the atmosphere a few hundred miles to the south, where Ian and I would rain death from above. I wondered if there were people in that locale looking at the same stars and pondering their place in the universe. I wondered if there were people in the target compound who were struggling with a monster that lived inside of them. Or perhaps they weren't. Maybe they had let their monsters consume them.

I looked down at the time display on the lower left side of my PFD. It was nearly an hour since I had left the condo. The sanitation crew was probably there by now, cleaning up the mess I had created. Sharona and the boys, Smith and Amrine, probably had Anne and were taking her to a place where she would be questioned. I knew I would be in debt to the CIA again. And again, they would be able to use that to call me into action. Part of me looked forward to making a difference, to making the world better. Another part of me hated myself for the inevitable violence I would cause.

But deep inside, the Darkness nodded its approval and even its eagerness for more action and more activity. For more death.

I turned onto the short taxiway that led to the beginning of runway 21 and reflexively reached for the OV's mic switch to make the standard position report over the airport's Unicom frequency. But I stopped myself before I activated it. No record of these flights should exist. Even the chance of a stray radio call was too great.

I turned out on to the runway, pushed the condition levers into T.O./ LAND, and moved the throttles forward to MILITARY. As soon as the engine RPM settled, I looked the engine instruments over and released brakes. The stubby propjet jumped ahead, eager to remove itself from the confines of the earth. As rotated the nose skyward a few seconds later, and looked at the stars through the HUD, I felt a strange sense of peace come over me. I was doing what I was meant to do.

CHAPTER TWENTY-NINE

Tuesday, December 1st
2300 Hours Local Time
Arming Area
North of Quartzite, Arizona, USA

It was one thing to watch these guys from afar and quite another to see them in action. I had no sooner landed on Highway 95 and turned into the roadside arming area, then I was marshaled into a parking spot, and directed to shut down my engines. I did as instructed, and the magic began.

I was reminded of the ICTs, the integrated combat turns, I had seen when I was stationed at RAF Bentwaters/ Woodbridge in the UK, many years ago. The maintenance personnel had practiced them for NATO Tactical Evaluations and USAF Operational Readiness Inspections. ICTs were a highly choreographed event involving refueling and rearming an aircraft in the shortest time possible, all while abiding by the strictest procedures. The entire process was closely observed by an evaluation team, the members of which would notice any discrepancy. I had participated as a pilot in many ICTs, some for practice, some for actual evaluations. I had seen ICT crews work the most intricate interactions of men and machine in their efforts.

But the ICT crews I had seen had nothing on Brooks' team. I was supposed to study my target materials, the photos and the 1:50,000 scale map that had been provided, but I found I had difficulty keeping my eyes off these guys as they worked.

In mere moments, an electrical power cart was connected to my airplane, so I could keep all my flight data loaded in the navigation system while the arming process was underway. First, the refueling truck topped off my wing tanks. Then, the napalm canisters were loaded onto the five sponson stations, and their arming wires were connected. After that was complete, the ECM pod was attached to the hard point underneath the left wing, and the gun turret was installed underneath my OV's nose. I sat in my cockpit, mouth agape, as I watched the process. It had all taken place in less than 25 minutes.

The leader of their ground crew climbed up the steps to my cockpit as his people cleared my aircraft.

"The napalm is radar proximity fused," he said. "With a 50-foot burst altitude. You can deliver it as low as you want as long as you're above 100 feet AGL to allow for the fuse to activate. A level delivery would probably be best. Don't worry about sight settings or CCIP. This stuff is very high drag. You can probably use the same sight picture as you did for high-drag bombs when you flew the A-10."

I took in his instructions and nodded at him slowly as I listened. Brooks had obviously briefed him on my background and given him advice to relay. The napalm canisters were relatively light and had no guidance fins. Once released into the airstream, they would tumble and perform as very high-drag munitions.

"How far is the boss in front of me?"

"About 45 minutes," the crew leader responded. "I tried to radio him when you landed, but he was out of range. There is a holding orbit east of the town of Ajo, he might be waiting for you there. But you know how he is."

I nodded. "I presume that point is in the navigation load?"

"Ajo is point four."

"Understood," I said. "Com frequency?"

"Winchester," he said. "3030, FM. The radio is encrypted. No one else can understand what you're saying."

"Got it."

The crew leader smiled at me. He was an older man, close to my age. His face told of many days in the elements arming and de-arming aircraft. I wondered if we'd ever get to trade war stories over a drink someday.

"Good hunting, sir," he said. "Give the bastards hell."

I nodded back at him. "That's the plan."

CHAPTER THIRTY

Tuesday, December 1st
2346 Hours Local Time
500 feet and 250 Knots
North of Interstate 8, West of Dateland, Arizona USA

Flying the clean OV-10A had spoiled me, particularly with the performance we got out of it during the winter months in the cooler climate of Sedona. Tonight, the D-model felt almost sluggish although it was sustaining a respectable 250 knots, in spite of the nearly 3,000 pounds of extra shit hanging on it.

I clicked the trim button on the stick forward a bit to keep the aircraft at low altitude and rechecked my engine gauges. The two PT-6 engines were performing superbly and generating the maximum torque they could, given the atmospheric conditions of the Arizona climate. I sat back in my seat a bit and surveyed the terrain around me in the NVGs. My last memory of flying an aircraft with a night-vision device had been five years ago in a CIA-owned F-35B. That experience had spoiled me because the helmet-mounted display in the F-35 had combined infrared, electro-optical, radar and synthetic vision in the same display, and all I, as the pilot, had to do was turn my head in the direction I wanted. The helmet did the rest. The NVGs I was flying with tonight seemed like a huge step backward in technology although they were similar to the goggles I had worn the last time I had flown low-level in Arizona; when I had flown an F-16 south of the border to bomb a target belonging to a different Mexican drug lord.

I shook my head as I recalled the memory. That had been Miguel Hidalgo, the same drug lord whose contract had generated the two men whom I had killed in my condo.

My thoughts then turned to Anne. I knew that the CIA would show her no quarter in the extraction of information and while she was a royal bitch and had betrayed both her brother and me, I felt a begrudging bit of sympathy toward her for reasons I didn't understand. Then the memory of my near rape of her flashed through my head, and I felt the Darkness laugh in the back of my mind.

Jesus, I thought. *This is getting out of control.*

But you love it, the Darkness responded. *You know you do.*

I nodded to myself in the cockpit. *I do*, I thought. *After five years, I still do. God help me.*

I raised my goggles as I saw the ribbon of light that was Interstate 8 just ahead of me. Sometimes, intense light from any source can wash out the display in NVGs and present too much brightness to the eyes looking through them. I preferred not to risk it. Interstate 8, running from the city of Casa Grande, Arizona to San Diego, California wasn't as well traveled as its cousin to the north, Interstate 10, but it still boasted a respectable traffic load tonight, the multiple headlight beams cutting through the darkness eastbound and westbound as the faceless drivers in the vehicles guided their vehicles to destinations unknown.

I had last driven that highway many years ago when I had been in the Air Force. I remembered driving a convertible Mustang rental car from Gila Bend to Tucson and using it to take a young life support sergeant out to dinner. Later that evening, we had retreated to her apartment and fucked each other's brains out. Those had been simpler, more sensual days. I missed them.

After I crossed the highway, the dark terrain loomed before me again, and I lowered the goggles. As the world appeared before me in the NVG's color scheme, I dismissed my thoughts of the sensual past and tried to recall something useful, my memories of the ZSU's capabilities.

During my days flying the A-10 in Western Europe during the Cold War, the ZSU-23-4 "Shilka" was the most-feared anti-aircraft artillery piece in the arsenal of the former Soviet Union. It consisted of a turret with four 23mm guns, mounted on a tracked vehicle. The four guns were in a square arrangement on the front of a turret, with a gunner's window mounted between the bottom two. Each gun could fire 23mm rounds at a rate of 800 to 1000 rounds per minute, which meant the ZSU could put up to 67 rounds per second into the air at a time. The 23mm projectile sported a muzzle velocity of about 3,000 feet per second and to make matters worse, the ZSU had an onboard radar to track targets and predict firing solutions so it could put rounds into the air one time-of-flight ahead of an unfortunate aircraft. Although, if that target was within half a mile of the ZSU, there wasn't much solution required.

When I flew the Warthog, we practiced engaging the ZSU with the jet's spectacular 30mm cannon, but even then, such an engagement required explicit knowledge of the position of the ZSU and very precise marksmanship indeed. Tonight, we'd be going up against a ZSU in an aircraft with lighter cannon, less speed and an even greater radar cross section, thanks to the two huge propellers on the front end. Our odds of getting in and out of the target area in one piece weren't good.

I banked the OV up to the left a bit and let the nose track slowly eastward. The route Ian had selected reflected his comfort at low altitude in the dark. The points provided were reference points more than they were steerpoints or waypoints. The pilot had to navigate to them visually, not directly, unlike the point-to-point navigation we had done in the F-16. As I traversed the distance between steerpoint three, just north of I-8, and steerpoint four, Ajo, I would need to negotiate the terrain between the two locations. At the moment, I flew south-southwest, along the west side of another rocky hill line, looking for a gap further to the south. When I reached the gap, I would turn east and fly across a small north-south valley and then between the hills that formed an east-west valley before I turned southeast again towards Ajo.

Fortunately, even with the lack of moon illumination this evening, the bright light from the stars gave the NVGs plenty of light to work with. The infrared capability of the NVGs enhanced the picture. I smiled to myself as I picked up the gap between the hill lines clearly and adjusted my course slightly to fly towards it. I actually didn't mind Ian's lack of precision in the route structure. I recognized the terrain easily. I was well acquainted with it.

I had spent a good portion of my USAF career flying in southern Arizona. As an OV-10 Forward Air Controller, we had conducted many an exercise in the Gila Bend Ranges, now known as the Barry Goldwater Range Complex. When I transitioned to the A-10, I trained at Davis-Monthan Air Force Base in Tucson, and we used the Gila Bend ranges as our working area, both for tactical navigation and for air-to-ground weapons delivery. When I trained in the F-16, at Luke Air Force Base in Phoenix, eight years later, again the Gila Bend Ranges were used. Then, when I came back to Luke as an instructor, I trained students in the same airspace.

Now, flying back over the same ground and in the same airspace, at slower speeds than I was used to, the familiar terrain almost seemed like home in an odd sort of way. I just hoped we didn't encounter some jets from Luke out here on a night mission. The USAF didn't train to fight at low altitude anymore, so the chance of encountering another aircraft at our altitude wasn't great, but it also wasn't zero. For the first time since flying for Brooks, I lamented the fact that I didn't have an air-to-air radar. I felt like I was flying blind and it made me slightly uneasy.

As the ridge on my left declined into the desert floor, I banked up and pulled the OV's nose to the left, aiming for the left side of the gap between this northern ridge and its counterpart to the south. The two ridges appeared as dark creatures, sleeping on a light expanse that stretched southward as far as I could see. As I rolled out, I spotted two small rock formations in the center of the valley that would take me to Ajo. They stood out as minor dark patches, in the middle of a larger area of lighter color, with the looming dark hills on either side. I guided the OV toward the left side of the hills and pushed the stick over slightly to take the propjet down to a lower altitude. At the slower speed I was maintaining, I was confident I could fly the aircraft comfortably much closer to the ground, and I wanted to avoid the odd F-16 or F-35 on a low-level night flight. They'd be at 500 feet and down the center of the valley if they were flying, and I planned to deconflict from them by both altitude and lateral space.

I leveled the OV off at 200 feet radar altitude. The plane felt solid and docile at the lower height. I peered forward, through the HUD and watched the sparse desert vegetation and cacti pass underneath me, the outlines of the flora surprisingly crisp in the NVGs. Even at full throttle, the rocky landmarks seemed to float by the aircraft in slow motion, giving me time to appreciate the desolate beauty of the desert, seemingly lonelier and more removed from the world at night than it was during the day.

I reached the other side of the north-south valley and turned the OV to the right to parallel the hill line north of the gap leading to Ajo. Ajo had been a well-known landmark during my days flying in the Gila Bend complex. A small town of some 3,000 residents, it lay at the southern end of the conventional range complex and was highly visible from the air due to the sizable white-colored containment pond on the northeast side of the town, and the copper mine pit to the south. The mine used to employ the population of the entire town until it closed in 1985. I wondered why anyone even remained there now. As I looked to my left, the color coding in the NVGs had turned the igneous hills a very dark shade, giving them a similar tint to the way they looked in the daytime. Many of the hills in the area were the product of volcanic activity countless years in the past, but the rough shape of the dark rock still provided a constant reminder of the violence of the acts that had produced the terrain.

I continued down the left side of the valley, on an east-southeasterly heading. About ten miles in front of me, I could see another dark hill formation, resembling a cork trying to seal the western end of the valley but leaving two gaps. One to the north of it, leading to the east and the other to the south of it, leading southeast toward Ajo. As the end of the valley approached, I realized that it was time to begin my turn towards the town. I started to apply pressure to the control stick to turn the OV, but I felt a sort of invisible hand stopping me from performing the act.

Instinct is one of the qualities that keeps experienced aviators from killing themselves. I honored it whenever I encountered it. I relaxed the pressure on the stick and took a breath. Immediately, two sets of lights appeared in the NVGs, moving very quickly from my right one o'clock to five o'clock position. I saw a flight of two Vipers, in perfect tactical formation, tearing through the valley to my immediate right, slightly higher and a lot faster than I was. I nodded to myself and waited a few seconds to see if there was a trailing element of an additional two aircraft. But the NVGs showed nothing, and I turned the aircraft towards the gap to Ajo.

As I rolled out, my FM radio barked in my ear, but the words were unintelligible. Brooks was talking, but our aircraft weren't line-of-sight with one another. He had already headed south.

"Well shit, Ian," I said to myself. "How can I save you if you don't fucking wait for me?" I checked the position of the transmit wafer switch and then keyed my mic. "Boxer One, Blazer One. Just north of Steerpoint Four, headed south."

The radio blared in response, but the words weren't comprehensible.

I keyed my mic again. "Boxer I can't support you if I can't catch you. Can you pull it back a little, so I can get some overtake on you?"

The radio crackled again, and I heard the words 'follow' and 'route.' I called up the waypoint list on the navigation display and looked at my map. The route from Ajo to Pitiquito followed Arizona Highway 85 to the Mexico/US border where it turned into Mexico Highway 2 and headed south to Caborca and then on to Pitiquito. A direct route to the target would be southeast. If Brooks followed the flight planned route, he'd provide me two corners to "cut" and gain some closure on him. I nodded to myself. He was going to intentionally create some geometry for me to use to catch him. I called up the target in my navigation display and clicked on it. Then I centered the steering cue and pushed the power levers up to MILITARY.

118 nautical miles to the target. A little over 28 minutes at my current speed. Brooks' route would be slightly longer at 132 nautical miles. That would take him just over 32 minutes.

I would have a four-minute time advantage on him as well as the geometric advantage of cutting across his circuitous route with my direct one. I didn't need to catch him, necessarily, just get within radio range and warn him off the attack before he was chewed up with 23mm anti-aircraft fire.

I hoped I could get close enough in time.

I climbed to 500 feet as the small town of Ajo went beneath me. The infrared capability of the NVGs provided a detailed view of the town. It was bounded by the dark-colored copper mine pit to the south and the white containment ponds to the northeast, still emitting residual heat after a day of absorbing the desert sun. Tonight, the town looked nearly dead, with only a few lights illuminated on the lonely streets.

As I passed the copper mine pit on the right side of my aircraft, I pushed forward on the control stick to return to low altitude and aimed the OV just to the left of the ridge of dark volcanic rock that lay to the southeast of the town. I leveled the propjet at 250 feet radar altitude. I could make out the scant light from the small village of Why at my left nine o'clock and the much brighter light of a casino complex that was southeast of the town.

I was cutting the first corner. Ian's route would have taken him from Ajo to Why and then turned southbound, which would take him over the top of my flight path. I keyed my mic.

"Boxer, Blazer, do you read?" I asked over the FM intraflight radio.

The radio blared in my headset but like before, the words were unintelligible.

"Shit," I said to myself. I could have made a radio call in the blind about the ZSU, but encryption notwithstanding, I wasn't sure if this frequency was being monitored, and I didn't want to reveal our intel about the ZSU to any unfriendly ears. I decided to keep the advisory to myself until I was sure he could hear me.

I crossed Arizona highway 85 a few minutes later. No headlights were visible, and the road barely emitted any IR energy, a testimony to the infrequency of its use. In front of me, I could see a valley formed by a mountain range to my left and a large rocky ridge to my right. I aimed the aircraft down the center of the valley and began a gradual ascent to maintain my separation from the rising terrain. My map told me that Estes Canyon was at the center of the valley and a trailhead for the pasture was at the north end of the canyon. I wondered if any cowboys had their herds grazing there this time of year. As I flew between the mountains to the left and ridge to the right, I marveled again at the fidelity of the NVGs. The detail and even the texture of the two geologic structures was clearly discernible, in spite of the tint generated by the googles. It truly made flying low level at night nearly as easy as flying during the daytime, with one noticeable difference - the lack of depth perception in the visual field. There was something about the way the light was gathered and displayed that eliminated the ability to the eyes to perceive the minor differences in distance between the two and provide the brain the resolution it needed to judge depth.

The rocky ridge on my right descended into the desert floor a few moments later, and now I paralleled the mountain range on my left as it extended southeast into northern Mexico. Once I crossed the border, I would be able to adjust my course a few more degrees to the southeast and directly to the target. As I looked to the left and ahead, the expanse of dark mountain rock seemed to point to the path ahead of me, deeper into the province of Sonora. Even through the display of the NVGs, the mountains seemed like an eerie portent for the journey southbound, a long, black finger directing me along my route. They looked ominous and unyielding.

I shook the image out of my consciousness and trained my eyes on the terrain in front of me. The U.S. – Mexico border was minutes ahead of me and at my altitude of 250' AGL, vehicles traveling along the border road, on either side, could be troublesome. As I looked forward, I saw a set of headlights rapidly moving from left to right ahead. I glanced down at my map and nodded to myself. There was an unimproved road that ran out of the mountains to my left and south to the border road. The vehicle was traveling along it. I felt for the EXTERIOR LTS MASTER switch next to the flap handle and double-checked that it was in the OFF position. While the OV wasn't a quiet aircraft, I was reasonably sure that the occupants of the vehicle wouldn't be able to pinpoint my position between my lack of illumination and the noise inside their vehicle.

But then the vehicle stopped, directly ahead of me, on the road. As I closed on it and watched, I could see the outline of a pick-up truck in the NVGs, and I could also see the occupants exiting the truck and looking in my direction.

"What the hell?" I asked myself in the intercom.

One of the occupants put something on his head, and then he pointed directly at me and said something to the other person he was with. The other person reached into the cab of the truck and retrieved a long object and put it on the hood of the truck. Then he deployed two legs of a bipod on one end of the object and got behind it. A few moments later, I saw the muzzle flash.

"Jesus!" I said to myself as I rolled left and pulled the OV into an aggressive left turn. "What the fuck?"

My complacency had almost killed me. I had been so fascinated by watching the truck, it had never occurred to me that it might be hostile. I didn't have time to consider whether the truck was US DEA trying to interdict drug smuggling or drug smugglers themselves, trying to knock down a competing operation or defending themselves.

But I was lucky. Hitting a flying aircraft with small arms

fire is difficult, especially when the gunner has no practice at the task. Bullets are unguided, so they must be aimed one time of flight in front of the target aircraft. With no precise range data for my aircraft and only a two-dimensional idea for my flight path, the gunner didn't have the information he needed to compute a firing solution.

But I wasn't going to stay predictable and make it easy for him. As soon as I was into the turn, I pushed forward on the stick to unload the OV, rolled to the right and applied back pressure again, reversing my direction of turn. Even as I settled into the right turn, another muzzle flash appeared in front of me. I immediately rolled to my left and oriented my wings about 45 degrees from the horizon in a left bank and applied back pressure. This movement generated a left, climbing turn and added a three-dimensional element to the maneuvering equation. As I made the turn, I glanced down at the armament panel and briefly considered arming the 20mm cannon and engaging the truck with it. But I disregarded it a moment later. I had no idea who or what was in the vehicle and/or who they were affiliated with. I wasn't going to risk the possibility of killing friendlies tonight.

After staying in the climbing turn for a few seconds, I rolled the OV to the right and pulled into a descending right turn. I maintained the turn for two seconds, then I rolled out and looked out my left. By this time, I was crossing the road that the truck was on, about half a mile to the south and west of it. As I looked to the left to regain sight of the vehicle, I saw three more muzzle flashes. Instinctively, I pushed forward on the control stick to change my flight path. The OV began a rapid descent.

My instinct saved my life. Even as the OV nosed over, I felt a thump in the nose area of the aircraft, then the HUD disintegrated in front of me, and I heard glass shatter above me.

"Jesus," I said to myself into the intercom. "This guy is good!"

"PULL-UP! PULL-UP!" the terrain warning system barked at me.

I leveled the aircraft off and continued straight and level and away from the truck. I scanned the landscape in front of me for some sort of natural obstacle to put between me and the truck, but the terrain was dismally flat. There was nothing to hide behind. I pushed over on the control stick and silenced the low-altitude alarm as I descended. Receding targets are challenging to hit with small arms fire because the aircraft's opening velocity away from the gunner can cause kinematic problems for the round; the bullet tends to run out of energy as it chases a target moving away from it. I did a little mental arithmetic. Assuming the gun was the biggest thing available, a .50 caliber Barrett or the like, it's maximum tactical effective range would be about two miles, 10,500 feet or so. At 425 feet per second, I'd be outside of that range in about 25 seconds – assuming I lived that long.

I guided the OV lower, as close to the ground as I could stand it, trying to increase the gunner's line of sight issues by using whatever variations in the terrain I could find. I was so low that I could see small arroyos and hills in front of me as well as cacti and other flora around me. I couldn't risk a look over my shoulder at the truck as I flew, a moment's inattention and I could hit the ground. I held my breath as the separation between the gunner and me increased. A tall chain-link fence with a roll of concertina wire across the top appeared in front of me, and I instinctively raised the nose to ensure the OV cleared it. As the fence flashed underneath me, I noticed two parallel dirt roads on either side it and I realized I had just crossed the international border. There were no vehicles or humans discernible in the NVGs, although the roads next to the border glowed with radiant infrared energy, testimony to the number of vehicles that had traveled them that day.

The time continued to increase without additional incident or projectile impact. After a minute or so, I eased back on the control stick and allowed the OV-10 to climb back to 250 feet, which by now had become an even more benign altitude. I could see a few lights from the small town of Reforma just to the left of the nose as I continued southeast bound and I banked the aircraft to the right about ten degrees to increase my separation from it.

I peered through the windscreen and what remained of the HUD. Apart from that scant illumination from the lights of Reforma, the terrain ahead appeared dark in front of me. After passing the town, I banked the OV back to the left. There was a formation of small, rocky hills directly ahead of me, and I wanted to put that formation between my aircraft and Mexico's Route 2 which paralleled the hills on the west side. After I passed these hills, I would be in open terrain for a few minutes, then I would encounter the more massive hill formation directly northwest of the target.

Twelve minutes to go. I reviewed the attack plan Ian and I had practiced. We would both ingress from the initial point, which was due west of the target. About seven miles to the target, and on the west side of the ridgeline between Caborca and Pitiquito, he would action left, and roll in right, attacking from the north, northwest. I would action south, extend to the south and roll in from the south, southwest. The goal was for his initial delivery of high-explosive bombs to daze and distract the defenders, and allow me to sneak in and deliver the napalm undetected. The elements of distraction and surprise were critical to my delivery since I'd have to maintain level flight at low altitude as I expended the ordnance, and I'd be extremely vulnerable to ground fire while I delivered.

But all of that seemed to be a moot point with a ZSU in the area. It would be suicide for us to attack with a gun like that on the ground.

The range of hills to my left ended, and the small valley opened up in front of me. At the end of the valley was the larger hill formation which would require a turn to the south. About 8 minutes to go. I looked down at my map for a few seconds to ensure I was precisely where I thought I was even though the OV's navigation system seemed to be keeping up just fine. Old habits die hard.

And then I remembered what I needed to do.

Jesus, Pearce! I thought. *You're an idiot!* I keyed my mic. "Boxer, Blazer. I'm 8 minutes out. Are you up?"

This time there was no corresponding blare of static from the radio. I repeated the transmission with the same results.

Fuck! What's going on? Why can't he hear me?

But then I looked to my right and saw the rocks of the hills that lined the southwest side of the valley, and I understood. I was at 250' on one side of the ridge and Brooks was at low altitude on the other side. FM was a short-range, line of sight radio. The rocks between us were blocking the transmission. We weren't going to be able to speak until we were nearly on top of the target. By then, he'd be eager to drop his bombs and inflict the destruction he had come here to do. I wondered if I'd have the time to talk him out of it.

As I glanced to the right, I saw a set of headlights appear among the rocks, and I looked down at my map. My flight path was converging with Route 2 now. Brooks' flight path, the pre-planned one, had him paralleling the highway on the other side of the ridgeline. The hills at the end of the valley loomed in front of me. Mere moments until I had to make the hard turn to the south that would place our aircraft near each other. I sighed to myself.

"Goddamn," I said. "This is going to be fucking tight."

I pulled the control stick to the right and banked the OV up to about sixty degrees. Then I applied 2 g's of backpressure to keep the plane level as I turned it to the south. The nose tracked smoothly across the desert horizon. I rolled out after a few seconds with Route 2 on my nose and the town of Caborca to my left. As I returned my vision to the front, an aircraft appeared in my NVGs, moving from right to left in front of me, at approximately my altitude and speed.

"Yes!" I screamed into the intercom. I keyed my mic. "Boxer, Blazer's visual, your left nine o'clock, five miles, level."

The radio blared in response, but yet again, the words were unintelligible. I reflexively checked my radio and mic settings to make sure I was transmitting and listening on the correct frequency. Sometimes, if a radio frequency is slightly mistuned, bleed over can occur between the mistuned frequency and the correct one. My settings were correct. I wondered if Ian's were.

"Boxer, Blazer, abort attack. Heavy triple-A in the target area. I say again, abort the attack. Heavy triple-A in the area."

Ian's aircraft was now left of my nose and headed to the action point, just south of the town of Caborca. Apparently, he wasn't dissuaded. Either he hadn't heard me, or he didn't care.

"Goddamn it, Ian," I muttered into my intercom. "You're going to get us both fucking killed." I keyed my mic again. "Boxer abort your attack. There's a fucking ZSU in the target area. For God's sake, Ian, abort the attack."

Silence from the radio. He wasn't even trying to answer. He didn't give a shit what was down there. He was still going to stick his nose in and kick ass.

I had a rare moment of clarity then. Very similar to when I had watched the flames rush toward me as I had been pinned inside of Ian's truck. Maybe this was my destiny. Maybe this was the way things were supposed to be. We might get chewed up by this fucking ZSU, but at least we'd die doing something that mattered. The Darkness would be satisfied, and I would be dead. Colleen would grow up without a father, but it wasn't like that would be a significant change for her.

I smiled as I pulled the OV's nose around and aimed for a place south of the action point to try to keep the timing as close as possible.

"So be it, Ian," I said into my intercom. "So fucking be it."

I checked the power levers all the way forward to ensure I was getting every ounce of speed I could get from the stubby propjet. Then I worked my way from right to left across the top of the OV's front console as I armed the aircraft. I flipped the switches on the upper right console from OFF to DROP. I moved to the upper left console, and I flipped the BOMB-FLARE switch from SAFE to NOSE & TAIL. Finally, I moved the MASTER ARM toggle switch to ARM. My weapons release or "pickle" button on the control stick was hot. The OV was ready to deal death.

Ian's OV was now well left of my nose. I could see the infrared glow of his aircraft clearly as it traveled just south of Caborca and toward the ridgeline west of the target area, a geologic structure composed of two rock formations with a gap in between them. Suddenly, his plane banked up and made a hard turn to the north. He was into his action. I nodded to myself as I approached the gap in the rocky hills. Amazingly, the geometry for the attack seemed like it was going to still work. Ian would have to begin his pop-up maneuver soon and climb up to his release altitude for the bombs. I, on the other hand, didn't have to pop-up to deliver the napalm. My current altitude of 250 feet would be perfect. That made his flight path to the target longer than mine and would allow me a few more seconds to close the time/distance between us.

I wasn't sure how I was going to put the napalm on target without a bombsight, since my HUD had been shot to pieces, but I had a feeling I'd be able to figure it out.

I reached the gap in the ridgeline and banked the OV left to split the distance between the northern and southern rock formations. The craggy desert terrain, still glowing with radiant IR energy, moved across my NVGs as I turned. The rocky landscape appeared as a ghostly sentinel, guarding the western approach to the target valley, ever watchful and intransigent. I looked to the north as I made the turn and saw the lights of the target area gleaming in the darkness. The collection of buildings, in the shadow of the ridge, seemed still, even tranquil.

In the distance, beyond the target, I could see the bright glow of Ian's aircraft as it rose above the northern end of the ridge, climbing to his pull-down altitude, where he would roll the aircraft, stop his climb and pull his nose to the target.

I glanced at my radar threat display. There were no radar symbols and no tell-tale sound of radar energy in my headset. I looked back at the target. The tranquility remained. No lights were flashing. No vehicles were moving. No activity at all.

She got it wrong, I thought. *Anne got it wrong. This is going to be a fucking cakewalk.*

I allowed a satisfied smile to sneak onto my face as I pulled the nose of my OV around to the north and watched Ian begin his roll-in. We had planned the parameters for the bombing passes together. He would only be straight and level on his pass for 3-5 seconds. In a few mere moments, he'd be off target, and 2,500 pounds of high-explosive would be on the way.

Thirty seconds later, I would deliver a like amount of hellfire and brimstone.

"We're going to kick their fucking asses," I said into my intercom. "They'll never know what hit them."

Then all hell broke loose.

CHAPTER THIRTY-ONE

Wednesday, December 2nd
0037 Hours Local Time
250 feet and 250 Knots
Near Pitiquito Municipality
Senora, Mexico

Three to five seconds can be a hell of a long time when temporal distortion sets in. And in twenty years of flying military aircraft, I had never seen a heavy anti-aircraft artillery piece in action. I had studied them, watched footage of them, but never experienced the effect for real.

The ZSU 23-4 appeared in my NVGs like it had been transported in from a parallel universe. One moment it wasn't there. And the next moment it was, with its four 23mm cannons blazing. It was positioned in a shadowed area of an open field, about halfway between the manor house and the warehouses and the turret was pointed north, directly at Ian's jet. The ZSU boasted a tactical effective range of 2,500 to 3,000 meters, and Ian was well inside of that. The trajectory of his bombing pass was such that he was descending slightly to the left of and into the ZSU, which made the targeting problem very simple for the gunner in the turret. I now realized why my radar warning receiver had remained silent. The gunner was either operating visually, or the target tracking radar was locked onto Ian and not emitting energy in my direction.

I continued my turn and rolled out with the warehouses directly in front of me, but I was barely aware of where my aircraft was headed. I was transfixed by the sight of the ZSU and the streams of tracer rounds it was firing into the night sky. The ZSU's gunner was too well trained to shoot at his quarry continually. The ZSU only carried 2,000 rounds onboard, about 30 seconds of trigger time for the four 23mm cannons. The gunner was mindful of his limited capacity, and he fired at intervals, allowing time for him to assess the effectiveness of his bursts. Four individual paths of illuminated rounds emerged from the cannons and reached into the heavens like four fingers of fiery death. And since tracer rounds were typically placed into the bullet stream about every 3-8 rounds, that meant that anywhere from 44 to 128 bullets were being fired with each burst. Unlike the gunner though, I could actually see the rounds travel through the air towards Ian's aircraft, and it was plain they were well in front of the OV-10 as it dived toward its target. But that wouldn't change the fact that there were still a hell of a lot of bullets headed his way. It was just a question of time before the gunner corrected and got him.

"Jesus," I muttered into the intercom. "He doesn't stand a fucking chance."

Well then do something about it, idiot!

The thought startled me from my reverie. I quickly reached up to my left armament panel to arm the gun turret and reign some 20mm destruction of my own on the ZSU, although I had no idea how I'd aim it without a HUD. But the master caution light glowed as soon as I pushed the gun switch to RDY. I looked down at the warning display. The GUN INOP light was illuminated.

"Well, shit!" I spat into the mic. "Fucking sniper!"

One of the rounds that had been fired at me north of the border had damaged the gun turret and made it incapable of firing. Ian was on his own.

"Goddamn it!" I cursed into the intercom.

Another three-dimensional rectangle of bullets arced into the sky. Closer to Ian this time. I was struck by the image of an illuminated hallway to hell. It was odd to see the rounds being fired but not actually hear the guns. Between my distance from the ZSU, the wind noise generated in the cockpit, and the two propellers twirling just behind me, I was deaf to any sound outside the cockpit.

More bullets headed skyward, and this time, they hit their target. The rounds that weren't tracers packed a small high-explosive incendiary warhead with a contact fuse. In my NVGs, I could see the multiple small flashes as the bullets impacted Ian's OV and exploded.

"Fuck!" I said to myself.

I knew the OV had foam-lined, self-sealing fuel tanks, but those were designed for small arms projectiles which might penetrate the fuel cells and cause a leak. I had no idea what good they would do against a high explosive shell. I didn't have to wait long to find out. A trail of fire erupted from Ian's left wing and spread to the engine attached to it. In my NVGs, I could see a trail of white flame behind the left wing, and as I watched, it grew longer and wider.

My left hand found the mic switch on the throttle, and my mouth was working before I willed it. "Jesus, Ian," screamed, "you're on fire! Get the fuck out!"

No response on the airwaves, but the OV continued to descend even as the fire engulfed the entire left side of the aircraft. I watched the immolation, mesmerized by it, wondering if Ian was still looking through his bombsight, watching the pipper track upward on the bomb fall line toward the target, or if he had been consumed by the fire.

But then something Ian had said in his kitchen, just a few nights ago, popped into my head.

"I'm like the fuckin' terminator," he had said.

I allowed myself to hope, just for a moment, that Ian might actually survive.

But the ZSU gunner seemed to have other plans. Another four-fingered burst went skyward and the infrared the view from my NVGs clearly showed the tracers and Ian's plane, and the rounds would hit the OV-10 squarely. There was no doubt. But the phenomenon of temporal distortion slowed the world down even further. In the fractions of a second before impact, my eyes detected the Mark-82s leaving the OV-10's sponsons, just the way the delivery had been planned, with two pairs of the 500-pound bombs, followed by a single. As soon as the bombs departed the aircraft, the high-drag ballute deployed, and the weapons began their descent towards the huge manor house below. The time of flight to impact would take mere seconds.

But as the ballute inflated behind the final bomb, the 23mm rounds from the latest burst impacted Ian's aircraft and chewed it to pieces. The OV-10 was immediately enveloped by a giant fireball that encompassed the entire aircraft, from nose to tail and from wingtip to wingtip. I held my breath, waiting for the inevitable explosion and it came, just a few milliseconds later, the flash clearly visible in the NVGs, and the hot pieces of the propjet spewed into the night sky, creating a shower of metal for the earth below.

But then I saw something else. A trail of fire departing the top of the fireball, accelerating heavenward – a trail of fire with a man and an ejection seat at the top of it. Ian had punched out.

"Holy fucking shit!" I exclaimed into the empty cockpit. "Holy fucking shit!"

Then the Mark-82s impacted and the entire north end

of the valley was illuminated as the bombs detonated. Two flashes, two flashes and then a single flash. Through my NVGs, I could see the manor house decimated by the explosions. Bricks, structural beams, and glass were propelled through the air and away from the blasts, their outlines and textures clearly visible in the goggles.

Then a random sentence I had read in a USAF armament manual popped into my head. *2520 feet in 9 seconds.* That was the top of the fragmentation envelope of a Mark-82 explosion and the amount of time the frag took to reach that altitude. And Ian was right in the middle of it. He might have ejected and escaped the explosion, but he was descending into his own frag, in a parachute.

"Jesus," I muttered to myself.

But then two things brought me back into the moment. The first was the realization that with the separation we had planned on our attacks, it would be time to release my ordnance on the warehouses in mere seconds. The second was the distinctive sound of a GUN DISH radar searching for my aircraft.

ZZZZIT. ZZZZIT. ZZZZIT. It was a high-pitched, momentary tone, generated by my radar warning receiver as the radar beam passed through my aircraft. Each tone separated by a second or two.

I nodded to myself as I heard it in my headset. "He's in acquisition mode," I said to myself.

Then, abruptly, the radar tone went solid and urgent in my headset. The ZSU's radar wasn't sweeping any longer. It was locked on to me. In my peripheral vision to the left, I saw another four-fingered burst generated, this time in my direction. I focused on the buildings in front of me. The warehouses were stretched out ahead, four long, rectangular buildings that were oriented perpendicular to my flight path. I didn't have a HUD, so I didn't have a bombsight. I was going to have to release my weapons based on sight picture or TLAR, as we used to call it – 'that looks about right.' It had been fifteen years since I had expended a high drag munition like napalm. But in my twenty years of USAF service, I had dropped a lot of them, and my brain retrieved the sight picture readily.

"Feet on the target," I said to myself. "Feet on the target."

Unguided low-drag bombs, delivered ballistically, typically impact the earth directly under the aircraft that drops them. But high-drag munitions, like napalm, impact behind the delivering aircraft to allow for separation from the explosion. The sight picture for a low-drag bomb looks more normal to the pilot. The bomb range is longer, and the aircraft is further away from the target. There is plenty of room in which to recover if things go wrong. With high drag delivery, the aircraft is much closer to the target at release, and the picture looks decidedly different. But I remembered it. Years later, I remembered it.

I saw another four fingers of flame to my left, but at that time, the first warehouse was just off OV's nose. I waited until it went under the nose and when it felt like it was under my feet, and I pressed the pickle button once. I felt the kick of the bomb rack ejecting the weapon as I felt the impacts of 23mm rounds hitting the tail end of my aircraft. I could feel the rudders vibrate through the pedals under my feet and the stick shuddered in my hand. But the OV still felt stable.

"Damn," I muttered. "That was fucking close."

The second warehouse went under my feet, and I punched the pickle button a second time. Another kick and another canister was away. The third warehouse came under my feet even as I saw another burst of ZSU fire headed my way. I hit the pickle button twice and sent two more canisters of napalm earthward while I braced myself for the impacts of more bullets in my aircraft. The OV vibrated behind my seat.

I heard the "tink" of glass breaking, and then I saw a flash in the cockpit behind me through my rear-view mirrors and felt something smack the back of my helmet.

The gunner was correcting from aft to front. He had led Ian too much on his dive and had to correct fore to aft. But Ian was headed towards him, with a low line-of-sight rate, and I was 90 degrees to him with a high line-of-sight rate. I hoped the gunner's temporary miscalculation would save me. The final warehouse went under my feet. I punched the last canister of napalm off and immediately rolled into a hard turn to the right, away from the ZSU and away from the target. I momentarily debated about whether to roll out to the east and attempt to fly over the small hills there or continue to the turn to the south. I elected to do the latter, if for no other reason but to reverse the ZSU gunner's targeting solution. I pulled the OV's nose around as rapidly as I could, silently praying that the rounds that had hit my aircraft hadn't completely taken my elevator and rudder away from me. As I pulled through 90 degrees of turn, I saw tracers fly under my aircraft and into the sky in front of me. My abrupt change in flight path had fooled the gunner, at least for the moment.

I continued my turn to the south, and I saw the damage that my ordnance had done. The napalm canisters had detonated into an inferno encompassing the entire warehouse complex and the surrounding buildings, vehicles, and terrain. It was a wall of raging flame that reached hundreds of feet into the sky.

I eased forward on my control stick as I rolled out and brought the OV closer to the ground for the second time that evening, hoping to use the flames and my low altitude as cover from the ZSU. My efforts were rewarded by the silence in my headset. The ZSU's GUN DISH radar had lost its lock on my aircraft. I breathed a small sigh of relief.

I leveled the OV at 100 feet above the desert floor and eyed the terrain in front of me through the NVGs. There was an undeveloped road that led out of the south end of the valley and deeper into Mexico. If I stayed on my present course, I'd fly right down it. And if the ZSU decided to go mobile and come after me, it could travel down the road as well. The ZSU could shoot on the move and wouldn't suffer much degradation of capability if it did. I could outrun it of course, but if it were moving at top speed and headed southward, I'd be inside of its effective range for an uncomfortable period of time.

I tried to get inside the ZSU gunner's head and consider what he might be thinking. I was sure he and the rest of his crew were under immense pressure to bring me down. They would be hungry to get bullets on my aircraft. At the moment, they had no radar or visual contact with my aircraft. They were blind. They knew I wasn't headed northbound any longer, so they had two options, wait to reacquire me as I emerged from the south end of the warehouse inferno, or fire random volleys at me and hope to get lucky. I nodded to myself. That gave me a few moments of uncertainty on their part that I might be able to exploit.

I rolled the OV up to the left and pulled the nose around to a southeastern heading, aiming for a gap in the rocky terrain in front of me. The moment I rolled out, a four-fingered volley of bullets appeared off my right wing, slightly higher than my aircraft. The tracers pierced the inferno from the warehouses and left trails of fire reaching into the darkness to the east. My change of direction had come just in time.

I nodded to myself, but there was no time for self-congratulation. I forced the OV even lower as I peered through the NVGs, trying to try to find a path through the hills that I could follow so I could get some terrain between me and the gun. I saw an unimproved road at the bottom of a shallow valley that led initially to the east and down the dry creek bed in front of me, then toward the northeast. It showed up in the NVGs as a trail of light color, thanks to the white sand's ability to retain the heat of the desert sun. I decided to track it into the hills, hoping there would be some sort of valley that I could use to pass through the rock obstacles between me and the valley beyond.

Another three-dimensional rectangle of tracers appeared to my left, paralleling my course to the east. Like the last volley, this one was above my altitude. I pushed the OV lower and guided it closer to the road, hoping to break line of sight with the ZSU. I glanced toward the northeast. I could see the dark terrain to the left of the nose and a clearly discernible gap between the nearest rocks. Only a few miles away.

"Perfect," I said to myself. "Now if we can only get there in time.

ZZZZIT. ZZZZIT. ZZZZIT. The GUN DISH was into acquisition mode, and my radar warning gear was picking up the signals – which meant the ZSU's radar had re-achieved line-of-sight with me. I didn't make sense to me, but I didn't have the time to think about it. It was everything I could do to keep the OV clear of the terrain. I had the fuselage as close to the dry sand of the road as I could stand it and the wings were barely clearing the vegetation on either side. I remembered from my days flying in Europe that the ZSU had issues with both the depression of its radar and its guns, so I hoped that would save me. I also knew that the radar warning gear detected side lobes of the radar beam as well as the main lobe, wherein my aircraft would generate a return, so it was possible the GUN DISH didn't see me yet. I hoped my luck would continue to hold.

The road made an abrupt bend to the left and another abrupt turn to the northeast. I banked the OV up to the left and tried to guide the stubby aircraft around the two turns without digging the left wingtip into the ground. A large mound of earth suddenly appeared in front of me, the light-colored image blocking the road and presenting a no-notice obstacle. I rolled out slightly and pulled back on the control stick as hard as I could. I barely cleared the mound, the twin propellers of my plane coming within mere feet of the top of the berm and the propwash kicking up twin clouds of dust from the sand below them. The OV shot skyward in a 30-degree climb, leaving the protection of the terrain behind and I was instantly, suddenly, exposed in the night sky.

ZZZZIT. ZZZZIT. ZZZZIT. The GUN DISH was searching for me. Mere seconds later, I heard the urgent tone of the target tracking mode in my headset.

"Fuck!" I screamed into the intercom.

I glanced to the left to see where the stream bed continued to the east and found it easily. Then I looked down at the radar altimeter display in my PDU. I was passing through 300 feet AGL and still climbing. I needed to get my ass back down before the ZSU did it for me. I pushed forward on the control stick slightly, to unload the aircraft, and rapidly rolled to my left, past 90 degrees of bank to about 135 degrees, my wings nearly inverted to the horizon. Then I applied back pressure and pulled the OV back to the desert floor, wondering how quickly the gunner would be able to get rounds on the way after the radar lock was established. I had my answer a few milliseconds after the OV's nose began to move towards the ground. Four fiery fingers emerged out from under the belly of my aircraft, piercing the exact piece of sky that had been occupying mere moments ago. I felt a mild thump on the right side of the OV, but the aircraft felt stable in my hands, so I ignored the impact.

I rolled out a few seconds later and pushed the stubby propjet back down and closer to the road, which was now aligned on a straight course to the northeast and into the hills. I leveled off a few feet above the surface, eager to put the small hill to my left between the ZSU and me. My headset went silent and I gazed at the path ahead. It seemed to offer sanctuary for my journey into the rocky terrain beyond. I breathed my second sigh of relief of the evening.

Then the right engine erupted in flames.

CHAPTER THIRTY-TWO

Wednesday, December 2nd
0055 Hours Local Time
20 feet and 250 Knots
Near Pitiquito Municipality
Senora, Mexico

FIRE. The red letters on the right engine T-handle illuminated just as I detected the glow of orange flames out of the corner of my right eye. At the extremely low altitude I was flying, I couldn't afford a slight glance at the number two engine, even though the temptation was almost overwhelming. I reached up with my left hand and pivoted my left rear-view mirror so that I could see the right engine nacelle. As I expected, flames were streaming from just behind the propeller and trailing down the entire nacelle.

Sadly, I was no stranger to ground fire. I had been shot out of the sky once in Iraq in an A-10 during the first gulf war, once in a T-38 six years ago and once in an F-16 a few months after that. One of the things I had learned through all of those scenarios is the damage inflicted by surface-to-air ordnance was unpredictable, and that swift action by the pilot was necessary. And yet the phenomenon of temporal distortion, where time seems to slow down radically in high-stress situations, always made me feel like I had a few extra moments to analyze the situation before I started throwing switches or levers.

The ENGINE FIRE IN-FLIGHT checklist called for me to shut down the right engine and feather the propeller. On any normal flight, where I had a lot more air underneath my ass, I wouldn't have hesitated. But I was flying at nearly 280 knots, mere feet above the dirt road and over rising terrain into the hills beyond. If I didn't have the thrust to maintain level flight with one engine shut down at my low altitude, the consequences would be every bit as disastrous as an engine fire burning out of control – and I would be equally screwed. As long as the burning engine continued to provide thrust, I was tempted to let it burn a while longer.

I glanced ahead and saw the first minor hills just off the nose at the entrance to a small valley – my passage to the other side of the rocks. I was almost there.

But then the OV made the shutdown decision for me. The propjet began yawing to the left and right, and I could hear the propeller randomly changing speed and pitch. The propeller governor was failing.

"Here goes nothing," I said to myself.

I put my left hand on both condition levers and then moved to the right one. I took the risk of taking a quick glimpse downward to make sure I had my hand on the correct lever and nodded to myself when I saw it was. I didn't want to be one of those pilots who accidentally shut down the good engine during an emergency. I pulled the right condition lever all the way aft to the FEATHER & FUEL SHUTOFF position. The right propeller stopped turning almost immediately as oil pressure was dumped from the propeller control unit and the compression washers inside the propeller hub and aerodynamic forces streamlined the propeller blades into the wind. The loss of thrust on the right was instantaneous, and the nose of the OV yawed hard to the right in response as the thrust from the left engine pushed the aircraft sideways. The left wing began to rise, and the right wing fell as the OV tried to roll into the dead engine. The yaw-roll coupling tendency of the OV was one of its few aerodynamic flaws, but it was a significant issue.

"Jesus," I said into the intercom.

I applied left rudder to stop the yaw and saw the right wingtip come within mere inches of the ground. But then the rudder took effect, and the OV righted itself. A mental image of the wingtip digging into the dirt and the aircraft cartwheeling into a ball of flame popped into my head, but I dismissed it. I glanced up at the mirror and saw the right engine nacelle still streaming flames, although not as brightly as before. Shutting the engine off had interrupted fuel flow to the engine, which had dampened the fire. But there was still work to do. I switched hands with the control stick and pulled the illuminated FIRE T-handle on the upper right side of the forward panel with my right hand. Then I shifted my hand to the FIRE EXT switch and moved it up to the AGENT position. Finally, I reached down to the FUEL EMERG SHUT OFF switches on the lower right panel, and after ensuring I had my hand on correct one, I actuated it. I glanced down at the engine gauges in my PFD. The torque, RPM, interstage turbine temperature and oil pressure for the number two engine were all decreasing. The engine seemed to be shutting down normally.

I looked at my airspeed in the PFD as I moved my right hand back to the stick and my left hand to the left power lever. As I expected, the airspeed was decreasing. I wondered how low it would go and whether I'd be able to make it through the hills on one engine.

"I guess we'll see," I said to the empty cockpit.

The small hill to my left disappeared, About a kilometer

of open ground remained before I reached the hills and disappeared behind them.

"Almost there," I said to myself. "Almost there."

ZZZZIT. ZZZZIT. ZZZZIT.

"Jesus!" I screamed in frustration. "Give it a rest you guys!"

But the ZSU crew was not to be dissuaded. The tone in my headset changed from acquisition to target tracking, and a sudden display of light to my left drew my gaze there. I glanced over quickly and saw something in the NVGs that I had only remembered from the televised opening of the first Gulf War. Four long fingers of fire were reaching for my aircraft. This wasn't a controlled burst. The gunner was emptying his magazine to get my aircraft before I made it to my sanctuary. A least a thousand rounds of 23mm were on a collision course with my aircraft.

My reactions were utterly reflexive. I applied back pressure to the control stick to get an upward vector on the OV-10 and reached between my legs for the ejection lanyard.

"Goddamn it," I said, "I can't fucking believe I'm doing this again."

Then I pulled the lanyard.

CHAPTER THIRTY-THREE

Wednesday, December 2nd
0110 Hours Local Time
Under Canopy
Near Pitiquito Municipality
Senora, Mexico

The OV-10's ejection seat performed as advertised and I found myself a few hundred feet above the plane and under a parachute canopy mere milliseconds later. Below me, I saw my aircraft perforated by a stream of 23mm rounds and shredded into pieces. A fire broke out on the left engine nacelle and spread impossibly quickly, burning the entire aircraft in seconds. The stubby propjet disintegrated into a fireball that initially kept its trajectory, then slowly descended to the desert floor, an arcing trail of orange flames that careened through the air and slammed into the hard terrain, creating a pool of fire about fifty yards across.

Right below me.

I pulled the right riser of the parachute as hard as I could to steer away from the fiery wreckage. Ordinarily, you try to land a parachute into the wind, just like an airplane. But I didn't have that luxury. I was barely going to clear the crash site and would have to take whatever the terrain gave me.

Amazingly, the NVG's were still attached to my head and still powered, so my view of the terrain below was much better than it would have been with just my eyesight in the early morning darkness. I saw a small clearing among several large rocks and guided the parachute towards that, hoping like hell I could get the chute down in the space.

I looked up at my canopy to check for rips and tears. The nylon parachute appeared light gray in the NVGs, probably a function of the warmth of the cockpit and the speed of the ejection sequence. I scanned it quickly in the few moments I had and nodded to myself. The canopy seemed to be intact.

As I continued my descent, I thought about releasing the survival kit but decided against it. The kit had vital supplies, but it was attached by a twenty-five-foot strap, and if I released it, the strap might tangle in a cactus or on a rock going in. That would be the last thing I needed.

The rocks were quite close now. I pulled my left riser slightly and guided myself between the tops of two huge boulders that were about fifty feet high. Then I released the left riser and pulled on the right one to realign myself with the broadest part of the clearing. As I drew nearer to the ground, I was able to see some foliage scattered throughout the open area. I breathed a sigh of relief when I realized none of them appeared to be cacti or Joshua trees.

Then it was time to land. I slammed my legs and feet together and just before they hit the ground, I pulled down on both risers as hard as I could. My feet hit the hard terrain first, then my left thigh and then my butt, all in a fraction of a second. I felt a sharp pain in my thigh as my body came to rest.

"Jesus," I said to myself. "All this and I land on a fucking rock."

Get moving, said an internal voice. *They'll be coming.*

I felt a tug at my shoulders from my parachute. The mild wind was partially inflating it and threatened to pull me along the ground. I quickly released one riser strap and was about to release the other, when I thought better of it. I stood up and detached the survival kit from my harness. Then, I got out of the harness and rolled the parachute and harness up together. It took me a few moments, but I had the parachute and harness condensed to the size of a small beach ball, which was going to have to do for the moment. I slung the survival kit over my shoulder, grabbed my bundle and made for the south side of the clearing as quickly as I could, trying to get as far away of the wreckage of my aircraft as possible. The bad guys would be arriving soon, and I wanted to be nowhere near this place.

Just past the south end of the clearing, I found what I was looking for, a group of several small rocks in a cluster formation. Hoping like hell that a rattlesnake wasn't coiled up inside the cluster, I pushed the bundle of parachute and harness down inside of it, trying to keep the olive-green parachute casing on top of it and the multi-colored parachute below and obscured.

The sound of a vehicle engine pierced the silence and grabbed my attention. I could hear it distinctly in the still night. It wasn't nearby at the moment, but it would be soon. The cartel's search party was inbound. I needed to get the hell out of here. I started moving southbound, to put some distance between me and the crash site, which was undoubtedly where they'd go first.

As I began to walk southward, the survival kit swung under my arm and I felt a hard object prod into my side. It occurred to me then that I had not inventoried what was in the kit and what I could make use of. I squatted down and unsnapped the latches of the plastic kit. Inside, arrayed in a custom cut Styrofoam tray, there were the usual survival items: ration bars, a few cans of water, a handheld radio, mirror and signal flares. But there appeared to be another layer underneath. I heard the vehicle noise getting louder and closer, but I took an extra moment to see what was there. When I peeled back the top layer of Styrofoam, I smiled at what I found. Ian had thought of everything.

##

Change of plan. About ten minutes later, I was ensconced on top of a large rock just north of the crash site and watching the OV's wreckage burn below me. The search party had arrived and were making their way to the site, down a path that stretched from the road I had been flying along to the area where the aircraft had come to rest. I could see them in the NVGs and hear them speaking to one another in Spanish, not taking any care to lower their voices or advance with caution. I counted four of them, and they carried their weapons carelessly at their sides, supremely confident that their quarry was no threat.

"¿Qué harán con el primer gringo?" I heard one of them say. "El que vivió. ¿El Grande?"

The first gringo, I thought. *The one that lived. The big one.* I nodded to myself as I watched them. *They've got Brooks, but they think you died in the crash.*

"El jefe dice que desarmará al gringo y venderá sus piezas," the one in the front responded.

Take him apart? Sell him? Jesus!

In my hands was an AR-15 pistol with a 7.5–inch barrel and a suppressor screwed onto the end it. That was Ian's surprise in the survival kit. He had apparently felt that if a bailout were necessary, he'd have to fight his way out of the place. When I had found the weapon, it occurred to me that having a vehicle to escape Mexico would be easier than walking the 100 some odd miles out of the country.

The AR had a single dot illuminated sight mounted on top

of the receiver, and as the search party approached, I pushed the NVGs back on my head and peered through the reticle. I could have avoided them and stolen the vehicle while they were at the crash site, but I didn't want to provide them the opportunity to sound the alarm or call for backup. Besides, some payback was in order tonight.

I intended to make use of a phenomenon that occurred at many crashes of fighter aircraft carrying cannon ammunition. I just hoped I'd actually have some luck tonight.

The first two search party members entered the clearing where the OV had impacted. The other two were just behind them on the trail. All were dressed in camouflage fatigues. For a moment, I thought they might be Mexican soldiers on retainer to the cartel. But these guys carried their weapons sloppily and carelessly, like men who had no formal training and who were arrogantly confident that the outcome of every mission could be taken for granted.

They were about to get a lesson.

POP! I was in luck. Out of my peripheral vision, I saw a small explosion emanate from inside the OVs wreckage, and a miniature fireball shot out of the burning aircraft and into the night sky above. The 20mm cannon rounds were cooking off in the fire. The shells were detonating due to the heat, and because there was no chamber around them, they were like small bombs with a single piece of shrapnel, the bullet, that didn't get far.

I watched the search party flinch at the sound, but then they pressed forward, more curious than frightened.

Perfect, I thought.

I centered the AR's aiming reference on the guy who was furthest back in their group and waited.

POP! POP! Two more 20mm rounds cooked off and I fired.

Suppressors aren't silencers, hence the name. They don't eliminate the report of a gunshot, they suppress it and hide the muzzle flash. For rounds that were supersonic, like the 5.56mm NATO that I was firing, they didn't do anything about muffling the sound of the bullet breaking the sound barrier. The AR sounded like a .22, a loud .22., so it wasn't quiet, but its report was masked by the 20mm rounds. Perfectly.

The search party member I had targeted fell backward quietly. I was already transitioning my aim to his partner, the next one forward in the group.

POP! POP! POP! POP! More 20mm rounds detonated into the night.

I fired two shots at my latest target, and he too fell into darkness. The leader of the group shrugged as he looked forward into the wreckage, apparently baffled as to where the sounds were coming from. He turned toward his followers and froze when he saw the two men in the rear squad were down. He started to raise his weapon and pivot back toward the wreckage. I put two bullets into his upper back, and at least one of them must have gone through him because the leader's partner, the last member of the group, fell to his knees as the leader hit the ground. I centered my reticle on the final group member's chest and fired twice more, just to be cautious. He fell to the ground with a surprised expression on his face.

I was off the rock and down with them in about thirty seconds. Perhaps a better man would have checked for pulses, bandaged wounds or tied up the injured. But I wasn't that guy. I made the rounds and shot each of them twice in the back of the head. Then I inventoried them for weapons, ammunition, and information. Their weaponry wasn't standardized, as was typical for criminal henchmen. The two in the front had AK-47s and only one extra magazine each. The leader did have a radio clipped to his belt. I took the radio and left the weapons behind. I made my way to the rear two and found an old GI AR-15 with the full stock and triangular hand guard. I helped myself to his two 30-round magazines. The last guy had a Thompson .45 ACP submachine gun and three spare magazines strapped to his chest.

"Never hurts to be prepared," I said to myself as I loaded up the gun and magazines. "It's a long way to the border."

I lowered my NVGs and headed back along the trail they had taken from their vehicle to the crash site. The trail was a light gray, like most I had seen in the NVGs tonight, and wound between several large dark-colored boulders. As I walked, I could see the texture of the sand and the rock clearly, and I wondered how much longer the battery charge in the NVGs would hold out. I was hoping to use them to drive the vehicle north into Arizona.

The trail ended abruptly at an unimproved two-lane road that seemed to extend to the northeast. It took me a second or two to get my bearings, but then I realized that it was the same road I had been flying over mere minutes ago. I heard the sound of an engine running and realized that the search party members must have left their vehicle in a hurry. I dropped to my chest and peered around the rocks at the intersection of the road and the trail to look at the vehicle. I saw the large, rectangular outline of a big, black SUV, probably a Hummer H1, by the look of it. The engine and the tires glowed white in the NVGs, as did certain parts of the chassis, but the rest of the vehicle was light gray. There didn't seem to be any other human beings nearby.

Rather than walking up the road to the Hummer, I took a more circuitous route, keeping some of the rocks between me and the vehicle until I was abeam it and about five yards away. Then I moved on it rapidly, AR at the ready position. Once my boots stopped walking on the desert sand, the only other sound that was audible came from the vehicle's engine. I made my way around the vehicle carefully, doing my best to ensure that no one else was lurking around it. Once I was satisfied, I opened the driver's door and entered the vehicle. I was surprised that the dome light didn't come on when I opened the door, but I realized that might have been the henchmens' one concession to tactical lighting. No use highlighting the contents of your assault vehicle while you were exiting it.

The Hummer H1 was the civilianized version of the Humvee military transport vehicle, which I had been well acquainted with during my time in the USAF. This one had been outfitted with a luxury interior, but now it was showing the signs of years of use and abuse. I wondered if it had once been a rich person's plaything and had been commandeered into service by the cartel. The black leather upholstery was torn in some spots and stained in others. The wood and plastic of the dashboard was scratched in several places, and there were cigarette burns here and there. But as I gazed at the instrument panel, I saw that it was full of gas, and that was all that mattered to me. I put the AR and the Thompson on the passenger seat and strapped in. Then I dug out my iPhone and consulted the maps app, which was surprisingly detailed for my current location. I found the road I was on and saw that it did indeed go into the next valley and joined a blacktop road that intersected with Mexico's Route 2.

Perfect, I thought.

I put the phone down, made sure the gain on the NVGs was set correctly and drove off into the hills.

CHAPTER THIRTY-FOUR

Wednesday, December 2nd
0230 Hours Local Time
On Highway 2, West of Altar
Sonora, Mexico

The trek through the hills had been slow, but uneventful. Eventually, I made it out to Highway 2, east of Pitiquito. Then I had a to make a decision. Take Highway 2 west, through Pitiquito and Caborca and back to the US border or go east and find a way into the US at Nogales, south of Tucson. I opted for the latter, even though I had no idea how I'd get into the US when the time came, especially in a stolen vehicle, with no passport and a cab full of weapons. I sighed. Another call to the CIA was in probably in my near future.

The traffic on Highway 2 was light but frequent enough that seeing other vehicles didn't make me suspicious. So far, I didn't feel like I was being followed, although it had been over an hour since I had ejected, and the search party had been dispatched for me. It was just a question of time before the cartel went into pursuit mode. I had to put as many miles between them and me as I could in the meantime. I gazed around the Hummer's interior as I drove and had a sinking realization. The Hummer was huge, and it was distinctive.

It wasn't like I was going to blend into the flow of traffic. Regardless of where I went, I would be easy to find.

"Well shit," I said to myself.

A dingy rectangular sign appeared on the side of the road just ahead. The NVGs were on the passenger seat next to me, so I had to squint slightly to read the print.

ALTAR 10KM.

I nodded to myself. About 6 miles away. I raised my phone to eye level and looked at the map. I had another decision to make when I reached Altar. I could stay on the main highway, Highway 2, to Santa Ana and then head north to catch Highway 15 into Nogales or I could take route 63/43 and drive a much more circuitous route to the border. Highways 2 and 15 would take me slightly out of my way but would probably be faster since they were both major roads. Routes 63 and 43 would take longer since they meandered and were secondary highways, but they might allow me more concealment from possible detection and observation.

I glanced down at the Hummer's fuel gauge. The vehicle had been nearly full when I had taken it. Now the needle was at the ¾ remaining mark.

"Jesus," I said to myself. "Does this thing suck gas."

Regardless of the route I chose, I had no idea how far it would be to the border or whether the Hummer could make it there without a fuel stop.

"Decisions, decisions," I said.

I flipped a mental coin and decided to chance the less traveled route. I looked into the darkness ahead of me and saw the few lights of the city or town or berg of Altar a few miles ahead. While I had been a passenger in various vans and taxis in Mexico several times before tonight, this was the first time I had actually driven a vehicle in Mexico. So far, the highway experience didn't seem much different from what I had experienced on rural highways in the US. I wondered what the back roads would be like. I nodded to myself as I looked at the map.

Couldn't be that much different, I thought.

As it turned out, having the phone up near my face might have saved my life.

Strangulation is a tricky kill mechanism and requires strength, skill, and tools on the part of the attacker. Although sometimes, it can only take a bit of luck.

I sensed the rope going over my head more than I actually felt it. There was a breeze of movement on my hair and my internal alarm system instantly went to high alert mode before I could even command it. My eyes detected a line of motion passing vertically before them, and temporal distortion kicked in. I was able to see that the line was a white rope of some sort, a short length of it, held between two small hands and wrapped around both wrists.

Not a pro, I thought.

I dropped the phone into my lap and grabbed the rope with my right hand before it had a chance to dig into my neck. As soon as the rope touched my hand, the attacker increased the tension on it, and my hand was slammed against my neck. But I could still breathe and think.

I glanced in the mirror to ensure there was no traffic directly behind, and stomped on the brake pedal as hard as I could, hoping like hell that the anti-skid system would function properly. The huge Hummer rapidly decelerated, and my attacker was thrown against the back of my seat. I heard a small, feminine cry of surprise.

I pulled the SUV over to the shoulder, and it skidded to a halt. As soon as I didn't need a hand for steering, I reached back over my head and grabbed the wrists of my attacker. Then, I leaned to the left, contracted my muscles and pulled as hard as I could. My hours in the gym paid off. A small woman with disheveled black hair came over my right shoulder. Her upper body landed in my lap, and her head hit the plastic steering wheel as she came to rest, sprawled across the front seat. Her dark eyes were dull for a moment, then they went wide in surprise as she came back to herself. Before she could react, I reached under my left arm with my right hand, retrieved the Colt .45 commander from the shoulder holster and pushed it up under her chin.

"Keep your hands where I can fucking see them," I commanded. "Now who are you and what the fuck are you doing here?"

Her eyes flashed in recognition as I spoke. She understood me. Her face went through a series of small contortions as she decided how to answer my question. She was young. Like mid to late 20s. Her face still had a look of innocence to it, not like the visage of a girl who had been artificially aged by use in a bar or on her back. She was clothed in something that looked like a uniform. I couldn't make out the color in the dim light. But there was something about the cut and style of the uniform that pulled a string inside my brain. I had seen it before.

I pushed the .45's muzzle into her chin a little harder to encourage her. "I'm losing patience," I said.

"You're American?" she asked. Her tone was one of relief and surprise.

I nodded. "And at the risk of sounding like a cliché, I'm asking the questions here. Who are you?" I looked up and down her body again and regarded the uniform. "And what are you?"

"My name is Maria Hernandez," she said in totally unaccented English. "*Agent* Maria Hernandez. I'm with the US Border Patrol. And you need to untie me."

I looked at the length of rope between her two hands. "We'll see about that," I said. "Besides, it looks like you've got a pretty good start on that already." I kept the pressure from the .45's muzzle against her chin. "And just so you know, this gun has a three and a half pound trigger so if you even twitch too hard, you'll be dead before your body stops moving. Do you understand me?"

She nodded, her eyes wide in comprehension.

"What's a Border Patrol agent doing in the back of cartel Hummer this far south of the border?"

She shrugged, and I saw a look of embarrassment seep onto her face. "I was captured near Nogales," she said. "They didn't kill me because..." She gestured towards her body. For the first time, I noticed the top button of her uniform blouse was unbuttoned and her large breasts were straining against the fabric of a black t-shirt underneath.

I nodded. "Because you're a woman." I removed the .45 from under her chin and replaced it in the shoulder holster under my left arm. "And you had other uses." Then I reached across to the passenger seat and grabbed the firearms and NVGs. I motioned to the right seat with my head. "Might be more comfortable for you over there," I said.

She nodded and attempted to resituate herself. But her posture made the process awkward. I held the firearms and NVGs against my chest with my left arm and offered her my right hand. She grabbed it with both of hers and pulled herself up and over the center console. She landed unceremoniously in the right seat, directly on top of the ammo magazines for the weapons.

"Sorry," I said. "I did some arms and ammo collecting earlier."

"What happened to them?" she asked as she pulled the magazines out from under her and placed them in a pile on the floor near her feet. Then she finished untying the rope around her wrists. It didn't take her long.

"Let's just say they won't be following us," I said. I raised my eyes to the rear-view mirror and saw a set of headlights in the distance behind us. "But that doesn't mean someone else won't." I handed her the AR-15 and put the Thompson behind her seat. Then I put the Hummer in gear and accelerated out on to the road. I glanced over at her. "I take it you're familiar with that weapon?"

She nodded as she looked the weapon over and ensured the safety switch was in the SAFE position. She handled the rifle with the casual confidence borne of thorough training. "Shorter barrel with a suppressor," she said, with a satisfied tone. "Very nice."

"I'm not sure how far you can reach out and touch someone with it," I said. "But it should be enough to engage the bad guys if we encounter some of them on the way back."

"This far into Mexico, it's probably not a question of if. It's a question of when."

I nodded as I watched the meager lights of Altar draw closer. "I was afraid you were going to say that." I retrieved my phone from my lap and handed it to her. "The code is 0622," I said. "Call up the map, and maybe you can pick the best route out of here."

She did as I instructed, and I saw the screen light up with the map page illuminated.

"The way it looked to me was that we could take the major highways, two and 15 or the smaller roads, routes 63 and 43. The highways would probably be faster, but this tank we're driving would have a larger chance of being spotted. The back roads would take longer, but we might stay a little more concealed, particularly this time of night."

Maria was nodding as she looked at the map while I spoke.

"What do you think?" I asked. "Or do you know of a better route?"

She shook her head slowly and then looked over at me. "I grew up in Flagstaff," she said. "I even went to Northern Arizona University there. Until getting snatched last night,

Nogales was the furthest south I'd ever been." She looked back at the map on my phone. "I think we should stick to the main roads," she said. "We'll run the risk of being seen, but if we take the back roads, we don't know how many of those small towns will have a cartel presence."

I nodded. "I didn't think about that. Good call. The last thing we'd need is to run into some more of those thugs and have no place to run."

She handed the phone back to me, and I placed it into one of the chest pockets on my flight suit. I could see her looking over at me, studying me like she was seeing me for the first time.

I watched the lights of Altar come and go down the left side of the Hummer at 70 miles per hour. I reminded myself to look out for a speed limit sign and to keep my velocity under the limit. The last thing we needed was to get pulled over by a Mexican cop.

"I've told you who I am," Maria said at last. "Who the hell are you and what are you doing in Mexico in a flight suit, NVGs and with all this hardware?"

I glanced over at her quickly before returning my eyes to the road. "Did you see the light show earlier?"

"You mean the bombs and the fire?" I could see her eyes widen in my peripheral vision.

"I was the fire. A friend of mine was the bombs. But the cartel had a very lethal anti-aircraft gun on the ground, and it shot us down. We both ejected. I obviously survived. I'm not sure if he did."

"But...but why?"

I shrugged and gave her a quick smile. "Seemed to be the thing to do at the time."

Maria was shaking her head. "It was a stupid thing to do!" These drug lords are crazy. You never know how they'll react to something like that. They could bomb something in the US!"

"No," I said. "They can't. At least not in an airplane. You know as well as I do we have tethered radar balloons all up and down the border looking southward at low altitude. And there's a least one set of F-16s on alert all the time at either Tucson or Luke to engage unidentified aircraft. The bad guys would never make it."

She was still shaking her head as I spoke. "You don't understand. The whole border thing might seem chaotic to you but there is a certain balance to it all. Something like this airstrike could disturb that balance."

"What about kidnapping a border patrol agent?" I countered. "Wouldn't that disturb the *balance* as well?"

Maria leaned back against the headrest and exhaled loudly. I could see her face in my peripheral vision, illuminated by the lights of the dash. Although disheveled by her abduction and subsequent treatment, she was quite attractive. She had high cheekbones and flawless skin. Her eyes were a lustrous brown and had long natural lashes.

"I guess that would disturb the balance too," she said.

"How'd you get snatched?"

She hung her head. "My partner and I were inspecting a section of fence about 20 miles west of Nogales. It appeared to have been cut open and then wired back together."

I glanced over at her.

"Happens all the time," she continued. "We were trying to see how large of a section would require replacement when a squad of heavily-armed cartel people appeared out of nowhere." She paused, and I could see her struggling to control her emotions. "We surrendered, and they put us both on our knees and tied our hands. Then the bastards just shot my partner for the fun of it. They did it slowly, one bullet at a time, in his legs and his arms and his..." her voice trailed off. "Then one of them said they had no time for this and shot him in the back of the head. I thought they were going to kill me too. I've never been so scared."

Maria hung her head, and I could see her shoulders shaking. "But they didn't kill me. They put me in the back of some truck, and we drove to the compound. I thought they were going to rape me, but the one in charge said I wasn't to be touched until the boss decided what to do with me. But that didn't stop them from..."

Maria looked down at her chest, and I understood. She had been *handled*. Multiple times.

"Anyway, we got to the compound, and everyone was scurrying around. They were very concerned about something." She looked across the Hummer at me. "And I guess that was you and your friend. Then that damn cannon started shooting, and they threw me in the back of this thing. As we drove away from the house, I felt the bombs go off. The explosions rocked the vehicle. Then, a few minutes later, I saw the fire. It was like daylight through the windows. The men driving me were terrified, and they were going fast, trying to get away from the flames. They hit a bump, and I got thrown into the side of the Hummer. I hit my head on something. That the last thing I remember before I woke up to find you in the front seat." She looked over at me sheepishly. "Sorry I tried to strangle you."

I flashed a quick smile at her. "No worries. I'm used to it. I have that effect on women."

I saw a road sign coming up on the right side of the car. SANTA ANA 30KM. "So about twenty miles to Santa Ana and then we'll turn north to Nogales." I glanced at Maria again. "Do you think you can get us through the checkpoints when we get there?"

She nodded. "If we get there." She looked around the Hummer's interior. "There can't be too many of these in this area of Mexico. At some point, someone is going to notice us."

I nodded in response. “I had the same thought earlier. Hopefully, our luck will hold.”

“Luck?” she asked with a bitter tone in her voice. “After what happened to both of us tonight, what in the hell would make you think we’re lucky?”

I looked over at her. “Because we’re still alive,” I said.

CHAPTER THIRTY-FIVE

Wednesday, December 2nd
0330 Hours Local Time
On Highway 15, North of Imuris
Senora, Mexico

Our luck ran out in the home stretch, 15 miles north of the town of Imuris, about thirty miles south of the border.

Until then, there had been few vehicles, and we had been able to stay within the flow of the traffic we encountered and avoided attracting attention to ourselves, in spite of our ostentatious vehicle. Once we turned north on Highway 15, we relaxed a bit. It was a divided highway that wound through a valley created by the Agua Caliente river, and there were no real opportunities for oncoming traffic to see us and make a U-turn to pursue us if they were so inclined.

That changed north of Imuris. At about the 15-mile point, the north and southbound lanes of the highway split and were only a few hundred feet apart. I guided the big SUV around a curve to the east and then I turned back to the north, following the road as it wound through rows of trees on either side of it, obscuring the view of anything immediately beyond the paved surface.

Then I saw the small road on the right side. It appeared

as I finished the turn, the entrance almost concealed by the roadside trees. I immediately thought that it would be a perfect hiding place for a cop lying in wait for speeding vehicles, and I took my foot off the gas.

But it wasn't the police I should have been worried about. A battered and dented Chevrolet pickup truck was parked about fifty feet off the highway. At first, I thought the vehicle was abandoned. But as the Hummer's headlights illuminated the truck, I could see two hard-looking men sitting in the front seat, observing the road carefully. I stomped on the gas pedal as soon as I saw them and the SUV's big engine roared, pushing the Hummer forward at higher speed.

"Looks like someone has been waiting for us," I said.

Maria was looking out of the right side of the Hummer, and she noticed the truck about the same time I did. I saw her nod in my peripheral vision. The radio I had taken from the guard earlier blared with a quick conversation in Spanish. I couldn't translate but the intent was clear enough.

"How in the hell did they know we'd be on this road?" I asked in exasperation.

"*Los Diablos* controls all of this area," Maria said flatly. "They've probably been rounding up the troops."

I felt a chill go up my spine. I had interactions with Los Diablos sometime back. "*Los Diablos?* The motorcycle gang?"

Maria nodded again. "They used to just be the muscle. They worked for a powerful drug lord named Miguel Hidalgo and were led by Miguel's younger brother, Ramon. Both of them were killed a little over five years ago. After that, there was a power vacuum and Miguel's son, Mariano, took over the gang and the entire cartel. Now they control all the provinces that border the US, Sonora, Chihuahua, and Coahuila, the northern part of Tamaulipas, and the entire Baja Peninsula."

We went by the pickup truck at about 80 miles per hour. We had no sooner passed it when the truck pulled out onto the highway behind us, creating a cloud of dust as its wheels churned up the dirt on the side road.

I barely noticed. The pieces of the last few days were all falling into place.

"Shit," I said unconsciously. The moment I had been dreading for five years had finally come to pass. It was one thing to ask for a cleaning crew. It was another to ask for a rescue.

"What?" Maria asked.

"This won't be the only vehicle they send against us." I motioned to the truck behind us. "If this guy has IDed us, and he probably has, he'll be on the phone to his buddies, and there will be more vehicles waiting for us as we go north."

Maria nodded thoughtfully. "Probably."

"We're going to have to call in the cavalry," I said. "Goddamn it."

"Cavalry? What cavalry?"

I looked over at her quickly and then glanced in the mirror. The truck was gaining.

"I know some people. They'll come and get us."

"Down here? And cause an international incident? That's crazy."

"Not for these guys," I said. "And trust me, we can't have Los Diablos catch us."

"Well no shit, I don't want them to catch us either, but what makes you think we're so special these friends of yours will take the risk?"

I opened my mouth to speak and then thought better of it. I dug my phone out of the breast pocket of my flight suit and tossed it to her again. "Remember the code?"

She nodded.

"Find a contact named Bruiser and open up a text message to him."

I glanced in the rearview, the headlights were getting

brighter.

"Got it," she said. "What do you want me to type?"

"Nine one one."

"That's it?"

I nodded as she typed the numbers into my phone and hit the SEND button. "That will be enough."

SMASH! The Hummer's rear window disintegrated as several bullets came through it, perforating the passenger compartment of our vehicle. I felt a series of impacts in the seat behind me and a pinching sensation in my lower right side.

"Oh," Maria said as the phone fell out of her hand and tumbled to the floorboard of the Hummer.

I glanced to my right. She had turned sideways in her seat and was facing me. She had her hand to her chest, and I could see dark frothy liquid coming from between her fingers. In front of her, there were several dents in the dashboard and a few holes in the windscreen.

"Damn!" I said. I looked into the rearview mirror. The truck was very close behind us, and I could see the occupant on the passenger side leaning out of his window with some sort of assault rifle.

There wasn't much time to consider options. We couldn't afford another volley of fire. I pushed the Hummer's brake pedal to the floor and guided the SUV with my left hand while reaching behind Maria's seat for the Thompson with my right, praying that the bolt was cocked. The pickup truck slammed into the rear bumper of the Hummer as my right hand found the Thompson's pistol grip. The force of the impact almost jarred the weapon from my grasp, but somehow, I held on to it. I looked behind and saw the truck's passenger thrown violently against the front frame of his side window and his weapon disappeared into the night. The driver was more prepared for the impact, and even though he was pushed forward into the straps of his shoulder harness, he kept his gaze on the interior of the Hummer, obviously straining to see us in the dim interior lighting. I raised the Thompson and swung it to the driver's side of the truck, pulled the trigger and held it down. The rate of fire was surprisingly slow for a fully-automatic weapon, but between the heavy weight of the gun and the light recoil of the .45ACP cartridge, it was very controllable. I didn't know if the slow-moving bullets would penetrate the pickup's windshield, but I didn't have another choice of weaponry at the moment.

I sprayed the driver's side with several shots. My worries about penetration turned out to be unfounded. This truck was manufactured to Mexican specifications, not U.S. ones. The bullets shattered the windshield and ripped into the driver. I watched his body shudder with the impact of the heavy bullets and his blood spatter onto the glass. I swept the weapon to the passenger side and saw the stunned passenger jerk as the slugs tore into him. Satisfied, I dropped the Thompson on the Hummer's back seat and moved my foot from the brake to the gas. As we pulled away, the pickup continued to creep forward, apparently in idle.

"One down," I said. "But there will be others."

Maria was silent. She was still strapped into her seat and had her right hand to her chest. Her eyes were wide. She coughed a few times, and I saw blood on her lips.

"How many times were you hit?" I asked her. "Any idea?"

She shook her head at me, and I could see her eyes beginning to glaze over.

"You're in shock," I said. "Try to recline your seat and lie down."

She looked at me blankly.

"Goddamn it," I said. I saw another unimproved road coming up on the right side of the highway. This road was out in the open, and I couldn't see any other vehicles waiting there for us, so I slowed the Hummer down to leave the highway. A few moments later, I made the turn onto the road and followed it for about a hundred yards before I stopped the vehicle and turned the lights off. Then, I retrieved the NVGs from the backseat, donned them and powered them on. The view was reassuring. The gray stream of road in front of me led through a small thicket of trees and then into a clearing with a few buildings that seemed to be abandoned. Behind the clearing, small hills rose into the night sky. The infrared energy I saw in the NVGs was natural, radiant heat from the terrain, vegetation, and objects. There was no man-made energy that I could detect. I breathed a sigh of relief and got the Hummer moving again.

I drove a few hundred yards down the road, through the clearing and parked the Hummer on the far side of one of the abandoned buildings. Then I exited the vehicle and made my way around to the passenger side. Maria was on her side, facing away from me and toward the driver's side. After opening her door, I reclined her seat and moved her on to her back. The NVGs were remarkable in their clarity. Without rearranging or removing any of her clothing, I could easily see the two bullet wounds in her body, mainly because the exit wounds were even warmer than the rest of her body, small white-hot holes, surrounded by the darker white outline of her torso. She had been hit twice, once in the right shoulder, and in the chest, just under her left breast.

"I'm sorry Maria," I said, "but this is probably going to hurt a bit."

I rolled her away from me and inspected her shoulders, back, and hips, looking for more wounds. The NVGs didn't find any other white holes, and I couldn't feel any with my hands. I did my best to be methodical. Depending on the weapons the bad guys were shooting, .22 or .30 caliber rounds could have left small entrance wounds. After a few moments,

I satisfied myself that the two injuries I had found were all she had suffered.

I removed the NVGs and rolled her face up.

“Okay,” I said to her in what I hoped was a reassuring voice, “it looks like you’ve been hit twice, but both rounds went through you, which is good. The shoulder wound has to be painful, but it’s probably not life-threatening. The other wound worries me. I think the bullet went through your left lung. Are you having any trouble breathing?”

She seemed to think for a moment and then shook her head very slightly.

I patted her shoulder. “Good. Now we’ve got to see if we can get you bandaged up. I’ll be right back.”

I walked around to the Hummer’s cargo door and opened it, hoping to find a first aid kit of some kind. If this vehicle had been commandeered, it was possible that the manufacturer’s kit was still stuck in a compartment in the cargo area. I searched around for a few minutes before I found the kit shoved into a niche along the left side. As I pulled it out, two bottles of booze tumbled out of the compartment and landed on the hard plastic of the cargo area’s floor. Neither of them broke. I grabbed the nearest one and looked at it.

“Tequila, of course,” I said to myself. “Probably hiding it from the boss.” I wasn’t tempted to unscrew one of the lids and smell the booze. I hated tequila, and the very aroma of it could make my stomach do somersaults. But then a thought occurred to me and I hefted the bottle in satisfaction. “This might actually come in handy,” I said.

I brought both bottles and the first aid kit to the passenger side of the vehicle. I inventoried the kit, and it seemed to have all the standard bandages and gauze that I’d need. I nodded to myself as donned a pair of latex gloves and began unbuttoning Maria’s shirt.

“What...what are you doing?” she said, in a voice that

was panicked but barely audible. I stopped immediately and almost smacked myself in the head. This woman had been groped and manhandled earlier tonight. The last thing she needed was a strange man taking her clothes off.

"I'm sorry, Maria," I said. "I know you've had a long night. But I'm going to need to get the clothes off your upper body so I can bandage you. If I don't, your wounds could get infected, and you could use a lot of blood. I'll try to be as gentle and as clinical as I can. OK?"

Her face was contorted in pain and discomfort, but it seemed to relax a little, and she nodded.

"Good. Thank you." I reached down to the floor of the front seat and raised one of the bottles. "Are you a tequila drinker?"

She nodded, and I thought a saw an outline of a small smile.

"Perfect. You need to drink some of this because what I'm about to do to you is going to hurt."

She reached for the bottle. I unscrewed it and handed it to her, lifting her body up a bit so she could drink it. She took a healthy sip and then grimaced.

"I guess it isn't Patron or the equivalent is it?"

She shook her head and took another long drink of the bottle, coughing as she finished it. There was more blood on her hand this time.

Shit, I thought.

Maria handed the bottle back to me. I lowered her body down and finished undoing her buttons. Fortunately, her uniform shirt wasn't tucked into her pants, so it was easy to get the shirt fully open. Then I used a pair of scissors from the first aid kit and cut her t-shirt from waist to collar and from center to her sleeves so I could pull it off of her. The right shoulder wound was revealed. I could see a ragged hole about the size of my finger just inside the right shoulder joint. The chest wound on the other side was more concerning. There, the hole was about a half inch wide under her left breast. The hole was oozing frothy blood. All that remained on her upper body was a lacy but functional brassiere that barely contained her breasts. I didn't know what the protocol called for in situations like this, but it seemed that I could bandage the wound without removing the bra, so I left it in place. My inspection complete, I used the shreds of the t-shirt to cover her breasts while I set about my tasks.

The chest wound was the first priority. I had planned to pour some tequila on it to sterilize it, but I didn't think it was a good idea to pour liquid into a lung wound. I poured some of the booze onto a gauze pad.

"Ok," I said. "So, here's where it's going to suck."

She nodded and closed her eyes.

I swabbed the wound with the tequila-infused gauze as gingerly as I could but the harsh alcohol hitting the sensitive nerves pulled her from her reverie of shock in milliseconds. She writhed in pain and cursed in a softly spoken but vehement stream of Spanish.

"I know this hurts," I said, softly. "But try not to talk." I put two gauze pads over the wound and taped them into place. Then, I rolled her onto her left side, lifted her shirt up and repeated the process on the lung entrance wound. She continued with her invective, but she was more mumbling than speaking now. The tequila she ingested earlier seemed to be taking effect.

Now it was time to bandage the shoulder wound. I used the scissors to cut the right sleeve off her uniform shirt. Then I sterilized and dressed the entrance and exit wounds on her shoulder as quickly as I could. The effect of the tequila on these wounds didn't seem to faze her at all. I rolled her onto her back again and buttoned her up. When I was finished, I offered her another drink of the tequila, and she accepted, taking the bottle with her left hand. After she took another long drink, she offered me the bottle in a motion that seemed to ask if I wanted a sip of the vile liquor.

I shook my head in response. “No, thank you. One of us needs to stay sober, and I hate that stuff.” I took the nearly empty bottle from her and put it on the floorboard. “Besides, I need to find out what’s up with our rescue.” I felt around on the floorboard for my phone and finally found it just under Maria’s seat. I unlocked it and looked at my text messages.

There was a response from Bruiser, Dave Smith. EX-FIL VIA HELO FROM DM. It was followed by a by another message that had been sent a few minutes later. ENROUTE.

I nodded as I typed a response into the phone. ETA?

I gazed down at Maria while I waited for the response. She seemed to be comfortable, at least for the moment. She was breathing steadily, and her face seemed less tense.

“Something...different...about your friend?” The words surprised me. Her voice was barely audible and sounded like she was in the midst of some sort of dream. She lifted her right hand up and opened her palm. I put my right hand into it, and she clenched it tightly. “Guards talked about him,” she continued, in the same soft voice. “Talking about taking him apart. Selling him. Like a machine.”

Jesus, I thought as I remembered the search team’s commentary earlier. *I guess my Spanish is better than I thought.*

“He’s still alive,” she continued. “Heard something before I got knocked out. Said they captured him.”

“He’s pretty hard to kill,” I said, without thinking. “And yes, he is...different.”

“Thank you for saving me,” Maria said as she squeezed my hand slightly.

“No thanks necessary. I seem to have gotten you shot. The least I can do is contain the damage.”

“Didn’t get me shot,” she said, her voice trailing off. “It

was the fucking Mexicans."

I smiled at that and squeezed her hand in response. At that same moment, the radio I had taken from the guards earlier blared with several streams of Spanish.

"Found the pickup," Maria said, translating. "They're coming."

In the distance, I heard the roar of truck engines at high RPM from the nearby highway.

"Fuck," I said. "If they come looking for us, they're going to find us."

She nodded. "They said they're tracking the GPS chip in the Hummer."

"Of course, they are," I said in disgust.

I rose from the seat, opened the rear doors and retrieved the Thompson. I swapped the magazine with a full one and put the others in my flight suit pocket. Then, I returned to the front seat, found the suppressed AR-15 and made sure a fully-loaded magazine was in place.

The radio blared again, and the sound of truck engines grew louder. "Turned off where we did," Maria murmured, struggling to speak. "Crew knows about this place."

The engine sounds were closer, and I could hear three separate vehicles. They were coming down the road from the highway to the clearing.

"Make a run for it?" Maria's voice was barely audible, and she coughed several times after she spoke.

I shook my head and looked down at her. "There's only one way in and one way out and we've got a GPS tracker on our ride. We wouldn't make it far. And we can't get far on foot because of your condition."

Maria was shaking her head in frustration and looking at me in wide-eyed disbelief. I could see the question she wanted to ask but couldn't because of her injuries.

I felt my phone buzz in my hand, and I glanced down at it.

I looked up from the screen and smiled at her. "Don't worry, I'm not going to try to hold them off by myself," I said. "I think I'll have some help." I typed a quick note into the phone, HOT LZ, and sent it.

The trucks roared into the clearing on the other side of the house and stopped. Doors opened, and I could hear many voices speaking urgently. Finally, one voice commanded the others into silence. After a moment, it spoke.

"Hey Gringo," the voice was nasal with a heavy Mexican accent. "I lost enough of my men to you tonight, eh? We know who you are. A little bird told me. You give yourself up, and we kill you quick, and we let the agent go. You make us fight you, and you both die very slowly and with much pain."

"I have a better idea," I said, yelling my response back with as much confidence in my voice as I could muster. "You all get back into your trucks and leave, and you'll stay alive." I looked down at my phone. "You've got about 30 seconds to decide."

There was a brief stream of Spanish and then a round of laughter. Apparently, my words had been translated for the crew. "I was hoping you would fight," the nasal voice said after a moment. "You killed my father and my uncle. I want to make you pay for what you did."

Maria's pain couldn't hide the curiosity in her face. And as she looked at me, the curiosity transitioned into realization. I saw her mouth open in shocked surprise.

"You mentioned Miguel and Ramon earlier," I said, looking back at her and shrugging. "I'm what happened to them."

"Hey gringo we come for you now," the leader's voice taunted, "we come for you now, and I will take you and make you beg for death before the end."

The phone buzzed in my hand again. I glanced down at it. RIFLE x 2, it said.

I nodded, reached into the Hummer and scooted Maria across the seat a few inches. Then I got into the vehicle with her, shut the passenger door behind me and wrapped my arms around her.

"What...you...doing?" she asked in bewilderment.

"Shut your eyes," I said.

"What?"

"Shut your eyes in case there's flying glass."

"Flying...glass? From...bullets?"

"No," I said as I caught sight of the fire trail from the first missile. I put my hand over her eyes and shut my own. "From the explosions."

WHUMP!

The first Hellfire missile impacted the vehicles on the other side of the building. The vibration and overpressure from the blast rocked the Hummer. It felt like we had driven into a hurricane.

WHUMP!

The second missile hit its target, and the Hummer was rocked so hard that it actually moved a few feet. Debris from building next to us pummeled the side of the vehicle and the glass windows shattered all around us. I felt a few minor stings in the back of my hand. The moment the vehicle's motion stopped, I released Maria and opened the passenger door. I donned the NVGs, slung the weapons over my shoulder and slid my arms under Maria's knees and back.

"Time to go," I said.

I lifted Maria and pulled her out of the Hummer. She grimaced with pain but remained silent. I carried her away from the vehicle as quickly as I could, hoping that all of our pursuers were either dead or immobilized. The NVGs revealed a path away from the clearing, and I moved along it rapidly, through a few scraggly trees, around a large boulder and then into and out of a shallow arroyo. My ears were ringing from the explosions, but I could still hear the muted "whop-whop-whop" sound of the inbound helo.

Maria lifted her head and tried to speak, but no sound came from her mouth. I saw her face take on a panicked look. She tried to raise one of her hands to her neck.

Shit, I thought. *She can't breathe. They better get here soon.*

I looked down at her and put on my best reassuring smile. "Our ride is almost here, Maria. Stay with me."

I made my way through a small gathering of tall cacti, taking care to ensure that I didn't accidentally brush Maria against any of the bristles. Finally, we found a group of three large rocks that lay on the edge of a clear area about thirty yards wide. The helo was very close now and I could hear the change in the sound of its blades as it transitioned from forward to vertical flight. The pilot was tracking the GPS coordinates of my phone. I looked into the night sky, and the NVGs showed me the rounded white and gray form of a UH-60 Blackhawk in the descent to hover.

I shook my head as I watched the aircraft come down to us. After five years of trying to avoid contact with the CIA and live a normal life, I was back in the middle of the action. The entire scenario tonight, from the encounter with the gangsters in my condo, through the flight south, the bombing, the ejection, the escape, the pursuit and now the rescue, seemed oddly normal. Disturbingly normal. Almost natural. A satisfied smile crept onto my face.

"Jesus," I said to myself. "I guess I did miss this shit."

The helo touched down in front of us and settled onto its wheels. The side door was open, and a crewman with a helmet and NVGs sat behind a mini-gun mounted on the forward end of the opening. He was scanning the area around and behind us. On the other side of the opening, another crewman held an M-4 in the ready position as he too studied the night. Between them, a familiar face appeared in my NVGs, a face I recognized even though I could only see an infrared image.

“Well, come on, Pearce,” Dave Smith said. “We haven’t got all fucking night.”

CHAPTER THIRTY-SIX

Wednesday, December 2nd
0355 Hours Local Time
300 feet and 170 Knots
Crossing the US-Mexico Border
30 Nautical Miles East of Nogales, Arizona

Maria was on a stretcher in the back of the Blackhawk's passenger compartment. A paramedic team was working on her furiously. I had my back to them, and I was not looking back there. I was in no mood see another woman die who had the misfortune of being in the same space I was.

I stared across the helo's interior at Operations Officer Dave Smith. He still had the same slim build, the same brown hair, and the same jade green eyes, but his face seemed harder than I had known it five years ago. Harder and older. I wondered what missions and/or events had happened since we had last worked together to make it so. Or maybe it was just the passage of time. We were approximately the same age, and the years hadn't been particularly kind to me either. We had been airborne for about ten minutes, and we were wearing headsets so we could easily converse, but so far silence had prevailed. It wasn't that I didn't want to talk. I just didn't know where to start.

Eventually, the words came to me.

"Looks like you were right about me," I said, looking at him. "I couldn't stay out of it."

He gave me a grim smile that was tainted with a tinge of sadness. "Actually," he said, "I was hoping you could, believe it or not." He looked over my shoulder at the paramedic, and his eyes grew distant. "It's difficult to get out of this line of work and make a clean break. You seemed like you had."

"You were keeping tabs on me all along."

He nodded. "Of course. You were an asset, and we're the CIA. It's what we do."

"I guess my false identity thing didn't fool you guys at all, did it?"

"Maybe for a few months. We knew you had swapped identities when you went off the grid. But we also knew you were stable and not looking for trouble. Finding you wasn't a priority, but we finally got to it. We only had to look as far as the FAA database. We knew you'd be flying."

"It is a bit of an addiction. I'm not sure what I'll do with myself the day that I can't get air under my ass anymore."

Smith nodded in response and smiled a second time, again with a tinge of sadness. He fixed his eyes on the floor between my feet. "But you didn't come back, Colin. We pulled you in. You probably figured that out by now.

I nodded as he spoke. "I did. I guess I don't understand the whole ruse with Sharona. You could have just asked."

Smith turned his hands palms up in a gesture of helplessness. "We had to observe you and question you in a way that wouldn't make you suspicious. For a while, we weren't sure exactly what Brooks was up to." He looked at me with a serious expression on his face. "I mean a former CIA operative with Ian's technology and closure record is out buying warplanes and weapons? And he happens to have a fighter pilot with your abilities working for him? We had to make sure you weren't in on it." He sighed. "The mechanism, or the play, if you will, was entirely Sharona's idea."

"Well, it worked. Obviously. I went for it. Hook, line and sinker."

He smiled. "John predicted that you would." John was John Amrine, Smith's partner.

"But now I am inside. I got inside, and I just bombed the shit out the cartel. Did you see that coming too?"

He nodded again. "We wanted that to happen. Once we understood what he was trying to do, we wanted him to continue it. The Los Diablos cartel changed their suppliers recently. They were getting their stuff from South America, but with all the unrest, the supply line became erratic, and the drugs became more expensive. The cartel found eager suppliers in countries that are state sponsors of terrorism, so their drug trade is funding groups like Hamas, ISIS, and Hezbollah, as well as several smaller, more radical groups."

"I guess I was aware that some of those countries were selling drugs to pay for terrorism, but I didn't realize the scale was so large."

Smith nodded.

"But you know that Ian doesn't give a shit about the whole terrorism thing. This is personal for him."

Smith nodded again. "The human trafficking thing is tragic," he said. "But we couldn't have allowed him to proceed without the terrorism angle. We would have had to stop him."

I eyed him. "My understanding is the last time you guys tried that it didn't work out well."

"His batteries aren't holding a charge very long these days," Smith said, looking away. "This time, we could probably outlast him."

"Probably?"

Smith shrugged in response.

I heard the noises of someone donning a headset. After a

moment or two, the paramedic spoke.

"She had a collapsed lung. That's why she couldn't talk. But we got a chest tube into her, and she's breathing just fine. She appears to be stable for the time being, but we need to get her to a hospital ASAP."

I nodded in response and turned to Smith, who was seated across from me. "Where are we going?" I asked.

"Davis-Monthan," he responded. "We've got an ambulance waiting to take her to the trauma center of the University of Arizona hospital."

I nodded again. "That will be handy," I said.

I saw Smith's eyebrows raise.

"We have to go back in and get Ian, Dave. He's alive. The guards were talking about chopping him up and selling his parts. The bad guys know something about what he is. Your personal feelings about the guy notwithstanding, I'm sure you don't want that technology falling into the wrong hands."

Smith was silent for a few moments and then nodded. "I never had a problem with Ian. I even worked with him a few times. He's a badass. Do you have any idea where they would take him?"

I shook my head and then motioned over my shoulder to Maria. "I don't. But she might."

"We've got another one of these birds on the ground at DM, along with a full assault team. We'll get the intel we need then go find him."

"You're going to need cover," I said. "They've got a ZSU 23-4 on the ground there. That's what took out both Ian and me."

Smith's eyes grew wide. "Damn," he said. "That's a bad-ass gun. And we don't have any more drone support with ordnance to use against it."

"We'll need to have a bigger gun to take it out. There's only one plane that's got one and DM is the schoolhouse."

Smith was nodding in agreement. He knew what I was going to say even before I uttered the words, but I said them anyway, just because I wanted to hear them.

"We need an A-10."

"Do you think you can still fly one of those things?"

I smiled at him. "Once a hog-driver, always a hog-driver."

CHAPTER THIRTY-SEVEN

Wednesday, December 2nd
0415 Hours Local Time
Base Operations
Davis-Monthan Air Force Base
Tucson, Arizona, USA

We touched down in front of the Base Operations building at Davis-Monthan Air Force Base about 20 minutes later. The vast expanse of pavement was practically empty. The only other transient aircraft at this end of the ramp was the other Blackhawk that Smith had mentioned.

As we had crossed the airfield boundary a few minutes earlier, at a few hundred feet, I had my first aerial look at the base in many years. Davis-Monthan had a long and storied history in the USAF. Named for two airmen who were Tucson natives and had died in separate aircraft crashes after World War I, the base had been a central training site for bomber crews during World War II. After the war ended, the base was allocated to the newly-formed Strategic Air Command and had been home to missile, bomber and tanker wings for several years until the base was transferred to what was then Tactical Air Command in 1976.

As I looked down at the configuration of the base, with

its single, long runway and the vast, rectangular ramp area that paralleled it, I was reminded of all the bomber bases I had seen in my flying career, either from the ground or from above as I had flown overhead. But DM had special meaning for me, as it did for all Hog Drivers. It was the home of the A-10 schoolhouse, and it was here that I had first flown the jet, way back in 1987.

After the Blackhawk's landing gear contacted the concrete on the ramp, the pilot took the load off the rotor disk, and the big helo settled onto its wheels. I glanced to my left and caught my breath at what I saw. There, at the north end of the ramp, were the A-10s of the 355th Fighter Wing, sitting in the darkness under their metal awnings. It had been over 20 years since I had seen so many A-10s at once. A lump rose in my throat, and I swallowed hard to subdue it.

The flash of lights from an emergency vehicle tore me from my reverie. An ambulance had driven onto the ramp and was pulling up to the right side of the Blackhawk. One of the aircraft's crewmen had opened the side door and was helping the paramedics unload Maria. I unfastened my safety belt and exited the helo as quickly as I could, leaving Smith behind me. My feet hit the ramp about the same time the medics moved Maria onto a gurney from the ambulance.

"Is she conscious? Can she talk?" I asked one of the medics.

The lead medic from the helo shrugged at me. He was a tall, slender man with black hair who looked barely old enough to drink, but his dark eyes were surprisingly world-weary. "She's been medicated," he said, sighing, "but she still appears to be conscious. I'm not sure if she can speak."

"I just need to ask her a quick question."

He motioned toward the gurney, and his fellow medics moved aside. I stepped forward and took Maria's right hand in mine and squeezed it. Her eyes opened lazily and fixed on me. I could see a small smile under the transparent plastic oxygen mask the medics had placed on her mouth and nose.

"They tell me you're going to make it," I said, smiling at her. "They must make you Border Patrol agents pretty tough."

She squeezed my hand weakly in response.

"Maria, we're going to need to go back down there and get my friend out. Do you have any idea where they would have taken him? We leveled the house and burned the warehouses, so they wouldn't have taken him there. Is there any other place you saw or heard about?"

For a second, I couldn't tell if she understood the question. The expression on her face appeared frozen, and her eyes seemed to look past me.

"Sir, we need to get her moving," the lead medic said. "She's stable, but she's not going to remain that way if we don't hurry."

I nodded in acknowledgment but kept my eyes on Maria's face. I could see an expression of helplessness creep over her features and my heart sank. She didn't know.

I squeezed her hand again and released it. Then I stepped back from the gurney and let the medics wheel her away.

"Damn," I said to myself. "Damn, damn, damn."

"Nothing, huh?" Smith said as he stepped up behind me.

I turned to him. "No. We'll have to wake up someone from the DEA, but they might not know either."

We began to walk toward the glass front doors of the Base Operations building. The desert air was surprisingly cool, and I could feel a slight chill on my skin. The adrenaline that had been fueling me for the past several hours was waning, and I could feel a combination of fatigue and hunger coming on.

"I don't know about you," I said to Smith, but I am in serious need of some coffee."

Smith wasn't listening to me. "We can't go get Ian if we don't know where the fuck they took him," he said. "We've got to get him out of there before..."

"I know," I said. "We need to get down there before they kill him."

"No," Smith answered, looking back at me. "We need to get down there before the failsafe device inside him detonates."

I froze and turned to Smith, my jaw was open, but my mouth wasn't working. Mental images of the final scene in the first Predator movie where the creature dies in a small mushroom cloud appeared in my brain.

Smith was looking back at me with an embarrassed expression on his face. I must have looked outraged or angry because he hurriedly raised his hands, palms toward me in a gesture of appeasement. "We didn't do that," he said. "The doctor who built him did. Something about making sure the technology wouldn't fall into the wrong hands."

"Jesus!" I said. Several thoughts and questions flew through my mind, but the most obvious one came out first. "He fucking knew that! He wanted them to catch him! He wanted to die! That's why he went down there without me!"

Smith shrugged. "Maybe. Ever since the cartel murdered his girlfriend and her daughter, he's had sort of a death wish."

"What is this damn thing and how is it triggered?" I asked.

"I don't have all the details," Smith answered, shaking his head. "But I know it is a small fission device – about the size of a man's shoe. It's embedded in his lower abdomen. It's triggered if the integrity of his system is suddenly interrupted and stays interrupted for several minutes."

"Like if someone takes him apart," I said, thinking aloud.

"Yes," Smith said, "There are a few other things that have to happen as well, but that's the gist of it. They can kill him, but if they disassemble him, the failsafe device will detonate, and we'll have a nuclear incident in Mexico. I'm not sure even we can cover that up."

"Well, I guess we better figure out where he is," I said.

"Sir!" One of the paramedics from the ambulance was

yelling and gesturing frantically at me.

I trotted over to him, and he motioned for me to get inside the ambulance. Maria had her eyes open and appeared to be quite agitated. She nodded when she saw me. The medics had removed her oxygen mask so she could speak. I took her right hand, and she pulled me down to her weakly. I turned my head so that my right ear was next to her mouth.

"Just remembered," she whispered. "Shelter."

"What?" I asked.

"Heard...them...talking...about...underground... shelter. They...were all...going there...before...bombing."

I nodded as she spoke. "Any idea where it is?"

She shook her head slightly and spoke again. "Must be close. They were walking...and...running to it."

I nodded again. My mind was racing. It would be just like a paranoid drug lord to have a place where he could hole up in the event of a police raid or more direct action. I wondered if the CIA could task a satellite to do a flyover and locate the shelter before we flew down there. I snapped out of my thoughts as I realized Maria had stopped talking.

"Hope...that...helps," she said.

"It sure does," I answered. "It helps a lot!" I tried to let go of her hand, but she held onto me and pulled me down to her. She raised her face slightly and brushed my cheek with her lips.

"Thanks...for...saving me," she said.

I squeezed her hand again. "I'm a contractor, ma'am. Comes with the service. No extra charge."

CHAPTER THIRTY-EIGHT

Wednesday, December 2nd
0435 Hours Local Time
Base Operations
Davis Monthan Air Force Base
Tucson, Arizona, USA

His name was Paul Preston. He was the Commander of the 355th Fighter Wing, and he was not happy.

Preston was a short man, maybe five feet five inches, with gray hair, gray eyes, and extremely white teeth. He had to continually look up to Smith, who was my height, while he spoke, and you could tell that irked the little man. I wondered if I looked up "Napoleon Complex" in the dictionary if I'd find his picture there. He seemed to be a living manifestation of the flaws in the USAF promotion system, where how one looked on paper made far more difference than how one performed. Another reason I was glad I was no longer in the military.

"If someone is going to fly one of my jets, it's going to be one of my pilots!" he had insisted. "Not," he motioned in my direction impatiently, "this...person."

We were in the conference room at Base Operations, the aircraft handling facility on every USAF base that deals with non-local aircraft. Dave Smith had made a call before we landed. The colonel had arrived 15 minutes after we walked into the building. He was wearing a wrinkle-free desert tan flight suit and boots so pristine they could have just come out of the box. It was apparent he didn't fly much. Real fighter pilots never looked that immaculate. The discussion had started with Smith introducing himself as a CIA operations officer and had gone downhill since then.

Smith studied the colonel for a moment and seemed to take a breath to steady himself. "Colonel," he began, "I've told you as much as I can. The clearance level for this mission is well above anyone on this base. Additionally, in the event something goes wrong, the US needs a degree of plausible deniability. Mr. Price," he gestured to me, "is a former A-10 pilot and a Fighter Weapons School graduate. But what's more important is that he works for us, not for you and not for the Air Force."

"So how is it that you and he get to commandeer one of my aircraft?" Preston had said, inching a little closer to Smith in the process. The two men were barely a foot apart. This was the fifth or sixth exchange between the two of them and the colonel had edged closer every time he spoke. I wondered if he thought it made him look taller.

I was leaning against the wall of the conference room, watching the two of them and shaking my head. Colonel Preston reeked of staff tours and paperwork. I wondered how much time he had spent behind a desk versus in operational positions. He was the complete opposite of Dave Smith who had lived his life in the field.

I had seen Smith interact with many different people in our previous associations. Usually, he was courteous to a fault and had the highest respect for military personnel, particularly USAF officers, since he was an Air Force Academy graduate himself.

Smith crossed his arms and smiled down at the colonel.

"Because," he said, "we're the CIA, and we get what we want."

"Who do you think you..."

Smith's phone rang, and he put his index finger to silence the colonel's next tirade as he answered. I could see Preston twitching with rage at the gesture. Smith listened for a moment, put the phone on speaker and turned it towards Preston. A deep voice came booming from the small speaker.

"PW, give him the fucking jet and get one of your star captains to give the pilot a crash course."

Preston was taken aback by the voice and the words. I assumed it was his boss, the 12th Air Force Commander, a two-star general, who also had a headquarters at the base. I wondered what the PW stood for.

"But sir, this is highly irregular..."

"Pee-wee, do you know who just called me? The Chairman of the Joint Chiefs. Not our chief of staff but the fucking Chairman of the JCS. In the middle of the fucking night. This is not fucking optional. Now, do you think I'm fucking kidding?"

"No sir, but..."

The general ignored him. "Get these guys over to the 357th. Now. Hook the pilot up with life support and the best IP you've got in the building. And if I get another call from the Chairman, you're going to be looking for a new fucking job in the morning. Copy?"

"Yes, general."

Smith put the phone back into his pocket and gave the colonel his best congenial smile. "So, Colonel Preston, where are we going?"

##

Ten minutes later we were walking into the doors of the 357th Fighter Squadron. There wasn't time to appreciate walking through the hallowed halls of a fighter squadron again, but I saw the usual fixtures that pulled the strings of nostalgia inside of me. Unit patches, unit photos, briefing rooms, and the ever-present squadron operations desk, which was coming to life a few hours before the first launch. My entire career flying fighters in the USAF went through my mind's eye in a flash. I felt a tug inside of me and the sting of a tear in my eye.

The squadron operations supervisor greeted us as we stopped in front of the desk. He was a major like I had once been, only he looked impossibly young. He had close-cropped prematurely gray hair, blue eyes, and an athletic build. I watched his eyes take in the three of us: the wing commander in his regulation flight suit and perfect boots, Smith in full black tactical gear with an assortment of weapons strapped to his body, and the smelly old guy in the dirty flight suit and dusty boots with a .45 automatic under his arm. He looked us over, and I could see the cogs turning behind his eyes, but his face stayed utterly impassive.

"Colonel Preston, gentlemen," he said as he raised a mug of steaming coffee to his lips, "what can I do for you?"

Preston and Smith didn't answer his question. Instead, they both turned their heads and looked at me. The supervisor followed their gaze, and our eyes met. In a millisecond, the unspoken communication that happens between fighter pilots occurred between us, and he nodded at me.

I stepped forward and spoke. "We need to send two helos into a hostile LZ tonight to rescue a high-value asset, and I need to escort them," I said. "In one of your jets."

The supervisor considered my words, but it was clear that he didn't have quite enough information to convince him. He looked at me and sipped his coffee.

The wing commander stepped forward, a tight but impatient expression on his face. His mouth opened but the supervisor kept his gaze on me, wanting more. I smiled at him. We understood each other.

"I was a Hog-driver in a former life, and I was a Sandy One in combat...a while ago," I said. "So, I've had a bit of practice at this. Oh, and a ZSU 23-4 is guarding the LZ. I need to take it out."

The supervisor gave me a knowing smile and the conversation was over.

The life-support fitting didn't take long. Once the technician saw that I was familiar with the helmet, harness and anti-g suit, it was just a matter of him tightening straps. He did make an observation as he was tucking away the excess straps.

"You're bleeding sir," he said, pointing to the right side of my flightsuit, just above the waist.

I looked down to see a red stain there and remembered the pinch I had felt when the shooter in the pickup truck had opened fire on Maria and me. There was also a small bullet hole in my flightsuit, right in the middle of the stain. A bullet had grazed me, and I had forgotten all about it.

"It's just a flesh wound," I said in my best British accent.

The technician looked at me blankly and raised his eyebrows.

"Monty Python?" I asked. "Holy Grail?"

The sergeant shook his head.

"Oh well," I said. "Before your time I guess."

After I completed donning my life support gear, I was led to the mission planning room and introduced to a young captain who was to be my instructor and escort. He was just a few inches shorter than I was and had a stocky build. He had fine blond hair, intense green eyes, and a quick, nervous smile.

"Mike Mangus," he said, throwing his hand out at me as I entered the room. "I go by Mung."

"Connor Price," I replied as I shook his hand. I felt

comfortable using my pseudonym since I was pretty sure I was going to have to do away with it after this excursion was over. "And I can't tell you what I go by because if I did, you might be able to find out my real name."

I sensed the presence of both Smith and the operations supervisor behind me. Colonel Preston seemed to have left the premises. I wondered if he had some paperwork calling to him.

I looked around the mission planning room, and it reminded me of all the others I had seen - large flat map tables and several desktop computers on a table at the far end. But next to the computers was a row of data transfer cartridges, stored in a rack against the wall to my left.

"DTCs?" I asked. "Like the Viper? Back in my day in the Hog, we would have considered that blasphemy."

Mung nodded and gave me a toothy smile. "Different day, sir."

"So, you're going to load waypoints and a navigation route into the DTC, so I can load them into the jet, right?"

Mung nodded again. "Along with a terrain and full waypoint data base, map display, threat information and a lot of other stuff. Pretty much whatever you want."

I turned to Smith. "For him to load the route, he's going to need to know where we're going. Are you okay with that?"

Smith nodded.

"I'm thinking of using the site where the house used to be as a reference."

Smith nodded again.

I turned back to Mangus. "Okay Mung, let's get in front of one of these computers, and I'll show you where we're going."

Mung nodded back at me. "What ordnance are you going to be carrying, sir?"

I looked at the operations supervisor.

He took his coffee mug down from his mouth. "Full load of

30mm TP and nothing else," he said. "It's the best we can do on short notice. We're not dropping lives this week, so none of the jets are configured with munitions."

"TP should be just fine against a ZSU," I said. "It's pretty lightly armored. Plus, we won't be leaving any of that telltale depleted uranium on the ground down there. It'll make it a little more difficult for the Federales to figure out what happened."

Smith nodded. "Good call," he said.

##

Fifteen minutes after that, I was strapped into an A-10C with the APU running. I had my helmet on, and Mangus was wearing a headset that plugged into the jet's intercom system. He was giving me the rundown on the upgraded cockpit and doing his best to explain how everything worked. I wanted to take it all in and learn as much as I could, but there wasn't time.

"Mung," I had said, interrupting him as politely as I could. "This is cool stuff, and I'd love to hear it all. But I've got a colleague about 120 miles south of here who is going to die unless I get this thing in the air and get to him as soon as possible. I can fly this jet. I really only need two things from you."

He looked like I had taken the wind out of his sails, but he nodded slowly at me.

"Show me how to get to where I'm going and how to turn the gun on. I'll figure out the rest."

CHAPTER THIRTY-NINE

Wednesday, December 2nd
0530 Hours Local Time
500 feet and 300 Knots
10 miles north of the US-Mexico Border
30 Nautical Miles Southwest of Tucson, Arizona

Time is a strange thing.

I was back in the mighty Hog, throttles parked in MILITARY power, watching the rugged terrain go by in the NVGs mounted on my helmet. I had a rough navigation route programmed into the jet's avionics, and I was following it to the extent I could at 500 feet. I maneuvered the jet around obstacles like hills, rocks, and the occasional mountain instead of climbing to clear them. Once I was past the obstacles, I corrected back to the route. And it all felt incredibly normal. Like I had never left the airplane.

The last time I had flown the Hog had been my end-of-tour flight at England Air Force Base, Louisiana in the spring of 1992. I remembered the sortie like it was yesterday. I had led a four-ship of A-10s on a short low-level navigation route, and then we had gone to the Claiborne gunnery range because the one thing all Hog-drivers live for is shooting the gun and dropping bombs. We dropped 9 BDU-33 practice bombs in various events and finished with the king of all gunnery events, low angle strafe using the A-10's GAU-8 30mm cannon. I could remember the names of the guys I had flown with, the weather conditions of the day, and even the radio calls we made as we came back into the traffic pattern for my final landing in the aircraft.

Now it was over 23 years later, but I felt at home in the roomy cockpit and had a lump in my throat that I couldn't quite explain. There's something about the Hog, or Hawg as we used to pronounce it, that endears it to the pilots that fly it. Part of that is about the mission, supporting engaged ground forces and bringing death from above to all who oppose them. But the other part of it is the jet itself. It's big. It's ugly. It's slow. And it's underpowered. But it can turn on a dime, carry 16,000 pounds of ordnance and, best of all, has the most lethal airborne gun system ever devised.

Most of my time in the Hog was during the Cold War, flying all over the U.K. and what was then West Germany, at 250 to 500 feet, practicing for the war that we all hoped would never come. Then there was Gulf War 1, where we had flown at medium to high altitude, except those of us who flew in the combat search and rescue or CSAR role. As a Sandy One, a CSAR flight lead, I spent a good portion of the war protecting helicopters that were performing rescue missions to retrieve downed pilots. It had been perhaps the most important flying I had done in the military and had even gotten me shot down once.

And here I was again. Doing the same thing. Twenty-three years later.

The technology in the jet had changed significantly since I last flew it. The cockpit functionality was more like the F-16 than the Hog I flew back in the day. The control stick looked like it had been taken from the Viper with the target management, display management, and countermeasures switches. The front panel of the jet had changed markedly. Gone was the large stores management panel and the monochrome TV display for the AGM-65 Maverick missile. Twin color multifunction displays now dominated the front panel and provided navigation information, complete with threat plots and targets as well as tactical communications, data links, stores management, and a host of other functions.

Even with the limited instruction I had received from young Captain Mangus, I found the avionics in the jet very intuitive thanks to my time in the Viper and my brief foray in the F-35. The two displays were like the ones I had in the Viper only these were color and had more functionality. I could call up anything I needed with the option select buttons, and toggle between the different display modes with the display management switch or DMS located on the control stick. Between the way the jet flew and the functionality of the cockpit, it all felt absurdly familiar.

At the moment, I had a tactical awareness display or TAD displayed on the left MFCD. The TAD provided navigation and threat information and was loaded with an overlay of the route to Pitiquito. Every hill, valley, town, road and other terrain feature was displayed clearly. On the right MFCD, I had the digital stores management system selected, and it indicated that the other thing loaded on the aircraft was 1,150 rounds of 30mm target practice ammunition. I needed to have the rounds counter displayed so I could keep track of how many bullets I had left. The GAU-8 fired at a rate of about 3,900 rounds per minute, about 65 bullets per second. The 1,150 rounds provided about 18 seconds of trigger time and I was going to need to make every second count.

I was enjoying the feel of the aircraft in my hands. I had forgotten how nimble the big jet was and how keenly it responded to my control inputs. Both the Viper and OV had been responsive in their own right, but the Hog, with its conventional hydraulic flight control system and long, straight wings, was different. It was like having the reins of an eager horse in my hand, ready to spring in the direction I wanted, the moment I desired to go there. I was having flashbacks to my time flying over Europe and Louisiana, and every time I banked up to turn the jet, a flood of wonderful memories was pouring into my brain. I couldn't wipe the smile off my face.

The USAF NVGs were superb in their rendering of the earth's surface in the mild light of the stars and radiant energy in the terrain, even better than the NVGs I had in the OV. Making my way along the route thus far had been easy. I hoped my luck would hold once I got south of the border.

My maneuvering notwithstanding, I was on time to make the rendezvous with the helos on the north side of a range of hills above Pitiquito. They had departed Davis-Monthan before I did, partially due to their slower speed but also because they didn't need a course of instruction about operating their aircraft.

The US-Mexico border went under the nose of the aircraft and then disappeared behind me, much more prominent on the map display than it had been on the actual terrain. I shook my head as it went by.

"Maybe we do need a wall," I said to myself.

I glanced down at the map display and then up through the HUD to survey the land in front of me. I was at the mouth of a long valley that would take me all the way to the town of Altar and then southeast to the cartel's headquarters.

Our attack plan had changed, and it was risky. Initially, we had thought that I'd go in first, locate and neutralize the ZSU. Then, the helos would ingress, engage, and make the pickup with me providing air cover. But no one consulted the sun when we conceived that plan, and it was not going to cooperate. Dawn would break at 0540 hours this morning, and sunrise would occur at 0705. Sometime during that interval, the two helicopters and my A-10 would become visible to observers on the ground, and we wouldn't be able to predict exactly when. Time had been a significant factor, to begin with. Now, with the cover of the night waning, time was critical.

We decided to go in simultaneously, the helos from the south and me from the north, and chance that the ZSU wasn't manned and ready for us. It had been several hours since the last air strike, and the bad guys had no reason to expect another, so it seemed reasonable the ZSU crew would not be in their vehicle and actively scanning the sky when we appeared. We hoped the sudden arrival of two helos and some well-placed 30mm might startle the bad guys enough to allow the ops team to disembark and accomplish their mission, while I found the ZSU and destroyed it.

It seemed like a feasible plan when we had thrown it together in the 357th's mission planning room. Now, as I flew the A-10 towards our rendezvous, I found myself doubting it. I called up the MESSAGE page on the right MFCD and ensured the text message that young Captain Mangus had preloaded was still there. FIVE MINUTES was displayed in the message grid, and the address for Smith's helo remained in the appropriate line. I nodded to myself. When the five-minute point came, I'd send the message, and the fun would start.

As I continued south, I tried to construct a mental model of the terrain around the cartel headquarters based on the maps I had studied, and the raid we had conducted earlier. I knew the valley was roughly V-shaped, with ridgelines comprising the arms of the V and the open end to the north, facing the town of Pitiquito. Based on Maria's information about the location of the cartel's shelter, and some satellite imagery that Smith had procured, we believed the underground facility was near the base of the V, close to the intersection of two unimproved roads. I was betting that the ZSU was parked nearby. If the ZSU came up before I was able to neutralize it, the gun's location and the configuration of the terrain were going to limit my avenues of attack. Attacking from the south was out because Pitiquito would be in the background and stray bullets could find their way into the town and kill innocents. Attacking from the east or the west were possibilities, and I could use the terrain for cover until the last minute, but I'd have to pop up, acquire the ZSU, pull down, roll-out and shoot. Popping up would highlight me to the radar, and while I was pulling my nose to the target, the ZSU could get its radar locked, compute a firing solution and engage me. Attacking from the north would be the best axis for me and would give me the opportunity to take a long-range shot at the ZSU, using the A-10's CCIP gunsight, outside of the ZSU's maximum range, but I had to be able to see it to engage it. If I pressed the attack too long, I'd enter the ZSU's envelope as a non-maneuvering target, and the gunner would have plenty of time to see me coming, get his radar locked on, and put rounds into the air and into my jet.

Shit, I thought as I flew south into the night, *if that damn thing comes up, how in the hell am I going to take it out?*

I glanced at the HUD and saw 05+15 in the time remaining display. I put my left finger over the OSB next to SEND and at 05+05 remaining, I punched the button.

ROGER. INBOUND. Came the reply in mere seconds. I nodded to myself. We were on.

I saw the meager lights of the small town of Altar ahead of me and remembered Maria and I driving by there earlier in the evening, hours ago. It felt like days had passed. I selected the DSMS option for the right MFCD, and the 30mm rounds counter reappeared. Then I moved my hand to the panel beneath the display and toggled the two topmost switches upward. Directly in front of my eyes, under the base of the

HUD, a light came on that I had not seen in 23 years. GUN READY, it said. An involuntary grin stretched the edges of my mouth.

In the HUD, the continuously computed impact point, or CCIP, gun reticle appeared in the upper portion of the display. It was a circle 50 milliradians or mils in diameter and 25 mils in radius. At the center, was the one-mil pipper, affectionately known as the 'death dot.' When the system ranged in, 30mm bullets would go through the center of the pipper and into any unfortunate target that lay underneath it.

Young Captain Mangus had tried to talk me out of using the reticle. "No one uses that anymore," he said. "They use the CCIP gun cross instead. That's what the jet defaults to."

"Just tell me how to get the reticle, Mung," I had said. "It's the last thing I remember from flying the Hog back in the day."

He had begrudgingly agreed.

Now I glanced to the lower left portion of the HUD, and I saw TP/1150. I smiled and shook my head in wonder.

"Jesus," I said. "That's handy."

The rounds counter in the HUD explained why young Captain Mangus had been perplexed by my insistence on displaying the DSMS in the right MFCD. It was a waste of the display.

"Oh well," I said to myself. "Live and learn and all that."

I reached the final turn point and banked the A-10 up to the right. I allowed the nose to float around the turn so that I could maintain my airspeed and waited the few seconds for the nose to settle onto a southwesterly heading. Once I had rolled out, I pushed the nose over a bit. It was time to get down to 100 feet and get dirty.

The Altar municipality went down the left side of my aircraft, and the few lights of Pitiquito appeared just to the right of the nose. The starlight remained bright and unimpeded by clouds, so the light gathering capability of the NVGs rendered the terrain ahead perfectly. The passive infrared energy emitted by the hills, rocks and desert floor provided additional depth to the picture, and it was easy to find a comfortable place close to the earth where I could let the Hog settle in.

The Hog had always been a very stable jet in the very low altitude environment. Between its slower airspeed, size, weight, and its straight, thick wings, the jet seemed content close to the ground. I eyed the radar altimeter display on the lower right side of the HUD and kept it between 100R and 150R. Any lower than 100 feet radar altitude and the Hog's ground collision avoidance system or GCAS would bitch at me.

Mexico's Highway 2 went under the nose, with no vehicles in sight for miles. It seemed a lonely morning in Sonora. Directly in front of me, I could see the square outlines of a group of farm fields, and beyond the fields, a finger of rocks that represented the northmost end of the eastern ridge of the target valley. I'd be actioning in mere moments.

"Tango Charlie, Delta Sierra is 1 minute out." Smith's said on the FM intraflight frequency.

I pushed the mic switch on the right throttle upward to respond. "Tango Charlie copies. I'll be up and in just before then. I'll roll in from the northeast and come off to the northwest."

"Delta Sierra copies."

"You seeing any AAA radar, Delta Sierra?" I asked.

"Delta Sierra negative."

I nodded to myself and smiled grimly under my oxygen mask. If the ZSU was up and its radar was scanning, it would detect the helos before it would see me. Maybe we were going to get lucky tonight. Maybe we would catch them unaware.

The ridgeline loomed in my forward vision. I banked the Hog up to the right and pulled the nose through about 45 degrees of turn.

"One thousand one, one thousand two, one thousand three," I said.

I pulled the A-10's control stick backward and settled the flight path marker at about 20 degrees of pitch. The jet shot skyward, leaving the sanctuary of low altitude and the cover of the rocky terrain behind.

I looked to my left and beheld the destruction we had wrought on the valley earlier that evening. The enormous main house had been reduced to a pile of rubble enshrouded in a cloud of lingering dust. Further south, the five rectangular warehouses were still smoldering from the napalm I had dispensed on them earlier. The entire warehouse area was bathed in a dull white, infrared glow in the NVGs and there were spots in the middle of the area that showed as intense white heat. Apparently, some of the jellied gasoline was still burning.

I rolled the A-10 onto its back and gently eased its nose down to earth, trying to float the vertical turn so that I could commit my nose on a possible target if I detected one. I continued to scan the valley, looking further southward to see any indication of the shelter's location or the position of the ZSU. Just beyond the southern end of the valley, my NVGs picked up the glow of the two helos, headed into the area at high speed. Our timing for the rendezvous seemed to have worked perfectly.

But the entire target area was strangely quiet. No vehicles were moving, no personnel were darting about, and no muzzle flashes or other indications of hostile fire were visible. The place was empty - no bad guys, no ZSU but most importantly, no Ian.

I shook my head in frustration. "Fuck!" I screamed into my oxygen mask.

But then, a particular sound seeped into my ears. It was

a sound generated by the A-10's ALR-69 radar homing and warning gear. A sound that I had heard earlier in the evening and had dreaded. But now, it was a sound that I was relieved to hear – a sound I almost welcomed.

ZZZZIT. ZZZZIT. ZZZZIT.

It was the sound of the GUN DISH radar, in acquisition mode, but it was very faint. I glanced at the ALR-69's azimuth indicator, next to the left MFCD. An A with three dots underneath it, the symbol for the GUN DISH, was blinking on the small scope, on an azimuth that placed it due south of here.

"Tango Charlie, Delta Sierra, we're not seeing anyone down here." The frustration in Dave Smith's voice was audible over the FM radio waves.

I keyed my mic to respond.

"That's because they're running, Delta Sierra. They're running south. You guys have the gas to follow them?"

"I'll have to get authorization," Smith said.

"You go ahead and do that," I said as I leveled the A-10 and put the GUN DISH symbol on the nose. "I'm going after those fuckers. I'll try to get them stopped for you."

"But you don't have authorization!"

"I don't need it," I replied while I checked the throttles in MIL and peered through the HUD to find the convoy of vehicles that I was sure was out there. "You've got plausible deniability. Remember?"

CHAPTER FORTY

Wednesday, December 2nd
0545 Hours Local Time
500 feet and 300 Knots
Somewhere South of the Pitiquito Municipality
Sonora, Mexico

It was one thing to hunt a ZSU 23-4. It was quite another to chase one. Especially when both of us were out in the open.

I was pursuing a convoy down an unimproved dirt road that ran down the middle of a wide valley. The road had exited the smaller valley where the cartel's main complex was, wound its way through a few smaller hills, then south into this larger valley. There was no terrain to hide behind for a few miles on either side of the road, so both the ZSU and I would be totally out in the open when the time came to engage each other. And since I was closing the distance between it and me by about four miles per minute, that time was coming soon.

Already, the radar tone in my headset had gone from intermittent to steady, although I could tell the gunner hadn't gone into target tracking mode yet. He was still keeping his eyes open for other possible intruders. Maybe he didn't know who or what I was, or whether I was a threat. It didn't matter. As the blip that represented my aircraft continued to march right down the center of his radar scope towards him, all would become clear to him before long.

I was only 500 feet above the ground, but I could see the first rays of the dawn sun creeping over the eastern horizon. Our time was running out. The more visible we became, the higher the risk that someone with a cell phone would take a video that would go viral and with all the recent talk about border security, the last thing the US government needed was a movie showing a US A-10 attacking ground targets well south of the national demarcation line.

"Tango Charlie, Delta Sierra, are you contact the convoy yet?"

I keyed my mic to respond. "Negative, but it won't be long. The radar strength is growing stronger."

"We're airborne behind you. We can continue the mission until 0615 local then we have to abort to maintain night cover."

I nodded to myself. "Copy that," I responded.

I peered ahead, through the HUD, and into the darkness of the valley beyond. It was evident that the vehicles ahead of me were driving with their lights off otherwise they would have been easily discernible by now. I was hoping that the NVGs would be able to pick up the IR signatures of the vehicles, but they seemed to be too small and too far ahead. I knew the ZSU was the limiting factor in their journey southward. It was mobile, but it could only move at about 30 miles per hour or so.

"I wonder where the hell they think they're going?" I asked myself.

The radar tone in my headset changed abruptly, and the familiar sound of the GUN DISH in target tracking mode filled my ears. I scoured my alcohol-soaked brain cells for any nuggets of ZSU knowledge that might be embedded there and was pleased to find the number I was looking for after only a few moments.

I keyed my mic. "Delta Sierra, Tango Charlie. The ZSU just went into target track. They're about six miles ahead of me. I'll be on them in about a minute and a half."

"Copy," Smith responded. "What's your plan?"

I snorted into my oxygen mask. "Good fucking question, Dave," I said to myself.

"Any chance you can by-pass the ZSU and get the lead vehicle? Stop the convoy?"

I didn't answer. Smith's question was a logical one. I just wasn't sure how I could get a shot at the lead vehicle without taking fire from the ZSU. To make matters more complicated, I wouldn't be able to take the ZSU out preemptively. The ZSU was probably the last vehicle in the convoy. I couldn't shoot at it and risk hitting Ian who would undoubtedly be in one of the vehicles further up.

"Damn," I said to myself. "I can't fucking kill it, and I can't get past it without probably getting killed." The irony was that the A-10 typically carried several types of ordnance that could accomplish the task at hand with no risk to either Ian or me. But none of them were loaded on the jet. It was just me and 1,150 rounds of 30mm TP ammo.

But as I peered ahead, the NVGs showed me something I wasn't counting on, and I allowed myself a moment of hope. Just ahead, the valley narrowed, and there was some rocky terrain on the western side. I glanced at the map display and nodded to myself.

"That will have to do," I said.

At that moment, I saw the fiery four-fingered rectangle of death emerge into the night sky. The ZSU gunner was firing at me. The bullets traveled at about 3,000 feet per second from the muzzle, so I was still far enough away that the time-of-flight was 5-6 seconds and I could easily avoid them. But the ZSU gunner's message was clear.

I know you're there, he seemed to be saying. *And I'm*

going to kill you if you get any closer.

"Fight's on pal," I said into the intercom.

I banked hard to the right and pulled the Hog's nose through about 35 degrees of turn. Then I pushed the stick forward to descend. I looked at the TAD on the left MFCD again. The rocky terrain I had seen was two, nearly parallel lines of small hills that parted and created a swale leading away from the road and down to a small lake. The hills would provide me both cover and concealment from the main road. Assuming the map was accurate, I'd have some turning room at low altitude to get my nose pointed at the road and onto the convoy. If I didn't run into the ground first.

I leveled at 100 feet and focused on the terrain ahead of me. I guided the jet between two small hills and followed a very narrow road or trail that would lead down to the lake. In the NVGs, it appeared as a thin, gray line, that seemed to be barely wide enough for a vehicle.

As the hills rose around the aircraft, the ZSU symbol vanished from the threat display, and my headset went silent. The radar lock was broken. I smiled under the oxygen mask as I imagined the ZSU crew frantically trying to reacquire me.

My brief excursion into very low altitude operations earlier had been over flat terrain. That had been relatively benign. But this terrain had more hills, arroyos, and rocks. It was quite a bit more challenging. In a fighter cockpit, there are myriad mission tasks that must be accomplished and often, the act of flying the aircraft takes place in the background. At 100 feet, over harsh terrain, with no autopilot or terrain-following radar to assist, all the pilot has time to do is fly the aircraft. No other tasks are possible. As I flew across the rugged ground at about 500 feet per second, just over one wing span's distance from the earth, I kept my eyes on the terrain ahead and my hands poised on the controls. A moment's distraction or inattention would mean disaster.

A small lake appeared in the NVGs before me, visible as an irregular black shape, just barely discernible using the low-light feature of the googles. Beyond it, I could see what appeared to be farm fields or irrigated land of some sort. It went under the nose, and I banked the A-10 up to the left and began a 3g level turn to the southeast. After clearing my flight path, I watched the symbology in the HUD carefully, making sure that the flight path marker stayed on or just above the horizon line. I rolled out a few seconds later, just south of a ridgeline that proceeded to the southeast and would offer cover and concealment as I re-approached the convoy from its right flank.

The terrain underneath me began to rise, and I applied very slight backpressure to the Hog's control stick to stay parallel with the earth but remain below the crest of the ridge just off my left wingtip. As I looked ahead, I could see the ridge on my left, merging with some terrain coming from the right. Even in the low light of early morning, the IR tones in the various strata of rock were visible. I knew the road was less than a mile from where the two ridges merged and I dreaded having to pop-up over the terrain to find the convoy and shoot, knowing it would expose me to the ZSU's radar and guns, well inside the lethal envelope of the system.

But there seemed to be no other choice. The convoy had to be stopped. I forced my mind into the usual compartments and verified the GUN READY light was still illuminated.

"Oh well," I said to myself. "I didn't want to live forever anyway."

But the universe smiled on me then. As I approached the point where the two ridgelines merged, a huge notch appeared in the rising terrain to my right. Without thinking, I banked the Hog up to the right, pulled the nose to the middle of the notch and rolled out. The Hog shot through the gap in the rocks in seconds. As soon as the ridgeline went behind me, I pulled the nose around to the left and paralleled it. Ahead of me, where the hills went down, and the terrain flattened, I could see the wide gray trough of the main road, about 5,000 feet away. The road extended for several miles to my right, and there were no vehicles visible, so they had to be coming from the left.

And then, as if on cue, a vehicle emerged from behind the ridgeline on my left and appeared on the road in front of me. Followed by another, then another and then a fourth one, and at the tail end of the convoy, the distinct profile of the ZSU 23-4.

At 500 feet per second, there wasn't much time to think. I banked to the right and moved the CCIP gun reticle to the lead vehicle. Since the vehicle was moving, I didn't center the pipper on it. Instead, I put the left moving target indicator on the middle of the vehicle, to allow lead for its motion, and I pulled the trigger. Beneath my feet, the GAU-8 Avenger 30mm cannon came to life, and 30mm bullets exited the weapon at 3,000 feet per second, headed toward a thin-skinned target that was just over one time-of-flight away. And for the first time in 23 years, I heard the sound that all Hog-Drivers live for, the mechanical roar of the gun.

BRRRRRRRRRRTT.

I released the trigger and recovered from the gun pass, applying about 4g's to the jet as I climbed away from the ground. Almost instantaneously, I heard the ZZZZIT of the GUN DISH radar in search mode, followed closely by the transition to target tracking mode. Bullets would be on their way in seconds, and I was in the real-time envelope of the gun. There was only one maneuver applicable in this environment, and I executed it like I had practiced it yesterday. I continued the aggressive move into the vertical, and as soon as the vector was fully established, I rolled the aircraft over to 135 degrees of bank, nearly inverted, and pulled the jet back down to the earth. Even as the nose began to move downward, a rectangle of anti-aircraft fire went underneath the belly of the Hog, perforating the air where my jet would have been if I hadn't changed its direction.

I glanced down at the convoy and saw the lead vehicle had been decimated by the bullets and had exploded. I was puzzled at that, given the TP bullets had no explosive charge. But there was no time to relish the kill.

I immediately rolled the Hog to wings level, broke the descent and pulled into the vertical again. Another stream of fiery death went underneath me.

"Jesus," I said to myself, "this guy is good."

I had to jink downward again, and the only two choices were to the left, where the terrain was flat, and there was little to hide behind, or to the right, where I might be able to get behind some hills or rocks. The choice was obvious to me, and I was betting it was apparent to the gunner as well. I unloaded the jet, rolled to the left and pulled downward. Four fingers of fire lanced through the air to where I would have been had I pulled to the right, and as I got the nose of the aircraft started downward, I did the one maneuver that was forbidden in the Hog at low altitude. I pushed forward on the stick to unload the aircraft, cracked the speed brakes to increase the roll rate and rolled underneath to the opposite direction, back toward the higher terrain to the west. The big jet pirouetted in midair like a ballerina, and as soon as my lift vector was oriented in a direction that wouldn't take me into the rocks, I pulled back on the stick for all I was worth and closed the speed brakes. The jet changed direction, and in a scant few seconds, I was back at 100 feet and safely hidden behind a small ridgeline, with another fiery trail of bullets streaking across the top of my canopy to remind me that I had again only cheated death by milliseconds.

I exhaled in relief as I followed the terrain to the west. I could feel sweat across my brow and down the center of my back.

"Where the fuck did they get these guys?" I asked myself.

"Tango Charlie, Delta Sierra," Dave Smith's voice was barely audible over the FM radio. My low altitude was interfering with the radio transmission.

I pulled back on the stick slightly and allowed the Hog to climb a few hundred feet. Then I keyed my mic. "Delta Sierra, this is Tango Charlie, go ahead."

"We're holding about three miles north. Say status."

"I got bullets into the lead vehicle and stopped it. But the ZSU is still up, and the crew is proficient."

"Copy ZSU still up. What's the play?"

Our options were limited. With its CCIP gunsight, the A-10's GAU-8 could destroy the ZSU outside of its maximum effective range, but because of the terrain, I couldn't get line of sight with the ZSU without increasing my altitude significantly and risking detection by Mexican Air Defense or Air Traffic Control. I had to remain at low-attitude, and that required me to engage the enemy at close range.

The ridgeline next to me descended into a shallow valley with a dry creek bed at the center of it. I eased the Hog into a turn to the north and flew just over the creek. The ridge I had just left behind was the southernmost of a series of three rock formations that resembled the crooked fingers of a decayed hand, reaching out to ensnare unsuspecting passersby.

I shook off the macabre imagery and pulled the Hog's throttles back, allowing the big jet to slow a bit as I gathered my thoughts. The helos were well inside the GUN DISH's acquisition and tracking range, so it was a sure bet that the ZSU crew knew the helos were there. The crew would have to assume the helicopters were carrying Hellfire missiles or the like. Now they had multiple threats to consider.

"Delta Sierra, Tango Charlie, I presume those helos have

radar warning gear?"

"Affirmative," Smith replied.

I nodded to myself and keyed the mic. We discussed the plan, and then Smith briefed the helo drivers.

"They're ready," he said a few moments later.

"Roger that," I replied. I shoved the Hog's throttles to MIL and pushed the stick forward to descend to lower altitude. "Tell them to start inbound."

"Roger," Smith said. "Headed inbound now."

I had turned into a slow 360-degree turn south of the lake I had crossed earlier while Smith and I discussed our attack plan. Now, as I prepared to exit my orbit, I suddenly felt a series of vibrations underneath my butt. Clunk-clunk, clunk-clunk, clunk-clunk. The gun was rotating. For a moment, I was startled. But then, my mind remembered what was happening and I smiled. The gun was cooling itself. Between firings, the gun rotated to allow cooling air equal access to all seven barrels.

I nodded to myself and eased the Hog's nose around to the southeast, rolling out along the same ridgeline that I paralleled for my first ingress. The rays of the morning sun were growing brighter now, and the only portions of the landscape that were staying shrouded in darkness were the valleys. Once again, time wasn't on our side. The only way our hastily-conceived plan would work was if the ZSU was forced into a radar tracking mode due to the environmental conditions.

"Tango Charlie, Delta Sierra is Dirt on the triple-A."

I nodded to myself. Dirt was an armed forces brevity code word which meant that the radar warning gear on the helos was detecting the GUN DISH radar in search mode.

"Copy Dirt," I replied.

The ZSU's maximum effective range, with radar guidance, was about 1.6 nautical miles. Once the helos came inside of two miles, the ZSU gunner would start throwing bullets their way. When helos didn't shoot back, the ZSU crew would know they weren't armed. We had to keep them confused in the meantime. I continued down the ridgeline and kept the Hog at 500 feet waiting for the cue I knew would come.

"Sierra Delta is Mud."

Mud was the brevity code that meant the GUN DISH had locked onto the helos, was in target tracking mode, but hadn't opened fire yet.

"Copy that," I answered. "Tango Charlie is up and in."

I banked the Hog to the left and pulled the nose toward the ridgeline to build a little turning room, and then pulled back on the control stick and sent the Hog skyward. As soon as the upward vector was established, I rolled the big jet into 135 degrees of right bank and looked out of the top of the canopy to find the convoy and the ZSU.

Initially, as I strained my eyes to find the convoy, the sun's rays washed out the NVGs and depicted the landscape below me as a harsh, white fuzz. But then, as my nose came through the horizon and blocked the sun, the NVGs adjusted to the darkness of the lower valley and rendered the scene below in the usual clarity. My eyes found the gray line of the main road and followed the road to the convoy and the ZSU.

The ZSU has an optical tracking capability that features a periscope mounted in the top of the turret and a window in the front of the turret. But the field of view through both is extremely limited, and I was betting that the ZSU crew wasn't relying solely on them for optical acquisition, especially with multiple hostile aircraft stalking them.

I was about one mile from the ZSU as I began my roll out. I wasn't committing my nose to him, but I wanted him to think I was. I strained my eyes to see detail in the top of the turret, and I saw the upper torso of a person, sitting in the hatch on top of the ZSU and scanning the horizon with binoculars. As soon as I noticed him, I could see movement from him as he seemed to motion frantically to his fellow crewmembers inside the turret.

"Delta Sierra is Naked," Smith's voice said in my ear a second later.

I nodded to myself and smiled. An odd choice of words in a normal conversation but in this case, they were the words I was expecting. Smith had just told me that the GUN DISH had broken radar lock with their aircraft and wasn't looking for them any longer. As the familiar sound of the radar in target tracking mode filled my headset, I aggressively pulled the nose of the A-10 down and to the right and away from the convoy, aiming for a cleft between two of the ridgelines in the fingers I had seen earlier.

"Tango Charlie is Mud," I said.

As my nose tracked down, I caught a glimpse of something bright and fiery and realized that another burst of 23mm fire had just missed my jet. Again.

I broke the A-10's descent at 100 feet. My headset was silent. I took another deep breath. Our luck was holding.

'Tango Charlie is Naked," I said.

"Delta Sierra is Dirt," Smith's voice intoned.

"Time for round two," I said to myself. "And you won't be so quick to go into target tracking mode this time, will you pal?"

I began a slow right turn to the north and allowed the Hog to climb a bit. I glanced down at my fuel totalizer. I had about 5,000 pounds of gas left. I needed to end this soon if I didn't want to eject out of an aircraft for the second time in less than a few hours.

I aimed the Hog's nose out over the valley to the west of the hills and allowed it to track further north to the lake I had crossed earlier. I rolled out for a few moments and looked down at the map display, evaluating the terrain approaches to the convoy. This next pass was designed to get the ZSU crew a little more nervous. I not only had to get them to track me, but I also needed to get a few bullets of my own headed their way.

I banked the Hog up the right and pulled the nose to the northeastern-most point of the lake and rolled out. I pushed over to descend and checked the throttles in MIL. This pass was going to be riskier. I did some mental math as I flew up a shallow swale that drained into the lake. I was going to come at the convoy from the north, approximately the same direction from which the helos were approaching. If Ian hadn't been in one of the vehicles further down the convoy, I would have used this avenue to take a long-range shot at the ZSU and kill it. But without knowing where he was, I couldn't take the chance. The swale rose into the flat terrain of the main valley. I followed a dirt road that came from my right, and headed into the valley, presumably to join the main road.

I was flying over a long hill that partially blocked the line-of-sight between my cockpit and the ZSU, but that obscuration was going to vanish in mere few seconds, and then I'd be out in the open and about 9,000 feet from the ZSU, right on the edge of its maximum range.

"Delta Sierra is MUD," Dave Smith said over the FM radio. "At two miles."

"Arc to the east, Delta Sierra. Maintain your distance."

"Delta Sierra copies," Smith replied.

In an instant, the terrain between my jet and the convoy vanished, and I was looking at the ZSU through the CCIP gun reticle in my HUD. I put the right moving target indicator on the ZSU, so my bullets would miss it to the left, and held the trigger down.

BRRRRRRRRRRRRRRRRRRRRTT.

The GAU-8 spat 100 rounds down range and into the dirt to the left of the ZSU. Before the crew could react, I pulled hard into the vertical, rolled 135 degrees to the left, and pulled the nose of the jet back to the earth.

"Delta Sierra is Naked," Smith said.

It took the ZSU crew longer this time. They didn't get their radar on me until I had completed the break and was recovering to level flight at low altitude.

"Tango Charlie is MUD," I said. But the lock didn't last long. I was down into the swale again, and out over the lake in seconds. The terrain between the radar and the Hog broke the line of sight. I keyed the mic. "Tango Charlie is Naked."

Now it was time for the knock-out punch. Smith and the helos would stay well outside of the ZSU's effective range and fly around the convoy to the east, hopefully distracting the ZSU crew, I would sneak in from the south and take the gun out.

I turned to the south and looked for the last ridgeline of the three fingers I had seen earlier.

"Copy," Smith said. "Turning inbound now."

I was so busy avoiding the rocks at low altitude that my brain didn't process Smith's radio call for a few seconds.

Why the hell were they headed inbound? That wasn't the plan!

"Jesus," I said to myself. "That fucking gun will chew you guys up in seconds over that flat terrain!" I keyed the mic. "Negative Delta Sierra!" I said "Maintain your distance! Maintain your distance."

"Delta Sierra is Naked," Smith wasn't hearing my radio call. I glanced to my left and saw the jagged rocks of the three fingers slightly above my altitude. The terrain was blocking my transmissions.

"Delta Sierra is still Naked," Smith said. His voice was almost casual. As far as he was concerned, all was going as planned.

I continued to the south, around the last of the three

fingers and found the small road that led back to the main one.

"Delta Sierra is MUD," Smith said. The tone of his voice wasn't casual any longer. He knew they were flying into the ZSU's effective range.

I almost keyed the mic but thought better of it at the last minute. If the gunner was focused on the helos, it might give me the extra second or two I needed.

"Delta Sierra is taking fire!"

There was no more time. "Tango Charlie is up and in," I said. "Get your asses out of there, Delta Sierra."

I pulled back on the control stick and urged my eager Hog up into the clear air of desert morning. The sun's light was now a wide swath of brightness across the eastern horizon, and it made the NVGs worthless. I ripped the goggles from my head as I rolled the Hog inverted and looked for my prey.

"Tango Charlie, Delta Sierra, still taking fire!"

"Shit!" I cursed into my oxygen mask.

The shapes of the convoy vehicles were barely visible in the last vestiges of the early morning darkness. I tracked the line of them with my eyeballs and found the ZSU at the northern end. It had ceased firing, for the moment, and as the first rays of the morning sun began to break up the darkness, I saw that its radar dish was oriented toward the east, where it had been firing at the helos. But as the light revealed more of the angular vehicle, I saw something I did not expect.

The four 23mm guns were pointing directly at me.

The gunner had completely suckered us. He was in full optical mode, and after firing two bursts to the east, he had pivoted the turret to the most likely direction for a new attack.

The ability of the mind to process information in time-critical situations never failed to amaze me. All sorts of things went through my head in the nanoseconds it took my brain to understand what was happening. I saw flashes of Sarah and Colleen as well as a host of other images.

But fortunately, my hands reacted more quickly than my brain did.

The first rectangle of fire left the four barrels and headed my way. Optical AAA fire is difficult for even the most seasoned AAA gunner. The bullets have to be fired one time of flight in front of the target aircraft, and with a radar providing the range of the target, the lead can be computed much more accurately. Without the radar, the gunner has to guess.

I pulled the Hog's nose earthward as the first volley of 23mm fire pierced the air just above me.

"Good guess," I mumbled into my oxygen mask.

A pop-up attack for a gun pass presents a fairly predictable geometry for a ground-based gunner, particularly if that gunner has seen it several times in the last few minutes. The only variables the gunner has to solve for are range to the target and g on the target. Based on what he'd seen before, the gunner was waiting for me to continue the pulldown maneuver and then roll out. Once I completed the rollout, my flight path would be the most predictable but also the most potentially lethal for him, because 30mm bullets would be headed his way milliseconds later.

He couldn't let me finish the rollout, so he had to shoot me before I got there.

Instinctively, I stopped pulling on the control stick and pushed forward for a moment, stopping the jet's nose movement and hanging it in midair. A long volley of fiery death passed underneath me, clearly visible through the canopy in my nearly inverted attitude. The evenly spaced tracer bullets passed below the plexiglass in a sort of odd slow motion.

The good news was that I had dodged another burst of 23mm fire. The bad news was that I was closing the distance to the ZSU at 500 feet per second and making the targeting problem easier for him with every passing moment. To make matters worse, I had ceased my nose track and made his job even simpler.

I had a fleeting thought about pulling the CCIP gun reticle to the ZSU while I was in my current attitude but the "X" in the middle of the reticle indicated that no CCIP solution was available and I didn't know how to turn the computer off and get the manual gun cross.

But then another idea came to mind.

I rolled the jet to 90 degrees of bank and stomped on the left rudder, shoving the nose of the aircraft violently to the left. Even as the nose moved, a stream of fire went by the right side of the jet, so close I could almost see the individual colors of the tracer rounds. I felt the right rudder pedal vibrate under my foot and I felt a slight yaw to the right. Out of the corner of my eyes, I saw the row of right engine gauges begin to fluctuate erratically.

"Tango Charlie, Delta Sierra, we're inbound with all souls and aircraft."

"Thanks for that, Dave," I said into the intercom.

I looked through the HUD at ZSU. The range had closed to 5000' feet, and I saw, much to my surprise, that the CCIP gun reticle had stabilized.

I didn't bother to roll out. I didn't have time. I applied back pressure to the control stick and dragged my nose across the ground even as the aircraft accelerated and the distance between the ZSU and me closed rapidly. I saw flame and smoke emanate from the barrels of the four cannons as the edge of the CCIP reticle reached the vehicle. I braced myself for the impact of more bullets, but nothing happened, and I realized that my nose movement in the horizontal plane had fooled the gunner and perhaps bought me a few milliseconds of time.

I hoped it would be enough.

The analog range bar in the circular reticle was sweeping

by the 3 o'clock position, indicating that I was 3,000 feet from the ZSU, and each mil in the reticle represented 3 feet on the ground. Watching the reticle track across the desert terrain was excruciating. As the one-mil pipper approached the chassis of the vehicle and began to move to the turret, I saw the turret itself pivot toward me as the gunner refined his aim for the final shot. I grimaced in anticipation of the 23mm rounds that I was sure would tear me to pieces in mere nanoseconds.

But then the hatch on top of the vehicle sprang open, and I saw a man's body scramble out of it, apparently abandoning the vehicle. I didn't know whether it was the gunner, an observer or another crewmember but he was years too late.

My finger came down on the trigger.

BRRRRRRRRRRRRRRRRRRRRRRRRRTT.

30mm TP rounds poured from the GAU-8 in a river of steel-jacketed death. They tore into the thin-skinned AAA vehicle and turned it into metallic swiss cheese, perforating the hull, turret, and radar dish, and exploding the human body on top into a cloud of red mist. I released the trigger and tracked the target for a fraction of second and found myself fascinated by the amount of raw carnage the gun had inflicted in a second's time.

Then, instincts took over, and I recovered from the gun pass. I rolled out of the bank, applied back pressure to the control stick and pulled the Hog's nose up, breaking the descent and pulling the jet's nose up into the desert dawn.

But even with 300 plus knots of airspeed, the Hog didn't respond as eagerly as it usually did. A glance down at the engine instruments provided the explanation. The right engine's interstage turbine temperature was above normal, and the core and fan RPM indications were low. The engine was damaged, possibly on the verge of a compressor stall. But, at the moment, it was still producing thrust, and I needed all it could give me.

I leveled off at 1,000 feet above the convoy and began a slow right orbit. Then I keyed my mic. “ZSU is down Delta Sierra,” I said. “Now go get our boy.”

CHAPTER FORTY-ONE

Wednesday, December 2nd
0605 Hours Local Time
1000 feet and 250 Knots
Somewhere South of the Pitiquito Municipality
Sonora, Mexico

The CIA Ops Team didn't waste any time. The helos had split from their two-ship formation and approached the row of vehicles from the north and south. They touched down quickly, the Ops Team members rapidly deployed, and the helos lifted off and moved away from the convoy to take up their orbits. As I looked down upon the two Blackhawks, I tried to see if I could detect traces of damage from their altercation with the ZSU earlier, but nothing was visible on either ship.

It was fascinating to observe the Team do their thing from an airborne vantage point. Sort of like watching an action adventure movie from a unique camera angle. The team members formed up into six groups of two and approached the convoy from each end, with the three groups from the north on the west side of the convoy and the three groups from the south on the east side.

"Clear fields of fire," I said to myself.

All had their weapons shouldered and in the ready position as they approached.

"Stay close, Tango Charlie," Dave Smith's voice said in my ear as I watched them. "If we have any squirters, we'll need to you get them."

I looked down at my engine gauges again. The right engine indications hadn't improved, but they also hadn't gotten any worse. I decided to keep my situation to myself. At least for now.

"Roger that," I said. "Standing by."

"Lead vehicle, clear," said a voice on the radio. The speaker sounded like he had grown up in South Carolina or Georgia.

"Trail vehicle, clear," said another voice a few moments later. This team member had a distinct New York City accent.

Both groups now converged on the center three vehicles. I found that I was holding my breath as I listened to them and watched them work. Ian would be in one of the remaining three vehicles. Hopefully in one piece. We'd be on our way soon.

Then a thought popped into my head that should have occurred to me several minutes earlier. *Why didn't the other vehicles make a run for it?* And as the team advanced on the remaining vehicles, there were no sudden eruptions of gunfire, no bad guys jumping out of the vehicles with weapons, no resistance at all.

We were missing something.

"Vehicle 2 is clear," said the southern voice. "One tango inside, the driver, but Jesus, his hands are wired to the steering wheel." There was a pause. "And he seems to be sitting on an explosive charge of some sort."

"Vehicle 4 same," said the New Yorker. "Probably a weight switch. Driver moves, and the charge detonates. Like some of the involuntary suicide bombers we saw in Afghanistan."

"By-pass and proceed to the center vehicle," Smith

commanded.

"Roger," North and South said in unison.

I had been so focused on the events below me that I hadn't performed the usual visual lookout that I would have typically accomplished in a CSAR situation. I tore my eyes from the drama below and swept the horizon for other air threats as I continued my wide orbit around the convoy. Then I turned my eyes to the land below the horizon to see if I could detect any movement there.

"Same deal with the driver in vehicle three," New York said. "But the Asset is here in the back seat. Alone. He seems to be unconscious."

I breathed a sigh of relief. They had found Ian.

"Oh, Jesus," said South Carolina. "But he's wired to another trigger."

Then there was a long moment of silence. I was tempted to break into the conversation and ask them what the hell was going on, but I was detecting clouds of dust south and west of the convoy and straining my eyes to see what was there. The longer I watched, the wider my eyes became. Vehicles were coming. More vehicles than I could count - traveling at high speed - headed right for us.

"What are we going to do, Chief?" New York asked.

"Reggie?" Smith asked. "Can you deal with this?"

"Probably," a deep African-American voice answered. "But it's going to take some time. The Asset is wired pretty good. And if he wakes up during the process, we're screwed."

"You have your tools, right?"

"Always," Reggie replied.

"You don't have time," I said into my mic.

"What are you talking about Tango Charlie?" Smith seemed startled and irritated by my interruption.

"They're coming," I said. "Like a hundred of them. And they'll be here in minutes. This whole thing was a trap."

CHAPTER FORTY-TWO

Wednesday, December 2nd
0620 Hours Local Time
1000 feet and 250 Knots
Somewhere South of the Pitiquito Municipality
Sonora, Mexico

It was worse than I thought. The bad guys were coming from three directions, not two. And there were a lot of them.

Smith was having trouble comprehending. “What are you seeing Tango Charlie?”

“We have three huge groups of fast-moving vehicles inbound. One from the south, one from the west and I just picked up one coming from the north. Close to 100 vehicles total.”

“Do they look official?”

I shook my head as I responded. “Negative. Too many different colors and models. Looks like the standard cartel fleet.”

“How far out are they?”

I watched all three convoys for a few seconds as I maintained my orbit. “Hard to say,” I answered. “Not far. Ten – fifteen minutes tops.”

“Roger,” Smith. “Air One and Air Two, either of you have

a sling?"

"Air One, roger," the CIA helo pilot answered. The vibration in his voice from the rotors was barely audible.

"Air One, cleared in. We're going to have to sling the vehicle and the asset out of here. Air two, maintain the perimeter and be prepared to collect the team."

"Air One, roger."

"Air Two, roger."

"You want me to ride with him, Boss?" Reggie asked.

"Negative, Reggie," Smith replied. "If we have to jettison the load, I don't want to lose you with it. Neutralize the driver and get out of there. Squad leaders, neutralize the drivers in the other vehicles."

South Carolina and New York acknowledged the order.

One of the helos approached the middle vehicle of the convoy and touched down. Two crew members exited the helo and pulled a cable apparatus from a storage compartment in the back. They divided the apparatus between themselves and some members of the Ops Team. The crew members set about fastening the cable to the underside of the helo while the Ops Team members began to attach the other part of the apparatus to the vehicle, a large, windowless Ford van.

I was only half watching the activity below me as I kept track of the incoming masses. It seemed that they were moving at different speeds. The vehicles coming from the south and west were driving faster, maintaining an almost frantic pace, while vehicles from the north were moving slower, more casually. I wondered if there was some sort of competition between the two faster groups.

I widened my orbit and studied the roads and terrain to the south and west. Both of the roads wound through some rock formations with very little clearance on either side of the road. The southern route was slightly wider than the western, but both would be easy to constrict when the time came. If I shot up the first few vehicles in each convoy, I'd restrict access for the vehicles that followed.

And the time would be soon. The western vehicles looked like they were about five miles away, the southern ones were a bit further. I glanced to the north. The northern vehicles were more like 10-12 miles away and moving deliberately southbound, but at a restrained pace.

I shook my head as I watched them. There was something else going on that I didn't understand.

I looked down at the activity below me. The sling apparatus seemed to be fitted to the van, and four of the team members had boarded the helo with the sling attachment. Two of the other team members had climbed on top of the van and were holding the sling apparatus taut. The helo slowly lifted off and rose to the height necessary to engage the loop on top of the sling apparatus. I nodded to myself as I watched. It wouldn't be long now.

I glanced towards the west and saw the clouds of dust much closer. I looked through the HUD and checked the display. I had 804 rounds left. It would have to be enough. Then I looked to the west again and noticed something I hadn't seen before. There was a smaller cloud of dust in front of the larger one. I pulled the A-10's nose around to the south so that I could see the road more clearly. Two Hummer-sized vehicles were approaching, and each had a gun turret in the roof that had a large automatic weapon mounted to it.

"Fifty cals," I said to myself in disbelief. "Holy shit."

"Delta Sierra, Tango Charlie, we have two vehicles approaching rapidly from the west. They're Hummers with heavy machine guns. You guys need to get moving. Now."

"Roger," Smith said. "Air Two, cleared in. I want everyone onboard except the hook crew."

The first Hummer had cleared the narrow rocks on the western road, followed closely by the second. The other vehicles on the road weren't far behind. I had waited too long.

"Goddamn it!" I spat into my oxygen mask.

I pushed the Hog's throttles up to MILITARY and mentally willed the right engine to keep producing thrust. Then I banked the Hog up to the right and pulled the nose to the right and down.

Strafing a moving vehicle that is coming directly towards the attacking aircraft is more difficult than it looks. The natural tendency was to put the gun reticle on the target and then push forward on the control stick to hold it there. But that created problems. Pushing forward on the stick steepened the dive angle and increased the altitude required for the recovery. It also tended to throw the bullets high of the target.

I had a better technique for it and the years between the last time I had attacked a moving target and the present went by in a flash. I rolled out and placed the CCIP gun reticle about fifty feet in front of the lead vehicle. I could see the gunner in the roof turret trying to slew his weapon towards my aircraft and raise the muzzle of his gun to engage me. He wasn't going to make it. As the Hummer approached the one-mil pipper, I opened fire and let the vehicle drive into the bullets.

BRRRRRRRRRRTT.

30MM bullets tore into the Hummer and stopped it in a cloud of white dust. I recovered from the gun pass, and once I had the A-10's nose above the horizon, I dropped the left wing to look down and inspect the damage. The first Hummer was thoroughly perforated, and the only thing that remained of the gunner in the turret was a wide red swath of blood and gore on the roof of the vehicle. As the dust cloud settled, the second Hummer emerged and barely evaded the first vehicle as it drove off the road to the right. The driver didn't stop to check on or assist his comrades in the first vehicle; instead he drove past the first Hummer, got back on the road and seemed to accelerate towards the convoy and helicopters ahead. I saw the gunner in the turret pull back the charging handle of his .50 caliber machine gun.

"Jesus Christ," I spat into my oxygen mask. "Some fucking air cover you turned out to be."

I pulled the nose of the Hog hard around to the left to keep the second vehicle in sight. As I turned, I could see one of the CIA helos hovering above the Ford van as the crew finished connecting the sling fastener. The helo began to rise slowly, and the Van's wheels left the ground. The two operators jumped off the van and made for the second helo, about fifty yards away.

"Delta Sierra you've got a leaker coming your way, a Hummer with a fifty on the roof. You guys need to get moving now."

"Copy," Smith replied. "Air One, head north now, max speed!"

"Air One copies," the helo pilot replied, "but we're limited with a sling load, Chief."

"Fuck the limits, Air One. Get north now."

"Roger."

By the time I got my nose around about 135 degrees, the second armed Hummer had almost made the intersection of the western road with the main road. There wasn't time to think or plan an attack geometry that took everything into account, like how close the good guys were or how quickly the bad guys would arrive. I stepped on the left rudder as I completed the turn, trying to get my nose below the horizon and on the truck as soon as I could. But the nose moved downward sluggishly, which was very uncharacteristic for the Hog with its huge rudders. I realized then that I hadn't checked on the health of the right engine in a while. An asymmetric thrust situation, with the left engine producing full thrust and the right providing little or no thrust would make the nose harder to move to the left.

"Idiot," I muttered to myself.

And, of course, that's when the FIRE light illuminated in the right engine T-handle.

""Two fucking engine fires in one day," I muttered. "How lucky can one guy be."

The second Hummer had reached the intersection and was turning on to the main road. Both CIA helos were barely out of the hover and nearly helpless. The 7.62 miniguns mounted in the side doors didn't have the range a .50 caliber machine gun did.

I reacted without thinking. I pulled both throttles to idle, negating the thrust asymmetry and stepped on the left rudder even harder. The nose fell quickly. I kept the Hog in a left bank and pulled the nose to a place where it was ahead of the second Hummer. The range between the vehicle and I had closed to less than 3,000 feet, and even at idle thrust, I was eating up the distance quickly. I lessened my bank angle and got the right moving target indicator on the vehicle as the range went through 2,500 feet. At that point, the gunner seemed to notice an airplane with a big gun pointing at him, and he began to swing the .50 away from the helos and towards me.

He didn't make it. I squeezed the trigger and held it down for an extra half second to make sure I stopped him.

BRRRRRRRRRRRRRRTT.

The Hummer disappeared into a cloud of dust as the 30mm bullets reduced it to a smoking hulk and flying metallic debris.

"PULL UP! PULL UP!"

A large "X" appeared in the HUD, and I realized that I had pressed the attack too far. The ground collision avoidance system was telling me I needed to recover to avoid hitting the ground. I shoved the left throttle to MIL and applied back pressure to the stick until I got the chopped tone from the angle of attack warning system. Fortunately, thrust limitations notwithstanding, I had enough energy on the jet to recover from the dive. The nose tracked upward quickly, and I released pressure to get back into the steady tone. As the nose stabilized above the horizon, the left TF-34 engine slowly wound up to MIL power. I dropped the left wing and began a slow turn to the north. Below me, the second Hummer was a perforated shell. Once again, there was no trace of the human being in the turret.

"You guys are clear," I said into the mic. "I'll follow you north. Stay as far as you can from the main road. As far east as possible."

"Delta Sierra Copies," Smith replied. "You almost busted your ass on that pass, Tango Charlie. This whole mission is for naught if you wind up dead down here."

"Thanks for the appreciation, Dave," I said to myself.

I rolled out of my turn at about 1,000 feet AGL and executed the first three steps of nearly every engine fire procedure I had learned – the same three steps I had performed earlier in the OV-10. I pulled the right throttle to OFF, lifting it over the detent in the process. Then I pulled the right T-handle which was conveniently labeled FIRE (R ENG) PULL. Finally, I moved the FIRE EXTING DISCH switch to the right. After a few moments, the light inside the R ENG T-handle extinguished. I swiftly reached down to the left console and hit the FIRE DETECT BLEED AIR LEAK TEST button. The system checked normally. The rest of the checklist could wait.

The two CIA helos were moving northward, edging towards the eastern ridgeline of the valley. The sun had risen higher in the sky, and there was very little shadow left on the ground. I noticed the helos staying as low as they could to take advantage of the terrain and avoid being highlighted by the sunrise. I followed behind them, with the Hog maintaining about 220 knots on one engine. I breathed yet another sigh of relief. It looked like we were going to make it.

But then I looked to the north, and I caught my breath. There was a thin arm of wispy white smoke emanating from one of the vehicles in the convoy and heading toward the helos. It looked like a skeletal finger of the grim reaper.

"Delta Sierra! MANPAD launch! Your left nine o'clock!"

"We got it," Smith replied calmly.

The cartel had acquired man-portable surface-to-air missiles. That was why the northern convoy had taken its time going down the valley. They were the backstop. If the ZSU or the wired explosives in the vans or the two southern convoys didn't get the job done, the northern convoy would play goalie, and make sure the gringos didn't make it north.

Jesus, I thought. *This whole thing hasn't been about Ian at all. It's been about shooting us down.*

The helos were dispensing infrared countermeasures, flares, and climbing into the morning sky to get the sun behind them so the seeker heads on the missile would be decoyed. And, in the process, probably framing themselves for a perfect photo, which would be a great consolation prize for the cartel. More SAMs were being fired. It was like the cartel had stockpiled them.

Without consciously willing it, I put the Hog into a gentle right turn as my mind sorted through some options. Unlike the helos, I didn't have any flares or other infrared countermeasures loaded on my aircraft. I couldn't decoy a missile if the cartel shot one at me. My only choice to stay alive was to follow the helos and run.

But I was getting tired of running. I was tired of getting manipulated, predicted and outsmarted. I was getting tired of these cartel fuckers thinking they could go anywhere and do anything they wanted. I was getting especially tired of them always coming after me. It was time for some fucking payback. I glanced at the rounds counter in the HUD. I had 632 rounds of 30mm revenge.

Kill them, said the Darkness in my ear. *Kill them all.*

"No shit," I said.

The left throttle was still parked in MIL. Losing an engine had decreased my fuel consumption somewhat so I hadn't burned gas as rapidly as I would have with two engines running. I still had 2900 pounds. It would have to be enough.

I completed my turn and rolled out headed northbound, along the road. I saw the northern convoy a few miles ahead. The vehicles were still, and several of them had discharged their occupants to watch the volleys of SAMs fired at the helos. A large group of people stood on the roadside, looking to the east. They seemed to be focused with rapt attention. The scene reminded me of a tailgate party, and that infuriated me.

The A-10 is an incredibly quiet aircraft for a fighter. The TF-34 engines are non-afterburning, high-bypass turbofans, similar in construction to those you'd find on a business jet or an airliner and they don't make very much noise at all, especially from the forward aspect. As a result, I wasn't attracting any attention as I approached.

I had the Hog level at about 300 feet. I was two miles from the first vehicle. The CCIP gunsight had ranged in and was providing a solution. I could have fired then. But I decided to wait. Just a bit longer. I wanted them to see it coming. I wanted them to know it was me.

The range indicator under the gunsight said 1.5 nautical miles from the target, about 9,000 feet. The first truck in the convoy must have been a large pickup because the one-mil gun pipper in the middle of the reticle was dwarfed by the vehicle. I refined my aim and placed the pipper in the middle of the truck's windshield. Still, no one on the ground noticed me.

Six thousand feet from the target now, onc nautical mile. The analog range counter had traced the circle down from 12 o'clock to six o'clock and was now making its way up the right side of the circle.

Suddenly there was activity on the ground as the people in front of me finally noticed that a gigantic, metallic bird of prey was descending upon them. There was frantic movement. Arms were waving, and people were pointing. Many of them running, some towards their vehicles, but the smarter ones were running away from the vehicles. Away from the targets. It wouldn't save them.

"Tango Charlie, Delta Sierra," Smith's concerned voice crackled in my ear. "We're safe and clear and headed home. Where are you? What are you doing?"

I didn't answer. The Darkness descended behind my eyes and took me. There would be no quarter. I smiled and began my work.

CHAPTER FORTY-THREE

Wednesday, December 2nd
0700 Hours Local Time
357th Fighter Squadron Ramp
Davis-Monthan Air Force Base
Tucson, Arizona, USA

I stayed in the cockpit of the crippled Hog as the USAF maintenance crew towed it back to the 357th. The crew had asked me if I wanted to ride in their vehicle, and I had declined. I just wasn't ready to get out of the big jet. Besides, I felt like I owed the squadron operations supervisor an apology. The gun was empty, the right engine was trashed, and the airframe was riddled with small arms fire. But the mighty Hog had gotten me home. It had proven its durability yet again.

When the jet was stopped and chocked, I deployed the internal boarding ladder, gathered my borrowed gear and made my way to the ground. The squadron supervisor and young Captain Mangus were there waiting for me. They looked the aircraft over as I unbuckled the leg straps on my parachute harness and secured them.

"I hope you gave more than you got," the supervisor said at last.

I nodded slowly. "I'm sorry that I can't tell you more of

the details, but there's a lot of dead shit down there, and we accomplished our mission."

"Gun empty?" he asked.

I nodded.

"Then the mission was complete," he said.

I turned to the massive airplane and ran my hand down its rough metal sides. I could feel the curved metal over each of the rivets that held the plates of the jet's skin to its framework. When the USAF had built the A-10, it had done so under protest and had spared every expense it possibly could have. The rivets were not made flush with the skin of the aircraft. That would have required more cost and more technology. Instead, the rivets protruded. They were covered by small half-globes of metal that were welded to the surface. It made the airplane uglier. And more endearing.

"I've missed this jet," I said to no one in particular.

"It has that effect," the supervisor answered. "My dad was one of the first pilots that flew it. He was responsible for nearly all of the tactics and the fighter weapons school syllabus that taught it. He loved the jet. He talked about it all the time when I was a kid. It's one of the reasons I wanted to fly it when I got into the Air Force."

I felt a lump form in my throat for the second time that night as I continued to run my hands over the jet's skin. Then a thought occurred to me and I turned to him.

"I might have known your dad," I said. "What was his name?"

"Al Moore," the supervisor said. "His callsign was Mud."

I nodded and smiled at him. "Best squadron commander I had while I was in," I said. "He taught me more about leadership than anyone else I've encountered, either before or since."

The supervisor smiled crookedly at me, but I could tell his eyes were shining. "You were at Bentwaters with him?"

I nodded again. “Loved every minute of it.” I looked at him closely. “Was that where you were born? He mentioned that had a son while he was there.”

The supervisor nodded in response.

“You’ve done pretty well for yourself,” I said. “He must be proud.”

The supervisor looked away. “He died in a plane crash in the late 90s. After he retired, he did tourist flights over the Grand Canyon.”

The news stunned me. The Al Moore I knew had seemed indestructible.

“I’m sorry,” I said after a few moments. “I’m truly sorry for you. He was a great man.” I looked around the hangar and tried to search for the right words, but I knew somehow that no matter how eloquent they might be, they’d never be good enough. “If it matters, there are very few people who I can remember, by name, who have made a huge impact on my life. Your dad was one of them.”

There was silence for a few moments, and the atmosphere became somber. I felt the need to lighten it.

“Well, anyway, I’m sorry I fucked up your jet,” I said. “It wasn’t intentional.”

The supervisor smiled at me, seemingly grateful that I had changed the direction of the conversation. “They’ll fix it,” he said. “We’ve seen a lot worse than this in the ‘Stan.”

“I bet you have,” I said.

The supervisor’s phone rang, and he pulled it from a leather holster strapped to his flightsuit. I got the impression it was an official duty phone. He took the call, listened and then finished with “Yes sir, I’ll tell him.” Then he hung up. He returned the phone to his holster and looked over at me. “Looks like your presence is required elsewhere,” he said. “They’re sending a helo for you. It’s going to pick you up at Base Ops. I’ll take you there in one of the line vans.”

I handed all my gear to young Captain Mangus who had been uncharacteristically silent during our conversation.

"Mung," I told him, "any information about this mission needs to be destroyed. You never saw it. You never helped, and you never met me. Do you understand?"

He nodded quickly.

"This is serious," I said. "The people I work for don't mess around, and they don't like loose ends. As long as you do what I ask, all will be well. But if any of the gun camera footage winds up on YouTube, things won't be pleasant. Get me?"

He nodded again.

I shook his hand. "Thanks for your help," I said. "I couldn't have done what I did tonight without you."

He smiled broadly, and the supervisor motioned me away to a waiting van, just outside the hangar doors. We rode in silence from the 357th's hangar down the flight line to Base Ops. As we arrived, I could see yet another anonymously marked Blackhawk helicopter idling on the tarmac, rotors turning. The van stopped, and I turned to the supervisor in the driver's seat.

"I can't tell you my name, but my handle was T.C. when I was in. If you do a little research, you'll find out who I am. I owe your dad a debt of gratitude I can never repay. And now I owe you too. If there's ever anything I can do for you, call this number." I reached inside my flightsuit and gave him one of my Brooks Air Service business cards. "That's not my real name. But it's close enough for contact purposes."

He took the card and extended his hand. "Al Moore the third," he said. Then he smiled broadly. "And like my dad, I go by Mud."

I shook his hand and smiled at him. "Glad to hear it!" I said. "The legacy lives on."

I released his hand and stepped out of the van. I walked down the tarmac to the waiting helo without looking back.

The evening had brought some warmth in spite of the grim proceedings.

And I was grateful for that.

CHAPTER FORTY-FOUR

Wednesday, December 2nd
0830 Hours Local Time
Banner University Medical Center
Phoenix, Arizona, USA

It was a good thing that I had been dropped off at the helipad on the roof of the Banner University Medical Center in downtown Phoenix. Judging by the looks I received as I roamed the halls to my destination, I probably wouldn't have been allowed through the front door. I caught a glimpse of myself in a mirrored wall. I wouldn't have blamed them for keeping me out. The desert brown flight suit was dirty, dusty and stained with sweat. There was also a healthy swath of blood on the right side of it, just above my hip. My cheeks were still creased from the oxygen mask I had clamped to my face when I was flying the Hog, and my visage looked worn and tired. The .45 auto hung from the shoulder holster under my left arm. Apart from the gun, I could have passed for a homeless person who had found a flightsuit to wear as temporary clothing.

I rounded a corner and came upon the room number I had been given. But as it turned out, the room number wasn't necessary. The room in question was the only one in the hospital with two heavily-armed men standing outside of it. Apparently, the CIA was more interested in security than secrecy.

The two men either knew who I was or had been briefed. They nodded at me as I approached and opened the door for me to enter. I nodded back at them and stepped inside.

The room seemed to be either a small operating room or a large patient room. I couldn't tell which. There was a large shape on a bed in the center of the room, which I presumed was Ian. He wasn't moving, and he was surrounded by medical personnel who seemed to be very busy. Smith, his partner Amrine, and Sharona stood off to one side. Smith was still in the tactical gear I had seen him in earlier. Amrine and Sharona were both dressed in business attire. Smith and Amrine had their gaze focused on the medical team. Sharona nodded at me as I approached and winked at me. I didn't wink back. I didn't know if I was pissed at being so thoroughly used or just tired. Maybe it was both.

I was tempted to utter a witticism as I approached them, like "so the gang's all here?" But I didn't. Instead, I inclined my head towards the bed and spoke. "How is he?" I asked.

"We don't know yet," Smith said. "We just got him here a few minutes ago."

I raised my eyebrows at him.

He answered without looking at me. "We had to set down on one of the Gila Bend ranges, so we could disarm the explosives in the truck," he said. "It took Reggie a while to do it, and we moved everyone out of range while he worked."

"Reggie's a brave guy," I said. "You need to give him a raise."

"Steady as a rock," Smith said, shifting his gaze to me. "He's probably one of the top IED technicians in the world."

"Good thing you had him around," I said.

Smith nodded. "What happened to him?" he asked,

motioning towards the bed. "The doctor said he was pretty messed up."

I looked at Smith blankly for a few moments while my mind rewound to the raid on the cartel headquarters the previous evening. It was then that I realized how long I had been awake. I felt a wave of fatigue go through me and I had to momentarily fight the urge to find a chair to collapse into. After a long moment, I retrieved the memory and answered him.

"That damn ZSU was waiting for us at the cartel's headquarters. I knew it was there, and I tried warning Ian off the pass, but he wasn't having any. I think he wanted to die in the act. The ZSU took a few bursts to get the range right, but then it opened up and chewed his OV to pieces. His aircraft blew up into a fireball, and he ejected from the middle of it. I'm not sure anyone else would have lived through it."

Smith and Amrine both nodded as I finished speaking.

"He's pretty tough," Amrine said at last.

"I have to know something," I said. "If he had this device implanted in him all along, why did you risk sending multiple teams against him in the past?"

Smith and Amrine looked at Sharona, and I realized that I had been had. Again.

"That part of the story might have been embellished a bit," she said. "Only one government team was ever sent against him, and we had nothing to do with it. It was the guy who built him, a Doctor Shelley. The good doctor had a remote control that could disarm the device inside of Ian. When Ian left us, Shelley was pissed. After Shelley found out where Ian was, he put together a contractor team to go after him."

"I see," I said. "And they didn't fare well."

Sharona nodded. "That part I told you about Ian breaking people apart was true, but it was only one person that he did that to."

I sighed. "Let me guess. Shelley."

There was silence for a few moments, and the three of them and I stared at each other.

"So why the subterfuge?" I asked after a long moment. "It's like I told Dave. You could have just asked. I didn't need to be," I deliberately looked away from Sharona's face, "courted."

"We wanted to leave Ian alone," Amrine said. "We signed an agreement with him, and we wanted to honor it. But then we started hearing intel chatter about the human trafficking business. Initially, it came through the DEA, but then we started hearing it through our channels. It seemed to be very focused."

"He did the first raid about a week before I flew with you," Sharona said. "We had to know what he was up to, and we had to make sure you weren't in on it. We know...how you are."

Smith was nodding in agreement as she spoke.

I raised my eyebrows at her.

"We know you care about things," she said. "In spite of how you like to pretend you don't. We knew if Ian made the right pitch to you, you'd respond."

It was my turn to nod. I looked at Smith. "I guess I'm predictable that way."

"We also knew you had...needs," Amrine said softly, looking right at me. "Even though you spent five years pretending you don't."

There was a long silence.

"What happened in the valley, T.C.?" Smith asked. His voice was no louder than a whisper. "You were flying a crippled jet, and we were clear."

I looked away from them and swallowed hard. It was a long time before I spoke. A line occurred to me that I had heard in a medieval-themed movie. "I left none alive," I said at last. "I killed them all. I had to kill them all."

All three of them were nodding at me, and it infuriated

me. I looked back at them defiantly. "You realize that we were all totally played, right?"

Smith, Amrine, and Sharona looked at me blankly.

"Oh, come on!" I said. "Really?"

More blank looks.

"Jesus!" I said. "It's like Smith always says to me. You guys are the CIA after all!" I looked between them, and it was still clear they didn't get it. "They fucking baited Ian!" I said. "They knew he was there, and they made him aware of something they knew he couldn't resist! They lured him down south, knowing you would come after him! They wanted an international incident, and we almost played right into their hands! And the one thing that stopped it, the one thing they didn't expect..." I let my voice trail off.

"Was an A-10," Smith said, shaking his head.

I nodded at him. "Exactly. The ZSU and the Man-Pads were there to shoot you guys down, not me. They knew you'd come after Ian because they knew what he was. You know that Miguel Hidalgo's son, Mariano, is running the cartel now, right?"

The three of them were now looking amongst each other. I could see questioning looks on their faces.

"Didn't you get anything out of Anne?" I asked. It exasperated me that they weren't keeping up. It seemed so incredibly clear to me. "She was their intel! The guys who came to Sedona knew who I was! They were after me, not Ian! They wanted Ian to get worked up and come south; it was me they wanted to contain!"

"But why..." Amrine spoke, but his voice trailed off.

"So Mariano could be seen defending Mexico against the invading Gringos," I said. "So he could capitalize on that act and use it as a PR ploy. Maybe he was trying to take over the country like his dad."

"But they could still do that," Sharona said. "The battle

still took place!"

I shook my head and looked at her. "You've forgotten the Mexican machismo," I said. "They would have had to win. They would have had to conquer the gringo invaders. Just fighting wouldn't have been enough. Mariano, like his dad, would need to look powerful."

"And now he doesn't," Smith said.

"Nope, he doesn't," I agreed. "Assuming he's still alive."

One of the doctors left the table and came over to us. His scrubs had very little blood on them for how intently they had all been working. But then it occurred to me that Ian probably had very little blood in his body.

The doctor removed his surgical mask as he approached.

"We've got power on him, and we've stabilized him," he said. "He's badly burned, but that's not the main issue. We can fix that. One of his batteries is leaking. The one in his lower right leg. He must have hit something."

"He ejected," I said, as much to myself as to those around me. "But he weighs twice as much as the seat is designed to handle. He must have landed too hard after the ejection. The seat didn't get him high enough, and the parachute couldn't handle his weight."

The doctor nodded. "The battery acid is poisoning him. But if we remove the battery, he'll die. It's a catch 22."

Silence ensued for a few minutes, and I found myself growing impatient the longer it went on. "What are you waiting for?" I asked them. "Replace the fucking batteries!"

"That will be expensive," Amrine said. "Really expensive."

Smith and Sharona were nodding.

"The government will want something in return for its money," Smith said.

I wasn't looking at him when he spoke, but after he uttered the words, I turned to him and found he, Amrine and Sharona all staring at me. The look on each of their faces was one of odd expectation. It took me a few moments to understand.

"You guys are unbelievable," I said, shaking my head at them. "Yes. I'll come back. I'll do anything you need me to. Just get Ian fixed, and get him home. I don't know much about his history, but I know who he is. He's a good man, and he deserves to live a normal life. Or as normal a life as he can."

Amrine nodded at the doctor. The doctor returned to the table, and I realized that once again, I had been played.

I turned my back on them and walked to the door.

"Pearce? We have more questions for you!" Amrine said.

"T.C.!" Smith said. "Come on!"

I didn't turn to look at them. I just waved my hand dismissively and went through the door.

Sharona caught up with me just as I reached the elevator. It was probably a good thing. I didn't have any idea which direction I was going to go. Down, to find a way back to Sedona, or up, to throw myself off the roof. At the moment, the two courses of action seemed equally appealing.

"Colin!" she said, as her hand reached my shoulder.

I sighed and turned around to face her. We stared at each other for an awkward few seconds before I decided to break the silence. "I'm going to regret asking this, and I hate sounding like a chick, but," I searched her beautiful face, "was any of it real?"

There was just a moment of telltale hesitation and then she looked down.

"Maybe," she said, quietly.

I nodded and exhaled simultaneously. "Okay," I replied. "I guess that's something."

"I made the decision to approach you the way we did," she said. She slowly raised her eyes to mine. "And I'm not sorry it happened that way."

I smiled at her tiredly. "It was...fun," I said.

She nodded at me and smiled back. "Yes," she said. "It

was. I enjoyed the hell out of it."

"Thanks for that," I answered. "Me too." I turned to go but then turned back to her. "I know you didn't come out here to tell me that, as much as I'd like to believe it."

The corners of her mouth turned down, and her smile took on similar notes of sadness and determination. "You asked about Anne," she said. "When we got to your condo, she wasn't there. Someone came and took her."

I felt my shoulders go slack in disappointment. I shook my head at her. "You realize she's the key to all of this," I said.

Sharona didn't react to my statement. Instead, she stepped forward and gave me a brief, unexpected kiss on the lips. "Be careful," she said.

CHAPTER FORTY-FIVE

Friday, December 18th
1830 Hours Local Time
Verde Valley Medical Center
Sedona, Arizona, USA

It was a beautiful December evening in Sedona. The air was a pleasant 52 degrees, and the sky was clear and moonlit. I glanced up at the heavens as I crossed the parking lot at the Verde Valley Medical Center. The stars gleamed down from dark sky cheerily, and I felt my heart lift a bit as I walked. It had been a good day. A long day, to be sure, but a good day.

With Ian and Anne out of the office, I was running Brooks Air Service these days. I was quoting and booking trips, greeting customers, playing Director of Operations and even flying once in a while. It was my first return to a leadership role since I had retired from the USAF, and I was enjoying the hell out of it. I was exhausted when I got into bed every night, but I went to work with a smile on my face every day. I wondered if I had found my true purpose in life.

Brooks' surgery had been extensive and had taken two days. The special doctors had been flown into Phoenix on CIA aircraft. They repaired Brooks' skin with a mixture of grafts and technology, replaced his batteries with smaller, more efficient units, and did some work on the nerve connections for his prosthetics. In the process, they reduced his weight by about 200 pounds. The doctors also managed to remove the failsafe device and a cleverly disguised nuclear containment team evacuated the bomb and took it to parts unknown.

After the surgery was completed, a young man arrived who looked like he was barely old enough to drink. He announced that he was a 'Company' software technician and it was his job to do some recoding and reprogramming. He spent two more days in Brooks' room, downloading code from Brooks' processors, reworking it and uploading it. When he was done, he announced that Brooks' prosthetics should now behave more naturally and efficiently. Then he had left.

We loaded Brooks into an ambulance and took him back to Sedona later that same day. A private room at the Verde Valley Medical Center had been reserved to provide a quiet place for him to recover. Since then, a team of CIA-provided personnel had been tending to Brooks as he recovered.

I had returned to work and called a meeting for all Brooks Air Service staff. I told them Brooks had been in an accident but was expected to fully recover and that I would be acting DO and charter manager in the meantime. There was relief at Brooks' recovery and some consternation at my new role, but the business quickly resumed, and we re-attained our former pace of operations quickly. Now we were humming along, and I was working my ass off to make it go, but also having more fun than I could remember in a long time.

Brooks, on the other hand, was not happy. He had regained consciousness about two days after his arrival in Sedona, and once the pain had subsided, he had wanted to get out of bed and back to work immediately. But that hadn't been possible. The CIA technician had installed a routine that limited the power to Brooks' prosthetic limbs and could only be deactivated by a code that he had given me. The aim had been to keep Brooks on his back until he was fully healed from his surgery. The doctors told me he needed at least two weeks' rest before he could be permitted to move around. That deadline was going to come soon, and he'd be up and about before Christmas. But that wasn't soon enough for Ian. He was chomping at the bit to get back to work.

Since he had regained consciousness, I had been visiting him every evening and briefing him on the day's events, as well as bringing him whatever meal he requested from a local restaurant. Tonight, Italian hoagies had been on the menu, and I had brought one from his favorite delicatessen.

I walked through the doors of the Medical Center, waved at the receptionist behind the front desk and made my way to Brooks' private room, which ironically, was only a few doors down from the room I had occupied during my brief stay here a few weeks ago.

The door to Brooks' room was closed as I approached it. Most hospital doors stayed open except when privacy was required in the rooms, but Brooks' door had stayed closed during his stay to reduce the possibility of curious onlookers. I knocked, using the code I had been given, and entered the room.

Brooks was awake, sitting up in bed with a scowl on his face. There seemed to be no one else in the room. I wondered if the CIA guard was down the hall making conversation at the nurse's station. But then I saw the two feet in white shoes, protruding from the aisle on the far side of Brooks' bed.

"Freeze fucker," said a cold British voice.

I didn't freeze. I knew the voice. The Darkness rose inside in an instant, and I turned toward the sound.

"I said freeze!" Anne said as I made eye contact with her. She was standing in an alcove on the side of the room's private bathroom with a Glock pistol in her hand, a long cylindrical suppressor attached to it. She was dressed in slacks, a button-down shirt, and a white lab coat. Her hair was pulled back behind her head, and she sported black-framed glasses which did a credible job of altering her appearance.

I looked her up and down and shook my head. "Damn," I said. "I was hoping like hell you were dead."

She looked back at me, defiantly, and a crooked smile etched its way onto her face. "Well, I'm not. I'm here to finish what I started, and this time, you're not going to stop me."

I shrugged at her. I looked around the room and didn't see anyone else there. I wanted to taunt her further and spur the Darkness into action, but a part of me, the more deliberate part of me, refrained. As I looked at the smug, priggish expression on her face, I knew at once that she wanted to tell me how smart she was. She needed to tell me how smart she was.

I raised the deli bag gently and inclined my head towards Ian. "Can I give them man his sandwich?" I asked. "You'll get to see my hands unimpeded."

She motioned towards the bed with the muzzle of her pistol. "Do it," she said. "He doesn't seem to be moving well anyway."

I nodded at her and walked towards the bed. "Ten sorties today, Ian," I said. "Four tours, five acro flights, and another photo shoot for our favorite photographer."

"Let me guess," he said, smiling at me. It was the first smile I had seen out of him since he had returned to consciousness. "You flew her."

I smiled back. "Yep. And of course, she had to pee a few times while we were up." I offered him the sandwich, and his arms reached for it, in the exaggerated slow motion typical of his reduced power profile. "And you know what I kept thinking the whole time she was in the airplane? The day that we would fly her the last time. The day we could say alpha-mike-foxtrot, adios mother-fucker."

"She's a good, paying customer, Pearce," he said, with an

admonishing tone to his voice. "We need to treat her well."

I shrugged as I placed his drink, a 12-ounce can of Coca-Cola, on the table next to him. "I know. You're right," I admitted. "But I just kept thinking alpha-mike-foxtrot."

This time, Brooks' eyebrows came together, and he looked at me with a quizzical expression on his face. Then a look of realization filled his eyes.

I winked at him and turned to Anne. "Tell us the story before you kill us," I said. "You know you want to. For starters, I know you were somewhere else before you were in London. And I'm betting it was somewhere south of the border."

Ian snorted. "That's putting it mildly. Her father was a Mexican gangster. Someone in the drug trade. He died when she was young, and her mother got remarried, to my father."

I looked back and forth between the two of them. "What happened then?"

"I joined the USAF, and my father died of alcoholism soon after," Ian said. Then he inclined his chin towards Anne. "Her mom moved them to England. She thought it would be further away from the drugs."

I did the relational math in my head for a second or two, and then I stated the obvious. "She's not your sister," I said. "She's your stepsister."

Ian nodded.

"No love lost?" I asked.

He shook his head. "No. She calls me out of the blue and tells me she wants to leave the UK and apply for US citizenship. She asked me if I'd sponsor her. I didn't want the bullshit between our parents or my previous issues with the drug cartel to interfere, so I tried to do the right thing. I gave her a job and sponsored her."

"How long ago?" I asked.

Ian seemed to think for a second. "About six years." He said. "Just after I got here. I needed help with the business, and I wanted to give Anne a chance. Let bygones be bygones."

I nodded and mentally commended myself on my assessment of Ian's character. He was a good man. Far better than I was. No wonder the work he had done for the CIA had given him pause.

I turned my gaze to Anne. "When did the Mexicans recruit you?" I asked.

She shrugged. "One of my cousins came up to visit a few years ago..."

"Yolanda?" Brooks asked, his voice incredulous.

Anne stuck her chin out in defiance. "Yes, Yolanda. Her husband runs distribution for Los Diablos in the western US."

"I knew there was a reason I didn't like that bitch," Brooks muttered.

I nodded to myself. More pieces of the puzzle were falling into place. "So whole human trafficking thing was a ruse, wasn't it? Whose idea was it? Yours?"

Anne's eyes glowed, and she smiled gleefully. "I knew he'd go for it," she said, inclining her head towards Ian. "He's such a sucker for little lost girls."

I could see Ian twitching out of the corner of my eye. I glanced at him and gestured for him to calm down.

"They were obviously planning this for some time," I said. "The convoys Ian bombed. Was there actually anything in them?"

Anne looked triumphant. "Illegal immigrants from Central America. They paid Los Diablos a fee to cross the border. We took their money and used them as bait."

"Jesus," Ian said with a long sigh. "Sweet Jesus. What have I done? Innocents. All those innocents..." his voice trailed off.

Welcome to my world, Ian, I thought. Then I spoke to him, softly but firmly, while I kept my eyes on Anne's face. "Ian, who was your intel source in the cartel?"

He didn't answer.

"Ian!"

"He called himself José," Ian said after a long moment. His voice was choked with emotion. "He told me he heard about what happened to Carina and her daughter and he wanted to help me get revenge."

"I'm sorry about that, Ian. I know the feeling. But I need to know how he contacted you."

Anne's smile was growing. I was reminded of the Cheshire Cat from Alice in Wonderland.

Ian paused again. There were drugs in his system, and his body was struggling to put itself back together, so his mental powers weren't as keen as they normally were, but he was assembling the pieces of the puzzle that had been constructed around him. He was discovering how thoroughly he had been played. I was sympathetic. No one likes finding out they've been manipulated and used. "Through Yolanda," he said, softly. "He was a friend of hers."

"Did this José have a heavy Spanish accent and speak with a sort of nasal voice?" I asked.

Ian didn't answer.

I glanced at him, and the answer was on his face. I turned back to Anne. "You were speaking with Mariano Hidalgo, son of the late Miguel Hidalgo, and leader of Los Diablos."

Anne looked positively radiant as I finished speaking. She was proud of the deception and proud of almost luring her stepbrother to his doom.

"That explains why you were after Ian," I said to her. "But it doesn't explain why you were after me." I paused for a moment to think.

"They recognized you," she said. "The team Mariano sent up here to monitor Ian. The day they met you in the parking lot. The team leader recognized you."

"And that's why they came for me on the street," I said. "And after that attempt failed, you thought you'd help them out by coming to get me at my condo."

She smiled at me, and a sensual glow filled her eyes. "I knew you couldn't resist me," she said.

"Of course, the ten-million-dollar bounty didn't hurt, right?" I said, ignoring her.

Anne's face took on a triumphant look again. "The same ten million I'm going to collect tonight. After I kill you. And this time, I won't have to share it with anyone. Funny how things work out."

"It certainly is," I agreed. "How did you get out of my condo?" I asked. "I gave you enough of that sedative shit to put you way under."

"The backup team came and got me," she said. "The ones you and your CIA friends never knew about."

I shrugged. "So, before you kill me and earn your ten million, answer a final question for me."

Anne nodded. The smug expression on her face made it clear that she thought she held all the cards.

"Was there anyone or anything actually in the hacienda or the warehouses? Or was that just more bait?"

"Mariano hasn't used that place in years," she said with a condescending tone in her voice. "The warehouses were empty and the only reason he had personnel there was to make the place look busy."

I shook my head. *He had not only fooled us,* I thought, *but he had also fooled the Border Patrol and probably the DEA as well. Damn.* I asked the question I already knew the answer to. "So, his goal in all of this was to consolidate his power by repelling a US attack and setting off an international incident, right?"

Anne nodded.

"Wow," I said. "The apple doesn't fall far from the tree. I guess megalomania is genetic. His old man wanted the same thing. That didn't end well either."

Anne's expression changed from confidence to anger in a millisecond. "What are you talking about?" she asked.

I ignored the question. "So where was your boy Mariano the night they tried to bring us down?"

She was ready for this question. "In the main convoy that came down from the complex," she said, defiantly. "He called me when the convoy with Ian headed south. He was waiting for the rescue. He wanted to be there to watch when the CIA pigs were killed or captured."

"Well apparently, he survived the two Hellfires the CIA fired at him and his crew when the CIA came to get me. I wonder how many of his people he used for human shields." I thought for a moment, tilted my head and looked at Anne. "He escapes death up north, only to find it in the convoy. I guess he's not as lucky as his old man was."

I could see Anne beginning to bristle a bit, but her eyes gave her away. The ire was as much about uncertainty as it was about indignation. She didn't know what had happened.

"When was the last time you heard from him?" I asked. "When was the last time you heard from any of them?"

She didn't answer.

"You've been holed-up in Ian's house waiting for weeks now, haven't you?" I asked.

She remained silent.

I mentally chastised myself for not checking on Brooks' house since we returned from Phoenix. I had meant to but just hadn't found the time. Anne had been under our very noses all along.

"So why now?" I asked. But I knew the answer. She wanted to get out of here. But she wanted her revenge, and her prize, first.

Anne stayed silent, but her right index finger moved from outside the trigger guard of the Glock to the inside and rested on the trigger. She was getting tired of talking. She had proven all that she needed.

"Well, it might interest you that I put several hundred rounds of 30mm bullets into that convoy on the day in question. And I was pretty damn precise about it if I do say so myself."

That was a lie. I had no idea how precise I had been. The Darkness had been in control of me. I barely remembered what had happened. All I knew was that when I was done, nothing and no one was moving. And the Darkness had been more sated than it ever had been. It was like an orgasm of death.

"If your boy Mariano was in that convoy, he's dead," I continued. "And so is anyone else that was with him."

Her face darkened, creating a mask of raw hatred. Sometimes, when people drop their emotional guard, it's like a window into their soul. You see who they are beneath the daily disguise they wear to conceal their true selves. I had no idea what childhood experiences had created the desolation inside of Anne's soul but the time for redemption had long past. As I watched her, she began to quiver with anger and frustration.

"There's no one left to pay you, Anne. You can kill us, but you won't get more than 20 miles before the CIA catches you. With any luck, you'll only get a life sentence in a public facility. But if luck isn't on your side," I paused for effect. "Anything could happen. You might not ever be seen or heard from again. It's what they do."

I looked back at Ian and then back to her.

"One of us is going to get you," I said. "I might not be fast enough, but Ian will be. Surrender now, and you might live through the night."

She exhaled in contempt and motioned the muzzle of her gun toward Ian. "What the fuck can he do?" she asked. Then she turned her attention to me. "What the fuck can you do?

You're both like all the pilots I've known. You think you're fucking superhuman." She paused and swallowed before continuing. "I don't give a shit about the money. I've got plenty stowed away. I skimmed it from Mr. Wonderful's business." She looked in Ian's direction disdainfully. "I'm going to kill you both just to show you how fucking pitiful you are."

"Last chance, Anne," I warned. "Put the gun down and surrender. You won't be harmed, and you'll be treated respectfully."

She laughed at me then. But it wasn't a normal laugh. It was one of hysteria and maniacal delusion, the laugh of someone who wasn't entirely sane. Her gun hand came up, and her finger tightened on the trigger. I hoped I wasn't too late.

"Now Ian," I said, as I dropped to the floor.

Two "boom" sounds occurred, nearly simultaneously. A huge hole appeared in the center of Anne's chest, a hole about the size of a soda can. The projectile went through her body and took flesh, bones, organ tissue and blood and spattered it on the wall behind her. Anne sank to her knees, and a look of disbelief passed over her face as her body began to shut down.

"You lived with him for years," I said, as I rose from the floor, shaking my head. "And you never knew what he was. Or what he could do. You've been used too, just like the rest of us."

Anne collapsed to the floor and lay still. As the life and emotion left her body, her face took on an expression of quiet peace. I looked at her and shook my head. She could have been a beautiful woman. But her inner anger had overshadowed that and turned her into an ugly caricature of who she was.

I felt Brooks standing next to me. I never heard him move. I looked over at him as he gazed down upon the remains of his stepsister, the woman he had just killed with a can of Coca-Cola. There was no emotion on his face. I regarded him carefully. One of the 'boom' sounds had been from Anne's gun, but he hadn't been hit. I was betting the bullet was buried in the wall behind us somewhere.

"The can broke the sound barrier when you threw it?" I asked.

Brooks nodded. "I used to be able to throw slowly enough to avoid that, but I haven't had any practice recently. And I'm not used to the new code they installed yet. You didn't give me much time. I hope I didn't screw up the mechanism in my shoulder." He turned to look at me. "Alpha-mike-foxtrot. Twice. That was the code to restore full power? How long have you known that?"

"Since we left Phoenix," I said.

"You son-of-a-bitch!" Brooks exclaimed. "You mean I've been in that bed for weeks when I could have been up and about?"

"I was given some pretty strict instructions where you were concerned," I said. "The docs were afraid that what they had done might have messed you up. They didn't want you back on your feet until you had completely stabilized. Besides," I gestured to Anne's body, "we needed to bring her out of hiding, on our terms, and find out what she knew."

"And I was bait?" Brooks asked.

I shrugged. "You were available. So was I. And we needed to create a situation where Anne thought she had the upper hand."

Brooks looked down at his stepsister again. "It still sucks," he said.

I nodded. "Welcome to government work," I said.

##

Two hours later, a CIA clean-up crew had cleaned up Anne and removed their comrade, who had been lying on the floor next to Brooks bed. He turned out to be just fine. Anne's bullet had struck his body armor and driven him to the floor, and he had been knocked unconscious by the impact.

Ian was back in bed and scowling at me.

"Why do I need to stay in here, Pearce?" he asked. "I'm fine. I'm ready to get out of here."

"I'm sure you feel great," I said, "But the docs told me a lot is going on inside your body. Some of your prosthetic code and all of your batteries have been replaced. You will be able to go three months without a charge now, although they recommended no longer than two. But the tricky thing is the nerve interfaces. They've been replaced and reprogrammed. They take a long time to heal and require minimal movement for the healing to take place. That's why you were placed on a low power mode. You need to stay in bed for another week to make sure everything knits up the way it should."

He seemed to accept the explanation begrudgingly. But then his face took on a baffled look. "That had to cost a fortune," he said. "Why would the government spend that kind of money on me? It's not like they can use me for wet work anymore. I won't do it."

"Just go with the flow, Ian," I said. "Sit on your ass and kid with the nurses for five more days. Then you're done."

He exhaled in resignation.

I nodded at him and turned to go. But then something occurred to me, and I turned back to him. "Oh, and they got the device out of you."

Ian raised his eyes to me with a bewildered expression on his face.

"Device?" he said. "What device?"

I shook my head and turned away. "Nothing," I said. "Must have been the cyborg in the next room."

As I exited the room and turned the corner, I ran right into Patricia Belmont, who was coming from another corridor.

"Conner!" she said. "What are you doing here?"

"Visiting Ian," I replied. "He had an accident. Now he's recovering."

A sad smile crossed her beautiful features. "I'm visiting a friend as well." She looked down at the floor and a few pregnant moments passed. "I haven't heard anything from you since Thanksgiving," she said at last.

"I've been...busy," I said.

She nodded. "I'm sure you have been," she said. "I've heard a lot of flying at the airport." She raised her eyes to mine, and I saw a hopeful smile on her face. "Would you like to go get a drink or something? Dahl and Delucca's is close by."

Several thoughts passed through my head as I stared back at her. She was beautiful and fun and had experience as the wife of a military pilot. There was much we had in common, and there was an electricity between us that was undeniable. But I couldn't allow myself to believe in it, and I couldn't let anyone get close enough to me where they'd be in danger. Especially given the recent promise I had made to the CIA.

Patricia watched me as I pondered her invitation and I could see her face falling into disappointment. She turned to go.

"Never mind," she said.

But then something occurred to me, and I reached out and grabbed her hand. She seemed surprised by the contact and turned back to me.

"I have paperwork to get to back to at the office," I said. "But I know someone who would really enjoy your company right about now."

She tilted her head and looked at me. "And who would that be?"

I interlocked my fingers with hers and squeezed her hand as I turned back towards Ian's room.

"Come with me," I said.

Epilogue

Wednesday, December 23rd
2100 Hours Local Time
Brooks' House
Sedona, Arizona, USA

I stood at the railing on Brooks' deck and nursed my first single malt of the evening, a nice pour of the Cu Bocan. The air was chilly but tolerable, and I was enjoying the moment of solitude as I contemplated the lights of the houses below and the dark silhouettes of the red rock monuments around me. For the first time in several weeks, I felt at peace.

The 6th Annual Brooks Air Service Holiday Party seemed to be a rousing success. Patricia Belmont and Myra Barnes had put the event together in record time, inviting employees and significant others as well as friends and family of the company. The event was both intimate and festive, and the food the two of them had prepared was spectacular.

Brooks had been in rare form as he played host and made the rounds of the room, with Patricia at his side. It seemed that the two of them had become inseparable in the week since I introduced them, and I couldn't have been happier for both. I had removed myself from the conversation groups and watched them work the crowd, talking to the guests. I could see genuine tenderness in their eyes, and that moved me with an incredible sense of happiness for them. But there was also a tiny tinge of jealousy inside me that I couldn't explain.

I took another sip of the smooth, peaty scotch and let it dance across my tongue as I looked up at the clear black sky above me, filled with millions of gleaming stars. I shook my head in wonder, yet again, that I could live in such a beautiful place.

"Penny for your thoughts," said a voice from beside me.

"I'm not sure they're worth that much," I replied without turning my head.

"Well, you're the president of the company now," Sharona said. "At least that's what Ian said in the announcement earlier. That's got to make them worth something."

"You might be surprised," I said, as I turned to her.

Sharona stood before me in a burgundy-colored sweater dress that accentuated her highly toned body and complimented her cappuccino complexion perfectly. She held a glass of wine that matched the dress.

"I don't think so," she said, watching my face. "I've come to know you well enough to know there's always something going on up there."

"Not all the time."

Sharona stepped past me and went to the railing. She looked out into the valley, and I turned and joined her.

"Does he know the terms?" she asked. "Of our agreement?"

"Who?" I responded, even though I knew the answer. "Brooks?"

I saw her nod in my peripheral vision.

"Somewhat. I told him that I'd be happy to run the company, but from 'time to time,' I might be called back to work for 'our' former employer. He didn't think that would be an issue."

Sharona nodded again. "That should work just fine. So

why did he decide to step aside?"

I shrugged. "We talked about it earlier today. He was pleased with the way I'd been running the business, and he said he wanted to be able to spend more time with Patricia."

"Seems reasonable."

"That's what I thought. He even offered me a substantial raise and some equity in the company."

Sharona laughed quietly and took a sip of her wine.

"What?" I asked.

"He obviously doesn't know that you don't need the money," she said.

"It's still nice to be working," I said. "Especially nice to be working at something that doesn't require me to kill people."

"Or take you to a dark place..." Sharona said softly.

I hung my head. She was right. The Darkness was like an unpredictable and uncontrollable disease that lived inside of me. In light of the recent business, it seemed more potent than ever. It had made me careless on a few occasions, and had almost led me to do something I would have regretted the rest of my life.

"Yes," I said at last. "You're right."

She put her hand on my arm. "We can hook you up with people who can help you to understand that part of you. People who can help you get it under control."

I looked down at my glass and exhaled heavily. "I should probably do that," I said after several minutes. "My dreams have been very dark of late."

Sharona squeezed my arm and put her mouth next to my ear. "You're not alone," she whispered.

I turned to her and looked her in the eyes. We held each other's gaze for several seconds. I felt a bond form between us in that time. It was incredibly strong but intangible, like fine lines of a spider's web that can't be seen from afar. I lost myself in it.

Sharona reached up and caressed my cheek with her left hand and then reached to the back of my neck and instead of pulling my lips to hers, she bowed her head slightly and pulled our foreheads together. It was an impossibly intimate gesture, and I felt a tear sting the corner of my left eye. We spent several seconds that way before she spoke.

"You're going to need to get to Chicago very soon, for several reasons," she said. "And in the meantime, I have a plane of my own to catch."

"Off for more adventures?" I asked.

She nodded. "I was hoping I could stay a while longer, but duty calls."

I found that I was oddly relieved by that statement. As fun as our brief time together had been, it was built on an element of deception that cheapened it. I wasn't sure I would have known what to do with that if she had stayed.

Sharona lifted her eyes to mine and stared into them for a moment or two. I could tell that she was thinking and feeling the same things. She nodded to me, raised her face and kissed me gently.

"Take care, cowboy," she said. Then she released me and headed for the door to the house. Just before going inside, she turned to me. "For what it's worth, I did buy one of those damn electric fireplaces for my apartment," she said. "Maybe you could come and see it sometime."

I smiled at her and nodded. "Maybe so."

Sharona smiled back and waved goodbye. Then she entered the house and was gone.

I turned back to the railing and pondered the sky above Sedona. As I looked up, a shooting star appeared and left a long, thin trail of fire across the heavens. The brilliant transition of solid matter to energy provided a spectacular reminder that anything could be reformed under the right circumstances. Even me.

COLIN PEARCE WILL RETURN IN

THE ENTERON CONTRACT

CPSIA information can be obtained
at www.ICGtesting.com
Printed in the USA
BVHW080851090119
537382BV00001B/2/P